THE BLACKOUT

A Novel
By David Alexander

HEIST

WWW.DAVIDALEXANDERBOOKS.COM

Triumvirate

Publications
New York • London • Sydney

THE BLACKOUT HEIST

A Triumvirate Publications International thriller novel.
Published by arrangement with the author.

For more about David Alexander:
www.davidalexanderbooks.com.

Copyright © David Alexander. All rights reserved.
ISBN-10: 0-9995493-3-2
ISBN-13: 978-0-9995493-3-9

Triumvirate Publications International
2001 Madison Avenue
New York NY 10035

DAVID ALEXANDER

Excerpts from Co-Co-Caleevio
A Mafia Novel
By David Alexander

Dominick "Dee" de Venise's textile warehouse has been in the family for generations, but he'll have to torch it for the insurance money. De Venise has no other choice. The Mezzatesta family is into him for boo-koo bucks and if he doesn't pay off, he's history.

The only other option de Venise has is to stage a big-money heist planned by his crooked lawyer friend Arnie, but he's already turned down that particular deal. Arnie's plan was too risky, and besides, de Venise knew Arnie long enough and well enough not to trust him. De Venise doesn't trust anyone to torch the business either. Wanting it done right, he plans to do it himself, then set up an ironclad alibi.

Everything goes like clockwork until the insurance company refuses to pay off on de Venise's policy, leaving him with no business to run and no money to buy off his wise guy creditors.

With no more cards to play at this point, de Venise agrees to do the heist for Arnie. If nothing else, it will get him out of the country, and if de Venise is really lucky and really smart, there's even an outside chance of him scoring the bucks he needs to get him straight with the mob and put him back in action. Just like when he was a kid, the name of the game is Co-Co-Caleevio – single, double, triple. Catch the ball to win.

The only difference now is that if de Venise winds up out, this time he could also wind up dead.

THE BLACKOUT HEIST

Crime Does Pay
Co-Co-Caleevio pulls the trigger with a bang!

Co-Co-Caleevio is a crime novel that begins and ends on the mean streets of Gravesend, the toughest neighborhood of New York City's toughest borough and the heart of notorious West Brooklyn. It's a place where organized crime still rules and where wise guys have to think fast, hit hard or get whacked. In between, the novel crosses international boundaries and time zones with the speed of sound as West Brooklyn's most accomplished safe and loft burglar takes on a European job in order to pay back the markers held on him by boss of bosses Tony the Pug. This is a caper novel to end all caper novels, a non-stop pager-turner from start to finish, and one of Author David Alexander's boldest books ever.

∎

"Where's the statuette? I've made a rather thorough ransack job of both cabins, but can't find anything. I'm assuming its inside the corpse you and the lady are transporting."

"It's not there. I have it in one of the drawers. I'll show --"

"Don't move. Tell the truth or I'll cause considerable pain."

"All right, I should have known better. Yes, the *Bambina* is inside the corpse in the casket we're taking back to New York."

"What happens then?"

"The funeral parlor gets it, opens up the stiff and takes it out."

"I see. How do I believe you?"

4

DAVID ALEXANDER

"If I tell you will you let us live?"

"That depends on whether you're honest with me or not. But if you don't give me what I need, I promise I will cause you and your whore pain. Her first, as you watch."

"No, okay. Yeah, I got the proof," de Venise said. "No problem."

"Where is it?"

"My phone. It's in my pocket. Cut the cable tie, and I'll get it."

"Tell me where it is."

"Okay. You win. The phone's in my back pants pocket. The right one."

"This better not explode in my face."

"It won't. I can do it for you."

"Shut up. I'm warning you."

He flipped it on and thumbed to the photo folder. He scanned the MRI they'd done of the Greek's remains to show the morticians at Bassamontagna where the statue was. The passenger in the white suit nodded.

"You didn't lie. That's good. I'll make it easy for you. After you die, I'll rape the bitch and make it look like you killed each other on drugs. One shot. You won't feel it."

"Wait, lemme smoke some grass. I got some joints rolled in a Baci tin."

"You get nothing."

"I can pay for it."

"How?"

"The cross around my neck. It's solid gold. I been wearing it all my life. It's worth a lot. You can have it."

The assassin reached for the crucifix. He fingered it, seeing it was pure gold, the real thing. With a tug he yanked it off the chain.

--excerpted from unrevised Co-Co-Caleevio chapter.

THE BLACKOUT HEIST

■

Today Brooklyn, tomorrow the world ... David Alexander has the names of two conquering heroes and Co-Co-Caleevio is world-class ... a thriller with style, guts and endless quantities of Brooklyn *chutzpah* applied as thickly as mozzerella cheese on a Brooklyn pizza. Alexander is an author who is going places. Hopefully one of them is not jail, as some of the criminal capers described in the novel read almost like he was present at the scene of the crime taking notes.

■

When he came in, hands free, the assassin was flopping on the bed, trying to get up. Blood pumped from his neck. He was still alive.

"You dumb prick."

The torso was still partially intact.

"You can see me right? You can understand, right?"

The killer's eyes registered that he did.

"You listen up. I was crying for Mario, who gave this to me. Now I'm sending you to wipe his fuckin' ass in heaven."

De Venise took off his sports coat then took off his shirt and pants. He stood naked with the gun in his right hand.

"I can wash your fuckin' blood off, and the powder grains will usually come off too. I'll give it three washes. They usually get the shit off your clothes anyway."

De Venise wrapped the butt of the assassin's silenced gun around his hand. He didn't have much longer. The eyes of the Infessura were rolling up in his head from shock. De Venise hoped he could still understand him.

"I hope you choke, you cocksucker," de Venise said, as he shoved the silenced muzzle into the killer's mouth as hard as he could, and jerked the trigger once with the killer's stubby forefinger. There wasn't much noise as the head jerked and the pillow was suddenly stained with glop from the brains that shot out the back end of his skull.

--excerpted from unrevised Co-Co-Caleevio chapter.

■

Could he also face a murder rap -- as a cop or JFK guard or customs officer was killed in the course of the robbery? It wasn't Dee's fault -- he never carried a gun -- but as an accessory to murder commited during a robbery he could get the hot shot.

There's this cop after him. For years already. He's like a stone in his fucking shoe, this cop. The cop hates him because he's half-Sicilian. He's some kind of fuckin' nut job.

The DA is is in league with the cops. The DA is on a vendetta against corruption with a holy zeal not seen since the Gotti trials. He's going after everybody.

Dee is smarter and more tech savvy than he appears at first glance.

The Boost is an old crony from even before the Aer Lingus heist days.

So there's a progression from the 1st safe and loft job in Red Hook (and from those that preceded it in back story) to the III-V job, and then it connects up with the *tombarolo's* "grave robbing" of ancient tombs. (Cracking safes is like cracking tombs in a way.)

Arnie may use his knowledge of Dee's involvement with the Aer Lingus heist as a lever to force his compliance with the III-V job -- and the rest that follows after the heist is eighty-sixed.

--excerpted from unrevised Co-Co-Caleevio author's notes.

■

Authors don't come any better than David Alexander, and his tough-as-nails global thriller Co-Co-Caleevio represents his taking the fine art of mayhem to an exciting new level of accomplishment. The depth of insight into the world of the Mafia, black intelligence ops, tomb raiding *tombaroli*, historical arcana, exotic military technologies and the inner mainsprings of political intrigue -- to name but a few of this book's points of focus -- seems at times close to envisaging actual   events.

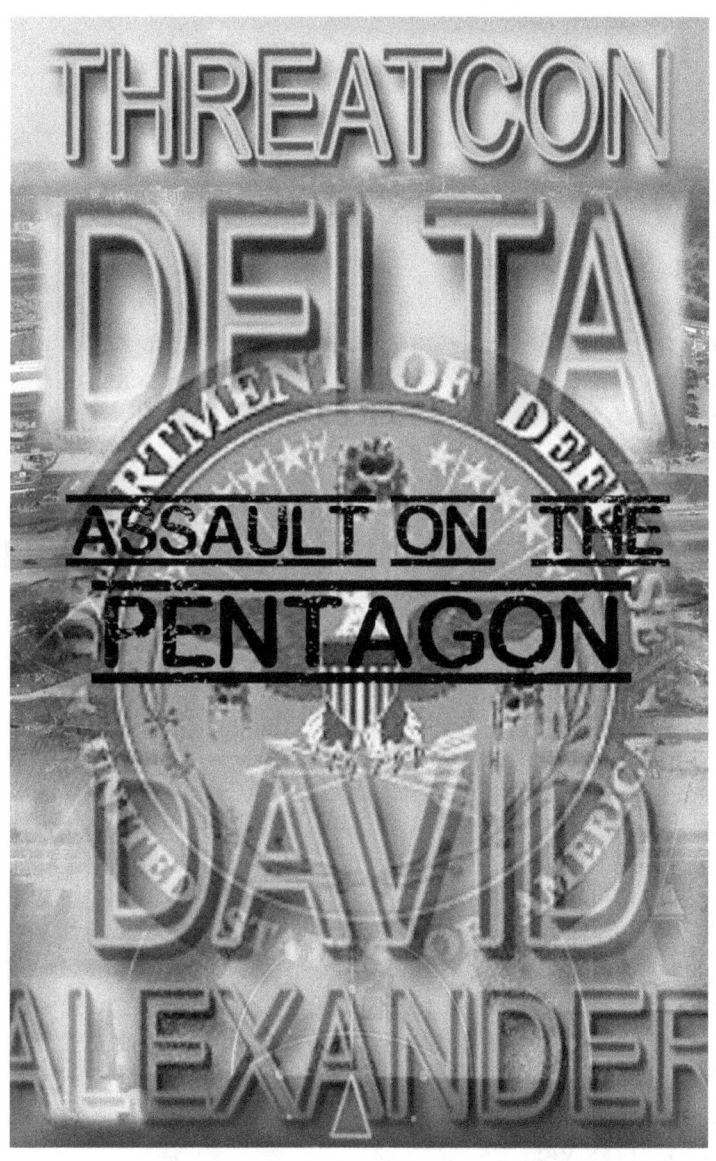

Chain Reaction

A Global Thriller
By David Alexander

In this superb achievement by a master storyteller, a New York City police detective caught in a web of international terrorism and global intrigue becomes the central focus of an expertly told story that's so exciting it may actually make you sweat.

Chain Reaction features scenes rich in gripping narrative, striking action and punchy dialog in a plot armed with superweapons and power-mad bad guys who rival or exceed any encountered in real life. This amazing thriller offers a feast of surprising twists and turns that suddenly appear with mind-boggling rapidity that make it a milestone in the annals of thriller fiction.

Carried along by a strong, clear and powerfully cinematic prose line that benefits from extremely accurate portrayals of all the elements of the cop's, spy's and soldiers' trades, Chain Reaction is top-notch writing and a great reading experience. The opening and closing chapters go off like a shock and awe campaign, and nothing in between gives readers enough time to even catch their breath. The cumulative effect of Chain Reaction is overwhelming in the sheer impact of the powerful prose and the slick, commercial, though uniquely original plot and style.

David Alexander is one of those rare authors who can write fiction that has the power to relentlessly carry the reader onward, and who can blend a wit and humor as sharp and cutting as a samurai sword and combine it with in-depth analysis and the deft touch of a master technician. David Alexander's superb thriller Chain Reaction is more than a great read, it's an awesome experience that is sure to keep readers on the edge of their seats, addictive adventure writing at its boldest and brightest -- the stuff from which great thrillers are made.

THE BLACKOUT HEIST

High Praise for The King of West Brooklyn

"The Mezzatestas, David Alexander's fictitious crime family in The King of West Brooklyn, are the new Corleones." -- USA Today

"If mob-related hits haven't already put Gravesend, the crime capital of West Brooklyn, on the map, The King of West Brooklyn is destined to do so." -- Daily News

"Today Brooklyn, tomorrow the world ... David Alexander has the names of two conquering heroes and The King of West Brooklyn is world-class ... a thriller with style, guts and endless quantities of Brooklyn chutzpah applied as thickly as mozzarella cheese on a Brooklyn pizza. Alexander is an author who is going places. Hopefully one of them is not jail, as some of the criminal capers described in the novel read almost like he was taking notes at the scene of the crime." -- L.A. Times

"If James Bond wore athletic shirts, spoke with a Brooklyn accent and drove a candy apple-red 1973 Plymouth Barracuda, he'd be Dominick de Venise, the edgy protagonist of David Alexander's smashing crime thriller The King of West Brooklyn." -- Kirkus Reviews

"Bestseller! Bestseller! Bestseller! The word should be shouted at least three times as a kind of Brooklyn cheer, because David Alexander's crime thriller The King of West Brooklyn has "Bestseller!" written all over it." -- NY Daily News

"... All muscle, no flab..." Daily News

DAVID ALEXANDER

"What Tom Clancy did for submarines, Alexander has done with the contemporary realities of global terrorism, high-tech weapons and the robotization of the battlefield." -- Jack Phelps / Independent Reviews

"This boat ride through the Tunnel of Fear nails you to your seat. Don't get on unless you have the guts to finish the ride!" -- Stun Gun Sam / Independent Reviews

High Praise for David Alexander's POTUS

"Perhaps the best thriller of its type to have come along all year!" -- New York Times

"Always the consummate prose stylist, David Alexander also speaks tech talk like no other. What's more, the tech specs are undoubtedly real, including those that pertain to ostensibly stolen or covertly obtained Russian and Chinese weapons that have been reverse-engineered by [US military technology development agency] DARPA. Alexander's security clearance is probably higher than the president's, and his knowledge of military systems better than any three members of the joint chiefs of staff." -- NY Newsday

"Among the possible three finest thriller authors today, Alexander takes first place." -- USA Today

"Here, as elsewhere, Alexander convincingly blends action, intrigue, adventure and startling glimpses behind the walls of the CIA, Oval Office and Pentagon that seem far too real to have been completely invented ...throughout he shows off the masterful skills that have placed him high amid the ranks of the world's thriller authors." --London Times

"Three R's for David Alexander's POTUS -- riveting, relevant, remarkable." -- The New Yorker

"A happening of a thriller. Alexander grand-slams the competition with this latest action-adventure masterpiece!" -- Village Voice

High Praise for Threatcon Delta: Assault on the Pentagon

"If you read no other technothrilller this year, read this awesome action yarn by David Alexander ... it's guaranteed to make you lose sleep."--Arlington Times

Critical Applause for Brothers of the Gun

"Brothers of the Gun is faster than a speeding bullet ... slicker than the slickest contender out there. Go and get this book today!" -- St. Paul Intelligencer

Critical Acclaim for Snake Handlers

"Alexander once again turns newspaper headlines into riveting high-tech military action fiction with that special combination of cinematic thrills and chills and fly-on-the-wall accounts of back room crisis management in the making ... surely one of the best technothrillers to come along in a great while." -- Salem Record

Critics Hail Under Attack

"Alexander is so far ahead of the pack that they must be howling like wolves running at his back, hungry for even just a taste of his immense writing talent. There's no doubt that in the action wolf pack Alexander is top dog, and the canine whose scent the others follow." -- F. C. Dubrow, Book Reviewer

Critical acclaim for Kill Chain

"Passenger jets disappear out of thin air ... terrorist armies drape black flags across failed states ... chaos in the streets of American cities ... and the threat of terrible doom gathers steam as this thriller draws to a powerful climax ... Alexander ... has thought of everything and then some...." -- Voice Book Reviews

"This is not just another novel; this is history in the making ... a game changing ... thriller." – Booklister

THE BLACKOUT HEIST

Also by David Alexander:

I Kinda Spy
Snake Handlers
Habu Patch
Under Attack
The King of West Brooklyn
Co-Co-Caleevio
Trainjack
War Pigs
Sword of the Mahdi
Death Pulse
Brooklynese
Bloodbath
Puzzle Palace (nonfiction)
Military-Industrial Complex (nonfiction)

DAVID ALEXANDER

O dark, dark, dark, amid the blaze of noon,
Irrecoverably dark, total eclipse,
Without all hope of day.
                    --Samson Agonistes/Milton

THE BLACKOUT HEIST

The Blackout Heist is a work of fiction. Names, characters, places and incidents either are the product of the author's imagination or are used fictitiously, and any resemblance to actual persons, living or dead, business establishments, events or locales is note even remotely intentional and entirely coincidental. Some place names and descriptions of locales, weaponry, and military procedures have been modified where necessary to suit the requirements of the narrative.

DAVID ALEXANDER

AUTHOR'S NOTE:
Although the events described in this book are fictitious, the possibility that the crisis around which the plot revolves may occur sometime in the not-too-distant future nevertheless exists. Recently, a number of real-life scenarios of urban disaster bearing frightening parallels to those created from the whole cloth of the imagination have taken place in major urban centers in the US and globally. Would a scenario that dwarfs even the nightmarish events of 911, such as the one portrayed here, lead to a nearly total collapse of society? No one, including myself, can say. Unfortunately, according to some experts, it's only a question of time before folly and greed collude to subvert technology and let the genie of doom out of his bottle.

THE BLACKOUT HEIST

Prolog:
Nazi Germany
1944

DAVID ALEXANDER

North Rhineland-Westphalia, Germany. Hjalmar Horace Greeley Schacht -- who had been brought up in Brooklyn, New York, but who currently served Adolph Hitler as Minister of Economics and overseer of the Reichbank of Nazi Germany -- exited the Daimler Benz limousine. The long, southward drive from Berlin over the Führer's newly constructed Autobahn had been a smooth one and the air of the Bavarian countryside refreshed him as he stretched his cramped and tired legs. Already in the parking area of Schloss Wewelsburg, the brooding twelfth century castle owned by Reichsfuhrer Heinrich Himmler, were the cars of several others Schacht knew had also been invited to the castle.

Schacht was a fastidious man. Given the matters for which he was responsible, he had to be. He took the opportunity before the meeting was to convene to go over some of the notes he had made on the drive and to collect his thoughts. He knew that Von Mantueffel was opposed to the plan, but that Skorzeny, Hitler's most trusted and able soldier, was strongly in favor. Kupsch of the OKW also was opposed. The rest did not count. Besides, it was Himmler's decision alone that held any weight, and it was Himmler's plan to begin with.

THE BLACKOUT HEIST

Hearing two staccato raps on the heavy oaken door of the room, Schacht went to answer.

"Bitte, mein herr," the servant -- who wore the snow white livery of the castle -- replied. Schacht noticed the man was tall and blond, one of the typical, or more accurately, Schact thought, "questionable" SS types that Himmler used for all serving staff at the *schloss*, meaning that Schacht considered them probably gay. "Your presence is requested."

"I shall be right with you," Schacht answered. He went back and placed his notes in their leather zipped folder. He would not need them as he knew the meeting would be largely ceremonial.

The SS man in the white domestic's uniform led Schacht down the echoing, flagstone-paved corridor whose walls bore huge paintings, medieval warfare implements and medieval suits of armor. The corridor ended in a flight of hewn stone steps leading up and down. Moving with quick, lithe steps and without turning around, the SS man took the upward flight. Schacht followed, slightly out of breath by the time they arrived at the floor on which the meeting chamber was located. The servant pulled open two heavy wooden doors to admit him.

Inside, Schacht found the expected sight. A square table dominated the room. A few electric bulbs burned feebly in grid-wire cages on the ceiling, but most of the interior light came from sconced torches in wall niches. The heavy oak table that dominated the room was square in shape, with Himmler sitting at its head and ten others seated around it. There was one vacant seat at the table. This, Schacht knew, belonged to him.

With a nod to the assemblage, Schacht took his seat between Colonel Otto Skorzeny and General Karl Heinrich Pohl. The first was Hitler's chief enforcer. The second, the Führer's chief tactician. Himmler nodded and rose. There were now twelve men seated around the table, the maximum number permitted by Himmler, whose superstitious imaginings attributed it to good fortune dictated by the Arthurian legends, and the later knockoffs of Von Eschenbach, that formed part of his bizarre code of ethics.

"Now the assemblage is complete," he announced, his nasal voice making his effort to inspire awe in the manner of his master, Hitler, seem laughable. "We must presently ask for spiritual guidance. I will begin the ceremony."

An ornate crystal goblet of blood-red Gewürztraminer was placed in front of each man at the table. Himmler opened an old-looking book bound in gold leaf containing runic symbols and began to read from the archaic German text that he had translated himself.

The purpose of the convocation was to communicate with the spirit of King Von Wevel, whom Himmler believed spoke to him in visions, during which he gave Himmler guidance and imparted higher knowledge of secrets kept hidden from common mortals. Glancing to one side, Schacht noticed the faintly mocking smile on Skorzeny's face and the now old *Schmisse* -- the dueling scars that snaked down the length of each tensed jowl -- which turned crimson whenever the Austrian brawler was angry or very bored.

The rest were stern-visaged, and although Schacht thought that it must be a great effort not to keep from breaking out laughing as the former Bavarian chicken farmer read his well-known mystical rubbish, Himmler's power to have any of them killed was genuine enough to convince each attendee to play the game to the hilt.

The freshly butchered venison from the Reichsfuhrer's private game preserves, and more of the good Rheinlander wine from the castle's amply stocked and quite extensive cellars, however, were anything but laughable. Schacht felt that the excellent fare at Himmler's table more than made up for the absurdities of his mystic pretensions. Besides, there was a purpose of genuinely vital importance to the Reich Finance Minister's visit to Schloss Wewelsburg for which Schacht would have been willing to put up with as much as Himmler's nonsense as need be.

The purpose concerned nothing less than the future of Germany after the war, a war that every man present at the castle, despite their own misgivings about other matters, was unanimously certain would soon be lost by Hitler's Germany and won by the Allied powers. Hitler had been a fool and a madman, but Germany had at first had no other choice. The Fatherland had needed a strong figure to lead it out of the crushing despair and maddening poverty that the Versailles treaty had subjected it to.

Buoyed with initial successes in politics and battle, Hitler's Deutschland had gotten off to a good start. But *Der Führer* had neither known nor cared to admit his limitations. His infectious megalomania, so necessary in the early days, was now a liability. His most trusted military experts, as well as Reich intelligence chief Reinhard Gehlen, had warned him about the Wermacht's inability to withstand a Russian onslaught from the East. Hitler had flown into one of his familiar rages and dismissed them both. When the inevitable had happened and von Manteuffel's Panzer army had been overrun on the Eastern Front, Germany's fate had been sealed. A few months, a year at the most, and Berlin would have fallen. The Third Reich's defeat was now inevitable and it was only Hitler himself alone who could not clearly see this.

Already Himmler's SS had made arrangements. Goods and currencies, men and materiél were already en route to safe havens abroad. Skorzeny was in the process of assembling his underground railroad for Nazis he called *die Spinne* -- the Spider. Germany would be defeated, but the Reich would only sleep. It would be awakened one day. No one could now say when that future day would come. But it would come eventually. This much was certain. Decades might pass, but it would surely arrive. To Schacht had fallen the task of insuring in his own way that a critical element of the plan would be carried out. When the ceremony was over, Himmler, with Skorzeny, took Schacht into a room hidden in the basement of Schloss Wewelsburg to show him the fruits of his labors.

Bars of gold were stacked almost to the ceiling. Schacht estimated that there must have been fifty tons of the bullion at least, each bar bearing the stamp of the Reicshbank and the Nazi eagle emblem, its wings outspread over a swastika bounded by an encompassing circle. The gold that had made up the bars had come from many sources. The concentration camps run by the SS were a chief source. Apart from the major ones, such as Auschwitz and Bergen-Belsen, there were hundreds of smaller ones across territory conquered by the Reich. From each flowed hundreds of kilos of gold taken from tooth fillings, wedding rings, items of personal jewelry and other sources. To these had been added the gold looted from the liquidated assets of cities and towns.

"It is astonishing!" cried Schacht.

"To those who commune with the Aryan spirits of the great, nothing is impossible," Himmler replied without a smile, his eyes dark smudges behind the thick lenses of his round bifocals.

"But how will it be moved from here?"

"To that task SS-Oberführer Skorzeny has devoted his considerable talents."

Skorzeny motioned Schacht to accompany him across the guarded storage vault and walk to one of the casement windows that overlooked an interior courtyard of the castle. The tall, broad-shouldered commando who had led his troops on a daredevil rescue of Benito Mussolini using gliders to reach an otherwise impenetrable mountain redoubt, towered over the prim Finance Minister and Himmler both as he pointed down through the window.

The courtyard was floodlit by powerful arc lamps. Within its confines Schacht could see frenzied activity taking place. Men were working on the trucks, some with pneumatically driven spraying devices, others painting the sides with brushes.

"You see those trucks, Herr Schacht?" asked Skorzeny. Schacht nodded his assent. "It is in those that the gold will be transported to its destination, the place of safety that we have all agreed upon."

"But how?" asked the Finance Minister. "The Americans and the British are positioned all around. Even a division would certainly be stopped at this point."

"*Nein*," Skorzeny answered, shaking his head. "Not these trucks. You may rest assured that they will get through."

Schacht turned his head. Himmler, he now saw, had come up beside them. The Reichsfuhrer was looking at him with a strange intensity. For the first time that evening, Schacht saw a smile begin to take form on Himmler's thin, pedant's lips.

***

The men of *SS-Jagdverbande 47* knew their mission well. They had been thoroughly drilled by Skorzeny himself on every possible contingency that might present itself. Each, in turn, was willing to sacrifice his life in combat to ensure that the mission was successful, and all knew that this might be necessary before they were done.

The convoy of six trucks had set out from Schloss Wewelsburg the previous day. None of the SS special warfare group so much as blinked an eye as Himmler blessed them, chanting in an arcane language said to be derived from ancient German conjurers' texts. They had learned that to win Himmler's favor his eccentricities had needed putting up with.

For most of the day, the trucks, which were painted white and whose flanks and roofs bore the highly visible red cross of the international relief organization, moved unimpeded across eastern Germany. At checkpoints set up by their own forces, the safe-conduct pass, signed by Adolf Hitler and countersigned by Himmler, insured that their passage would not even be questioned.

So far, there had been no trouble, but then again, it was still early on. This part of Germany, although perilously close to the front, was for the time being still securely held by Wehrmacht and Waffen SS forces and would by all accounts continue to be so for some time to come. But only a few kilometers beyond Germany's front lines, the Americans were gaining ground day by day. Now the true test would come, because the convoy had just entered American territory.

The leader had passed the word for his men to be on high alert just after they had passed the small mountain town of Regensberg. Soon after leaving the last German checkpoint there, the convoy found immediate signs of American military presence. It was not long before they were challenged by the sudden appearance of an American mechanized column made up of a tank, two half tracks a two-and-a-half ton truck containing a company of GIs and a scout car.

"We are Red Cross," the driver of the lead truck told the unshaven American soldier who leaned across the front of the truck eying the interior curiously.

"Where you boys going?" the soldier asked. The American bore lieutenant's chevrons on his shoulder. The patch identified him as being a member of the 47th Infantry Division and his accent identified him as a Kentucky farm boy. He spat a gob of chewing tobacco out of the side of his mouth. The driver, an SS captain, would have liked to show this insolent *untermensch* that one does not address an officer of the German *Schutzstaffel* in such a brazen manner, but he had no choice than to put on a deferential smile and continue the act.

"We have wounded and medical supplies bound for a field hospital in Brandenburg," he hastily told the soldier. "We must not be impeded. It is urgent that safe conduct is honored by your men."

"Lot of shit hitting the fan over the next ridge, Hans," the lieutenant told the driver. "I'd advise you boys to wait it out."

"My name is not 'Hans,' lieutenant," the driver retorted, struggling to keep his anger from showing on his face, "and we will accept the risks. Please allow us to pass."

The GI thought that over for a minute.

"Gonna have to have a look inside these here vehicles first, Hans," he said. "You boys just sit tight till we're through."

The driver could not suppress a sidelong glance at the other commando in the seat beside him. He saw the American lieutenant gesture to his men and heard the sounds of the other GIs jumping from the transport truck. Neither the twenty millimeter cannon of the Sherman nor the .50 caliber Brownings of the half track were trained on them, however. There were still seconds in which to move.

The driver had made his decision. He acted with the cool efficiency for which he had been trained. The American's face barely had a chance to express shock as the P-38 pistol was whipped from concealment and the *Jagdverbande* commando pumped three rounds into his head and throat. The bloodied face dropped from view as the driver whipped the steering wheel and floored the gas pedal at the same instant that the SS-man beside him produced a Schmeisser from under his seat and, shoving its snout out the window, sprayed the troops emerging from the transport with nine millimeter automatic fire.

By now the rear doors of the "ambulance" had opened exposing two men inside, one of whom opened up with the 7.62 millimeter MP-32 field machinegun mounted on a moveable pintle welded to the floor of the truck. Originally manufactured by the Czechs and produced in quantity by the Germans when they took over, the weapon could crank out withering firepower. Fire was pouring from the other two trucks as well. Caught in the deadly crossfire, those Americans who had not been killed in the initial seconds of the attack and had managed to find cover, opened up with their Garands and M1s.

The three trucks had split up as they were trained to do upon such a contingency. They now took to the road, still firing. But their escape was short-lived. The Sherman had swung around its main gun and fired a projectile on a flat-trajectory at the trucks. The shell hit the rear truck broadside, blowing half its roof off and overturning it. The truck rolled over the edge of a gully and lay on its side, wreathed in crackling flames and acrid black smoke. The heavy machineguns on the half track added to the firepower. Within a matter of minutes the remaining two trucks with Red Cross markings had been stopped cold and all Germans inside them killed.

Sergeant Pee-Wee Malone of Hoboken, New Jersey, was the first GI to reach the nearest of the three trucks. Unlike the other two ahead of it on the road, it was no longer burning. Pee-Wee half-walked, half-skidded down the embankment and looked inside. The body of one SS man had gone tumbling from the truck on impact and lay sprawled in a mud puddle a few feet away. The other man was dead inside the rear, slumped over the Czech machinegun.

***

Pee-Wee climbed inside and gasped at what he saw. Behind the dead kraut, the truck was full of wooden crates bearing the emblem of the German Reichshbank in black stencil. A few of the crates had been jarred open by impact, and from within the shattered wood slats, Pee-Wee saw something gleaming dully, something that had come spilling from inside the crates when the truck had gone rolling over the embankment. In a moment Pee-Wee realized what he was looking at. It was gold, millions in gold.

THE BLACKOUT HEIST

"Holy shit!" he shouted to his radioman, Hoot Kelso. "Quick, we gotta get G-2 on the line."

"What is it, Sarge?" asked Kelso.

"Never you mind what," Pee-Wee yelled back. "Just do like I tell you. There's gonna be medals for us all when this here's over."

As the radioman got cracking, Pee-Wee turned back and looked inside the truck, pushing the pockmarked steel pot helmet back across his mop of curly brown hair and letting out a long, low whistle.

DAVID ALEXANDER

Book One:
Things Fall Apart

Things fall apart;
The center will not hold
-- W.B. Yeats; *The Second Coming*

THE BLACKOUT HEIST

Chapter One:
Light of Day

DAVID ALEXANDER

Petrov, Baikonur Cosmodrone, CIS. Vassily Petrov, chief flight engineer of the Baikonur Cosmodrome at the Tayuratam Space Center was awakened from a dreamless yet fitful sleep by the persistent burring of the in-house phone on the bureau beside his head.

Reaching muzzily toward the source of the bothersome chiming and flashing, Petrov idly noticed the time on the luminous red LCD display of his bedside clock as numb fingers raised the handset to his lips.

"Sorry to disturb you, sir," the voice of Gennadi Zuhbin, Petrov's deputy director on the other end of the line said, "however you left instructions to be alerted the moment that weather conditions showed any signs of improvement."

Petrov muttered a Ukranian peasant's oath he had learned at his father's knee into the keypad as he rose to a sitting position and combed his lank blond hair with his bony fingers. It had been hands too finely fashioned to properly hold a plow or woodcutter's ax that had been the crude beginnings of Petrov's present career.

THE BLACKOUT HEIST

That and an inquisitive mind that had led to a scholarship to Moscow's University of Engineering where his talents had not gone unnoticed by those who ran the Kremlin's military space program, one kept contained from Russia's lucrative multinational space partnerships with clients such as the Americans and the EU.

"Meteorology section reports that the winds have calmed to forty knots. Upper stratospheric conditions have improved as well. It is estimated that weather patterns will remain stabilized for at least another three hours."

Willing his sleep-drugged mind to function, Petrov considered for a moment. The launch of *Pichuga* or "Little Bird," a new *Yarkaya Zvezdya (YZ*-class*)* -- Bright Star class intelligence, reconnaissance and surveillance satellite -- onboard the mammoth Proton booster rocket, had on Petrov's order, been frozen at T-minus-one hundred fifty-five minutes due to severe atmospheric turbulence over the barren steppes caused by the approach of a sudden winter squall.

Delaying the launch had presented considerable difficulty for Petrov. Ordinarily the chief flight engineer's decision went unquestioned.

A liaison of technical observers from Moscow was conspicuously present in the launch control room (the intelligence men were younger and less self-important than they had once been although the fact that Moscow's technical people still called the shots was not in question) but the rigid protocols that had once characterized all facets of the lumbering Soviet bureaucracy were largely a thing of the past and, at any rate, they had never been as singularly applied to aerospace as elsewhere. For Petrov it was business as usual. While the FSB and SVR had replaced the old KGB, the acronym was still used as commonly in Russia as the American practice of still referring to their post-Homeland Security Act multi-agency intelligence apparatus as the CIA.

During this present launch, however, the regular KGB observer detachment had been augmented by a group of "technical advisors" attached to Soviet GRU or military intelligence who had completely cowed their KGB counterparts into a timid silence.

Whatever else they might be, the state security personnel were not now, and had even in the past rarely been, ideological zealots. But while the state's intelligence bureaucracy had been restructured, the ruling hierarchy of the Commonwealth had trodden more lightly where the military was concerned. To Petrov's mind, the GRU people still bore the light of Soviet fanaticism in their eyes.

The GRU party had swept in without warning the day before the launch, ostensibly conducting a routine inspection of facilities for the launch of the YZ-class military surveillance satellite scheduled for liftoff from the Cosmodrome that week.

Petrov had not believed the fiction that they were engaging in a routine launch inspection for a moment.

Although the new surveillance satellite was a military launch and therefore by nature classified, it was nonetheless an otherwise routine procedure that in itself should present no cause for the intense interest now being shown in it. Besides, even in today's Commonwealth of Independent States (as was much the same in America as well) virtually all space shots were by definition military undertakings.

On the contrary, the intense scrutiny to which the Cosmodrome had been subjected and the replacement of key members of Petrov's launch control staff by GRU technical experts were all indications that the launch of the YZ-*class* spy satellite was anything but a routine undertaking.

Petrov suspected that the GRU was clandestinely lifting some new, sophisticated military payload into orbit onboard *Pichuga*. More than suspected: he was certain that this was so.

Despite their stated rhetoric, the Americans had never ceased research and development on their Strategic Defense Initiative, nor had they paid more than lip service to joint, multinational control of an orbital ballistic missile shield. Each Space Shuttle launch brought the Pentagon's current PATRIOT Shield program's updated space weapons technology a step closer to completion and broadened the United States' dominance of orbital space.

The Americans had never killed Star Wars, only repackaged it into a less conspicuous form, first as the Ballistic Missile Defense Organization (BMDO) of subsequent White House administrations to its current incarnation as the US Missile Defense Agency (MDA). In response, the Russian Republic (and with it the Commonwealth) had stepped up its own SDI experiments even as they, like China, invited America's Fortune 500 corporate elite to sup at their table.

Most of the military payloads carried by the boosters that rose from the Tayuratam Space Center at Baikonur in Kazakhstan carried military space weapons technology of one sort or another. This was an open secret. So was the fact that much of it was devoted to develop countermeasures capable of penetrating the US PATRIOT Shield using advanced stealth capabilities.

That the *Yarkaya Zvezdya* launch contained some radically new, highly classified, and significantly advanced next-generation stealth technology, went a long way toward explaining both the unannounced appearance of the GRU inspection team and their eagerness to see the bird launched, despite the miserable weather.

While officially the Russian Space Forces, which jointly control Baikonur with the civilian Federal Space Agency, oversee all military space missions for the CIS, the open presence of the "big hats" from the GRU's sprawling headquarters building athwart Khoroshevskiy Highway in the Moscow exurb of Khodynke argued differently. So did the company-sized contingent of *spetsnaz* that Petrov knew had arrived with the big hats and which was armed to the teeth.

In any case, the very emblem of the GRU -- a great black bat, hovering over the globe with its wings outstretched -- symbolized the Russian military's long-standing preoccupation with *maskirovka*, the tactical arts of stealth, secrecy and deception, that underpinned the foundation of all Russian strategic and tactical thinking and policy-making. Whether intentional or not, the juxtaposition of the Russian bat to the American eagle spoke volumes about the mindsets of the two world powers.

Nevertheless, Petrov had been adamant, patiently explaining to his stone-faced, uniformed and bemedaled guests that to launch now would be a virtual guarantee of failure. He reminded them of the costly lessons that the Americans had learned in the wake of their own recent blunders on the launch pad.

Finally, they had been forced to accede to Petrov's decision to freeze the countdown, but Petrov knew that they would insist on a launch at the first available opportunity. Now that opportunity had presented itself.

Petrov rubbed sleep from the corner of one bloodshot eye and felt a sudden urgency in his bladder.

"I'm coming down," the chief flight engineer said into the telephone mouthpiece. "Order the countdown resumed at once."

TWO

Petrov, Baikonur Cosmodrone, CIS. The Baikonur Cosmodrome's mission control center was situated at the heart of an underground installation that stretched for many hundreds of meters beneath the partially frozen plains of the Central Asian steppes of southeastern Kazakhstan. The launch facility held the distinction of being the largest operational space facility in the world, as well as the first of its kind. Its layout resembled that of an amphitheater, with tiers of telemetry console stations arranged in a series of concentric circles that spiraled downward to a central bank.

Command, control and communications (C3) consoles requiring the highest security clearances made up the central ring of the control center, with the outer tiers -- each built one level above the next -- devoted to progressively lower-level functions and redundant backup systems.

Occupying most of one hemispherical wall was a series of giant view screens. Directly across the vast bunker, glass-paneled observation rooms and offices looked out at the screens and the proceedings below. Petrov's office was situated in one of those glass-paneled rooms.

Now, precisely one hour and fifteen minutes after being awakened by his deputy's call, the chief flight engineer stood holding a mug of steaming

43

black instant coffee and looking down on the furious activity in the command center below as the final minutes of the launch ticked away.

Opposite Petrov's window, on the curved wall of the darkened command center, the giant viewing screens showed the aluminum-hulled leviathan that was the multistage Proton-K workhorse launch vehicle steaming on its pad. Since their introduction Proton-class vehicles had become the standard platforms for lofting satellite payloads, including commercial satellites, into orbit from Russian space centers.

Wreathed in thin of smoke caused by pre-launch degradation of the otherwise stable hypergolic fuel that filled its capacious tanks and garishly lit by searchlights on tracked vehicles surrounding it, the Proton-K resembled some prehistoric monster newly risen from a million-year sleep beneath the ice-covered steppes.

Petrov's phone burred in a one-two cadence of high-low tones. The space center's director crossed to his desk and picked up the handset. Zuhbin, his deputy, was again on the line, issuing a fresh warning from meteorology about a newly formed storm cell that was rapidly closing in over southeastern Kazakhstan. Revised estimates now gave them only half the time previously allotted in which to launch the bird.

The director had no alternative but to order the launch to continue, however. The weather was one matter, politics another entirely, and a small army of trigger-happy *spetsnaz* no doubt getting drunk on vodka just outside the facility's doors was a compelling third. Petrov was well aware that politically the mission had long-since passed the point of no-return.

It was clearly apparent that the GRU overseers would not tolerate any further delay in the countdown. They would order the launch resumed in any case, Petrov knew. Cradling the telephone handset, Petrov returned to the picture window of his office.

Looking down on the launch control center, his glance now came to rest on the section of telemetry consoles in the central ring that was isolated from the rest of the area; consoles manned by the special technical personnel that the GRU party had brought with them from "the Aquarium," their headquarters' nickname.

Cordoned off by a detail of military police armed with Makarov side arms and AK-74 assault rifles, the operations of the GRU special section were screened from the view of all the other members of the launch control team including the director himself.

Petrov's lips tightened dourly. Whatever their purpose, he knew that the military men and the spooks would stop at nothing to achieve it. Like it or not, and despite the clear risk of lightning strikes from the steadily worsening electrical storm that raged across the steppes, the launch would continue.

***

During the final ninety seconds preceding liftoff, all launch control functions were shunted to high-speed blade server clusters which overrode all human control. The technology for the computers had been stolen, almost component by component, from a variety of American -- and purchased outright from some Japanese -- defense contracting firms.

Sensors attached to thickly shielded electrical cables that snaked from the launch gantry to the thirty-story Proton-K launch vehicle like monstrous umbilical cords constantly input data to the computers which monitored every element of the immense booster rocket's propulsion and navigational systems.

Had there been any glitches discovered in the thousands of individual components that together comprised the three-stage launch vehicle, the computers would have automatically halted the countdown, and thus saving Petrov a great deal of trouble.

They did not, however. The final seconds of the launch ticked off uneventfully. A tense hush fell over the control room as the eyes off all technicians immediately went to the giant view screens that flashed the televised image from cameras monitoring the launch.

Each member of the ground control crew knew that it would be a rough launch, filled with peril. The storm cell's outer edge was now only ten kilometers from the Space Center's perimeter, picking up speed and force with each kilometer it covered, with significant lightning strikes already reported that were increasing in tempo and electrical impact.

Wind velocity had already risen by three knots and large flakes of moisture-laden snow swirled around the skeletal launch gantries and the wall-like phased array radar banks and prefabricated Quonset huts that topped the command bunkers located nearby. The bird was scheduled to liftoff mere minutes ahead of the leading edge of the vicious blizzard that had swept down from Siberia like some invading army.

A few seconds too late, and the Proton's flight path could very well be altered to the point where it could no longer be controlled, in which case it would have to be destroyed in the air.

More snow began falling as the final seconds ticked off and the launch computer triggered the ignition of the giant chemical combustion engines by mixing the two-component hypergolic fuel that powered the booster stage of the Proton.

Inside the launch control room, the giant video view screens showed the blinding white fireball that suddenly blossomed beneath the boost stage's behemoth propulsion nacelles.

The rumble of the ground beneath the millions of cubic pounds of thrust was felt within the control room itself as the booster stage shuddered on its pad for a moment before beginning its liftoff.

Brighter now beneath the slowly rising nacelles, the sun ball of incandescent gasses elongated into a mammoth geyser of flame as the computer launch system released the latches securing the umbilical cables from the rocket to the launch gantry.

Within moments, the Proton-K had cleared the gantry on a pedestal of fire, beginning to climb vertically at a rate of over two hundred feet per second. If all went according to schedule, it would continue to climb steadily until it reached an altitude of one mile.

Minutes later, when the spacecraft had reached that point, a telemetry signal from the control room blew the explosive toggles releasing the spent booster stage and initiated a second stage burn.

Lighter now by some five tons, the Proton launch vehicle continued to gain altitude at almost twice its original speed until it was only a black speck on the command center's television view screens.

Moments later, it was completely out of visual range, having reached the upper limits of the earth's atmosphere. There its second stage was ejected. A third burn sent its final stage into orbital trajectory at over two thousand miles per hour, the velocity required to escape the pull of earth's gravitational field.

Less than twenty minutes after the spacecraft had lifted off its launch pad, its payload was ejected at a telemetric command from Baikonur's launch control computer bank.

A cheer went up from the ground crew as telemetry was received that the mission had been successful as a series of small burns parked the satellite into a low, stable geosynchronous orbit two hundred miles above the earth.

THREE

Baikonur-Khodynke, CIS. The high-resolution plasma display cast glowing bands of violet across the boney face and hard gray eyes of the GRU technical officer seated before it as he keystroked a coded command sequence that was instantaneously transmitted by microwave uplink into the fringes of orbital space.

Attached to the Tenth Directorate of the Russian GRU which was tasked with SIGINT or signals intelligence duties, the technician was a member of an elite group of military intelligence personnel whose security clearances extended to the highest operational levels.

Screened not only from the ordinary personnel of the Baikonur Cosmodrome launch control room, but from the support personnel who had accompanied the GRU team to the base, the technician reported directly to the Chief Security Officer of the GRU based in military intelligence headquarters in the Yasenevo area just southwest of Moscow and not far from the main GRU complex at Khodynke.

The limitations that had been placed on the technician's contacts went hand-in-hand with the role he played in his country's clandestine military space program. One that coexisted with the main business at Baikonur, which was purely commercial in practice and multinational in scope.

The procedures he was now in the process of implementing were in direct violation of bilateral treaties against deployment of space-based nuclear weapons. Indeed, their existence, if made public, might very well spell the end of the fragile agreements and protocols against military exploitation of space between the White House and the Kremlin that had recently been established between the former components of the disintegrated Soviet empire.

In a worst-case scenario, they could potentially sow the seeds of an East-West confrontation that would make the debacle of a Cuban Missile Crisis, or North Korean Nuclear Surprise of the Obama administration's second term, appear inconsequential by comparison.

But there had been no alternative to this risky gamble. Whatever the American or European Union intentions, the new hierarchy of the Commonwealth with its strong tie-lines to a still conservative military establishment could not sit idly by and allow the superior technology of the West to tilt the balance of power so precariously in the favor of the United States and its strategic defense partners in Europe and Southwest Asia.

When a muted though well-funded lobbying effort against US PATRIOT Shield deployment, followed by prolonged negotiations both public and secret, had failed to soften the resolve of the

American military and political establishment to deploy advanced third-generation Star Wars technology in space, Moscow had decided that measures of the most stringent nature were immediately called for.

Unable to match the Americans on the technological front, the Russians would have to engage in subterfuge. If not by strength, then they would succeed by guile, if not by the power of the eagle, then through the stealth of the bat. But subterfuge was an old Russian tactic, and a successful one as well, and adroitness at conspiracy still ran deep in the Russian soul.

In conventional warfare, the Russians had termed the strategy *maskirovka*, a much more sophisticated application of what to the west was known as stealth and force multiplication, and combining them both. During the Cold War thousands of dummy tanks, aircraft and weapons systems had been constructed to fool the CIA's surveillance satellites in orbit above the USSR into providing the raw data for estimates of Soviet military strength that were far in excess of the actual numbers.

The Commonwealth's new counterstrategy to American PATRIOT (Patrol and Reconnaissance In Orbit) Shield space-based weapon arrays would be a variation on this time-tested gambit. Guile would give the Russian people the decisive edge over the technologically superior though politically naive Americans.

Muted bands of primary color now shifted and played across the operator's face as the control sequence was completed and the screen flashed a graphic display which showed the operator the new system parameters.

A keystroke and mouse click shifted the display to a series of sine-wave graphs superimposed above a map of the western hemisphere that gave the apogees and perigees of the satellite's projected orbital transits. Another sequence corrected the satellite's course to place it in its final orbit.

At that point, the technician began to key-in the final instruction sequence that would complete his mission at Baikonur. Having performed this operation, the clandestine payload that the Pichuga surveillance satellite carried would become activated.

Trained in Moscow's GRU school for elite intelligence officers, the technician showed not the slightest sign of wavering as he input the complex command code string at the computer keyboard. Although aware of the implications of the task he now performed, it would have been alien to him to question for a moment what his superiors had ordered him to do. In a few moments, the sequence had been completed.

It was a sequence that armed the sixty kiloton nuclear explosive onboard the satellite.

Once armed, the Russian counterstrategy would be fully in place. It would ensure that the no present or future hardliners in the West could exploit its PATRIOT Shield defensive umbrella to launch a preemptive nuclear strike against the Commonwealth's vulnerable heartland.

Despite any technological superiority it possessed, the West would find itself completely vulnerable to nuclear counterattack should it attempt such an action. The strategy was simple, yet effective.

While American intercontinental ballistic missiles and nuclear bombers would have to travel halfway across the globe to reach their targets within the Russian heartland, the phased array of three YZ-class surveillance satellites would already be within the American strike zone. Until initialized, they would attract no attention. Indeed, as part of strategic nuclear treaties cosigned by both the US and all member states of the newly created CIS, such orbital spy platforms were required by both sides to monitor each others' compliance.

When detonated, each of the nuclear explosives onboard the three spy satellites would blanket a section of the North American continent with a wave of electromagnetic particles.

These EMPs would destroy communications, electrical systems; anything not sufficiently protected against them. In America, the Russians well knew, few things were. The West's SDI shield would in one fell stroke be cut off from ground control, effectively neutralized.

Now, armed and ready for another control sequence that might one day trigger them, the nuclear explosives would remain undetected onboard the satellites they rode through the airless black skies above earth's atmosphere. If they were never needed, they would never be deployed. But should the West ever attack the Commonwealth's heartland (and to the hardliners in its military establishment the possibility of this occurring was still held as an article of faith), they would be used -- blinding the American Cyclops before a thermonuclear stake was hammered through its heart.

The military intelligence officer logged off and rose from his seat in the darkened command center. At that moment the crash of thunder boomed across the steppes and lights dimmed as a forked bolt of raw electrical energy jabbed like a cosmic pitchfork into Baikonur's main operations building. *That was a bad one*, the GRU man thought as he lit a cigarette and reached to the side of his belt for his cell phone in order to inform the big hats of the mission's successful accomplishment.

DAVID ALEXANDER

FOUR

Skerrit, Manhattan. Rick Skerrit hit the snooze button on the buzzing alarm clock that had blasted him reluctantly awake at six o'clock on a cold Tuesday morning in late January.

On the rumpled sheets of the bed beside him, he caught a flash of bare breast and dark nipple as the woman turned over on her side, showing him her dark pubic triangle, and incoherently muttered something in her sleep.

Skerrit felt his flaccid pecker get hard again at the sight of her creamy white ass and her hirsute cunt. He wanted a little morning delight but he'd wait until she woke up to start the usual preliminaries to making the beast with two backs. For now, Skerrit sat up, finger-combed his straight black hair and went into the bathroom to answer nature's call.

Slipping on a blue terry robe, Skerrit padded downstairs to the kitchen of his house in Riverdale, New York and got a cup of coffee from the old Black and Decker machine that had survived a million mornings of repeated use as he watched the Hudson flow past only a few hundred yards from his kitchen window.

THE BLACKOUT HEIST

When he returned to his bedroom, his bed partner was already awake. Shyanne Robbins, another man's wife, lay propped on the pillows, her coils of dirty blonde hair in glorious disarray in the rays of dusty morning sunlight that slanted in through the high dormer windows of the old Victorian mansion.

Skerrit and Shyanne had been having an affair for the past year, ever since the pretty newswoman for New York CableMedia's Manhattan Channel had met him while covering the blackout that had plunged most of Harlem and the adjoining west Bronx into darkness the previous year.

The chemistry between them was immediate and explosive. After a few vodka martinis at the hotel bar of the Giraffe, near Grand Central Station, he knew they'd both agreed to have sex without a word having been exchanged or a liaison having been mentioned. Since the bar was conveniently located in the small but luxuriously appointed lobby of the Giraffe, they were enjoying one anothers' bodies only a few minutes later. To Skerrit's delight, Shyanne's tastes in lovemaking ran parallel to his own.

Before they'd even had time to warm the sheets, she had knelt between his legs, the tips of her long blonde hair dancing on Skerrit's abdomen as she enveloped the head of his organ with her lips, encouraging him to ejaculate on her breasts before their lovemaking proceeded any further. When he'd protested that he might not be ready to satisfy her, she'd laughed and told him not to worry. She could guarantee he'd be hard again in minutes.

56

Shyanne had proven to be every bit as good as her word.

Long afterward, when they lay spent in one anothers' sweaty arms, she had confessed that she had been entertaining thoughts of taking on a lover for many months. Following her husband's prostate surgery, he had been unable to sustain an erection, even with liberal doses of Viagra, and was spent too quickly to bring her to climax.

Skerrit had called room service for champagne and then had helped Shyanne make up for lost time.

***

Skerrit now got into bed beside Shyanne and kissed her on the lips -- lips she'd never admitted to having had "done" but which were to his thinking too good to be true, or at any rate, too plump to be real.

"Good morning," he told her. "Sleep well?"

"Like a hibernating bear," she told him, putting her arms around his neck and earnestly kissing him back. "And I need me some honey."

Skerrit felt the nipples of her breasts erected against his chest. She'd admitted to having those "fixed" but Skerrit was no purist. He could smell the musky odors rising from her hair and the nape of her neck, arousing him again immediately. Nothing fake about that good old androgen rush, and that's what counts, he thought. Shyanne smiled as her hand reached under his robe and skillfully manipulated the erection that had sprouted there.

"In a rush?" she asked with a laugh.

THE BLACKOUT HEIST

"Depends what you have in mind," he answered, his voice husky.

Removing her hand from where it was and laying him gently down on his back, Shyanne parted his robe and, bending her head, began showing him exactly what she had in mind for the next half hour.

***

At 7:45 AM, Rick Skerrit was crawling at twenty miles per hour in his four hundred horsepower Corvette ZR1 down the Henry Hudson Parkway toward the lower tip of Manhattan. Below 72nd Street, he was on the part of the Parkway that New Yorkers persisted in calling the West Side Highway, where traffic was backed up for miles in both directions. Nothing moved and drivers were ready to kill. Just another typical Tuesday morning in the Apple.

The sight of the scummy brown smog of airborne industrial pollutants that hovered over the island, chopping off the tops of skyscrapers except during exceptionally windy days, filled him with a mixture of emotions, none of which were pleasant. The fact -- which he had learned in high school and always recalled at times like these -- that smog was the gaseous equivalent of a bottle containing a shaken-up mixture of dirt and water didn't improve his outlook any.

Skerrit's stomach rumbled. His extended sexcapades with Shyanne had left him satisfied but had cost him vital commuting time, putting him in the midst of the worst of the morning's inbound rush-hour traffic.

DAVID ALEXANDER

He would have to stop at the Acropolis deli on 57th Street after he got off the West Side Highway at Seventh Avenue and grab himself a take-out breakfast. A western omelet, whole wheat toast, black coffee, cardiac-arresting home fries piled on the side. And ketchup. Plentiful ketchup. The kind of greasy-spoon morning junk food you could get nowhere else but in New York, eaten in a booth amid the inevitable smells from the griddle filling the entire place.

Skerrit had the radio on, listening to the morning news on the Country-Western station he liked because its inane and repetitive playlist was the perfect music by which to drive: While it screened out traffic noises, you never paid enough attention to its nasal vocals and whiny steel guitars to distract you from things that actually mattered.

A new wave of attacks by Philippine terrorists on Manilla, a serial killer in California preying on transvestite whores, a man wanted in Wisconsin for slaughtering brown bears for the alleged aphrodisiac properties of their testicles, and a failed space shot by the Neo-Soviet Union, as some of Washington's more outspoken denizens had begun calling the Russian Commonwealth, comprised the bulk of the morning's headlines.

Bored with the news, Skerrit switched over to another station that played C&W music and listened to Johnny Cash do "Ring of Fire."

The song's lyrics described a man caught in a love triangle, the metaphor of encircling flames symbolic of the precariousness of the illicit affair.

THE BLACKOUT HEIST

Skerrit was that man, sharing the circle with Shyanne. The flames were on the perimeter, drawing closer every day. One day -- Skerrit didn't know precisely when, but he knew that the day would arrive sooner than later -- those flames would be licking at his feet.

Their relationship could not go on much longer without discovery, if her husband had not already found out. But that wasn't the main problem. The danger of discovery to the contrary, Skerrit wasn't certain that he wanted to continue the affair.

Early on, he had decided that he had been drawn into it because he had been going through an early mid-life crisis. Shyanne was in her late twenties, he in his early forties. He had been attracted to her physically, indeed still was, but had grown tired of the relationship months ago. No, not tired. *Exhausted* was the better word.

There was a word for what Shyanne was, and that word, although currently out of fashion and politically incorrect, was nymphomaniac. Her sexual hunger was a second flame, burning at the center of the tightening ring of fire. Skerrit had lately grown weary of satisfying her unquenchable thirst for his cock and the semen that she milked from it more skillfully yet more insatiably than any lover he had ever known before. He was tired of playing the eternal swan to Shyanne's perpetual Ledo. Ultimately and finally, Skerrit needed a rest, and Shyanne -- well, she needed some therapy and probably some meds as well.

DAVID ALEXANDER

When you started thinking with your cock, Skerrit told himself, *it was a sure sign that something was wrong.*

Mid-life crisis was as good an explanation as any. Maybe it also explained why he had stuck his neck on the chopping block with MetroCon, the sprawling East Coast power utility for which he worked.

A graduate cum laude of MIT's School of Engineering, Rick Skerrit had been one of Metropolitan Consolidated Electric's youngest rising stars. Deputy director of electrical systems, Skerrit had been a sure bet to occupy the number one corporate position before the year was out.

He was, that is, until he had been commissioned to head the New York City Critical Energy Infrastructure Security Study Program, or CEISSP, which its critics in the media and government, leveling charges of political patronage, to Mayor Charles DeKeyser's corporate cronies, frequently conflated as "Cesspool."

Though local in application, the program was national in scope, funded by huge federal budget allocations for the current fiscal year as part of several critical infrastructure protection initiatives at the federal level. One of these was the Department of Homeland Security's Critical Energy Infrastructure Protection Program, established as a counter-terrorism initiative. This, among other things, meant that the federal pizza pie was the deluxe kind with pepperoni, mushrooms and extra cheese. The kind of pie that Washington baked in its big money oven and which made the mouths of

61

the friends of Mayor DeKeyser water for a hot, cheesy slice.

The bill establishing Cesspool had been passed in the Senate after New York State Senators and city Congresspersons ramrodded it through the House. Its impetus had been a sudden and widespread power outage that had slammed the city on the eve of the tenth anniversary of the September 11th, 2001, terrorist attack. The blackout had been popularly viewed as another terrorist strike, and even in its aftermath most city residents refused to believe otherwise, despite every fact to the contrary.

Though minor by comparison to the two landmark power failures that New York City had sustained in 1964, 1977 and 2003, the 2011 blackout had reminded many of the horrors the city had suffered through in the past. Black leaders had been especially incensed that Harlem could be without electricity or light or sewage treatment facilities for almost twenty-four hours. And in the Bronx they were Bronx-cheering City Hall from the Third Avenue Hub to Marble Hill, with Bronx Boro President Emmanuel Eboue shouting the boro's official motto *ne cede malis* -- do not give way to evil -- as the boro's rallying cry against the DeKeyser administration.

Charges of racism and criminal negligence echoed through the halls of city government. Part of the citywide blackout had hit Wall Street too, and the New York Stock Exchange cried conspiracy. In fact, across the length and breadth of New York's five boros, every business, ethnic and economic community had some other charge to level against City Hall. The city cried foul and the already embattled "Kaiser," "Colonel Klink" and sundry other cognomens, set to run for a fourth term as mayor, was once again put on the defensive.

The upshot had been a sweeping and unprecedented study of New York City's ability to withstand -- and proactively prevent -- another massive power outage of the magnitude of its two most serious cases. Sensing political capital to be made, the mayor himself had insisted on the study. The power utility had been forced to bow to the pressure from City Hall. The study had been implemented.

At the outset, Skerrit had been made to understand that, as his superior would be stepping down within the next twelve months, his performance at the head of the mayor's task force would influence his selection for the soon-to-be vacant spot.

At first, Skerrit had been ready to play the game, to turn in the whitewash that the utility, the mayor and the city government would have wanted, indeed had expected.

Skerrit continued to be ready to play the game. Until the facts began coming in. Facts that horrified him. Facts that had convinced him, in the end, that another major blackout of New York City would spell nothing short of utter catastrophe.

Then Skerrit had changed. He had decided that he could no longer play the shill for the city's corporate and political power brokers. And because he had not done so, because he had failed to lie to assure his own advancement, he was now facing the ax.

His mouth turning down in a grim line, Skerrit suddenly snapped off the radio dial.

There was no use in playing games with his head any longer.

Today the ax would fall.

Suddenly he had no stomach for music any more.

FIVE

Inskeep, the Bronx. At 8:15 A.M. the Metropolitan Transit Authority Subway Yard at 180th Street and Dyre Avenue in the Bronx hummed with activity.

Weekday morning rush-hour activity was nearing its peak usage load level, straining the city's mass transit system's already hypertensive passenger arteries to the point of coronary overload.

The train yard serviced the IRT lines that connected Manhattan with the Bronx by means of a network of tunnels, bridges and elevated trackways.

Its rolling stock was made up mostly of trains that had been scheduled for phase-out as far back as the early seventies but had been retained for active service throughout decades of fiscal mismanagement by Albany and City Hall. The longtime champ and title holder for being oldest and most rickety in the city was the IRT line, which still held the title against all contenders, and which still ran subway trains with graffiti throw-ups on individual cars. Consequently, the IRT line was also the one most chronically prone to accidents, breakdowns and slowdowns, to say nothing of mugging, flashing and purse-snatching.

Possibly to illustrate their determination to upgrade the obsolescent and decaying system, the MTA administration had selected the IRT lines to be among the first to receive the benefits of a massive transit modernization effort financed by a multi-million dollar bond issue.

Truckloads of cash had been poured into purchasing shiny new monel-nickel alloy-hulled cars from the giant French contracting firm Battignolles -- which not inconsequentially based large corporate plant facilities in Brooklyn and Queens, with US corporate headquarters in Lower Manhattan's Wall Street district -- the refurbishment of tunnels and track, the installation of new direction and route signs and a beefed-up security force to guard the trainyards from vandals and graffiti artists at night.

Despite this massive shot in the arm, and because it had been a victim of neglect for so long, however, the IRT system still had a long way to travel.

Apart from having been allowed to sink into the worst state of disrepair of all the rest of the city's underground railway lines, the IRT had been constructed in an era when commuter traffic levels had been far lower.

Designed for shorter trains that moved at slower cruising speeds and which carried fewer passengers than more recent models, the tunnels were narrow, labyrinthine and full of often surprising twists and turns that made them among the most treacherous underground thoroughfares in the entire system.

Consequently, trains negotiating many stretches of subterranean track were often forced to proceed at speeds far below normal.

Nothing short of completely rebuilding the tunnels would change the IRT's root problems. And that, of course, was out of the question.

***

Willie Inskeep climbed into the motorman's seat in the cab of the first car of subway run number 911, the three-digit-sequence standing for its time of departure at eleven minutes after nine that particular Tuesday morning. The ten-car train was to run from the 149th Street and Bay Avenue terminal in the Bronx and straight across Manhattan to the South Ferry terminal at the boro's southern tip near Battery Park. As Inskeep switched on his radio and started his pre-run checklist, he also began the enactment of a cosmic contradiction known only to himself.

The roots of the contradiction lay in Inskeep's two-year hitch in Surinam during the Malaysian War, where he'd served as a member of a tunnel interdiction team, the mission of which was to burrow like human rats into Al Qaeda-linked Kumpulan Mujahideen rebel tunnels and neutralize the warrens of booby-trapped passageways. It was a job that earned the teams the name of tunnel rats.

Waging subterranean warfare in the dark, confining netherworld of the Surinam tunnels for two years had left him scarred for life. But it had not

67

kept him down. His psyche had been scarred again on 911, when he'd spent the better part of a day trapped in an IRT beneath Lower Manhattan mere blocks from the stricken World Trade Center towers, struggling to maintain order and calm among the passengers. The number of this morning's run was an irony not lost on him, but he shrugged it off like everything else that stood in the way of the job he had to get done. Shit happened. So the run was numbered with a nine and a one and another one after that? So what? It was just numbers, that's all.

Inskeep inserted the L-bracket between the cab's door and the jamb to keep the door open a regulation two inches. That was all the MTA allowed its motormen for purposes of ventilation in the confining subway cabs that were little larger -- and not much more comfortable -- than a conventional broom closet.

Usually, though, it was more than most MTA motormen themselves permitted. Two inches, after all, was ample space to allow in enough marijuana smoke to get you high by the end of your run. More importantly, it afforded sufficient clearance for the barrel of a semiautomatic pistol, submachinegun or sawed-off Mossberg to be stuck in and a wallet, jewelry or a wristwatch to be passed back out.

New York's prevalent subway crime and other risks didn't strike passengers exclusively. In addition to the threat of terrorist human-bombs blowing themselves and a carload of straphangers to pieces, motormen were also being robbed in ever-increasing numbers.

DAVID ALEXANDER

It had become standard procedure to check out the first car before entering the trainyard in order to determine if anybody bent on mugging the motorman was lying in wait. In increasing numbers, motormen, conductors and other transit authority personnel were applying for -- and being granted -- full-carry pistol permits.

Some of this weaponry would give Arab terrorists pause for concern. It was not uncommon for compact Uzis or Ingram M-11 submachineguns to be carried by motormen beneath their regulation pinstripe overalls or by conductors beneath their navy blue tunics.

Motorman Inskeep had never applied for a pistol permit, however, nor did he have any intention of doing so. He did not like guns. So far he hadn't had any trouble. Sure, there had been minor problems.

Once an irate passenger had punched him square in the face because the passenger been angered that the train was stuck in a tunnel. But that had been all. Even though that passenger had been a woman, she had hit him hard enough to bloody his nose, and had run out of the car fast enough to lose herself on the crowded platform.

In over ten years of driving MTA rolling stock, he had worked on every line there was, and hadn't yet found himself in a life-threatening situation. Maybe it was a question of attitude. Inskeep had a theory: if you worried about it, the predators sensed your nervousness. Like dogs smelling fear, they were then more likely to attack.

THE BLACKOUT HEIST

Pulling out the train's clutch, Inskeep heard the intercom in his cab crackle as his conductor came on-line, announcing to passengers that the IRT train was about to depart from the station.

"This is a number six local," the voice of conductor La Dollicia Shavers crackled over the intercom. "First stop will be Baychester Avenue where you can change for the Number 7 Flushing Line and the Number 4 IRT Express. Watch the closing doors and thank you for riding with the New York City Transit Authority."

A moment later, motorman Inskeep heard the two short buzzes which told him that the conductor had successfully closed every one of the train's twenty-four passenger-access doors. According to the MTA safety code, a train was not permitted to depart from a station if even a single door remained open.

This rule was not always honored, however, and it was not uncommon for passengers finding themselves stuck between the doors to be dragged along the platform as the train pulled out.

As Inskeep heard the buzzes, the red indication light simultaneously glowed on the console in front of him, signifying that the doors were closed. The train was now ready to pull out of the station.

Letting out the clutch, motorman Inskeep slowly eased back on the brake, watching the signals change from red to green as far down the trackway as he could see.

Moments later, he was on the elevated track bed that connected the subway yards with the first station on a run that would eventually take him across the island of Manhattan and beneath the East River into the boros of Queens and Brooklyn.

THE BLACKOUT HEIST

Applebaum, The Bronx. Mott Haven City was a middle-income housing complex that had been erected in the middle of the nineteen sixties. From the leveled earth from which an entire neighborhood had been converted into three million cubic tons of landfill sold by New York to the municipality of Shreveport, Louisiana, twelve high-rise towers of poured concrete and structural steel each rose sixty stories into the air, stone colossi dominating the skyline for miles around.

Each soaring, sky-challenging concrete tower housed six hundred apartment units. A security station, an underground parking garage and a post office were also located on-premises by the architects and the city planners.

The complex had been planned as the centerpiece of an urban renewal project for the entire eastern sector of the South Bronx that was to have included shopping malls, office buildings, new schools and a sewage treatment facility. Instead, the area had continued to slide inexorably down the

72

slope of urban decay into the bottomless pit of inner-city blight that yawned at its bottom.

With the onset of the seventies, however, as the surrounding sections had degenerated neighborhood-by-neighborhood into rubble-strewn wastelands resembling the aftermath of the World War Two bombing of Dresden rather than the twenty-first century urban utopia that the city planners had envisioned, the South Bronx had been all-but-abandoned. The money had run out by then, and with it, the will to continue.

Mott Haven City now stood in the geographic center of one of the hardest-hit urban areas in the country.

Its middle-class occupants were forced to negotiate through ghetto streets that were little better than demilitarized zones in order to reach the dubious sanctuary of their homes every evening; streets divided into turf ruled and fought over by drug dealers, streets walked by prostitutes, patrolled by vicious crack gangs and watered with the blood of the gangstas, or g's, and their victims alike.

Few ventured outside the housing complex after dark and few even during the daylight hours, except within the relative safety of automobiles with the doors locked and the windows rolled up tightly.

Despite the skeleton staff of city housing police which was charged with patrolling Mott Haven, muggings, push-in robberies, rapes and other violent street crimes were common occurrences within the environs of the complex.

THE BLACKOUT HEIST

Its occupants lived in a state of perpetual fear. They knew that the housing cops were little better, and often worse, than the street animals they were supposed to protect them from. The message of the savages were clear: the streets belong to us g's, and Mott Haven City belongs to the streets.

As a result of the conditions of life in the complex, there had been a slow attrition over the course of the last decade. For every three families that moved out, only one moved in.

Even in a time of acute housing shortages, there were vacant apartments on practically every floor of every building in the sprawling multiunit complex.

The vacant apartments quickly became transformed into heroin shooting galleries, crack houses and trysting places for prostitutes and their tricks. Less often, though with increasing frequency, they had become execution chambers for those caught in the crossfire of the city's never-ending crack wars.

Few of the hallways were adequately lit, and some not at all; since light bulbs were smashed as soon as they were installed, the management rarely bothered anymore. Graffiti throw-ups covered many of the olive-drab interior walls of the complex with the ugly modern equivalent of primitive cave paintings.

Small wonder that to the inhabitants of the complex, Mott Haven City was called by a name other than that which its planners had intended.

The Bronx Zoo.

***

DAVID ALEXANDER

Marty Applebaum palmed a magazine containing thirty-two 5.56-millimeter hollowpoint rounds into the receiver of the Heckler-Koch MP5 submachinegun and pulled back the charging handle located just behind the barrel, cranking a live round into the weapon's firing chamber.

Dressed in camo fatigues, Applebaum thumbed the select-fire lever of the HK to safety position and walked across the rooftop of Building Five of the Bronx Zoo.

When he had reached a position adjacent to the rooftop entrance door, Applebaum brought the subgun to hip position, thumbed the select-fire lever to full-auto and squeezed off a three-round burst at the human figure he had chalked on the entrance door.

Flame belched from the MP5's muzzle as bullets were ejected in a figure-eight pattern, leaving a jagged line of petaled holes in the concrete wall across the upper torso of the outline of the figure.

Applebaum laughed and squeezed off the remaining rounds in the magazine into the steel-plate of the rooftop door, enjoying the sight of puncture flowers of metal appearing around the holes in its rusty surface, then slung the subgun over his shoulder by its bandolier strap.

At first they'd called the cops, but there was nothing anybody could do. Applebaum had a legal right to own any kind of firearm he wanted, even in New York City where the laws for weapon possession were the toughest anywhere in the country. Applebaum had found the loophole in the law.

He was a licensed federal gun dealer. All he'd needed to do was to fill out a Bureau of Alcohol, Tobacco and Firearms application form and pay the government a hefty registration fee. Presto! -- he was legitimate. The cops couldn't take any of his weapons away. All they could do was fine him for firing them illegally within the city limits. To Applebaum, the fines were part of the cost of doing business.

After awhile, the neighbors didn't bother complaining. Ultimately it had sunk into their heads that with "Mad" Marty Applebaum running around the rooftops of Mott Haven City armed to the teeth with sophisticated small arms, and spraying everything with bullets, the punks who perpetually mugged them, knifed them and raped their sons and daughters would be less inclined to be there too.

Nobody bothered "Mad Marty" anymore. He was even respected, after a fashion, by his fellow tenants.

Applebaum slung the once German, now all-American, submachinegun over his shoulder and lit a cigarette as he leaned over the concrete parapet and looked over the bombed out wreckage of the South Bronx below him.

Unlike the rest of the Bronx Zoo's terrified residents, Applebaum went anywhere he wanted, at anytime, day or night.

Below him was a war zone. It was as much of a combat zone as had existed in any war ever fought. Down there was the Tet Offensive in the Season of the Witch. Down there was the Normandy beachhead, down there was the Valley of the Shadow of Death.

Mad Marty Applebaum called it home base. The rent-controlled apartment he lived in was inexpensive, subsidized by the city and no problem to vacate in a hurry, no questions asked. Plus, his gas and electricity were free. You couldn't beat a deal like that.

That was important for a guy in Marty's line of work. A professional mercenary had always to be ready to make tracks fast when the call to action came his way.

Although the only mercenary work Marty had gotten so far was a short stint as a bodyguard for an aging Borscht Belt comedian who'd experienced a final spurt of fame on the way to the graveyard that had led to a national tour and bad reviews, he had hopes that some day soon he'd be called upon for active duty in a covert fire zone in some exotic, faraway place.

It was hard to get merc work, Marty knew, unless you were hooked up with one of the "old boy" networks of Iraq vets. But Marty had made up his mind that he was in the merc business for the long pull. At the merc school in Alabama that he'd attended the year before, he'd gotten a taste of the lifestyle led by real-life soldiers of fortune and had decided that it was for him.

Marty was confident that something would come his way soon. He had been running display advertisements in International Mercenary

Magazine. Any day now, one of his ads on Craigslist or his résumé on Linkedin were sure to be answered by a prospective client -- a client, it need not be added, who would hire Marty as soon as he got a look at the weapons and know-how that his money would buy. That day, Marty knew, was not far off.

For the immediate present, though, he'd console himself with firing off another couple of rounds on the graffiti-covered rooftop of Building Five of the Bronx Zoo.

SEVEN

Amoroso, Manhattan. Ellis Amoroso was about to hit the jackpot. He'd been trying to hit it, in one form or another, for most of his life. Now he was about to hit it and hit it big.

Earlier that morning, Amoroso had begun the commute from his ranch-style home in Massapequa, Long Island, to his job as chief clerk at the payroll processing firm in Manhattan that he had worked at for the past nine years. But today marked the start of a permanent break with routine.

Left behind inside the top drawer of the dresser in his bedroom, where in time it was sure to be discovered atop a pile of his wife's underwear, was a note he'd left behind.

Addressed to his wife, Amoroso's note stated that by the time she would read it he would already be on his way out of the country with a million dollars of receipts he had embezzled from his firm. The note also went on to say that Amoroso had changed his identity and was starting an entirely new life far away from Massapequa, Long Island.

Amoroso's note had ended by expressing hopes that his wife would understand what he was doing and that she would find happiness. The note didn't, however, say exactly *how*. That would be up to her to figure out. Well, thought Amoroso, fuck the bitch anyway. Happiness sounded nice but was probably unattainable.

Now, as Amoroso exited the E-line shuttle on the subway platform one level beneath the Battery Park Commerce Towers promenade, after an hour's commute on the Long Island Railroad from his Massapequa ranch home, he experienced a numbing sense of panic that forced him to rethink the entire plan.

The plan was simple in execution and design but highly daring in concept. It was almost a surefire guarantee to work. All it would take was a little bit of luck to see Amoroso through.

The key to Amoroso's plan lay in the priority access codes to the firm's MVS computer servers that Amoroso had tricked the company's mainframe into supplying with despite his only having entry-level access. In some cases, Amoroso had generated bogus login credentials of his own to allow him to get into areas of the system that nobody else but he himself knew about.

With the illicitly obtained access codes and login credentials, Amoroso had two things at his fingertips that he had never had before: *power* and *control*. Possession of the keys to the digital kingdom had allowed him to penetrate to the nucleus of the corporate computer system. *Once you had the software by the balls*, Amoroso had often snickered to himself, *the computer's heart and mind will follow.*

Once there, he could perform what he thought of as his "dirty little miracles." Profitable miracles. Miracles that other people, not blessed with

Amoroso's gift for poetic metaphor, might call by another, more prosaic name: computer disbursement fraud.

The central organizing principle behind computer disbursement fraud is a simple one: its central objective is to fool the computer into issuing checks to people and companies that don't really exist.

An experienced programmer with a natural gift for manipulating the tricky logic of computer hardware and software, Amoroso possessed the background to make his "dirty little miracles" happen. All that had been lacking was motive.

That had come when Amoroso had discovered that Lacey, his wife of ten years had been having a steamy love affair with the manager of a local supermarket, who happened to wear a turban and robe as part of some arcane West Indian religious obligation that Amoroso had trouble understanding, but figured had to do with voodoo. But one thing he'd found easy to understand -- betrayal. He had caught them together one afternoon when he had returned home early.

They had been so engrossed in their fucking and sucking, and his wife's moans of passion had been so exuberantly loud, that they had not even noticed him standing in the bedroom door, watching them perform their sexual acrobatics. Then Amoroso had noticed the webcam on a tripod that was pointed at the bed and the little red light glowing next to the zoom lens.

He had left his house with the image of his wife on her knees, the black woman's large, pendulous breasts flopping from side to side as she penetrated Lacey's vagina with a strap-on rubber dildo -- which matched her skin tone -- and the grunts and cries of both women as they copulated ecstatically on the bed, oblivious to everything else in the world but their lesbian pleasure.

Amoroso's motive to embark on a life of crime had been further bolstered when Amoroso had been passed over for promotion and his twenty-five-year-old junior assistant, Mego Eagle, late of the Cayman Islands, promoted in his place. Amoroso had started drinking shortly thereafter. Drinking heavily. His life, he realized, was caving in around his ears. He was convinced that he would never be able to dig himself out of the wreckage.

Then he began thinking about the money that flowed past him every day. Thousands of dollars every hour, millions every week, the flow of cash reflected in the figures that danced across the screen at his work station in glowing green characters.

And suddenly one day, as Amoroso stared into the money stream that raged past him like the swollen rush of a river in spate, he beheld his image trembling on the surface of the flow. The image was one of a rich man, a man who could afford to take life as it came, a man who had no worries at all.

And Amoroso saw that it was good.

But when Amoroso tried to touch the image, he found, like Sisyphus, that the stream into which he'd cast his expectant gaze might as well have been on another planet, a million light years away. Enough money passed him by to provide him with a dozen lifetimes of ease and comfort in the company of women who made Lacey look like the stale dog shit she was. But none of the dream was his to keep.

If only he could dip into the stream and take a small piece of the wealth he coveted so desperately. Say, a million dollars. Who would notice? A million dollars wasn't as much as it used to be, but it was still enough to allow him to live comfortably for the rest of his life in another country where the cost of living was lower. So what if that country was Azerbaijan or Sudan? Anything was better than Massapequa and the bitch he'd married.

Fantasy had soon hardened firmly into conviction. Amoroso swore that he would find a way to dip his bucket into the money stream, to smash his fist into the mocking Cyclopean cyber eye of his computer terminal and come out clutching a thick sheaf of purloined greenbacks.

After that, he would go away. Forever. Amoroso had decided on the island of Majorca, off the coast of eastern Spain. Life was cheap there, even today. He'd spent a few months there in the late sixties, dealing heroin and hashish brought up from the hill country of Morocco where the Berbers of the Southern Sahara fed it to their children and camels like tahini halva. Though pitifully brief, it had been the best time of his life. It could be again. He could disappear and nobody would find him. Not in a million lifetimes.

He would let his hair and beard grow again, walk around in faded jeans and stay stoned on good Libyan kif smuggled across the Med in freighters and trucks all day long. It would be just like the late sixties all over again. Free and easy. The twenty-some years in between would mean nothing. It wouldn't mean jack fuckin' shit.

Often Amoroso had looked at himself in the mirror and wondered how he had changed into what he was today: a bored-to-shit working stiff who sipped his lunch out of a highball glass and contemplated suicide on the way to work each morning, with a two-story ranch home he couldn't pay for and an unfaithful wife that he no longer loved.

When had the change begun to take effect? When was the moment that the freewheeling, free-loving drug dealer had begun the slow, Kafkaesque metamorphosis into the cockroach-body of the middle-aged loser he was today? Sometimes Amoroso believed that if he could just fix that moment in time, pinpoint its exact onset, then he could free himself from the curse that had ultimately become his lot.

But he had never been able to, and when he'd finally given it up, the drinking had started in an attempt to forget. The booze didn't bring forgetfulness, though. Instead it inflamed his mind all the more, sparked wild fantasies of dropping out, assuming another identity, and disappearing forever.

On one of those drunken binges, he had begun to idly consider ripping off the payroll receipts in order to finance his disappearance. A man couldn't drop out without funds, after all. And what better place to steal money than from a payroll processor?

DAVID ALEXANDER

The plan had begun to take shape in his mind as a purely hypothetical exercise, but soon Amoroso began to realize that he was already on the road to planning his cyber crime in earnest.

Over a period of eighteen months, Amoroso had succeeded in channeling close to one million dollars in computer-generated checks, purchase orders, payment vouchers, requisition slips and advices of credit to a succession of dummy companies, pension funds and fictitious private individuals. The funds were then wire-transferred to bank accounts near Amoroso's job he'd had opened in order to park the funds until he was ready to retrieve them.

This week would be the final week of the scam. Amoroso now had all the money he felt was necessary to begin his new life. He had already booked a flight out of the country. By tomorrow morning, he would be in Amsterdam, the next day, Madrid. And then it was on to Majorca and his well-earned reward. The thought of it made him shiver with excitement. And visions of the ripe brown melon tits on young Moorish beauties that would be his for the plucking made his dick get hard.

To make absolutely certain that suspicion would not fall on him until it was much too late for anyone to interdict him, Amoroso had timed his disappearance to coincide with the start of a two-week vacation. A vacation that only Amoroso knew would last for the rest of his life.

He had already bought tickets for a direct flight to Holland, from where a flight to Spain and another brief charter hop would wing him to his final destination.

As Amoroso rode one of the large passenger elevators up to the seventy-sixth floor of the Commerce Towers' East Tower where his office was located, he again felt reassured. This plan wasn't the mere product of a drunk's imagination. It could -- and would -- work.

By seven o'clock this evening, Amoroso would be on his way to a new life with over one million dollars in his suitcase. His cheating lesbian wife and his treadmill job would be long forgotten, part of another incarnation.

Stepping off the elevator, Amoroso pushed through the high, glass-paneled doors and walked across the gray industrial carpet toward the small cubicle in which he had a desk and a phone and a computer terminal that flashed him tantalizing visions of another life, his only regret that he had forgotten to include a pink dildo with the note he had left in his wife's underwear drawer.

EIGHT

Kendricks, Washington, DC. Traffic moved sluggishly across the cross-Potomac Arlington Memorial Bridge connecting the Washington, DC metropolitan area to the outlying suburbs of Fairfax County, Virginia via the Beltway. Marshall Kendricks sat behind the wheel of the cream Toyota listening to a Baltimore hip-hop station as he wrestled with the problem that had keep him from getting to sleep all the previous night.

Kendricks had been given the task of coordinating the consolidation of the CIA's files with those of the DHS, the Department of Homeland Security. The fragmentation of the system, using up to six different databases, had contributed to the degradation of the intelligence agency's capacity to gather information. The Senate's Intelligence Oversight Committee had mandated a review of the data filing and acquisitions procedure and had determined above the protests of Director of CIA Lambert Edwards, that a streamlining of this important facet of the intelligence cycle was long overdue.

In the course of Kendrick's work, he had begun to see disquieting patterns emerging. These patterns were subtle at first but soon became clearly apparent. He had just learned of an operation by a secret cadre within the agency. There might have otherwise been time to go through channels, but Kendricks knew that he could not remain silent as was traditional policy. Iran-Contra, the Watergate mess and even the Cold War itself could have been averted if the fetish for secrecy had not been in force. Kendricks had decided to take his suspicions directly to the top. He had asked for an appointment with the Deputy Director of Operations and would lay out his findings there.

Kendricks rode the Beltway past the entrance to Fort Murphy, the training ground for CIA field personnel called the Village, and continued on toward the CIA Campus at nearby Langley, Virginia. He took the turnoff and went down the two-lane highway. It was the hour for the morning rush and Kendricks slowed his car to queue up behind a Ford that like himself, indeed like most of the drivers in the line, were bound for the checkpoint leading into the Langley headquarters of the Central Intelligence Agency.

Preoccupied with his own thoughts, Kendricks was only half paying attention to events taking place around him. Only when the horror struck him did he realize that a man wielding a short barreled Krinkov type AK rifle had stepped from one of the cars. Kendricks could only sit in the state psychologists call frozen fear as the gunman swung the AK into the open driver's side window of a vehicle four car lengths down and pumped a burst of 7.62 millimeter slugs into the heads of the two passengers in the front seat.

The gunman had begun walking and firing. His next burst shattered the windshield glass of the car behind the first vehicle. The next burst caught a man and a woman who were in the process of attempting to flee their own car. To Kendrick's horror he saw that the gunman was approaching him as he struggled to unfasten his seat belt buckle finding that it would not budge, which was odd since he had never had any trouble with it before.

By his car, the gunman paused for a moment. His eyes locked on Kendricks and the CIA analyst thought he saw a smile on the man's face accompanied by a look of recognition in the hard gray-brown eyes. Then the muzzle swung against his face and the world exploded in a spitting shower of hot yellow flame.

The gunman saw the driver hurled backwards by the force of the blast. For good measure, he pumped another three round burst into the twitching corpse making it shiver in its seat. He moved on and emptied the rest of his clip into the car behind Kendricks' vehicle. Then he ran along the embankment and disappeared.

More than twelve hours later, the shooter had gone to ground as planned in the small town of Mecklen in the South Tyrol region of Austria, only a stone's throw from the Italian border. His presence was not missed. Odessa, the underground fraternal organization of Nazi SS members, had seen to it that a man resembling the shooter was visible at all times. He had performed his work well, and the

THE BLACKOUT HEIST

Odessa's American members of the neo-Nazi *kameradershaftung* or fraternity, would have a clear field in which to perform their end of the long-awaited master plan.

<u>NINE</u>

Bingham, Manhattan. "Spa' fiftuh cints? Uhm trine tuh git 'nuf togethuh fo'a meal."

The wino was directly in front of Bingham's path. He stank. His bloodshot eyes bugged in a face so scarred and pitted that it looked as though it had been gnawed on by a family of hungry rats.

Bingham carefully walked around the beggar, watching the guy out of the corner of one eye. You never knew. They might attack. If no one were looking and they thought they could get away with it, then they *would* attack. Bingham had no doubts about this happening.

"Ga' bless yuh, suh," Bingham heard the derelict wheeze as he put some distance between himself and the panhandler.

It might not be so bad if it had been like before, when there were only the usual number of homeless people on the street. Bul not anymore.

Ever since the city, in its infinite wisdom, had decided to put a drop-in center for the homeless in Bingham's Upper East Side neighborhood, the streets had begun to resemble more the slums of Calcutta than the urban Mecca of New York's yuppies.

THE BLACKOUT HEIST

Oh, sure, there had been the pickets, the lobbying, the court actions, the playing to the media -- all of the by-now familiar NIMBI street theater common to such occasions. In a neighborhood where the average annual income ran to the six figures, there was plenty of clout with the local politicians. The mayor's office had been petitioned more than once, but the mayor had held firm. This happened to be one of the Kaiser's pet projects.

All New Yorkers, regardless of personal income, the mayor had proclaimed, would now have to share the burden of the homeless problem that grew with each passing day. It was a problem, he'd gone on, that would not go away by itself. Every citizen of the city would have to shoulder part of the burden, do his or her individual bit.

The concept behind the five drop-in centers that the mayor's plan had called for was to provide the homeless with places where they could find temporary shelter, a hot meal and facilities to shower and do their laundry before moving on.

Long committed to permanent shelters as a solution to the homeless crisis, the mayor had shifted his priorities after it had become clear that the homeless shunned the centers like healthy people shunned leper colonies.

The drop-in center on the Upper East Side had become a cornerstone of the mayor's new policy. It would demonstrate, he had claimed, that no neighborhood of the city was exempt from doing its fair share.

The pleas of residents that the influx of hordes of homeless would create the danger of rampant crime fell on deaf ears. Like Pharaoh before him, the more they pleaded, the harder the Kaiser's heart had become.

And so the center had turned into a reality for the residents of one of the Upper East Side's ritziest neighborhoods. Like a magnet, it seemed to draw in the homeless from every corner of the city.

By the hundreds, each day, they flowed into the neighborhood's streets. Within a week after the drop-in center's opening, street crime and burglaries had jumped by an alarming fifty percent.

Bingham felt himself cursed by fate. He had dreamed of owning a duplex apartment in a brand-new luxury co-op from the moment he'd arrived in New York six years before.

Despite two stock market crashes and a severe contraction of the New York financial market, his position as a Wall Street stock broker with a prestigious investment banking firm had given him the means of realizing his dream.

He had purchased a duplex co-op in the Borealis, a giant sliver high rise in the Upper Eighties. His apartment gave him a magnificent view of the East River. It had a terrace on which he threw lavish parties. It was his own little slice of Valhalla.

Until, that is, the brownstone across the street had been turned into a Mecca for every scum person in the entire world. Now Bingham had to make an end-run around scores of beggars that filled the once quiet, tree-lined streets of the neighborhood. It was a problem, he reflected as he reached the building's lobby, that would now probably never go away.

"Hey dude, spare five bucks so I can get a hand job?"

The wino's face seemed acid-washed, his breath could stop a charging rhino at a hundred paces.

Cornered, Bingham was reaching into his pocket for an obolus to Charon before he realized that the wino had somehow managed to slip past the doorman and hide himself in the elevator. Bingham tipped the doorman instead and stood in the lobby watching the elevator ascend. He hoped the fucker robbed them all blind.

***

Mayor Charles DeKeyser held out his arm and spread two fingers to form a "V." To millions of New Yorkers, and to the world at large, this trademark gesture meant that the mayor was signaling victory. To City Hall insiders, however, it had another meaning entirely.

To the insiders, the "V" meant that the mayor wanted another blue ten-milligram Valium. On the double.

The reason for the mayor's sudden gesture was on the TV screen in front of him in his City Hall executive office.

The arrogant, patrician face, aggressively contorted lips, pig-like eyes and comb-over hairdo of real estate baron Roland Stone was usually enough in itself to give the mayor agita. But when Stone started working his mouth, it could send the mayor's pulse right through the ceiling.

DAVID ALEXANDER

"Francisco," the mayor hollered, "get your ass in here on the double." Francisco Zapata was the mayor's aide. He was also the mayor's longtime lover, but although the relationship of the two men was an open secret in city government as well as to the members of the press, it was not openly talked about.

The mayor had strong feelings about being gay. He did not feel that it had anything to do with his political life and believed that his private life was nobody's business but his own. He had made it clear from the outset that anybody who tried to make it an issue would feel the full force of his righteous anger. So far, nobody had dared raise it.

Zapata came in with the rubber tubes of a blood pressure measuring unit dangling from one hand and a prescription vial of Valium in the other. He already knew the reason behind the mayor's shout. Roland Stone was on television. He and the mayor had been having another of their public pissing matches this week. This time it had been over the mayor's new pet project, drop-in centers for the homeless.

As Zapata strapped the belt over the mayor's arm, the press conference Stone had held the previous night at Stone Mountain, the mammoth skyscraper in the heart of Midtown that was the real estate czar's world headquarters and personal Taj Mahal, was broadcast.

His mouth haughtily screwed up in arch contempt, Stone told with obvious glee that he thought the mayor's plan was not only ridiculous, but had been aimed directly at him personally.

THE BLACKOUT HEIST

Why else did the mayor's plan call for constructing the five drop-in centers directly adjacent to the sites of buildings owned by Stone, than to lower real estate values and personally discredit him?

As Zapata pumped up the blood pressure meter's flexible rubber cuff, DeKeyser watched as newswoman Shyanne Robbins, reputed to pay for her news information by giving the best blow jobs in the city, asked Stone what motive the mayor might have to cause him embarrassment.

Stone laughed. He had obviously been waiting for the question. He replied that the mayor was infuriated by Stone's showing him up for what he was: an inept idiot, a base fool, a clown prince of jesters.

Stone, after all, had demonstrated this on several occasions beyond all shadow of doubt, the most recent of which had been when his own personal construction staff had saved the Brooklyn Bridge from collapsing into the East River after city inspectors had declared that nothing short of a massive federal bailout could save the iconic structure from doom.

Now, with this newest campaign declared Stone, the mayor was getting back at him for showing him up. The drop-in centers would act as magnets for the homeless, drawing them into the best neighborhoods of the city in the same way that doggie doo attracts the flies of summer. This would not do anything to genuinely relieve their suffering except to offer a band-aid solution.

It would, however, have a lasting negative impact on city real estate properties. Wasn't New York deteriorating enough as it was? asked Stone. Did we really need a city policy that encouraged further urban decay?

Mayor DeKeyser suddenly lurched from his chair and snapped off the TV, almost ripping the blood pressure machine from his aide's hand.

"Chuckie, be careful," Zapata said. "Now I'll have to take the reading all over again."

"Fuck the reading," the mayor shouted, popping a handful Valium tablets into his mouth. "I've got some heavy shit to think about. Now get your nellie ass out of my sight."

THE BLACKOUT HEIST

TEN

Suckdog, Staten Island. The Mall was situated only a few miles from the Verrazano Bridge which connected the city's fifth boro of Staten Island with southern Brooklyn.

The Mall boasted an Alexander's and a Macy's branch as well as an Arnold Schwarzenegger health spa that was popular with housewives between shopping and taking the kids to and from school. There were also numerous small specialty shops lining its two shopping levels that sold everything from acid-washed jean ensembles to imported goat cheese from Yugoslavia.

The Mall also had a quadplex theater that showed two matinees daily and a multilevel indoor parking garage that had a capacity of five thousand automobiles.

Although the Mall had just opened for the day, it was already rapidly filling up with shoppers from the middle-class bedroom communities that surrounded it in every direction.

The Spread 'N Buns Food Court was crowded with mothers and young children eating breakfast while seated at pastel-colored Formica furniture. The Strut Your Sass leather boutique which was running a post-Christmas sale on winter coats and jackets was doing a record business, as was the

98

Sonic City Record and Tapes Metropolis franchise located next door to it.

Canned music tinkled softly from artfully concealed public address speakers located every few yards. The music -- like the warm color scheme of the Mall -- was designed to put the shoppers at ease while they browsed the Mall's many small specialty shops and had also been shown to have a deterrent effect on shoplifters, pickpockets and other criminal offenders.

In the event that a threat materialized which was beyond the ability of the music or warm, friendly colors to deal with, the Mall also had a permanent security staff of thirty rent-a-cops under the direction of Chief Security Officer John Henry Parrish.

Armed with .38 caliber revolvers and able to deploy Ithaca riot shotguns in the event of emergency, the Mall's uniformed security guards were otherwise courteous and occupied themselves largely with providing directions to confused shoppers, reuniting lost children with their frantic mothers, lost pets with equally frantic children, and performing other related services.

Sipping a hot cup of fresh coffee from the food court as he gnawed a danish, security guard Parrish watched the shoppers enter through the Mall's south entrance gate and smiled wryly. It looked like the start of another ordinary business day at the Mall.

Ordinary, Parrish thought, and above all, *safe*. And, yeah, he had to admit it, *boring* as the sight of his wife's flat tire tits.

THE BLACKOUT HEIST

***

Suckdog Reich awoke and staggered from the army surplus sleeping bag on the floor of the abandoned Sanitation Department truck maintenance depot he called home, collapsing to the cold, dirty concrete before he got three feet.

He picked himself up, staggered to the sink and stuck his cueball-clean head under the cold stream of rusty brown water that gushed from the faucet with belching noises, as though the presence of his head in the basin were giving the sink heartburn.

The stream of icy water splashed across the Nazi swastikas that had been drawn with black indelible marker on the naked scalp. Brown water sluiced down the planes of Suckdog's cheeks and gurgled into his be-ringed ears.

Removing his head from the sink, Reich wiped his face on a dirty towel and turned on the Blaupunkt tape deck he'd smashed the window of some asshole's parked Mercedes to get. The raucous strains of a Sex Pistols song called "Belsen was a Gas" screamed from the overdriven -- and also purloined -- speakers that the deck was wired to.

The song jarred Suckdog's mind back into working order. But it wasn't quite enough to get all the gears turning. Groping in the pocket of the camo fatigue jacket draped over a chair, Suckdog fished out a Vicks inhaler filled with a mixture of cocaine and speed the Hells Angels called crank. A couple of snorts of the crank and Suckdog felt alive again.

DAVID ALEXANDER

Last night, he and his twelve-man strong Aryan Death Squad had run wild in the Jewish cemetery, overturning kike headstones and getting stoned on Wild Irish Rose, a case of which they'd lifted from a Paki's grocery before setting out for the cemetery and pissed back out all over the graves of the hebe motherfuckers who were buried there.

Drunk out of their faces and laughing hysterically, they'd gone out and boosted a station wagon from some fuckin' wetback neighborhood. They spent the hours between midnight and dawn driving around and spray painting swastikas on the wall of any building near the sites of their numerous open-air piss stops.

When the Aryan Death Squad had grown tired of emblazoning Staten Island with Nazi regalia, they had crowned the night's revelries by engaging in combat to preserve the honor of their beloved Fuhrer which had been assailed by a black man walking a small dog on a dark and lonely street in a run-down section of New Dorp in the northern part of the boro.

Despite the near-impossible odds presented by the profaner of the Fuhrer's name, Suckdog's intrepid Aryan warriors had succeeded in killing the dog and leaving the nigger lying in a pool of blood, minus his wallet to finance the purchase of another round of Wild Irish Rose.

Now Suckdog wondered what he would do today as he sat down on the bare planks of the floor of the condemned building he called home.

Maybe, he figured, he'd go the Mall. Yeah, that seemed like a real good idea. Go to the Mall, do a

THE BLACKOUT HEIST

little window shopping, steal a can of Red Devil,
spray paint a couple of swastikas....

DAVID ALEXANDER

ELEVEN

Khodynke, Moscow. The Sixth Directorate of the GRU was the Russian intelligence organ closest in charter and composition to the American National Security Agency both in the mission it was tasked to perform and in the territory it covered since, in large part, it oversaw intel collection operations in the US, UK, Canada and Latin America.

In order to accomplish its mission, the directorate was charged with monitoring the bewildering array of surveillance platforms in place both on the ground and in orbit around the earth to eavesdrop on the West's sprawling global information infrastructure. It performed this function largely via the GRU's Cosmic Intelligence Directorate, responsible for space-based intelligence, surveillance and reconnaissance activities.

In a darkened room, facing multiple banks of rack-mounted screens, veteran intelligence analysts monitored the Gordian tangle of orbital spy technology that crisscrossed the planet on a twenty-four-hour-a-day basis like busy electrons speeding around an atomic nucleus.

Of special interest now was the new YZ-class surveillance satellite that had been launched only a few weeks ago. It was the final satellite in a triad of newly constructed space observation platforms. The satellites were hybrid platforms capable of monitoring microwave transmissions as well as providing high-resolution real-time photoimagery and synthetic aperture radar imagery, the latter enabling viewing of earthbound surveillance targets through cloud cover.

Even the high-security clearances which the Cosmic Intelligence Directorate's technical officers possessed, however, did not make them privy to the fact that each of the *Pichugas* also carried onboard a clandestine nuclear device.

That information was shared only by a select few which included the Russian president and high-echelon members of the CIS military command.

In the event that it should ever become necessary, the technical officer would receive the necessary command sequences required to arm and detonate the sixty-kiloton thermonuclear explosive device and be ordered to input them to the tactical server cluster that monitored and controlled the functions of the *YZ-class* orbiters.

Until such time as the order was given, the GRU technical officers would suspect nothing regarding the dual role played by the surveillance satellites whose coded telemetry they routinely monitored.

As sophisticated as the high-speed computers and phased-array radars were which monitored the satellites, however, they were not infallible. The self-diagnostic functions built into the satellite's electronic circuits did not always perform correctly.

This was now the case with the final *Pichuga* satellite. Unknown to its ground controllers in the Sixth Directorate of the GRU, a microchip located within the system's launch arming microprocessor module was slowly failing.

It would continue to degrade at a steadily increasing rate until it no longer functioned dependably. The operations performed by the microprocessor chip were many. It controlled the scanning devices onboard the satellite and a host of other functions.

One function, however, was critical to the performance of the orbiting spy platform. The microprocessor also controlled the protocols for triggering the clandestine nuclear device that was carried onboard the satellite.

When the chip failed beyond a minimum performance threshold its effect on the satellite would be similar to that of the human brain activating the body's hiccup mechanism -- with one notable exception. In this case, the first hiccup would trigger the detonation of a sixty-kiloton belch. The last thing they didn't know was that it had been the lightning over Baikonur that had sent electrical transients snaking into the skin of the Proton-K launch vehicle that had been responsible, and that the entire orbital system was rapidly approaching a point of critical malfunction.

THE BLACKOUT HEIST

Chapter Two
Out of the Loop

DAVID ALEXANDER

Skerrit, Manhattan. Having slotted his ZR1 into the reserved parking space at the main offices of MetroCon on Beekman Street, Rick Skerrit clipped his laminated security tag to the outer breast pocket of his tweed sport coat. He entered through the building's main floor level into a carpeted reception area.

In the cavernous underground sublevel situated beneath the granite-walled modern building, huge generators hummed around the clock.

These generators fed electrical power to the grid of step-down transformers that converted the direct current generated by them into alternating, or AC, current which was used in the five boros of New York City as it was everywhere else in the continental United States.

In cavernous rooms resembling the command and control centers of nuclear missile battle stations, banks of data screens monitored the functioning of the branching power grid.

The on-line computer network was among the most sophisticated in non-government use. The heart of the system was a cluster of IBM AS/400 mainframe servers constituting an aggregate number-cruncher capable of performing twenty-six million operations per second.

The power utility could tell at a glance what was happening at any point in the power grid and what to do in relation to the ever-changing patterns of current flow that fluctuated in relation to millions of utility customers going off and on line every hour.

But the server cluster and its smaller clients performed most of the actual work. They could instantly sense when power use slacked off in one area and when it increased in another, and immediately allocate differing amounts of electricity to one zone of usage or the other.

With the computers running the show, humans were largely restricted to support roles. No longer at the controls of the system, they monitored its pulses and rhythms and only stepped in during emergencies.

As the techs put it, man was no longer "in the loop."

Skerrit took the elevator up to the second floor of the sixteen story building and walked a few score yards of soundproofed carpeted corridor to his office.

He had barely had a chance to grab a cup of coffee from the coin machine in a refreshment alcove just off the elevator bank and seat himself at his desk when his office phone rang.

"Mr. Gay wants to see you in his office, Mr. Skerrit," the female voice said. The tension in the voice was obvious, despite the forced cheerfulness.

"Be right there," Skerrit returned, cradling the handset.

The voice had belonged to Bob Gay's secretary.

Gay was the Director of Electrical Systems and Skerrit's boss.

Skerrit knew without having to be told that he was about to face the ax due to his damning report.

***

"I have only one question for you, Rick," Gay said as Skerrit seated himself in front of his boss' desk. "Why? Why in hell did you do it?"

Gay's office was large and well-appointed, filled with mementos of a long and distinguished career at the helm of one of the utility's most important divisions.

Daylight streamed in through the long rectangular window behind him. A tank stocked with exotic tropical fish stood on a cast-iron frame against one wall. The picture window behind Gay's desk gave a view of the Williamsburg Bridge, the river stretching below it and the busy highway along Manhattan's East River shoreline.

Skerrit could see tanker traffic on the river, heading out toward the Atlantic beyond the lower tip of Manhattan island.

"Analyzing the situation, Bob," Skerrit returned, carefully choosing his words, "I arrived at the only conclusion possible. The system was clearly in trouble. The core of the problem is supercomputers that take human operators out of the loop. Mothballing the last vestiges of manual switching systems leaves the entire grid vulnerable to mass

109

shutdown. There was just no way around that without a total whitewash. And you didn't want that, did you?"

"No, Rick," Gay returned without meeting Skerrit's glance, "nobody wanted a whitewash. But, damn it, did you have to veer off so precipitously in the opposite direction?"

Gay slammed the thick, Velobound copy of Skerrit's report on the glass top surface of his desk.

"This isn't a report," he went on, "this is Joan of Arc against the Inquisition; this is Savonarola against Pope Innocent the Seventh. This is a scathing condemnation of a multi-billion dollar federal program implemented over the last decade. Some of the best minds in government, science and private industry were behind its development. Couldn't you see that? Didn't you realize the implications of that?"

Skerrit looked Gay in the eye. Suddenly he didn't care anymore. If he was about to lose his job anyway, than he wouldn't cringe before Gay.

Anger rose in Skerrit's chest like a molten column of white hot metal as he replied, "I'm not Savonarola and this isn't the motherfucking Spanish Inquisition, Bob. To give you the short answer, let's just say I got tired of perpetually wetting my dick and holding it into the wind.

"That research study took over a year of grueling work and is meticulously documented. If it hadn't been, nobody would have gotten pissed off and I wouldn't be called on the carpet right now. So let's cut the bullshit. You didn't haul me in for a meeting to hash around my reasons for writing the report. You called in to tell me I'm fired. So say it fast and let me get out."

Gay shook his head, a schoolmaster disappointed in a bright pupil who had failed a crucial test. In reality the older man admired Skerrit, wishing he had half his guts but glad he had a better instinct for self-preservation.

"Okay," he returned, "You called it. The Board of Directors wants your resignation, Rick," he went on. "I tried to reign them in or at least make them take a softer line, but there was nothing I could do. They're hell-bent on cutting you off at the knees.

"They've got thunder up their butts, Rick. What your report recommended was nothing short of completely scrapping our new and very costly system upgrades, or at any rate, the better part of them."

"My recommendations were to retrofit, not redesign," Skerrit interrupted, knowing it wouldn't do him any good.

"Same animal. Your idea of retrofitting meant completely redesigning all computer hardware and software, massive EMP hardening of power installations, replacement of critical microprocessors with vacuum-tube based technology -- tantamount to junking everything presently on-line.

"Of course, that also means the replacement of cost-effective off-the-shelf components with astronomically more expensive boutique electronics. Most of that stuff would need to be custom-made, I'd imagine. Where would we get it? How long would it take to implement? No, Rick. It could never work. You should have known that going in."

Skerrit was silent for a few long beats.

"You know what, Bob?" he finally asked.

"No Rick, what?"

"Shame on you," Skerrit replied softly, and walked out of Gay's office without bothering to shut the door behind him. "Shame on you all."

***

Skerrit had been wrong. Like Savonarola, he had indeed incanted what was tantamount to modern-day heresy before corporate technology's high priests.

Right or wrong, it could not have resulted in anything less than the fate of all other heretics who had been burned at the stake.

Ever since the mammoth power failure of 1977, New York City's energy infrastructure had begun a process of complete overhaul of its existing facilities. Outmoded vacuum tube and transformer technology had been replaced with high-speed integrated circuit chips. Fallible human operators had been phased out in favor of supposedly infallible machines.

Sophisticated computer systems now switched power from one part of the regional power grid to another at speeds that no human operator could ever hope to be capable of duplicating. In the event of an overload, these mechanisms were capable of tripping circuit breakers to shut down power lines in the space of millionths of a second.

The computer systems were faster, better and more efficient at protecting and maintaining the power company's grid network than any human being or groups of human beings. Or so MetroCon's reasoning went. Skerrit had discovered, however, that it was precisely in this fact that their weakness lay.

The very ultra-high speed at which digital systems could detect potential failures and malfunctions and shut down parts of the power network could -- and in several instances already had -- created a domino effect that laid the groundwork for a blackout many times more severe than any before it.

In the same way that the stock market's computerized trading network generated a domino effect leading to the crash of 1987, the power utility's computerized switching system could crash just as easily. The consequences of such a crash today, however, would be far more severe than at any previous time in history.

In the wake of the blackout of 1977, Skerrit's research had noted, violent crime had risen dramatically for the duration of the crisis.

Looting, murder, arson, rape and other felony offenses had registered a dramatic tenfold increase in the space of only twenty-four hours.

But society had changed appreciably in the approximate four decades that had passed since the blackout of seventy-seven. Changed for the worse.

School children now carried Uzis to class, and there were squads of armed cops in every elementary school in the city, drug dealers had invaded even gentrified neighborhoods, while the streets and subways of New York City were danger zones even at the best of times. Statistical projections showed that the aftermath of a major blackout upon contemporary society would be nothing less than massive civil disorder on a scale approaching total anarchy.

Another weakness of computer switching systems over electromechanical systems under at least partial human control was their susceptibility to a phenomenon known as electromagnetic pulse, or EMP.

Such a pulse could be produced by high-voltage lightning strikes. It overloaded and burned-out electronic circuitry, wiped out cellular, cable and other digital information systems, even stopped heavy machinery in its tracks.

By all accounts, EMP was a death pulse.

While it occurred naturally to some extent, the greatest EMP hazard existed under threat of war or terrorist attack. Nuclear blasts were capable of generating EMPs, and both the United States' and the former Soviet Union's battle plans had once called for the triggering of nuclear death pulses in the upper atmosphere to blanket enemy nations with EMP as a prelude to main thermonuclear strikes.

In an era of regional wars, EMP attack plans continued to be made, especially by rogue states like Iran and North Korea, who, realizing that a small exoatmospheric nuclear detonation could produce devastating consequences across a large section of the United States and other Western nations, considered EMP as a cheap but effective weapon of mass destruction.

Although EMP attack was not an important aspect of Skerrit's report, in his opinion the other risk factors to the electrical grid system that posed a threat to civilization were even more frightening. They were utterly terrifying simply because, in a vastly changed world order, they were far more liable to happen.

THIRTEEN

Richie, Cancun, Mexico.
"Italiano, si?"

The shopkeeper with the face of a priest of *Chapultapek* turned the small golden figurine this way and that, intending it to catch the light of the subequatorial sun that slanted into the windows of the store. Richie had to admit the golden idol was unique. It had caught his attention after he had wandered idly into the shop in the sprawling open air market-bazaar that runs along the east side of Tulum Avenue in downtown Cancun, not meaning to buy anything.

"Si, Italiano," Richie answered with a slight nod. "How much? *Cuánto dinero?"*

Richie Block was used to being taken for an Italian, though he was one only through osmosis. His father had migrated to America from Romania by way of Auschwitz and Bergen-Belsen and the old man would have become a rabbi had not his green card arrived before the rabbinical school that had sponsored him as an émigré ordained him. Richie's identity crisis was a result of genes and locality. His hard face and muscular build meshed perfectly with the cock-of-the-walk body language that could have given Mussolini a few lessons in pugnacity.

116

DAVID ALEXANDER

Brooklyn's Gravesend-Bensonhurst section were he'd grown up had more Italians per capita than Palermo. Organized crime had made the neighborhood the most heavily Mafia-penetrated area in the United States, according to FBI statistics, but no kid coming up in those streets needed to be informed of that.

The storefront social clubs under the Sea Beach elevated with locked steel doors, the nocturnal car chases observed from pizzerias on 86th Street, the snap, crackle and pop of gunfire echoing off the walls of brown brick buildings on unlit avenues late at night, all clearly advertised the presence of the wise guys.

Unlike his brother Eddie, Richie's transformation into the black sheep of the family was apparent at an early age. By the time Richie and Eddie were in their twenties, Richie was on his way to being an accomplished thief, specializing in taking off trucks, while Eddie was on his way to being an accountant.

In the closing years of the Afghanistan War, and the start of the campaign in Malaysia, Richie decided to enlist to avoid being implicated in a string of robberies he had engineered. The heat was on and Richie preferred drop zones into Kumpulan Mujahideen Jungle strongholds in Surinam to doing time at Greenhaven, Attica or Dannemora. As it turned out, he spent less time in Malaysia than he did in Tora-Bora, where special forces were engaged in some of the most intensive fighting of the conflict.

THE BLACKOUT HEIST

"Para usted, señor, cincuenta pesos." The Mexican saw nothing in this one's eyes, no hint of interest. *"Un precio especial, señor, sólo para ti."*

The gringo picked up the gold figurine and held it at eye level in the hollow of his hand, examining it closely. The shopkeeper watched him carefully, hoping to discern the extent of his interest and set his price accordingly.

The war was over for Richie before his two-year contract with Uncle Sam expired. He had served a year and a half. But in that time he had learned some hard lessons about the world and himself. Richie did not want to do time. Any kind of time. Job time. Relationship time. Dues paying time. None of that shit was worth what you paid to get it, defend it and hold onto it.

The occasional job for quick cash had become a necessity in recent years, however, as building in the New York area ground to a halt and the construction jobs that had been Richie's bread and butter and insured him a comfortable standard of living got fewer and farther between. Since dealing drugs was out and Richie wouldn't accept a dime of charity from his family or the few friends he had somehow managed to acquire, he'd gone back to being a thief.

Richie's main criminal activity had been stealing high-priced vehicles. The cars and vans were easy to boost, despite all the security crap they loaded them with, and he stole them custom-ordered. You wanted a white Porsche with cruise control, you came to Richie. You wanted a Chevy van with a sun roof, you came to Richie. You wanted an ejector seat or a blowjob machine attached to the steering column, you came to Richie.

Whatever you wanted in the way of low-priced, high-end vehicles in peak condition, freshly heisted from the streets of the city and environs, Richie was the man who could supply it. In a short while in this line of work, Richie's fortunes had improved. He lived in a duplex condo in a high-rise building in Bay Ridge with a Verrazano Bridge view and had enough left over to build up a comfortable nest egg in banks in Zurich and Grand Cayman.

Richie put the trinket down and pointed out another one through the top of the glass display case.

"*Y para esto?*" he asked the *Indio*, "*cuánto?*" The shopkeeper placed the second golden charm into Richie's hand. "*Esto es setenta pesos, señor,*" he replied, wondering if he had asked too much.

Eddie had always tried to talk him out of it, work on him, appeal to Richie's nobler side.

"You're just fucking yourself, babe," Eddie would tell him as they sat in one of the lower Manhattan watering holes at the Seaport Eddie favored on his lunch hours from his job with the Federal Reserve Bank of New York. "One day you're going to get caught. And then you'll do hard prison time."

"Ain't nobody gonna catch me," Richie would say.

"Mark my word, Richie," Eddie would warn him, "day's gonna come when nobody can help you, not me, not anybody."

THE BLACKOUT HEIST

Eddie had thought that maybe a nice Jewish girl was what his brother Richie needed to help him settle down. Since one of those happened to be handy, in the form of a lawyer employed at the Fed, Eddie had introduced them.

Richie had been surprised that Maddie's face was not what he'd figured a nice Jewish girl would look like, but that of a Pre-Raphaelite Madonna. She filled out her bra pretty good too, an attribute that definitely scored with Richie. For Maddie's part, Richie was quite a bit different from the accountants and dentists that had been her usual dating fodder.

She liked the cruel smirk that Richie's mouth could twist itself into when the need arose, liked the way people made room for Richie on the street, liked the way he had quickly wiped the smirks off the faces of the two assholes in suits who had made a remark in a Chinese restaurant about her tee-shirt one day.

Maddie knew that Richie was a man who made the others look like puny little faggots. But she knew that she couldn't change him, nobody could change anybody else. Still, she was glad that Eddie had brought them together. As for Richie, he'd been forced to admit that Eddie had been correct in his judgment. Maddie was the angel on Richie's right shoulder. She balanced the demon on his left. Eddie had walked the straight and narrow. He'd shown Richie the light.

So why, Richie asked himself, why the fuck was Eddie now six feet underground? Why had Richie stood in some shit hole cemetery out in Queens somewhere with cold rain falling on his head, watching some schmuck rabbi who had never even known Eddie mouth some bullshit, color-by-number words over his grave?

Why had Eddie's wife, Marcy, and their two kids stood like zombies watching a husband and father who had died at the age of forty-two leave them for the last time? And why had the family had to pull strings and grease palms so that Eddie could be buried with the headstone placed in its normal position and not at his feet?

Eddie's death had been declared a suicide by the cops and Jewish law forbade those who had taken their own lives from receiving normal burial rites. Eddie had left a note saying that he was depressed over business problems, that he had confessed to embezzling almost two million dollars from the bank.

They had found the body in the motel room overlooking the Belt Parkway, a sleazy motor inn used by hookers and guys cheating on their wives. The gun lay at the foot of the bed and the cops had said that Eddie had shoved it into his mouth, pulled the trigger, and blown away the back of his skull.

Richie knew this was all bullshit. Eddie would never kill himself, not that way. Even if the part about the money problems were true, he wouldn't have done it that way. He wouldn't have stolen the money. He would have figured something out: Eddie was just too straight to be any kind of thief.

"*Voy a tomar dos,*" Richie told the shopkeeper, not wanting to bargain, although he knew perfectly well that he could easily have knocked down the price by as much as thirty percent. But the last time he had gone to Cancun six or seven years before, he'd bargained down the price of a rug that he hadn't really wanted just to see how low he could make the Mexican go.

As it turned out, he'd gotten the rug for next to nothing, but it was too late to offer the *Indio* full price, his honor would have never permitted him to accept it. Richie had never forgotten the look on the merchant's face as he'd handed him the rug. It was like a dog that had just been kicked. Richie bid good-day to the shopkeeper and walked back out into the baking sun and broiling heat of a Cancun afternoon.

He had flown down to Mexico after the funeral, leaving Maddie behind.

"I've gotta be alone," he'd explained to her.

She'd told him she'd understood and that it would be all right, but Richie wasn't fooled. Just the same, he knew that if he didn't get away long enough to work the anger out of his system, he would be impossible to be around.

He'd picked Cancun because, despite its touristy facade, the town had a wild side to it, a raw edge that appealed to Richie's sense of needing to tread the edge while his anger cooled. That and the fact that it had some of the best reef diving in all of Mexico. For the past seven days, Richie had been out in the lagoon every day, jumping off a rented fishing boat and snorkeling on the wrecks that littered the shoals of coral heads that crisscrossed the azure waters off the Gulf coast.

At night he'd sit drinking at the bars the tourists went to, carefully avoiding the ones he knew in the back streets off Tulum Avenue where the locals drank tequila and kept guns and switchblades as close as their shakers of salt; Richie had not come to Cancun to prove anything to anybody. He avoided the women too, the local *mujerzuelas* and the bored gringo housewives looking for some action alike, although opportunities had presented themselves more than once during his week-long stay. He had not come to Cancun to prove his manhood in any one of the two usual ways either.

Richie consulted his wristwatch as he approached the intersection where he had arranged to have the taxi driver who had taken him into town pick him up again. There was no sign of a cab, but he still had five minutes left. As Richie stood and waited, a green taxi braked to a top directly in front of him.

"You need a ride?" the driver asked in good English, leaning toward the passenger side window.

"In five minutes I might."

"You waiting for a taxi, *si?*"

"Uh-huh."

"Man, he never going to show," the driver said with a mocking laugh, shaking his head. "Be smart. You're not in New York, man. Get in. I take you wherever you want."

"He's still got three minutes, babe."

The taxi driver threw his car into park and sat there shaking his head at his gringo who was too stupid to discount the word of a Mexican cab driver as worthless. It would be worth the wait, because the first cabbie would never return.

THE BLACKOUT HEIST

In precisely three minutes, a second green taxi pulled up behind the first one. Richie grinned as the second cabbie cursed at the first one in rapid Spanish, then leaned on the horn until the skeptic roared off in anger.

"*Vamos*," Richie told the cabby with a smile, "*a mi hotel*." Richie knew at that moment that he'd had enough of Mexico for awhile. It was time to return to New York. He fingered the gold figurine in his pocket. Maddie would like it, he thought.

DAVID ALEXANDER

FOURTEEN

Amoroso, Lower Manhattan. Ellis Amoroso could almost see himself on a Spanish beach in Majorca. Although his memories of his early caravan years were lost in a drug haze to the point where they were comprised of equal parts of fiction and fact, he still fantasized a vivid image of what it would be like.

Palm trees would encircle the stretch of pristine white sand that merged with crystalline blue waters. There would be native fishing boats out at sea and Amoroso would watch them trawl their nets for the day's fishing run.

And of course, there would be women in the village. Their skin would be chestnut brown, their breasts firm and large. His American dollars would ensure him of as much companionship as he could ever want. His member grew rigid in his pants as he thought about a three-way menage with one girl riding his face cunt-saddle while the other sucked his erect penis deep into her throat.

"Hey, buddy, what are you smiling about?"

Amoroso almost jumped out of his chair at the sound of the voice and the hand on his shoulder. As the fantasy image blinked off in his mind, Amoroso forced the smile from his face with great difficulty.

THE BLACKOUT HEIST

Billy the Ear was standing beside his chair. The Ear was the office asshole. He was a middle-aged guy who dressed too young for his age and had a drinking problem that made Amoroso's own look tame by comparison. Rumor had it that he wore women's panties beneath his clothes; established certainty, that he was the most dreaded of all corporate creatures: *the office spy.*

Amoroso looked at the Ear with veiled contempt. The thought that in only a few hours he'd be light years away from Billy and creeps like him was the only thing that prevented Amoroso from anointing his milky little gopher's face with a rancid gob of phlegm on more than one occasion.

"Smiling?" Amoroso asked, trying to sound cheerful. "Was I smiling? Me smile? No way, Jose. I never smile. Smiling makes the heart pump piss, a team of noted French researchers just found it out."

"Yeah," Billy returned, ignoring Amoroso's remarks, "you had the biggest shiteating grin on your face I ever saw. In fact," he continued, "you had the distinct look of a man contemplating the great American pussy. You're not cheating on your wife, are you?" the Ear asked finally, showing carnivorous yellow teeth.

"Well, Billy, you never know," Amoroso returned, still mock-cheerful. "Maybe I was even thinking about cheating with *your* wife," he told the Ear. The older man's face suddenly got a cringing look all over it.

Billy the Ear walked away. Amoroso had another smile on his face. The smile of genuine triumph that is impossible to fake. But this genuine smile all too suddenly evaporated when Amoroso noticed that his boss was staring at him.

Although his boss was standing across the office, Amoroso could feel his eyes heavily on him. Amoroso didn't know how long he'd been watching. He would have to make a mental note to be more careful. That shouldn't be too hard. After all, he'd only have to keep it up for the rest of the day.

***

Murray Jackman, Amoroso's boss, suspected that his employee was ripping the company off by means of a fairly imaginative computer disbursement fraud scam. He had already reported this observation to his superiors and they had been watching Amoroso for months.

Shortly after the allegations had been made, the firm had hired a troubleshooter who specialized in sniffing out the perpetrators of computer fraud. He'd identified the source of the discrepancies in a few days. Ever since, many hidden eyes had been watching Amoroso.

The problem with computer crime, however, was the relative difficulty in conclusively nailing its perpetrators, especially when one was dealing with sophisticated fraud schemes.

Amoroso could have set up dummy accounts, dummy serial numbers; puzzle boxes within puzzle boxes. Only time and luck would allow the hunters to get to the bottom of the scam.

Amoroso's boss had the feeling that Amoroso was about to skip, though. He could smell rabbit in the air. Not that this in itself would pose a major problem.

THE BLACKOUT HEIST

The police and FBI had been alerted and would apprehend him as he soon as he reached any of the city's airports or otherwise attempted to leave town. The danger lay in the possibility that Amoroso might not be carrying all his ill-gotten proceeds with him. In that event, both the company and the authorities would feel compelled to offer Amoroso a deal.

But Amoroso's boss didn't want to offer Amoroso a deal. He wanted to catch him dead-bang. It would be a goddamned shame, he thought, if the scumbag got off.

***

The pub on Maiden Lane was crowded with men and women in conservative business attire as Amoroso sat down at the bar for a couple of drinks and a fast Montecristo sandwich stuffed with fried ham, turkey and Swiss cheese, and topped with yogurt and strawberry preserves.

While he sloppily munched his Montecristo, Amoroso chanced to eavesdrop on a conversation taking place at a table directly behind him. Amoroso enjoyed listening to overheard lunchtime conversations. Like reprogramming computers for fun and profit, it was one of his hobbies.

This particular overheard exchange concerned an embezzler who had been recently caught trying to steal two hundred thousand dollars from his company.

He had managed to steal the money in unmarked bills taken directly from the counting room right under the eye of the surveillance camera, and faked his death by leaving his car behind him with a suicide note on the front seat. But he had been identified soon after in another state with a new wife. He hadn't even bothered to grow a beard.

Amoroso smiled.

Those were careless, stupid mistakes. Stupid with a capital "S." Careless with a capital "C."

No way in the world would they ever happen to him. No fucking way.

***

Having bought four cheap leather-look vinyl suitcases from a Korean street vendor on Battery Park, Amoroso spent the rest of his lunch hour closing out the bank accounts he had opened under a variety of dummy names with the misappropriated checks he had deposited.

The suitcases came folded flat in clear plastic bags and the four of them fit snugly into Amoroso's hardshell attache case.

There was approximately two hundred fifty thousand dollars in each of the four accounts Amoroso kept at four different banks in the Wall Street area.

With each trip, Amoroso left the bank with a bulging suitcase, secreting each in a different rental locker located in one of the tunnels of the sprawling City Hall subway complex nearby.

At the end of the business day, Amoroso would remove the four plastic suitcases from their lockers and exit to street level.

From there he would hail a cab to JFK International where he would catch his evening flight to Amsterdam, Holland.

THE BLACKOUT HEIST

Wiping the sweat from his brow after stuffing the final plastic suitcase into the locker, Amoroso turned to see a group of winos watching him. They had smiles on their faces and the light of alcohol-induced dementia in their eyes. Their attention was nothing to be concerned with.

Amoroso turned and walked away. The odds of their successfully jimmying open the locker door at this hour of the day were miniscule, he decided. The money would be safe for a few hours more. Amoroso also decided that there was minimal risk of a mugging attempt when he removed them.

It would be rush hour and hundreds of people would be hurrying past each second. They wouldn't dare risk it in such a tight crowd situation.

Out of the corner of his eye, Amoroso watched the three hispanic-looking men in shabby clothes whisper to one another as he left the grime-covered subway platform on his way back to work.

He did not suspect that the homeless derelicts in rags were really members of the NYPD's Manhattan South Safe and Loft Squad's Major Crimes Unit who knew exactly what Amoroso had stashed in the lockers.

DAVID ALEXANDER

The Bronx, Applebaum. The musky fragrance of Yolanda's lubricating snatch filled Applebaum's nostrils like the scent of tropical jacaranda on a summer night. Sitting astride his hips, with her wet cunt pressed into his face and her ass propped on his heaving chest, Applebaum ran his tongue around the contour of the dense pubic hair and between the moist pinkness between it.

At Marty's urging, Yolanda had shaven her bush into the shape of a valentine. The edges of the valentine were now bristly on Applebaum's tongue. He found this *frisson* highly stimulating. His tool was as hard as an iron bar as she reached behind her back and jerked him off with her hand.

Yolanda Montoya liked what Marty was doing to her as well. As Applebaum used his forefingers to spread the thick outer lips of her pussy she threw back her head and purred like a cat.

Inserting his tongue into the pink interior of the wet cunt in front of him, Applebaum felt Yolanda's body begin to quiver like a subway platform does with an express about to enter from the tunnel.

THE BLACKOUT HEIST

Now, grasping her tight buttocks in each hand, he probed deeper with his tongue, tasting the pungency of her salivating vagina as he felt her reach behind beneath his balls to insert her finger in his anus.

Suddenly she came with a groan, crying out in Spanish. Yolanda then got on her knees and let Applebaum enter her from behind, in the doggie position.

As they began pumping against one another more furiously, Yolanda climaxed another time, and Applebaum had little choice but to explode inside her.

"God damn it!" Yolanda cried out, moments later. "Your fucking come is dripping out of my pussy like a fucking jellyfish died down there or some shit!"

Yolanda grabbed a couple of Kleenex sheets from a box beside the bed and wedged them between her legs.

Moments later she was up and running for the bathroom, hurling Spanish epithets at the peeling apartment walls.

Applebaum heard more cursing in Spanish and the not very musical sounds of the semen he had ejaculated into her being expelled into the water in the bowl above which she sat.

Laughing, Applebaum wiped the jelly from the tip of his rod with the bed sheet, reached for a cigarette in the pack in the pocket of his jeans slung across a nearby chair, lit up and dragged deeply, exhaling the creamy smoke through his nostrils.

DAVID ALEXANDER

Naked, Yolanda came back in and got on the bed beside him. She and Applebaum had been having sex on and off for about three months.

Her husband was a city housing cop who had lost his sex drive after a year on the job. She suspected that he was a homosexual. That would have been all right with her, as long as he was giving it to her regularly. The problem was, he wasn't.

Yolanda was considering getting a divorce before Applebaum had come along. The Jew was a little crazy in the head, but he could keep it up for a long time and he was fun to be around.

Applebaum had plenty of time to kill. A former high school social studies teacher, he had been on medical disability after a fall he had suffered in the school cafeteria had permanently injured his back.

Applebaum's back injury had done nothing to affect his sexual performance and he liked affairs with married women because there were fewer strings attached.

After a few minutes, Applebaum said he was going down to get some beer at the supermarket. Yolanda asked him to pick up a pack of Marlboro Silver Ultra-Lights and a big bag of Herr's sour cream and onion potato chips. Applebaum pinched the nipple of one breast and left the apartment.

He surfed the elevator down to the main lobby of Building Number Five and walked out into the main plaza of the Bronx Zoo.

Black and Hispanic teenagers loitered on benches, openly smoking crack, ghetto blasters blaring thudding, bass-heavy music that reverberated off the graffiti-covered walls with the force of punches to the head. A couple of kids were playing basketball in one of the fenced off courts nearby, oblivious to everything but their game, while others were pitting snarling, snapping bulldogs against each other, holding the dogs barely apart by heavy chain leashes.

The teenagers looked Applebaum over, noted the camouflage fatigues, the army surplus jacket, the lace-up steel-toed boots and the insane light that gleamed in the perpetually wary eyes and quickly looked away. Mad Marty got no props in the hood, but he was grudgingly respected by all -- and feared by many.

Applebaum stuck his hands into the pockets of his fatigue jacket as he left the Zoo and went into the bombed-out streets of Mott Haven that surrounded the complex.

As he headed for a nearby bodega, Applebaum checked out the activity on the street. In a black Lincoln Continental with its tailpipe smoking as it sat parked by a curb, a pimp took money from one of his hookers and sent her out to work Mott Avenue at the turnoff to the expressway.

Crack dealers stood their territories. Applebaum passed one who, with a lengthy handshake, transferred a small plastic vial to a young girl who walked quickly away without even looking back, dragging a small screaming child by the wrist.

Applebaum shook his head in disgust. He wondered, as he sometimes did, what in the name of hell he was doing here, in this place, on these mean streets. He had some money put away. He could afford to live somewhere else, someplace better.

Why in the name of God Almighty did he choose to remain at the Zoo? Who knew? Maybe the bottom line was because Mad Marty Applebaum was just another breed of street animal who needed to be with his own kind.

Shrugging, Applebaum went into the bodega and picked up a six pack of Coors Light and the other stuff that Yolanda wanted. He wanted to pick up a tube of K-Y too, but the drug store was a couple of blocks away and he didn't feel like walking.

She sometimes let him fuck her in the ass, and he had a feeling that she'd be in the mood when he got back. Marty decided he'd have to use Vaseline and a little tender loving care if he got lucky.

The cold wind New Yorkers called "The Hawk" whipped around the streets when he came out again, sinking icy talons that cut right through the fabric of his surplus camo jacket.

Applebaum zipped up, idly noticing as he did that the pimpmobile was gone as he turned and trudged back toward the Zoo, a brown paper sack in his hands.

SIXTEEN

Manhattan, Inskeep. Motorman Willie Inskeep saw the Whitehall Street station loom directly ahead of him. The tunnel lights were red, though, as he rounded the bend in the tunnel before the final stretch of tracks that would whip him around into the station.

Inskeep slowed the IRT local from its top cruising speed of forty miles per hour to half that velocity.

When the red signal changed to green, Inskeep increased speed and entered the station, his cab passing ranks of passengers that were waiting for the train to stop, open its doors and receive them.

Now he could see the final car of the train that had been in the station ahead of him pulling into the darkness of the tunnel beyond.

That explained the few passengers waiting on the platform. Most had already boarded the one that had left before his had arrived.

Inskeep heard the lady conductor announce the stop as the doors slid open. "Whitehall Street, ladies and gentlemen," the conductor, LaDollicia

Shavers, said, "watch your step getting off and have a pleasant afternoon."

Inskeep smiled. He could always tell the new fish from the way they read from the Suggested Announcement List that the MTA provided its conductors. The veterans lost that eager-beaver inflection in the voice that he now detected.

A few minutes later, Inskeep heard the two short buzzes that signaled that the train was ready to move. Over the intercom, LaDollicia added, "Motorman, you may now proceed with the train's departure."

A snort of laughter escaped Inskeep's lips. *Proceed with the train's departure.* Damn. He'd have to remember that one; it was a classic.

Seeing green signals all down the line and still grinning, Inskeep eased the train into the yawning mouth of the dark station looming directly ahead.

***

One stop before the end of his second run of the day, Inskeep started feeling unusually nervous and peered through the crack in the partially open door of the motorman's cab.

In the car beyond, Inskeep saw a wino of indeterminate age and sex sprawled lengthwise across a pastel blue bench seat. Curled up in a fetal position, the wino's hands were deep in his or her pockets, clutching whatever valuables he or she possessed in case they'd be rolled by a roving wolf pack.

Two young Oriental women sat talking and laughing in one of the smaller seats nearest him, one of them eating nuts from a cellophane bag, the other sipping something out of a paper cup that might or might not be coffee.

The only potential problem that Inskeep could make out was the dude in the black motorcycle jacket and punk haircut who sat with his legs jutting straight out on the bench seat across from the sleeping wino and repeatedly banging the side of his head against the window.

The dude had heavy chains strung through the epaulets of the jacket. Although there was the possibility that he might be trouble, most of the leather and chains bit was probably only window dressing within which lived a chickenshit trying to get over in a world he never made. Inskeep would remember to check him out carefully before exiting the cab, though.

Inskeep slowed the IRT local as he pulled into the Nostrand Avenue trainyard, noting that the signals were green all the way and that a Manhattan-bound Pelham Bay local was across the station awaiting his train's arrival before embarking on its run back toward the boro of Brooklyn.

Easing down on the throttle, Inskeep brought the IRT local to a full stop at the end of the berth and felt the train shudder as he switched off the engine.

Leaning sideways in his seat, Inskeep prepared to again peer through the crack in the door to see if the punk with the chains looked like he might be a badass. If it looked like there would be any danger, Inskeep would radio for a Transit Police patrolman to hustle over on the double.

The punk, like the other occupants of the car, however, exited Inskeep's train the minute that the doors opened up. The wino had already left too.

Inskeep unscrewed the throttle from the steering rod and put it in the pocket of his beat-up leather jacket.

He picked up his portable communications pack and pushed open the motorman's cab door and walked down the now empty car's aisle toward the final door and exited onto the platform with an empty belly and a full bladder.

**

During the one-hour break he had before he was scheduled to begin his final run of the day, Inskeep bought a hot cup of lousy tasting instant coffee and a ham sandwich from an Oriental sidewalk vendor who did business out of a truck near the trainyards.

Flashing his MTA employee's pass, Inskeep reentered the trainyard past the security booth and walked up the flight of concrete stairs to the platform level.

From there, he ascended another flight of stairs into the MTA personnel area that had been set up where an old trainyard controller's building once had stood.

Inskeep sipped at the rapidly cooling and coppery-tasting coffee while he munched the ham sandwich and skimmed the sports page of the Daily News.

The heavyweight fight was canceled due to yet another accident involving the champ. In this particular incident he'd broken three of the knuckles in his right hand in a streetcorner brawl. New York wasn't doing too well in the football playoffs and another major drug scandal was hinted at for a well-known basketball star with an already turbulent history of womanizing and drug abuse.

Somebody sat down beside Inskeep and when Inskeep looked up he noticed that it was a friend of his who worked in track maintenance.

"How's it going, my man," the maintenance man asked Inskeep.

"Can't complain," Inskeep returned. "You?"

"Same bullshit, different day," he replied with a laugh, lighting up a cigarette and offering Inskeep one which Inskeep took from the half-empty pack of Luckies.

"You hear about Artie Banks?" the track maintenance man asked Inskeep. Banks, Inskeep knew, was another motorman.

"No," Inskeep returned. "What happened?"

"Got shot yesterday," he answered. "Happened on the Broadway Line up in Washington Heights. He was on storm watch there, right? Well, couple of kids get on in Spanish Harlem, see the car's empty and go for Artie's radio. Artie puts up a fight and one of those kids stabs him with a nine-inch combat knife."

"Like they say, shit happens," Inskeep returned, sipping some more coffee, "especially when a guy decides to play hero."

"This is true," answered the maintenance worker. "Anyway, they got him up at Bellevue with nine stab wounds and a hundred stitches in his chest and arms. Another inch to the right and they'd have gotten him straight through the heart."

Inskeep reciprocated by telling the track walker about the funny thing his new lady conductor had said on the run in to the yard. Both men cracked up over her remark, and the phrase *Proceed with the train's departure* would be assured of being telegraphed to all corners of the city via the MTA's jungle drums before the week was out.

The maintenance man got up and walked away, waving at Inskeep. Inskeep finished the last of his cigarette and went back to sipping his now lukewarm coffee, turning to the front section of the News.

When he had completed scanning the lead stories, Inskeep checked his cell phone for the time. It was another ten minutes to the start of his run.

Inskeep got up and lumbered down the stairs to the platform where the train he would drive on its return run was just pulling into its berth in the station.

THE BLACKOUT HEIST

SEVENTEEN

Richie, Brooklyn. The sun was bright on the west end of Avenue U, though the morning air still had the bite of winter. Spring was in the air. Richie could see the green buds swelling on the trees. New life was returning to Gravesend, Brooklyn. But not for those who Eddie had left behind. And not for Richie himself.

A piece of his heart had been taken away when his brother died. The week in Mexico had done some good, but he was still a long way from healed. But there was business to take care of. Family business. Richie got his car out of the building's underground lot and bumped the Camaro onto the street, heading for the on-ramp to the Belt.

Sunday morning traffic was light on the LIE. The three hundred sixty-eight Detroit stallions underneath the Camaro's hood didn't even break a sweat as Richie cruised past the Elmhurst gas tanks that flanked the Long Island expressway, taking sips from a cup of hot Greek coffee he had bought on a whim at the station back on Avenue U where he'd gassed up before heading out into the 'burbs. The black coffee would make him have to piss a fuckin' river, but he could always water a couple of bushes off the shoulder if he needed to.

DAVID ALEXANDER

The radio station was playing a rap song that sampled an old Donovan tune that spoke about changes on many levels. Yeah, the man had got that shit right. Richie was going through some new changes. For some reason known only to his brother, Eddie had appointed Richie in his will as executor of his estate. Why he hadn't appointed his own wife, Richie didn't know, but executor he was and that's how he would act.

The other reason he was driving out into the bedroom community in Greenport, Long Island, where Eddie had lived, was to see what kind of a line he could get on Eddie's death. Richie wasn't buying the line about Eddie doing himself in. If that were true, it meant that some third party had dropped the hammer on his brother. If Richie could find that third party, then the person or persons were going to pay heavyweight dues for whacking Eddie.

There was an unmarked Buick parked outside that had cop written all over it. Richie got out and spotted the empty milk bottle on the filthy floor. That confirmed his guess. As he went up the walk two big-bellied detective types were coming out the door. The cops were talking to one another out of the sides of their mouths, and when they got a look at Richie's face, they immediately shut up and gave him a by-now-familiar stare. Richie kept walking and made them turn aside as he went to the front door and rang the bell. He didn't turn around but he knew the cops were staring at him. Well, let the fuckers watch his ass, that's the kind of guys they were.

THE BLACKOUT HEIST

Marcy answered the door. She was still wearing black and she still looked like she was in shock. Her eyes were ringed from crying. Tears came to them as she let Richie in. The kids were somber. They came lackadaisically to their Uncle Richie who patted their heads. He had brought along presents from Cancun and would have given them out already, except for the cops at the door. He needed some questions answered first.

"What did the cops want?" he asked Marcy.

"They wanted to know things about Eddie," she told him, bleary-eyed.

"Uh-huh," he returned with a nod. "Like what exactly?"

"They asked things like did Eddie have any bank accounts in his own name or in foreign countries and they wanted to know if I would let them look around the house."

"You told them no, right?"

She nodded.

"But they had a warrant. They looked anyway."

Richie went over to the window and chinked the thin slats of the pale blue Levolors. The copmobile was no longer out front.

"They find the safe?" he asked.

"No," she said. "I don't think so."

"I hope you're right," Richie said, "or all of us could be fucked."

In the basement of the ranch house, Eddie had sunk a cylindrical fire safe into the concrete of the foundation. The safe was hidden by the boiler. Richie moved it aside and spun the combination dial.

Soon Richie was in possession of a manila envelope containing the articles found on Eddie's person when the forensic team came to investigate the crime scene. Richie went through them. There was a wallet, a small electronic appointment book and a key on a chain. Richie studied the key. It looked like the kind used with safe deposit boxes.

"Do you recognize the key?" he asked.

Marcy inspected it closely and shook her head no.

"Did Eddie have a safe, any special place he kept papers, things like that?" he asked.

"He has his office in the back room," she said.

"Can I take a look inside?" he asked.

Richie was soon in his brother's study. Tears came suddenly to his eyes as he saw the picture of both of them together on Eddie's littered desk. He remembered it well. That summer they had been closer than every before.

Richie studied the articles in the room, wiping at the corners of his eyes. There wasn't anything there. Then, in a small fireproof storage box in a bottom drawer, he found a notebook. It was in code. He took the notebook home with him after he said good-bye to Marcy and the kids.

EIGHTEEN

Parrish, Staten Island. The Richmond Mall's multilevel parking garage was crammed to the bursting with cars and vans of every size and make, just as the stores that lined its duplex walkways were filled to capacity with shoppers and browsers of every race and creed.

Waiting by one of the four gigantic passenger elevators that serviced the Mall, Chief Security Guard John Henry Parrish watched teenage girls giggle as they inspected a store window displaying lace merry-widows and other sexy undergarments.

Nearby, under the watchful glances of their teachers, a class of schoolchildren was filing in a well-organized line into the Mall's movie theater that was showing a special Disney matinee.

Parrish watched the escalators that were ferrying a constant stream of shoppers up and down the two main floors of the center.

Courteously waiting until the elevator had emptied of shoppers, Parrish helped an old woman enter for the ride to the floor above, and gave her directions to the Spread 'N Buns Shoppe when they had both exited the car a few moments later.

146

DAVID ALEXANDER

On the Mall's upper level, as on the one below it, people moved about in a constant, disorganized flow, hurrying from shop to shop like insects pollinating a field of gaudily colored flowers.

Although Parrish had never before seen most of the faces of the shoppers and would probably never again, there were nevertheless some faces that were familiar. Faces he had seen since beginning his job fifteen years before.

Somehow, watching the crowd had always given Parrish a warm feeling deep down inside that he could never consciously explain, let alone articulate.

There was a cleanness and health in the bustling activity, and -- as Parrish circulated within the mass of shoppers, listening to them talk of their daily hopes, dreams and problems, watching them consider making their purchases or choosing what to have for lunch at one of the Mall's eating places, there was also a sense of belonging to the commonalty of man, a sense of being part of an extended human family.

Guarding the Mall was more than just a job to John Henry Parrish. It was his avocation in life. The people who shopped there were his personal responsibility. The Mall nourished him spiritually and emotionally.

The Mall was alive, thought Parrish. It was alive and it was a vital resource that the members of the communities surrounding it had come to depend on.

The mall was a source of sustenance and entertainment. It was an intrinsic part of their world.

THE BLACKOUT HEIST

An integral part of Parrish's world too. Finally and ultimately, it was one of the few places in a turbulent world that was both orderly and yet in the midst of constant activity at the same time.

***

The Aryan Death Squad assembled at the abandoned Sanitation Department depot in which Suckdog lived. There were ten of them in all. They sat on the scarred floorboards smoking crack and snorting crank.

One of the skinheads picked a fight with another one. They fell grappling on the filthy concrete floor, rolling and thrashing around until two other skins began kicking both combatants, breaking up the fight, but leaving the two grapplers bloodied and sullen.

"Let's go to the Mall," somebody offered.

That was a good idea, all the others agreed. Running out of the warehouse, the Aryan Death Squad looked around for new worlds to conquer. But first they needed a car to steal.

They found their chariot parked near a supermarket a few blocks away. A beat-up station wagon. Suckdog smashed the driver's side window with a fifteen-pound sash weight wrapped in silver duct tape that he carried on him, and the rest of the crew piled noisily into the stolen vehicle.

Ducking under the dashboard, Pooch, the group's resident auto heist expert, cut into the underside of the dash with a portable Sears sawzall, yanked out the ignition wires, and tore off strips of plastic insulation with his thumbnail.

DAVID ALEXANDER

The bare leads sparked as he touched them together and twisted them around one another as the engine caught and turned over.

Pushing Pooch aside, Suckdog climbed behind the wheel, threw the gearshift lever into drive and roared the stolen station wagon down the street with a screech of tortured Michelin rubber.

***

Swastikas were like playing lead guitar. Looked easy until you tried to do it. Then you found out that it was a lot harder than it appeared.

Suckdog had plenty of practice spray painting them, though. He'd painted swastikas all over the place, especially on gravestones in kike cemeteries all over town.

Suckdog held the can of luminous spray paint and began the giant red swastika he was painting on the plate glass window of the big black Caddy Seville parked on the sky level of the Mall's parking garage. Big car like that, probably belonged to some rich kike's J.A.P. wife.

"Hey! What the fuck you doing?" two gruff voices suddenly shouted from one of the entranceways to the spacious garage.

The group of Aryan skinheads didn't want to mess around with the beefy guys that were now running at them, shaking their fists and shouting Sicilian epithets. They hustled into the relative safety of the Mall's interior.

There was plenty of action there and a big crowd to get lost in. The Mall was full of post-Christmas shoppers taking advantage of extended sales. Despite the crowd, though, Suckdog and his

149

crew of skins attracted plenty of stares as their military surplus jungle boots stomped the floor, the impact of the hard rubber ripples against the tiles sounding like the crack of gunfire.

"There they are!" Suckdog turned to see the two guys who'd chased his crew from the car they'd spray painted coming after them with a Mall security guard.

"Okay," Parrish told the skins, hand on the butt of his .38 caliber revolver. "Let's take a walk."

He then rounded them up and ejected them from the Mall.

An hour later, though, after wandering the streets nearby, Suckdog and his skinhead rude boys had sneaked back in, ready for some more action.

DAVID ALEXANDER

<u>NINETEEN</u>

Kesselman, underneath Manhattan. Bernard Kesselman was on the final few steps of the stairway leading down to the IRT local platform when he was jostled by a man in a brown leather jacket and black woolen ski cap taking the steps two at a time while shouting obscenities at the top of his blustery voice.

Kesselman said nothing as he grabbed the polished steel hand rail to keep from completely toppling over.

He was sixty-two years-old, wore a pacemaker and believed that it was far healthier for a man to keep his mouth shut than to have somebody shut it for him. Better a live coward than a dead hero, was a motto he often repeated to himself at times like these.

Other crazy people followed close behind the heels of the man who had jostled him in a frantic dash to get to the platform before the train departed. Although Kesselman knew the reason behind all the running, he nevertheless couldn't understand it.

Already he could hear the deafening rumble as the Pelham Bay local thundered into the IRT station and smelled the characteristic odor of burnt popcorn blow in on smelly gusts of wind made by the train and hear the klaxoning of the new signals they had installed on the mezzanine level above that flashed cute little messages like *Subway Tracks are Dangerous ... Don't Walk On Them!* between arriving trains.

What was the good of these cute little messages when *mishuggeners* ran around too quickly to even stop and pay any attention to them? That was the trouble with New York, wonderful, beautiful city that it otherwise was.

Everybody moved too fast for their own good. Rushing, rushing, rushing. So much *fercockter* rushing. So fast that they hardly paid attention to the other eleven million poor schleps all around them who just so happened to be rushing around like crazy people too.

Let the rest of them live life in the fast lane. Kesselman was in no great hurry. If he missed the train, another would be along right behind it. So he might have to stand a few extra minutes. So what was such a big deal?

Better to stand the little while longer than to trip and break your neck charging down the stairs like some wild horse in a cowboy picture, the kind they always show jumping over a corral fence and running away into the sagebrush.

There was the pacemaker too, of course. Ever since the doctors had installed it, he was self-conscious of the little metal thing inside his chest that continued jolting his bad heart into reluctantly pumping the blood through his sludge-clogged veins.

Kesselman was afraid that if he exerted himself too much then the little thing inside him maybe might decide to stop working. Like the garbage collectors and the cops did, it might decide to go on strike.

And if the little thing went on strike then -- poof -- it would be all over for Bernie Kesselman just like that. He would be dead like a fly. Like a fly swatted by a rolled-up newspaper. Like a dead mosquito.

Dropping dead was bad enough, but to drop dead on a filthy subway platform with a bunch of wild animals and *mishuggeh* people stepping on his broken carcass just to get a seat on a *fercockter* train and ride two lousy stops, this was surely the ultimate indignity.

The local was beginning to pull out of the station as Kesselman finally reached the windy platform.

He watched the people inside the brightly lit cars speed past and become elongated horizontal blurs as the train gathered velocity, leaving a gust of foul-smelling wind behind as it rumbled into the mouth of the tunnel that gaped wide at the end of the station, its glowing red taillights winking out as it vanished around a bend in the tracks.

As soon as the train had gone, though, Kesselman felt another sudden gust of rancid-smelling wind at his back.

Turning, then stepping carefully to the edge of the platform, for he did not want to trip and fall now that he had safely negotiated the steep flight of stairs, he saw -- miracle of miracles -- the dusting of pale light on the track rails that meant another IRT train was right behind the one that had pulled out only moments before.

A small grin crossed Kesselman's wrinkled face as the second local slid noisily into the station like some enormous silver snake and he saw to his surprise and delight that it not only was almost completely empty but that it was one of those shiny new ones they had just put into service. Nice, clean, beautiful. Not a speck of graffiti anywhere on it. A pleasure to ride.

This was renewed proof that the Almighty One looked out for the old and the weak. Yes, this was a blessing. A blessing for a tired old man with a pacemaker in his chest.

Kesselman smiled at another passenger standing nearby as the IRT local slowed to a full stop with a shriek of tortured metal as the motorman applied his brakes.

He was certain that behind the blank face of the man who did not return his smile and zipped his fly as he stepped from a quickly spreading puddle there nevertheless existed a mutual sense of joy, satisfaction and mute awe at the innate justice that prevailed in an outwardly wicked world.

"Beautiful, this train," Kesselman said to the man, smiling and nodding his head while he gestured limply toward its gleaming hull. The only reply the man made, as the doors slid open, was to belch and scratch his moisture-stained crotch.

***

DAVID ALEXANDER

In the darkened cab of the spanking-new French-made Pelham Bay local that Bernard Kesselman had just boarded singing the Almighty's praises, motorman Willie Inskeep heard conductor La Dollicia Shavers, she of newly-minted "Proceed with the train's departure" fame, sound the two short buzzes that signaled the train's readiness to depart from the station.

Inskeep eased in the clutch while he let up on the brake and started the train smoothly rolling from the station into the yawning mouth of the dark subway tunnel that stretched beneath the bustling streets of lower Broadway more than three stories above.

Due to congestion caused by a train ahead of him onboard which the rear car had needed to be isolated, Inskeep was running over ten minutes behind schedule.

The problem, Inskeep had heard on his radio, was the overheating of the motor in the car of the train before him, the "leader," in MTA vernacular, of the backed-up column of subway trains which followed in slow succession. The burning motor had filled the tunnel with thick, acrid smelling oil-smoke.

The leader's motorman had radioed ahead for a Road Car Inspector to meet the train at the next station. There, the RCI had ordered the train to dump its passengers and lay up for the Flatbush Avenue yard.

Although he was annoyed at the delay, Inskeep knew that it could have been worse. The veteran motorman could remember being backed up in tunnels for half-hour stretches when traffic really became jammed.

On the ancient IRT line, such backups occurred far more frequently than anywhere else in the sprawling New York City subway system.

Once, there had been a serious track fire that had filled the tunnel with choking black clouds of noxious smoke. The smoke had been so thick that they had sent fire department paramedics into the tunnels to distribute oxygen masks to the trapped passengers.

There was some consolation, however. As soon as Inskeep completed this run, he was finished for the day.

It would be home for a hot shower, a cold brew and some serious football watching. Although his job prevented him from viewing the games in real-time, he'd set his DVR to record off Sports Channel.

Inskeep was now three stops away from entering the long, ruler-straight tunnel that stretched for three miles beneath the East River.

After that he'd be in Brooklyn. And after that, it was home, sweet home.

***

On the second car of the departing IRT local, the same car in which Kesselman had taken a seat, Jing Duk Soo sat reading the Bible as he returned home from his job as a floater for a Midtown messenger service.

The holy scriptures were an inspiration to him. Since emigrating to America from Seoul, South Korea, and beginning life in this great and noble metropolis, the words of the Gospels had given him an anchor in life that he would not have otherwise possessed.

Religion, though, was not on Patty Scarfone's mind. Makeup was. She had left her thousand-dollar-a-month, broom-closet sized East Village apartment in a hurry that morning and, as happened all too frequently, was now forced to apply her mascara while riding the jostling, swaying subway train.

To make matters worse, the legal secretary had awakened with periodic cramps that morning and the train ride was making her feel nauseous.

Of course, it might have been worse; she often had to perform this delicate exercise while both nauseous *and* standing. Now at least, she was sitting down.

Two seats away from the legal secretary's seat, Sterling Dupree, a twenty-four-year old printer's apprentice and aspiring rap superstar known to intimates as "SD Mackin'," sat playing a game of electronic pinball on his iPhone.

The smart phone's ap produced The assortment of beeps, buzzes and synthesized voices as virtual pinballs whizzed across the liquid-crystal screen, hitting bumpers and lighting up numbers at the deft manipulation of virtual keys on the phone's virtual game display. It was all obvious bullshit to the annoyed man sitting beside the wannabe SD Mackin'.

Frank "Buddy" Coyne was tired. He was a construction worker who was returning home to his white working class enclave in Brooklyn from a late shift at a high-rise building site in Midtown. But although there were plenty of seats on the uncrowded subway car, Coyne was too bagged-out to get up and change his seat.

Although the kid didn't look like he'd put up any trouble, Coyne was also reluctant to say anything to him. You never knew. Not with these fuckin' punks.

There had just been a story on the eleven o'clock news the night before about some sixteen-year-old shit who pulled out a gun and shot a guy in the face because he'd looked at him wrong.

In the end, Coyne settled for thinking about that cold Bud that was awaiting him in the refrigerator of his apartment in Brooklyn's Bay Ridge.

Coyne would have to transfer at DeKalb Avenue, but that was okay. It would also mean he'd be away from the punk with the faggot phone in only a few more stops. He could put up with the racket until then, he reasoned.

Walking toward the first car, was a group of four machine-shop students from a vocational high school who sashayed across the precariously swaying deck of the rocking, juddering train with the ease and grace of practiced tightrope walkers.

The first one carried an iPod-equipped ghetto blaster playing a Sheek Louch rap track at full volume, so loud that the music was clearly audible even above the deafening roar made by the train's wheels as it clattered through the tunnel at its top cruising speed.

Nobody among the passengers watching as they passed would have suspected as much from the looks on their faces, however.

Their faces revealed a studied obliviousness to everything going on around them.

Even a nuclear blast, one might suspect, would do nothing to effect the blank looks on their mask-like faces.

THE BLACKOUT HEIST

TWENTY

Skerrit, Manhattan. Rick Skerrit began winding down his work day.

Now that he had received the expected notice of his termination, the crushing weight of responsibility had suddenly been lifted from his shoulders leaving, him feeling oddly and uncharacteristically at peace with himself.

Whether or not he would have done things differently had he been given a second chance was now irrelevant.

He had acted in accordance with the dictates of his conscience. Now, whatever price those actions demanded, he would have to pay it.

For the moment, Skerrit occupied himself in the control room of the power station with the day's affairs.

Regardless of whether or not he was just marking time until his resignation became effective, he would continue to perform his duties to the best of his ability. If Skerrit was anything, he was a detail man.

The control room was a hive of activity as computer screens sifting data from sensors along the city's energy grid flashed a steady spate of readouts from points across the city, giving the moment-by-moment fluctuations of voltage as usage crosscut between different sectors of the grid.

Skerrit paused to note the graph curve on a screen at one of the consoles showing sudden increasing activity in the north sector of midtown Manhattan, a normal usage pattern at this time of year when the days were still growing short and night, though falling earlier each day, still arrived in late afternoon.

"How are your readings for sector seven-oh-eight-four?" Skerrit asked one of the technicians seated at one of the large room's many console screens.

Seven-oh-eight-four was a predominantly residential section of Inwood in upper Manhattan. There would be a surplus of power here that could be channeled elsewhere to make up for the increasing usage in the many business offices in the midtown sector.

"Normal usage pattern," the tech replied. "Oh, maybe a point or so off-scale, but otherwise same-old, same-old. Computer'll probably be kicking in any second now," she continued. Suddenly the graph's curve leveled out on the screen. "There you go," she told Skerrit with a smile and lit up a cigarette.

In less time than it took for a thought to form in the human brain, the mainframe computer servers had calculated the number of kilowatts available against those required, sucked them from parts of the sprawling energy grid where surplus existed, and shunted them to those areas which currently reported energy deficits.

The system was now again in a state of equilibrium. On an average day, Skerrit knew, the energy utility's servers would perform this operation at least fifty thousand times.

What frightened Skerrit was not so much the awesome power of the system to effect every household in the city, but the fact that it did not need to ask any human being whether to do so or not.

***

"How about celebrating?"

"What for?"

"My just getting fired," Skerrit returned as he spoke into the mouthpiece of his cellular phone while driving the ZR1 uptown across Broadway from the power utility's lower Manhattan headquarters.

"Oh Rick," Shyanne returned, "I'm so damn sorry."

"Don't be," he told her. "Because I'm not. In fact this is the best I've felt in months. Something about kissing ass doesn't agree with me, I suppose, and I was doing a hell of a lot of that when I should have been fighting the bastards every step of the way right from the start."

Shyanne's voice took on a sensual huskiness as she asked, "Where would you like to celebrate? My place or yours."

Skerrit laughed. Somehow, though, the thought of servicing her sexually filled him with a vague sense of being used. "Plenty of time to decide which. Right now how about meeting me at the Top of the Sevens for dinner?"

"Sounds great," Shyanne replied, thrilled to be having dinner at the swank midtown restaurant.

"Fine, I'll be the guy in the gorilla suit with the pink carnation between his teeth. If you still can't find me, just ask the waiter."

***

Lafcadio served the two diners their drinks. A Bloody Mary, heavy on the pepper for the lady, a vodka martini, light on the vermouth, for the gentleman.

Lafcadio had been in America for only seven months. Too soon yet to get his green card. Although he had been a doctor in his native Colombia, he was now forced to earn his living waiting tables.

This, however, was far superior to being lined up against a wall and shot, and so Lafcadio performed his duties both diligently and cheerfully. As a citizen, he would be able to set himself up in a small storefront clinic in Queens. With Medicaid money and insurance company retainers, he could very soon be doing quite well for himself.

Skerrit sat across the table from Shyanne as they sipped their drinks. The table faced the wrap-around window at the restaurant on the penthouse level of the high-rise office building at 777 Park Avenue. Everywhere across the city, lights were winking on, piecing together bright mosaics against the hulking black, and vaguely sinister shapes of the skyscrapers at night.

THE BLACKOUT HEIST

"What do you think you'll do now?" Shyanne asked him, reaching beneath the table to stroke the inside of his thigh, her eyes bright and wantonly moist.

"Too soon to tell," Skerrit replied, feeling his dick get hard despite his unwillingness do respond to her seduction. "Maybe I'll just decide to chuck it all and pack my things and hop a slow freighter for Christmas Island."

"Where's Christmas Island?" Her hand was now on his fly, the fingers tracing the ridge of his dickhead beneath the stretched fabric.

"Don't know where it is," Skerrit returned, his own voice growing husky now, "only that it's someplace remote and has a population somewhere under three."

"That'll make you a quarter of the population." Shyanne's fingers were tugging down on Skerrit's zipper.

"Be tough around census time," he said, finally pushing her hand away, seeing her expression quickly turn from excited to hurt, and feeling guilty despite himself. "I'm sorry," he said. "Not now, okay?"

Beneath the attempt at cheerful repartee, Skerrit was an angry man. He was not in the mood for handjobs beneath the dinner table right now.

He was angry at being shitcanned for no good reason. Maybe he could fight it, he supposed.

Even in New York State with some of the most lax hiring and firing laws on the books, wrongful dismissal suits were becoming more common.

Sure, he could fight it all right. *Like I could turn shit into wine*, he finally decided.

Skerrit sat and drank his drink, watching more lights flash on in the windows of skyscrapers as the twilight sky deepened to indigo and the belly of a jet plane, heading westward, caught the last glimmer of the almost hidden sun.

For six years Skerrit had played an integral part in lighting up those thousands upon thousands of commercial and domestic windows every day and every night. Homes where people lived, businesses where people worked, hospitals where doctors and nurses cared for the sick.

A part of him had reached out to every corner of the city, investing it with energy and light. Now that would all abruptly end, simply because Skerrit had found the courage -- or surrendered to the stupidity -- to speak truth to power. Where would he go? What would he do? How would he live with himself?

Sure, he could find work in another city. But Seattle, Denver or even Los Angeles wouldn't even come close to where he was right now. He'd come to love New York, felt a deep and abiding bond with the vibrancy and energy of the Big Apple. Nothing, he realized, would or could ever be the same again.

Raising his hand as he caught the waiter's eye, Skerrit signaled for another round of drinks.

TWENTY-ONE

Richie, Brooklyn. It was all there in the papers Eddie had left behind. Richie had been a competent accountant and an honest employee. His notes had clearly shown that he had found out early on that embezzlement of Fed funds was taking place at high organizational levels of the federal government's main banking establishment and a gold repository second in size only to Fort Knox.

Little by little, Eddie had realized that Norman Judson, his boss and a ranking corporate officer, was responsible for the missing money.

"Whether or not to confront him?" was one entry, dated June 1st of the previous year. A later one, written in August, read, "Have let him know that I know. Concerned about the outcome."

The diary broke off in early November. For some three weeks before Eddie's death, there were no entries at all. Richie was determined to put all of the puzzle pieces together. And the key to making that happen was Judson.

Richie was going to make Judson the focus of his attention. Before he was finished, there was nothing about the man that Richie would not know.

***

Maddie closed the office door. Norman Judson sat behind the desk with a smirk on his patrician face. Judson had been coming on to Maddie since she'd been hired, which made it almost a solid year of sexual harassment.

At first Maddie had ignored it, hoping, but not believing that the problem would go away. Sexual harassment usually did not just disappear, but Maddie waited until there was no option left except to confront him and call his bluff.

Among the options she had initially considered was to let Richie have a man-to-man talk with her boss, though she rejected that on the grounds that she might then be a party to homicide or at least aggravated assault. In the end, Maddie Robbins decided to do what her father in Vermont had taught her to do at an early age: take care of her own problems herself.

"Norm," she said, as she went to his desk, "I think we should talk."

"Good idea," he replied. "How about over dinner. I can see you in a lacy peignoir sipping a bubbly French wine while I kiss your big beautiful, and yes, *bubbly* tits."

"That's an interesting idea, Norm," she said as she grabbed Judson's tie and suddenly yanked it hard. Judson's head hit the rubber blotter on his teakwood desk. She was on top of him in a second, kneeing him in the rib cage. His cries were muffled by the blotter, but loud enough for a secretary to open the door.

"Is there -- "

The secretary felt silent, her eyes wide as she saw what was going on inside Judson's office.

"We're just having a talk," Maddie told her. The secretary understood. She closed the door and walked out. Maddie was glad. Now what happened would be all over the building but confined to a tactful stage whisper in the corridors. The prick would never live it down.

"Let me up!" Norman grunted.

Maddie pushed him back in the chair. She was breathing hard as she said, "Now you listen to me you bastard and listen good. You and I are both going to forget this shit ever happened. From now on we are going to have a model professional relationship, one attorney to another. Is that clear?"

"You fucking bitch!" he cursed. "You didn't have to do that."

"Norman, I asked you a question," Maddie repeated. "I want an answer." She pulled harder on his tie hearing him make gargling sounds.

"Okay, okay, it's clear," he agreed.

Maddie eased up on her grip. "Fine," she said. "Now I'm going back to my desk. We'll just start out fresh and hope things work out right."

She walked out, leaving the door open. Through the entranceway Judson saw his secretary looking in with a half-smile on her face. Judson glared at Jo Ann, who quickly looked away, busying herself with some papers on her desk. He thought: you haven't seen the last of me yet. But he knew he would have to bide his time.

Things had changed since he was a kid fresh out of law school. Even before the notorious Sluts of the Senate scandal made porn star Dong Deluxe a household word, women's harassment claims were

168

being taken seriously. And Maddie was an attorney, she knew as much about the law as he did. There would be no bluffing her. But the bitch had put her hands on him, and Judson didn't take that shit from anybody. He would get the dirty little slut, but in his own time, and in his own way.

"Jo Ann," he called out.

"Yes, Mr. Judson," replied his secretary, the question mark implicit in her tone of voice.

"I'm leaving for the day," he advised her. "Call the garage and tell them to have my car ready."

"Yes, Mr. Judson," she said, relieved to see the bastard heading for the elevators.

Parked on Maiden Lane just off the intersection with Liberty Street, Richie saw his target come out of one of the Federal Reserve Building's rear entrances which were restricted to staff use only. Although he was sure that Judson had never more than glanced at him in passing, and therefore wouldn't recognize him on sight, Richie had caught a good look at Judson not too long before when he had picked up Maddie for a lunch date.

Richie was glad Judson had shown. Apart from the fact that his ass was getting sore from prolonged sitting in the car, he had begun thinking about Maddie, whom he would have rather been waiting for had things been different. But he had phoned her after coming home, telling her he had to go out of town on business for a day or two after reading Eddie's diary. He didn't want to see her until he had figured out what to do about Eddie and knew what he was going to tell her. Richie didn't want to involve Maddie in a family affair.

THE BLACKOUT HEIST

Judson got his car out of a nearby garage on Maiden lane. It was a cream Mercedes SLR McLaren with gull-wing doors, not brand new but a custom model that would still command a high resale value. A car like that would stand out, making it easier to tail Judson. Richie followed the Mercedes onto the East River Drive.

Judson took it north to the Triboro, then turned onto the Bruckner. He was heading north, into Riverdale, in the Bronx. Close to rush hour, commuter traffic had been heavy on the highways, but once on the tree-lined streets north of Manhattan, it thinned out. Judson pulled the Mercedes into the driveway of an A-frame house with a well-manicured lawn in an expensive section of the suburban community that was physically attached to the Bronx but had never actually been a part of the large, grimy boro to its south.

Richie drove around, unobtrusively examining the suburban neighborhood with a professional thief's practiced eye. He returned and parked a few houses down, far enough away to avoid notice, but close enough to keep the house in view. He was going to get to know Judson better than Judson knew himself.

TWENTY-TWO

Richie, Lower Manhattan. It was raining when Richie met Maddie for dinner at the South Street Seaport three weeks after coming back from Cancun and staking out Maddie's boss. He had been getting to know Norm Judson very well during that time, and he had reached the juncture where he wanted to stop and take stock of his impressions.

It was not a very difficult matter to get vital statistics on just about anybody if you knew where to look. The day after staking out Judson's house in Riverdale, Richie had gone to a copy shop and had letterhead printed up. The same shop was also a cyber cafe, and rented out mailboxes, voice mail and fax numbers.

Now as "Kingsboro Credit Systems," Richie had given himself access to most of the databases in the country. He could have done his checking faster and easier using a computer, but not without leaving far more footprints behind in cyberspace than the old-fashioned way. He preferred leaving no tracks to the ease and simplicity of using internet snoop sites any day of the week.

"Kingsboro's" first inquiries had gone to the New York City Department of Motor Vehicles. The DMVs of every city and town were the largest brokers of information in the country.

The data on drivers license applications could be purchased by anybody for a small fee. "Kingsboro" paid that fee and soon Richie had Judson's social security number, date of birth, marital status and other information. The two big commercial brokers, Equifax and TRW, were next on his list. Through them, "Kingsboro" was able to obtain detailed credit information including transactions on Judson's American Express and Visa credit cards during the past twelve months.

Other sources had yielded more information. In a locked drawer of a filing cabinet in Richie's apartment, a folder was getting thicker by the day as Richie filled it with the paperwork detailing Judson's life. Judson might get a notice in the mail telling him that some outfit named Kingsboro had accessed his credit file, but Richie could not be traceable.

He had rented the box, the voice mail and the fax under a phony name and had paid for everything in cash. He had worn sunglasses and a ball cap when he had come in to apply initially and had made certain that no security cameras were on him when he stopped by to pick up mail and faxes in his mailbox.

The rent was paid for the next month, but Richie would never come back to the box again after the week was up. "Kingsboro Credit Systems" would vanish into thin air.

***

DAVID ALEXANDER

The Chinese restaurant had come highly recommended from one of Maddie's coworkers. The place was too small but Richie had reserved a corner table. The waiter brought two salads with lobster rolls that were superb.

"Are you all right?" she asked him.

"Yeah, why do you ask?"

"You haven't threatened to punch anybody out yet tonight," she explained. "That's a first."

"Give me a chance," Richie answered, "I'm just getting warmed up."

"I wonder what I see in you sometimes, Richie," she told him as she sipped some jasmine tea. "In a lot of ways you're bad news."

"Then what are you doing hanging around with me?" he asked. The salad had not yielded to the fork and he had begun to eat it with his fingers.

"I don't know," she said. "But when I figure it out, it could be hasta la vista."

"Okay by me," he said as the waiter arrived with the main course and asked them if they wanted to share. He meant it too. As much as he cared for and needed Maddie, if she went, then she went. Richie would never pay heartbreak dues for any woman, no matter how important she was in his life.

After the meal, Richie and Maddie walked along Fifth Avenue. The rain continued but had tapered off to a heavy drizzle. Now a dense cottony fog had rolled in from the East River and blanketed the streets in a billowing gray mist.

They walked along the empty avenues and side-streets, first looking for a cab, but when one was not in sight, continuing to walk. By the time they

173

realized they had reached Fourteenth Street, there was no reason for a cab any longer. Maddie's apartment was only a few blocks away.

Maddie's place in the Village overlooked Lower Broadway. Richie glanced out the window. The street was empty. A lashing rain had developed to replace the heavy fog, and the drab Manhattan asphalt now glistened under the streetlights and the headlight beams of passing crosstown traffic.

Hours later, he awakened. A glance at the lighted blue numerals of the digital clock on Maddie's bureau told Richie that it was 4:16 A.M. He looked over at her. One of her breasts was exposed from beneath the quilt, and she murmured in her sleep and rolled toward him, flinging an arm around Richie's chest.

He extricated himself from her slumbering embrace and padded naked from the bed. Stripes of light from the street lamps outside daubed his body as he went to the window and chinked two metal slats of the downward-slanted venetian blinds to have a look outside. Rain still fell and the street was quiet, but for a fleeting moment, a flicker of motion from inside the van parked directly below the window at curbside caught Richie's eye. He continued to stare at the immobile vehicle but saw nothing more. Yet something at the back of his mind was bothering him, tugging on a rope of thought, as if to ring a distant bell.

Shrugging it off to mere paranoia, Richie found his clothes and dressed quickly and quietly in the dark. Maddie was still sleeping as he kissed her on the forehead and stole toward the door of the apartment, locking it behind him as he stepped into the fluorescent-lit hallway and walked across the carpeted floor toward the elevator.

Night rain continued falling, and the helium-argon street lighting cast iridescent reflections on the wet hoods of parked cars and painted reflected colors across the streets and sidewalks, giving them a Cinderella quality they didn't deserve. Richie lit a cigarette and pulled up the collar of his black leather jacket against the weather. He walked to his car and saw two home boys looking it over, casing it, in fact. They saw him and booked like jackrabbits.

Richie's fingers closed around the butt of the .38 revolver in his pocket as he chased them back down the block. The homies piled into the parked van he'd spotted on the curbside below Maddie's window, which was no longer immobile. With a shriek of rubber, the van sped off down the street and disappeared around the corner onto Canal after traveling a block.

Richie checked his car for signs of vandalism but found nothing. Either he had stopped them before they could rip him off or there was another explanation for their presence, one he preferred not to consider for the time being, though the little bell at the back of his mind still rang softly and, for the moment, distantly.

TWENTY-THREE

Amoroso, Manhattan. Mary Koslowski worked three desks away from Ellis Amoroso. At sixty-three and having been employed with the firm for thirty-one years, she was a month away from mandatory retirement with full pension benefits. Although they had tried to conceal it from her, Mary knew that her coworkers had been planning a bon voyage party for several weeks.

Tomorrow was her last day on the job. From the way they'd been behaving all day long and the nervous glances that had been directed her way, Mary knew that the party would certainly take place this afternoon.

She had stayed on only long enough to train a bright young twenty-four-year-old girl in her office function. Danielle had caught on quickly. Mary had felt vindicated in hiring her. She knew that her replacement would do fine in her position and it pleased her to know that she would leave the company with a spotless record to commence her long-awaited golden years.

Mary glanced again at Amoroso who was busy keystroking at his workstation nearby. Such a nice young man. He reminded her a lot of her son, Peter. With his short brown hair and piercing blue eyes, Amoroso looked just like Peter had when he'd gone to Iraq decades before to die in some godforsaken cinderblock village in the desert somewhere.

Mary couldn't believe that such a nice young man could be in such big trouble. Yet, Amoroso was, Mary knew. He was in very big trouble indeed.

She suspected that he was involved in something dangerous, something that might result in his being fired, or much worse.

She had accidentally been in a position to eavesdrop on their boss, Murray Jackman, as Jackman discussed Amoroso with someone else, someone she sensed was with the police department.

What was Amoroso up to?

Mary had no idea.

However, she had been grappling with the question of whether or not to warn him. It was not the act of warning Amoroso that troubled Mary so much as the potential of spoiling her own perfect record in some way.

Mary was well aware that her firm was involved in shady dealings and had been from day one. Even if Amoroso had been stealing from the firm, it didn't make him any more of a criminal in her eyes than the greedy bastards who he worked for. Indeed, the people at the top were the ones who, by rights, should be arrested.

Mary would continue to make up her mind concerning what to do about Amoroso. She had this feeling, though, that time was running out. If he stayed for the "surprise" party, Mary would tell him, she decided. If he did not, then whatever happened would be in the hands of God.

***

Panic was starting to boil like a kettle in Amoroso's gut as the last few hours stretched by like slowly pulled taffy. He tried not to glance at his watch too often, but the temptation was too great to resist.

Go! Go! a little voice kept shouting in his head. *Don't press your luck a minute longer. You're living on borrowed time, my friend. Get out while the getting is good!*

Theoretically Amoroso knew that he could walk that very minute. He could quit the office for the men's room and never come back again.

But another voice contended against the one that cried out for him to leave immediately. This other voice urged caution. It told him to follow his plan through to the end, to leave at the end of the day without arousing anyone's suspicion.

In the end, Amoroso decided that the second voice, the cautious voice, was the right one to listen to. He would go away on his vacation and be too far from them to do anything about it once they discovered that the money was missing except bitch and cuss.

The company would pinpoint him, of course. But that was already factored into Amoroso's criminal equation.

There was no way to stop the company from finding that he had embezzled over a million dollars from the firm. But Amoroso didn't need to stop them. That was the entire point of his plan, the beautiful gimmick that would insure that it could not fail.

All he needed to do was be on the other side of the world when the realization came home to them.

With a new identity and a few superficial cosmetic changes, Amoroso would be completely beyond the grasp of the company and the police.

He might even be able to return to the States at some point in time. Even today, no one would argue that a million dollars was not a great deal of money. But neither was it, however, on a par with the really big rip-offs being pulled every day.

Not when wheeler-dealers on Wall Street could walk with twenty times that amount just handed to them in the form of government bail-outs when their screw-ups lost billions, and just stuff the federal cash in their pockets.

Not when the papers had just run a story about a stockbroker at a major investment banking firm who'd milked his clients out of eight million dollars by conning them into investing in phony stock and bond issues.

And certainly not when a story about a multi-million dollar rip-off rated no more than a sidebar on page twenty-three of the New York Post.

Amoroso was counting on the fact that a million bucks was a sizable enough sum to keep the heat on him for a year, maybe two, but not such a big chunk of currency that he'd be hounded for the rest of his life.

Add to this the fact that the firm he worked for was up to its eyeballs in money laundering scams at the highest executive levels, and Amoroso figured his chances of being able to walk the streets of Manhattan in the not too distant future were better than average.

And even if it turned out that he could never return, what of it? Life in this town wasn't all it was cracked up to be. Once, maybe. But the city had turned into a toilet bowl since Amoroso had been a kid. He'd give his regards to Broadway, but keep his ass in the wind.

The streets belonged to punks, savages and the mentally defective. Even the so-called "decent people" were at best deeply neurotic, at worst as bad as the crazies out on the street, albeit better-dressed and on more expensive pharmaceuticals.

Everybody did drugs and nobody gave a solitary fuck about anybody else. Most not even about themselves. That was the nitty-gritty on New York City.

It had gotten so bad that you either stayed locked away in your overpriced co-op apartment cuddling with your cable box and only ventured out for more beer and more sushi or you left town completely.

As far as Amoroso was concerned, the city and everyone in it could go straight to hell.

Then he realized that this wasn't possible. Amoroso smiled. The city had already gone there a long, long time ago.

***

Each of the Battery Park Commerce Towers' two skyscraper office buildings soared nearly a quarter mile into the sky of lower Manhattan, a sky that was often the exact color and texture of the streets below.

The towers held over ten million square feet of rentable office space, almost forty-five thousand windows comprising six hundred thousand feet of plate glass and almost two thousand cars daily in its underground garage.

More than one million cubic tons of earth and rock were excavated to make way for the global financial center, including the wreckage of what the media had called "Ground Zero" and the rescue workers who'd dug for bodies had dubbed "the Pile," creating almost twenty-five acres of landfill for adjacent Battery Park.

In excess of fifty thousand men and women every business day worked within the vast structures, not the tallest -- but among the tallest -- in the world.

On the observation promenade on the West Tower's one hundred tenth floor, visitors to New York could take in a panoramic view of the five boros, Liberty Island and the South Jersey shore.

Also located on the hundred seventh floor was the Pinnacle restaurant, from which diners could view the city from their tables while dining on international cuisine. The Battery Park Commerce Towers also housed a wide variety of businesses.

There were many government offices located there as well. US Customs had its Eastern Regional Headquarters at the tower complex, as did the trade missions of several foreign nations.

THE BLACKOUT HEIST

On Amoroso's floor were also located the Visitors' Bureau of Thailand and a major commodities trading firm.

On the floors above and below that of Amoroso's firm, were the offices of a movie production company, a firm that manufactured automobile hood ornaments and a large telecommunications and cable company.

Although the employees of these businesses passed one another regularly while going to and from their jobs, either in the spacious lobbies, the trains which ran below them or the huge elevators which serviced the Battery Park Commerce Towers, few of them formed lasting acquaintances, let alone acknowledged one anothers' presence.

As the two main buildings of the tower complex had been designed to be completely fireproof, there was no established procedure for evacuation in case of emergency.

The security staff of the immense office complex discounted this possibility anyway.

Nothing short of a major catastrophe equaling the 911 attacks could cause any significant problems for the Battery Park Commerce Towers. And in such a scenario, of course, it would be too late to do anything for anybody.

The upshot of this line of reasoning was that no emergency plans for evacuation of the Towers in case of major emergency existed at all. The events of 911 had proved that total evacuation was impossible, and that even partial evacuation was highly problematic.

There was one workable plan, though. And it was one that was based on the oldest rule there was.

In case of emergency, the plan was: every man for himself and devil take the hindmost.

TWENTY-FOUR

Applebaum, The Bronx. Mad Marty Applebaum's crisis room had been originally designed as a walk-in closet. Its door was concealed behind a bookcase that swung outward on hinges. He had done the carpentry work himself.

Lead sheeting rendered the crisis room impervious to electronic surveillance and nuclear fallout. It also made it soundproof and eavesdrop-proof.

Applebaum stored his valuable collection of weapons, ammo and electronic security devices inside the crisis room. The guns Applebaum had bought over the years were kept in a large gun safe that took up most of one wall. He'd ordered the gun safe from Sears. Privately, he called his gun safe "the Iron Maiden."

The arsenal in Marty's Iron Maiden included an M60E4 Squad Automatic Weapon, a machinegun that fired NATO-caliber bullets and was fed by a belt of hundreds of rounds that was folded inside a metal box hooked to the weapon's underside; an over-under combination Colt Commando submachinegun and M203 grenade launcher which could fire both 5.56-millimeter ammo and 40-

millimeter grenades, as well as other exotic hardware.

Also in Applebaum's arsenal was a pair of Litton ANVIS night-seeing goggles. The goggles were capable of electronically amplifying the tiny photons of light that were present even in pitch darkness so that the wearer could see his target in the dark.

He'd gotten them on the cheap because US military specifications had changed and the company had discontinued them.

In addition to the goggles, Applebaum was the proud possessor of an Armson laser scope. The Armson scope pinpointed targets in an ultra-fine beam of ruby-colored light -- pulling the trigger guaranteed a hit wherever the light touched. Also for night shooting, Applebaum had a British-made Pilkington scope which could be mounted atop any of his automatic rifles.

Unlike the weapons, for which Applebaum had needed to get a federal dealer's license to legitimately possess, the night-amplification equipment was legal anywhere. All you needed was the asking price and it was yours for the taking.

All in all, Applebaum's weapons arsenal had cost him a couple of years' pay as a high school social studies teacher and had forced him to moonlight at odd jobs after class. He considered these acquisitions worth it, however.

Applebaum was dead serious about being a professional soldier of fortune. In the two years since going on disability from the city school system, he'd trained hard.

185

THE BLACKOUT HEIST

With his first assignment, he knew, word would start to spread like wildfire that he was a merc's merc. Pretty soon, he'd begin to get the really choice and meaty assignments. Commando raids, palace coups, covert terrorist executions, the whole nine yards.

Applebaum poured himself a shot of Jack Daniels from the half-pint bottle in his fatigue pocket that he'd bought at the neighborhood bodega earlier that day. This was a big moment and it called for a ceremonial libation.

While he'd been out before, he'd picked up a copy of International Mercenary, a magazine in which mercenary soldiers advertised for contracts. Applebaum had placed a display ad in the magazine.

Flipping through the pages of International Mercenary, Applebaum spotted his ad which was sandwiched in the middle of the magazine between an article on hand grenades and a photo-spread of busty women in torn tee-shirts firing submachineguns. The ad read:

***

Experienced Mercenary For Hire
Bronx, New York-based soldier of fortune with the guts and know-how to tackle any job, clean or dirty, near or far, large or small.

Will travel anywhere for any reason at moment's notice. Can operate on solo missions or as member of select team of crisis management experts.

DAVID ALEXANDER

Services include the latest in sophisticated weaponry, surveillance electronics and covert operations tactics. Write with details for price quote.

***

Leaving his crisis room, Applebaum padlocked the door behind him. The dinginess of his housing projects apartment suddenly hit him full-force and made him want to puke. He hoped he'd get an answer to his advertisement soon. For the moment, he settled for knocking back another slug of the Black Jack.

He'd give it a week, then check the post office box he'd rented from an independent mail service for the offers he knew would soon come pouring in.

Right now, though, looking around his terminally messy apartment made Applebaum feel like a ticking bomb. He wanted out of this scum-pit of a city so bad he could taste it.

If the money was right, Applebaum would gladly relocate somewhere else in the world.

Maybe to Africa or someplace in the Pacific rim, one of those little island republics with names like Bonaire whose governments were always teetering on the edge of overthrowal. Yeah, Bonaire had a good sound to it, a right nice ring. He'd have to remember to look it up in his atlas and find out exactly where the fuck it was. For now, Applebaum decided to flip on the tube.

The garbage they were showing on cable brought him down even more. There was nothing but trash news programs, soaps and talk shows geared to the mental level of retards on at this hour. Of course, there was nothing on at any hour,

187

despite his having paid extra for the upgrade from standard cable to the enhanced plan.

Daytime TV was the pits. But by the time they'd change the rules about allowing dish TV in the projects, Applebaum knew he'd be old, gray and probably blind.

Applebaum was growing steadily more depressed as he kept zapping across the channels, trying to find something to take his mind off his problems.

In frustration he snapped off the television and pulled the bottle of sour mash whiskey from a side pocket of his camo pants. Tilting back for a healthy slug, he drained the bottle and finally started feeling just a little bit better.

Chapter Three
Live Cowards, Dead Heroes

THE BLACKOUT HEIST

Richie, Manhattan. All Richie's ducks were in line. His next move was to put the pieces together and turn his plan into a reality. He had assembled an extensive database on Norman Judson. The database contained photographs and all the personal history items he'd been able to turn up. All of this was tucked neatly away in his netbook and the paper files sitting in a locked cabinet in his apartment.

Richie was not about to leave telltale evidence lying around for anybody to see. He could call every fact about Judson up whenever he needed it, but if an unauthorized person tried to access the computer without knowing the login password and username, it would lock up.

If they tried to circumvent the login credentials, then the solid state disk drive would automatically erase itself and a few grams of C4 he'd wired inside to blow on tampering would give trespassers a nasty little surprise, like blowing off a nose or two. To be safe, Richie kept the palmtop locked in a hidden vault where it was impermeable to fire and not easily found.

Richie's plan called for a few good men to back him up. He had his own areas of expertise, but he was limited to being in only one place at a single time.

Letting others in on what he planned carried major risks. One of Richie's cardinal rules was to never work with partners. Partners talked when caught, talked at the drop of a hat. Partners sold you out. But the kind of caper he had in mind could not be handled alone.

***

Gun Hill Road in the Morrisania section of the Bronx. A mean neighborhood, one that had continued to belie decades of posturing by City Hall about urban renaissance. Richie peeled off a twenty and handed it to the gypsy cab driver, a Haitian with a big, bald head who had driven him there.

"You sure you want to get off here, mon?" he asked.

"I wouldn't have told you to drive me here if I wasn't," he replied. "No, you keep the change," he added before the hack driver could break the bill.

"Okay, you take care, mon," he said and made a fast U-turn out of there.

Richie couldn't blame the guy. He was in the midst of one of the worst urban centers in the entire city, maybe the country. On either side were immense lots filled with rubble and the occasional section of brick structural wall left standing when the tenements that had occupied the lots were demolished thirty-odd years before. Despite gentrification and overdevelopment elsewhere in the boros, the Bronx was still the dark side of the New York moon.

Richie began walking, feeling the stares of unseen hostiles on his back. A wino slouched in a corner by a row of garbage pails looked at him with baleful yellow eyes and held out his hand.

Richie bent down and waved a fifty dollar bill in his face. The wino's reaction was predictable. His yellow eyes lit up and he got a shrewd, hustler's look in his yellow-cornered brown eyes.

"This is yours. I'm looking for somebody. Maybe you've seen him," he said.

"Lotta people looking for lotta other people," replied the wino. "Who you looking to kill?"

"Want to find somebody. Black man. Big motherfucker. Goes by the name of Deacon. You'd know him if you saw him."

"Don't know no Deacon," the wino retorted. "But there's a bad muthafucka name Sister John fits the description of yo' boy."

He reached out to grab the fifty. Richie yanked it away.

"Where?" he asked.

"I'll show you," he told him, "free of charge."

This time Richie let the guy pull the rectangular green-tinged slip of paper from his grasp.

Before long they were standing in front of a locked plate steel armored door. There was an armored security camera mounted on a pole overhead that was trained on the street right in front and a speaker grille linked to an intercom inside. The wino pushed one of the unmarked buttons on a row of five.

"Who there?" a woman's voice tinged with the street inflections of San Juan, Puerto Rico, answered.

"Yo, dis Rasheem Abdul," the wino said at the speaker. "Mah boy here wants Sister John."

"Ain't no 'Sister John' here," the voice growled.

"Shit! Come on, mah boy, be cool. Best let us in, girl."

The door buzzed in response. Rasheed pushed it in and went inside with Richie following close behind him. A long corridor with dingy blue walls led toward a second door.

Another camera on the ceiling covered every inch of the corridor. The door opened and a big black guy stood glowering down at Rasheed and Richie.

"Been a long time, Deacon," Richie said.

***

Deacon nodded. Richie had explained the basic parameters of his plan. He had already told Deacon enough to put him away for a long time, but there was no way around it. He had taken a calculated risk by coming here to begin with.

"You are still as crazy now as you were back in the New 'Nam, Richie," Deacon, who preferred to be called 'Sister John,' his new street name, replied, referring to what grunts called the War In Surinam. "This shit will never fly."

"Yes it will," Richie told him. "If we do it right, it'll fly. And it will make us all wealthy."

"Wealthy ain't gonna do nobody no good stretched in the fucking pen, my dog," Sister John retorted.

THE BLACKOUT HEIST

"Nobody's going to prison," Richie advised, shaking his head. "I got all the moves planned out. But before I tell you more, I got to know if you're in or not."

Sister John thought it over for awhile. As the gears turned upstairs, Richie looked out the window of the diner open late on Morrisania Avenue. Cars passed in the rain, and across the street, in front of the local Blockbuster, a women who looked like one of the whores from whom Sister John made his living as a "hawkeye" or bodyguard, was being harassed by a group of street kids wielding lengths of bicycle chain.

"Yeah, shit, I'm in," he said and reached across the table. "Gimme your plate."

***

The small town of Hollis, Pennsylvania, sat amid brooding hills. The coal mines that had led to a boom in the area a hundred years before were largely silent now, but coal still was the major industry of Hollis, especially so since GM and the major automobile manufacturers had closed down their plants.

Jace Kingsley was among the fortunate few who still had himself a steady job which paid enough to keep up the mortgage payments on the saltbox house in the hills he'd bought and put groceries on the table. His skills with things electrical learned in the Army had enabled him to continue working as an electrician for the Oriskany Valley Power and Light as a lineman.

A car stopped by his parked utility company truck. Kingsley was up in the gantry, working on

194

high tension cables that had sustained some damage during a recent storm. He saw the two men approach and heard one of them call up to him.

"Hey, Witchitaw lineman!"

Kingsley figured he was being hassled by some punks. He pretended not to have heard them. People in his line of work were targets of thieves for whom uniforms, tool kits and especially power company ID cards were highly prized. Kingsley did not reach for the .38 caliber Walther automatic holstered inside a hideaway rig in the small of his back. He hoped they would go away before he had to use the piece.

"Hey, Kingsley, you dickhead faggot!" the shout came again. "You deaf or you a chickenshit!"

Kingsley heard laughter too and a suddenly familiarity with the speaker's voice made him look down in surprise. After a moment or two, the surprise turned to recognition. Both of the men standing at the base of the thirty-foot-high pitch covered wooden pole were laughing at the third man perched high overhead.

"Richie! Deacon!" he shouted down. "You sons of bitches ... I was gonna shoot your fucking asses straight to hell!"

"Get on down here, Kingsley," shouted Sister John. "We need to talk, my dog."

"Give me a couple of minutes to finish up, then I'll be down," he shouted back.

Kingsley climbed down after completing his splice. He had aged a great deal in the years since Richie had seen him after returning from Bad Tolz, their special forces station in Germany after

Afghanistan and Surinam. He was big in the gut and gone jowly. Richie read the signs of a man who had found his niche in life and would not leave it. He did not think that Kingsley could be recruited but needed to pitch his line anyway.

This they did at Kingsley's house where his wife Martha served an early dinner. On short notice she had cooked up a side of beef and made something out of potatoes that Richie did not know the name for but tasted of onions and garlic.

"Come on out front," Kingsley said. "We'll sit on the porch and talk."

Richie gave Kingsley his pitch. Kingsley's face changed as he thought it over. He went silent and looked away.

"What about it?" asked Richie.

"I'm sorry, man," he replied with a shake of his head. "But I can't do it. I dream about doing something like you have in mind. I dream about it every day. But I don't have the guts and I can't leave what I've built here."

"I knew you'd feel that way, Kingsley," Richie replied, clapping him on the shoulder. "I won't press you. But if you change your mind, you let me know."

He gave Kingsley his voice mail number, the untraceable one at the cyber cafe that had come along with the box and the fax line. Richie and Sister John got up and climbed into their car. They had a long drive back to New York ahead of them.

"Kingsley, he's settled in here. Got his self a life," Sister John observed. "I kind of envy the dude."

"Yeah, me too," Richie admitted. "Too bad, though. He has the skills essential to bringing off the caper the way I planned it. Kingsley's going to be hard to replace."

***

Kingsley's wife Martha got dressed.

"Don't go, not tonight," he told her.

"I can't stay cooped up in here," she answered him.

Martha was fishing in her purse for the car keys. Kingsley felt the sick feeling build up inside, the same way it always did at such times.

He would see the car leave the driveway. Martha would head for one of several cheap bars she frequented. She might call him and then again she might not. Either way, she would come home late, or not at all. But if she came home she would be stinking of liquor and stale smoke.

"Please, you promised me you wouldn't," he was red in the face from the sudden spike in blood pressure. "You told me you loved me, Martha."

"I do love you," she said. "But I'm going out tonight."

"You bitch," he said, shaking his fist. "I ought to -- "

" -- You ought to *what*?" she retorted, laughing in his face. "You lay a hand on me and I'm out of here for good. You don't want that, do you?"

"Honey, I ... just please, listen to me!"

But it was already too late. The front door was slamming. Martha's high-heeled footsteps clacked on the wood planking of the front porch as her perfume lingered in the air. Kingsley turned away in frustrated anger, promising himself he would not look out the window and see the car pull out of the driveway and go down the road until the tail lights disappeared around the bend. But Kingsley did just that, despite all of his resolve.

Then he sat down on the bed and cradled his head in his hands, his elbows digging into the fleshy part of his thighs. He locked his fingers around the back of his neck. The nape felt hot, so did his face. Kingsley went into the bathroom and ran cold water on his hair, cheeks, eyes and throat. It did little good. Hell, it never worked. He stared at his reflection in the medicine cabinet mirror and saw a gaunt, lined face etched deeply with the acids of pain that stared back at him like the visage of a doomed wraith.

Kingsley made his decision then and there. He would not take this any longer. He stalked out of the bathroom and picked up the phone. He dialed the number that Richie had given him. When the beeptone followed the digital message, Kingsley spoke two words.

"I'm in."

DAVID ALEXANDER

Judson, Wall Street District. The psychiatrist's office had never looked to Judson like what it was supposed to be. This, of course, was deliberate, he knew. The shrink wanted to put his patients at ease. The soft lighting, pastel walls and pleasant-looking faux Impressionist paintings had all been carefully selected to diffuse the anxieties of those who came to the psychiatrist for treatment.

Even the waiting was different. He could not recall ever being received by a dentist or general practitioner at the exact time of his appointment; there had been the inevitable backups, the added time lost due to an emergency case to be taken care of -- that sort of expectable though frustrating happenstance. Not here, though. Each forty-five minute session began and ended precisely when it was supposed to play out. He had asked Dr. Placidus about that and was told that it had therapeutic value.

Placidus now sat across from Judson on a comfortable chair of black Italian leather. For his own part, Judson reclined on a couch covered with

199

the same material, one hand draped across the rear of the couch as he began his weekly session.

"And you say these compulsions to have sex with the woman in your office have grown stronger after your confrontation?" the doctor inquired.

"That's correct," Judson replied. "I can't get what happened out of my mind. I know she had every right to do what she did, but ... I guess I don't like being dominated."

"But your intention was to do the same to the woman, wasn't it?" the doctor replied. "Domination, yes?"

"Yes," Judson said, "but it's different. Nobody does that to me. I hate it. I think it had something to do with what happened to me last night."

"Want to share that with me?"

"I went out. It was around nine o'clock, maybe a little later."

Judson broke eye contact with the doctor and looked up at the ceiling, trying to collect his thoughts.

"Well, I found myself in Fruit City, you know where that is, right?"

"I believe so, yes."

"Right, in the Meat Packing District, east of the West Side Highway," Judson clarified. "Anyway, I went into a gay bar and had a drink. I'm not gay, by the way. But I just found myself inside there. A guy came onto me. I had an erection which he noticed. I let him take me to his place which was a few blocks away."

Judson shook his head and laughed. He perfunctorily inspected his fingernails, and said, "I don't know if I want to go on."

"You don't have to if you don't want to."

There was a silence in which neither spoke.

"Okay, okay," Judson said. "I guess you want me to continue, right?"

"I said you don't have to," Dr. Placidus replied with professional complacence.

"But obviously I've said to much to stop now. Okay, so I go to this faggot's place and he wants me to tie him up, wants, you know, rough trade. So I tell him, 'I'll give you the kind of beating you won't forget,' those were my exact words."

Judson went on to describe how he had tied up the young man and began to beat him mercilessly, not stopping until he had drawn blood. He told Placidus next that, having noticed a jar containing condoms and a squeeze tube of lubricant, he'd slipped a rubber over his erect penis and then coated it heavily with jelly from the tube.

"And as I, well, sodomized this disgusting faggot, all I could think about was that I was doing this to Maddie and that I was video-recording everything and that when I came I could stab -- "

"Well, our time's up for today," Dr. Placidus interrupted, concluding the session as Judson was in the middle of telling the shrink about his fantasy. Judson hated being cut off like that, and whether or not it was part of the therapy, he thought the doctor must be thinking that he was a fool. He would have liked to hurt the doctor, he realized at that moment.

THE BLACKOUT HEIST

As he left the medical building, he wondered if he should tell him about that, maybe at his next visit.

Judson did not have to tell the psychiatrist that he would have liked to have done him physical harm. Dr. Placidus already knew all about his patient's violent delusions and predispositions, in addition to the many other things he knew about the working of Judson's aberrant mind, overactive libido and infantile fantasy life. Judson was a classic sociopath, with powerful schizo-paranoid tendencies. He was running across more and more of the type in recent years, a sign, he felt, that society was degenerating into a jungle fit only for savages and beasts.

This case, however, was somewhat different than others with which he was familiar. Dr. Placidus needed to report to his case officer about his findings. He picked up the desk telephone that was kept locked in a top desk drawer. The modular unit was connected to a digital encryption/decryption multiplexer device that would scramble voice input and descramble output from the other end of a tactical VOIP connection across standard coaxial cable.

"This is Majister," he stated matter-of-factly to the voice of nondescript gender that answered the call after a single ring.

"Yes, Majister," the voice replied. "I take it that Sunbird has been in for his weekly chat."

"He has," said the Doctor. "I feel that I should warn you about the subject. Sunbird's delusions are taking on a reality of their own. He is growing increasingly unstable."

202

"Sunbird's services will not be required very much longer," the intelligence officer's genderless voice told Placidus.

"Be that as it may, he has developed what I would call a sexual obsession with a female attorney working in his office. In my opinion Sunbird could act on his fantasies and cause physical harm."

"I see," replied the voice of the case officer, now taking on a different, and more thoughtful, tone. "And your recommendation?"

"Would be to terminate his involvement with the operation. Terminate immediately."

"That may not be as simple in practice as in theory," the intelligence officer returned. "However I will pass your information along to its proper recipients. Thank you, Majister. Please continue to keep me informed."

Placidus hung up the secure phone and put it and its accompanying twenty thousand dollar communication security device back into the drawer, locking it, then pocketing the key. He checked his watch and noted that his next patient was due to arrive any minute.

She was an interesting case. A nymphomaniac whose fixation centered on a figurative coating of her breasts with human excrement. Placidus wet his lips. He would enjoy this next one, he anticipated.

***

Late winter chill still hung in the city air. Maddie pulled her collar up to protect against the Hawk as the cold wind again made another of its unwanted appearances. A miniature tornado carrying bits of cellophane, sheets of newspaper, empty potato bag chips and other urban detritus whipped around her legs as she made her way up Maiden Lane toward the Federal Reserve Bank of New York's office headquarters building.

Maddie was preoccupied. Richie had been acting strange lately. He was withdrawn. He hadn't been eating and the color had seemed to have drained from his normally ruddy face. She had been having difficulties of her own. Judson had been acting up again. She believed that it had reached the point where she needed to tell somebody -- professionally. Though she didn't want to involve Richie, she needed his insights. She considered herself lucky to have hailed a yellow cab on her first try and was soon heading across the Brooklyn Bridge.

***

Richie came up the Promenade wrapped in his black leather coat against the wind. They had lunch at a nearby fish restaurant above which the underside of the Brooklyn Bridge loomed like the underbelly of a colossus that bestrode the nearby Hudson river.

"Let's take a walk," he told her.

They went together and stood against the railing.

"Richie, I've been having trouble with a creep at work and I'd like your help."

"Sure, what's the problem," he replied.

"The guy is my supervisor," she related. "At first it was the old story. He was trying to get me to go out with him. I thought I had read the bastard the riot act until recently. I've been getting threatening phone calls ... and *these*."

She held out some pictures. Richie took them. They did not show Maddie, but the resemblance was close enough to cast doubt.

"What's his name?" asked Richie.

"Norman Judson," she replied.

Richie nodded. He had already suspected as much. Richie had been thinking about a way of luring Judson to the safe house he'd already set up for the heist across the river in Jersey where he could be kept on ice. Idly, he had considered the possibility of using Maddie to lure Judson there, but had rejected the idea out of hand. He had not wanted her involved at all. Richie had always considered Judson -- and the dues he owed him for having set up Eddie to take the fall for him -- as his personal problem. Now he made a split-second decision to tell Maddie everything.

"Maddie, listen to me," Richie began. "I'm going to tell you something about Judson nobody else knows. And then I'm going to ask you if you want to do something about it."

Leaning against the railing of the Promenade, Richie began to tell Maddie about Judson and what he had done to Eddie, and next about the plan he was putting into operation to even the score.

"I'll help you," Maddie said after Richie was finished and she knew as much as he had deemed it safe to tell her. "The bastard deserves whatever happens to him."

TWENTY-SEVEN

Kreuger, Berlin.

The speech Kreuger had delivered had gone over well. The followers in their brown shirts and shaven heads had saluted like robots with the familiar precision of events gone past.

Kreuger was thirsty after the speech, and exhausted too. But when Sturmer arrived he admitted him immediately.

"You saw them out there?" he asked. "What did you think?"

"I think that they are the dregs of the earth," he said. "But Hitler started with less. As momentum builds we will be able to find those of a higher caliber."

"This, of course, is what our friends are helping us to do."

"Correct," Sturmer said.

Kreuger stood up from the chair and heaved a sigh. He went over to the window. He stood and looked out onto the Kurfurstendamm that was alight with the neon glow of countless sex shops. All this would change when the time came.

Turning to face Sturmer who had been watching him, Kreuger said, "Your courage in the action against the CIA man was courageous. In daring only the deeds of a Skorzeny can compare."

He was referring to the murder of five people that had been carried out by Sturmer outside of the entrance to the Central Intelligence Agency's Langley Campus.

The FBI, which had jurisdiction in the continental United States, was openly calling the act one that had been carried out by a lone hitman tied to Hezbollah fanatics in Iran. Privately, they had doubts, although the truth that Sturmer had been sent in to execute Kendricks the previous month was buried too deeply to ever surface.

"You are flattering," he said.

He knew that there was a reason for his being summoned from his safe ground in the South Tyrol to meet with Kreuger and it had not been simply to chat.

"I am not given to making statements I do not mean," Kreuger insisted. "But I want to get to why you are here today. There may be another use for your talents."

"In America?"

"Yes, in America," Kreuger acknowledged with a curt nod.

"When do I leave?"

"You might not have to go at all," Kreuger told the killer. "It all depends on how the Americans fare in coming to terms with the individual who may represent trouble."

"How long before I know?" asked Sturmer.

Kreuger smiled. "You are like a dog straining on a leash, jah?" He went and clapped the other man on the shoulder. "Don't worry, Sturmer, I will let you know as soon as possible. In the mean time, be my guest."

***

The two men moved with quick, practiced strides. Richie caught sight of them and in a split-instant saw that they had expertly bracketed him. He knew by their way of moving who they were and had a fair idea concerning what it was that they wanted of him.

"Mr. Block," said the first one, "we wonder if you could spare a minute to talk."

Richie shoved past them and walked on. His brackets kept following. One grabbed his arm. Richie turned and glared at the man. The guy quickly removed his hand.

"I've got nothing to say," Richie snapped.

"Fair enough," the first one said. "You don't have to say a thing. We'll do the talking. You see, we know about what you have in mind."

"What would that be?"

"Come on now, Richie," the second man said. "You don't want us to spell it out for you, do you?"

"Maybe in invisible ink."

"That's good. Invisible ink. But seriously, we know what happened to your brother. It was regrettable. But listen to our promise: the man responsible will be made to pay and do so in the most severe manner possible. We can even arrange for you to see a video recording of -- "

"Screw you, cocksucker."

Richie was already moving past them. The first spook grabbed Richie's arm again. He had made a mistake.

Spinning quickly on his heels, Richie jacked a hard right knuckle punch straight into the man's kisser. Blood spurted from his ruptured nose. As he made a groaning sound and began to wobble on rubber knees, Richie saw the second man dip inside his jacket pocket.

Richie moved quickly, locking the gun hand and driving his right knee repeatedly into the spook's testicles. Breathing heavily as the man went down, Richie spun quickly. He looked around but could not spot any backup in the vicinity. This did not necessarily mean that none were present, though, only that he saw none.

Richie started moving away before rubberneckers and bystanders could collect or even try to get in his way. He reached his apartment and broke out the bottle of Old Grand Dad from underneath the bar and poured himself a stiff shot.

"You blew it!" he cursed aloud.

Maybe there would have been some other way to get around the spooks, but he had blown his cool and lost whatever opportunity for compromise might have existed. Richie realized that he had burned all his bridges and that there was no way back now.

By now they would have branded him "beyond salvage" or some other bull-crap operational term currently in vogue among spooks to denote a guy who was on an official hit list. What did that mean to his plans for the caper?

Nothing, Richie realized after a moment's consideration. The spooks stood to lose a lot by burning him to the cops. If they did, then Eddie's secret diaries, revealing the covert complicity of

209

intelligence agents, among whom numbered Judson as a non-operational contact -- CIA slang for stringer -- would be made public.

As Richie's pulse rate returned to something like normal, he saw that the situation was essentially a standoff with neither side able to do anything to the other. The spooks wanted to get Judson out of the way too and their knowledge of the specifics of his operation might be limited. Richie needed to be careful, but damned if he was going to quit now.

***

At the safe house in Jersey, the group gathered to hear Richie outline his heist plans. Richie had connected his netbook via USB to a wall projector. The slide show dealt with the procedure for robbing the most heavily guarded bank in the world of its most valuable stockpiles of gold on a step-by-step basis.

First, Judson must be kidnapped and brought to the safe house. There he'd be stashed away under guard. Whenever the house is not in use, motion sensors would trigger booby traps that would kill him if he attempted escape.

Maddie should be critical in this initial phase of the operation. Under the pretense of being a willing partner to Judson's seduction fantasies, she would lure him to where Richie and Sister John could restrain him and capture him.

On the day that the heist went down, Sister John would be on the second floor of the Federal Reserve Bank building, ostensibly there to purchase US Savings Bonds. His strength would be necessary to carry sacks of currency and manhandle heavy pallets piled with gold bullion to the rooftop of the building -- which even on wheels required two men for the job -- via one of the Fed's freight elevators.

Richie and would be posing as tourists taking the tour of the building. Kingsley and Ace, a MetroCon electrical worker who needed fast money to save his home from foreclosure, would be standing by to cut the power to the building, just as the car bombs they'd have planted in the area exploded, throwing everything into confusion on the heels of a mock "terrorist" attack.

At that moment, the chopper flown by former Bangladesh resident Harry Krishnah, late of Cable New York News after having been fired without good cause, and painted in bogus search and rescue colors, was to hover a foot above the rooftop, receiving Richie and Sister John and take off for their hideout. Six tons of stacked gold bullion on a steel pallet was the crew's real prize, but enough currency -- whose serial numbers would have been recorded by the Fed -- would be planted near the drugged Judson to implicate him in the robbery as police, acting on a secret tip, close in to apprehend him.

By this point in time, the gang would be long gone from the scene. The police, having been given a convenient scapegoat, would declare victory. Sooner, rather than later, the CIA, standing to lose much, would as a matter of course arrange for Judson to catch a few bullets Lee Oswald style. And as for Richie and his crew -- they would remain silent about the high-level plot that Eddie's diary had uncovered and they'd helped stop in return for keeping the proceeds of their hard day's work in the fertile vineyards of high-stakes crime. The incident would be hushed up in the end. At any rate, so Richie hoped.

***

From a distance, a covert surveillance team scoped out the safe house. Thanks to the use of laser eavesdropping technology and infrared sensors the intelligence operatives soon had a fairly good idea of the unfolding plan that Richie had outlined to his crew.

***

Richie walked into his apartment. Nothing seemed outwardly amiss. However, he was instantly on the alert. As his eyes grew accustomed to the darkness of the flat's interior, he realized someone was in there with him.

"Turn on these lightings," the voice intoned. "I can see you. I haf got a gun pointed directly at your head."

His voice was foreign-accented, not German but something like it.

Richie did as he had been instructed to do. In the lighted apartment he now saw the speaker. The gunman had a plain-looking face with hair gone to gray that was worn long but swept back from the sides of his head. The eyes too were gray -- and unblinking. It was hard to tell how tall the man was because he was seated, though Richie judged him to be approximately the same size as himself.

"Put your hands up," the gunman now went on, gesturing upward with the barrel of the 9 millimeter

Walther automatic he clutched. "Very good," he said when Richie complied. "You keep a nice place."

"Glad you like it," he answered.

"I mean this," the gunman said. Now he got up from the chair. "That painting is a Manet, jah?" Richie nodded. "I thought so. Everything well kept. It is a pity I will have to kill you. Our tastes, they seem quite ... similar."

The gunman came close and patted Richie down while he kept the Walther trained on him. He expertly pulled the small .45 caliber Colt Richie wore in his shoulder holster beneath his jacket and jammed it into his own belt. Richie's boot knife came next.

"You won't be needing these items," the gun wielder said with a smile as he kicked the weapons beneath the couch where they could not be gotten at.

The gun safe keyed to his fingerprints where he kept his Sig-Sauer P250 flashed in Richie's mind. It was highly unlikely that the killer would have found it. And even if he had, there was no way this side of growing a set of identical prints to Richie's own that he would have been able to open it and get out the Sig.

"If you want the painting, take it, guy," Richie said. "I'll give you money too. None of it's worth dying for."

The gunman shook his head and clucked his tongue at Richie. "My dear Mr. Block, don't you think that playing dumb is beneath you?"

"I'm not playing anything, my dude," Richie said, trying to look puzzled. "You're robbing my place and

I'm not dumb enough to argue with a guy holding a fuckin' pistol on me."

"Then you are not the man I had taken you for," Sturmer replied. "You know you are going to die. Do so bravely and mit some honor, jah? Or do so in any way you wish. It is, as you say, your funeral."

Sturmer gestured with the gun toward the rear of the building. A window was already open. Richie could now began to see how the hit would play itself out. Sturmer would make it look like a bungled break-in and robbery attempt. A few items would be taken to make it seem legitimate in the eyes of the cops, who didn't need much evidence when they could easily wrap up a case with little effort.

"Honor?" asked Richie. "What's that mean?"

"It means -- "

Sturmer moved a fraction, but it was enough to for him to catch a fast snap kick to the arm that sent his gun sprawling. Richie had not time to grab his Sig from the gun safe, and diving for Sturmer's dropped gun wasn't an option either. Richie made the only possible move, which was to run for the window, wrestle it open, and jump onto the fire escape.

As he hunched low to take the ladder, Richie knew his decision had been right. Sturmer had either retrieved the gun that Richie had knocked from his hand or had a backup. Either way, silenced bullets were now punching through window glass and spanging off the metal bars of the emergency platform attached to the building's wall.

Richie dodged down the ladder and took the pavement harder than anticipated, the force of a crash landing against the hard concrete sending him sprawling. Regaining his footing with bullets bouncing off the sidewalk, Richie ran across Fourth Avenue as the traffic light at the corner turned from red to green and an instant before the oncoming traffic in both lanes from across the Verrazano Bridge began its normally crazed rush.

Winded as he sprinted around the corner of the opposite block, Richie heard the screech of tires and the crash of splintering metal. He continued running, then stopped short. Turning slowly, he saw the scene of the accident directly outside his building, and cautiously retraced his path. Reaching the scene where a city bus heading toward the Verrazano Bridge had collided with a Fedex delivery truck, Richie saw Sturmer's crushed and bleeding body sandwiched between the wreckage.

"What happened?" a woman in a pink jogging suit with a blood pressure meter strapped to one arm asked, sidling up beside him.

"Guess he got hit by a bus," Richie answered, adding. "The guy was probably a foreigner."

TWENTY-EIGHT

Maddie, Queens, Long Island. Maddie knew what was expected of her. After having come on to Judson, she was to get him to drive her to a certain spot on Long Island's North Shore. This was to throw any surveillance off the scent and to help establish Judson's whereabouts. As a backup she wore a compact 9 millimeter handgun that Richie had given her and saw to it that she learned how to use well.

Richie and Sister John were waiting for them at the appointed place with Mike and Vinh, the final two crew dogs brought in by Richie, trailing in their own vehicle. The group kept in touch via secure cellular phone links.

"Richie we've lost them!" suddenly came Mike's message.

"What!"

"I'm sorry, but they took a wrong turn."

***

"You thought you were going to outsmart me, didn't you?" Judson said. Maddie saw the mad gleam in his eyes. He had wrenched the wheel of the car as he highballed down the road missing the turnoff onto the hot sheet motel that was supposed to have been their destination.

"Where are you going?" Maddie had protested.

216

"Someplace else," Judson said.

He whipped out a large, serrated knife with such speed and raised it to Maddie's throat so fast that she had no time to make a grab for the gun. He stopped the car and frisked her.

"You bitch!" he snarled and began slapping her across the face. "You fucking bitch! You were trying to set me up!"

"No, Judson," she protested. "No, I wasn't, believe me."

"You are going to fucking pay for this," he shouted.

Judson grabbed Maddie by the arm and dragged her back into the sedan. He drove with the revolver held in his lap with one hand and its muzzle pointed at Maddie's midriff.

If she tried anything, there was no way to avoid being shot. She knew nothing about guns but she knew enough to realize that a .357 magnum bullet hitting her at such close range would be fatal.

"Now get out!" Judson shouted after turning off the secondary road and barreling the car across a harrow dirt track into the woods beyond.

***

"I think we spotted the bastard again!"

Ace's voice came over Richie's cellular phone. He and Sister John were in the van cruising down the highway in the general vicinity where they had last placed the car, hoping against hope to find Maddie.

"Thank you!" Richie shouted with relief. "Where are they?"

THE BLACKOUT HEIST

"On the North Access Road," Mike's voice replied over the flip phone. "Spotted the taillights and the tag number a few seconds ago turning into a small side track, leads into some scrubby woods. I'm going in after them."

"Kill your lights and block the road. Don't drive right up," Richie said. "Judson's got a gun and he's a dangerous psychopath."

"You got it, man," Mike replied and severed the contact.

A few minutes later, Richie and Sister John reached the scene. They spotted Mike's car blocking the roadway. Killing their engine they parked right behind the vehicle, moving carefully up the rutted dirt track into the woods beyond the asphalt.

They found Judson standing over Maddie with the magnum revolver. He had ripped open the front of her dress with a blade and had his pants unbelted and pulled down around his jockies.

"Judson!" Richie shouted.

Judson whirled around and without saying a word cut loose with three fast pistol shots. Before he could squeeze off a fourth .357 round, Sister John had tackled him. Vinh and Mike were piling on top of the downed man as Richie ran up to the scene and knelt beside Maddie.

"Are you all right?" he asked her.

She was shuddering as she collapsed against him. Richie crushed her body against his and kissed her hair as he heard her sobbing against his face.

"Yeah, I'm okay," she managed to say.

Richie let go of her and went over to Judson. They had hauled him to his feet and Vinh handed Judson's revolver over to Richie. Richie shoved the captured pistol in his belt.

"Bring the bastard over here," Richie ordered.

He already head a plastic carrying case open on a table and was getting out a hypodermic syringe and an ampoule containing a scopolamine-amobarbital mixture that he would use to inject Judson with a double truth serum and knockout shot.

"This cocksucker has just run out of rope," Joey said as he finished squirting fluid from the needle's tip to prevent the risk of an air embolism, and jammed the hypo's sharp end hard into the big dorsal vein on the inside of Judson's right arm.

***

They brought Judson to the safe house. Heavily sedated, and fed intravenously, Judson would be kept on ice until the bank job was over, then summarily thrown to the dogs. In order to keep him safely on ice, Richie used Mike's exceptional forger's skills to produce believable letters from the financier lawyer requesting vacation time for Judson to attend to emergency family matters in Arizona.

Zero hour approached. The operation was on schedule, and the chopper, critical to pulling off the ambitious heist, with the gear it carried onboard, was ready. Richie glanced at Judson and prepared to go into action, but knew something was wrong when he saw Harry Krishnah, their pilot, walking back across the field between the woods and the safe house.

"I got bad news, Richie," Harry Krishnah told him. "The chopper angle won't play."

"Why not?"

"Because they have instituted regular airborne patrols," he said. "There's an AWACs plane on station as part of a new experimental police program to protect the city against terrorism. I just got the word. But there's something else that we never considered. There's what's called low-altitude downbursts. It means this particular chopper can't hover over the rooftop like we need. I just found this out from a trusted friend who's a pilot. We'll never make this happen."

"I don't believe this," Richie shouted. "Not after all this -- hell, there's got to be a way."

"You've got to accept it, kid," Harry said, shaking his head. "There is just no way." He went on. "The Aircrane we're using is not just the only type that can do the job but the only super-heavy hauler commercially available, so we can get one without the cops or the feds becoming curious. But we didn't count on flying conditions above those Wall Street canyons. With the gigantic load we're supposed to haul ... well, we're just gonna crash, and hasta la vista."

Richie nodded.

"Keep me posted," he said.

***

Judson was to say on ice for the time being while Richie mulled things over. Turning Judson loose, even after his kidnapping, would pose few risks, as Richie has plenty to hold against him if he tried making any trouble. Enough damning evidence against Judson, in fact, to put him away for a long stretch if it came down to that. But there was anyway to stage the heist, Richie swore he wouldn't turn back.

TWENTY-NINE

Richie, New Jersey. "There has got to be a way to beat this wind thing," Richie told Krishnah. "The first way I had it is the only way. We need to use the Aircrane."

"There isn't, Richie. I wouldn't lie to you," Krishnah protested.

"I know that," he returned, "but maybe we're not looking at the problem in the right way. Maybe we're missing something. Go back over it from the top."

"Okay, it's like this," Harry began. "One: the wind is blowing south-southeast at thirty knots. Two: the chopper won't remain stable in such wind conditions. Three: we can't use a different kind of chopper for a variety of reasons, number one being that there's no other bird in the world with a twenty-ton lift capacity and a cargo bay in its middle that's just the right size for the load we want to steal."

"Why will the wind act the way it does?" asked Richie.

"It's complicated. Based on engineering dynamics. Shit like aerodynamic drag coefficients."

"Give me the layman's explanation," Richie asked.

Harry drew a diagram with a lot of arrows point down at the Fed's rooftop.

"That's what downbursts do. They push down hard on aircraft. They're a kind of wind shear phenomenon. The problem is the payload. Once we've got it gaffed we'll not only be six tons heavier but take on a lot of extra drag. The wind will knock the bird over."

"You've been telling me that these downbursts affect choppers flying at FAA-mandated altitudes, right?"

"Yeah, that's what I said."

"So why do we have to do that?" Richie continued. "Why not fly out the load at a low altitude. Would that stand a shot of working?"

"It might, but it would be pretty risky," Harry said. "There are some tall buildings in the way, know what I mean? We could just go splat."

"I know what you mean," Richie told him. "I know it's risky. But would it work?"

"Yeah," mused Krishnah, rubbing his chin. "It might work out like that. Even if it did, though, it would be a tight squeeze, but I can see maybe being able to do it."

"You're sure?"

"No promises yet, but I'll let you know," Harry Krishnah reluctantly agreed and went off to think the matter over.

***

A little while later, Krishnah had thought it over, and had deemed it doable. Albeit behind schedule, the Aircrane was again ready. And so were all the members of the heist crew that Richie had assembled. The additional equipment was ready too, including some diversionary pyrotechnics that

223

THE BLACKOUT HEIST

were designed to cover, and to maximize, their chances of a clean getaway.

And then it was game time.

DAVID ALEXANDER

THIRTY

Petrov, Baikonur Cosmodrome, CIS. One hundred fifty miles above the planet, the *Pichuga* surveillance satellite arced through the blackness of space just beyond the translucent mantle of the earth's atmosphere. Shaped like an elongated drum, with a cluster of imaging sensors at one end pointing downward towards earth, the satellite sprouted twin, wing-like solar cell panels at its sides.

Since the outset of their space program, the Russians had routinely placed radioisotope thermoelectric batteries, or RTGs, onboard their satellites as power plants. Such nuclear batteries commonly contained cores of Plutonium 238. NASA, instead, mainly used the sun's energy to generate electric power for US satellites. Pichuga's solar panels provided auxiliary power for the Russian recon bird. Its power plant, however, was nuclear.

Beneath the satellite, feathery patterns of swirling cloud systems imperfectly masked the vibrant blue of earth's vast oceans and the washed-out brown of its continental land masses.

225

THE BLACKOUT HEIST

To its ground controllers, which received around-the-clock telemetry via coded microwave transmission, all onboard systems appeared to be functioning normally.

Indeed, they had been showing positive indication ever since the sophisticated new orbital spy device had been payloaded from the Baikonur Cosmodrome some forty-eight hours before.

However, as the intelligence satellite's looping trajectory arced it high above the Atlantic Ocean at an azimuth of three-hundred twenty degrees, and it crossed from the earth's sunlit side into the half that was now shrouded in twilight, a critical component, damaged by lightning during the Proton's boost phase, began to fail. That component was a small wafer of silicon on a module among several identical in appearance nestled in a line along a passive backplane mount. But it was a critical component and its worsening degradation had a snowball effect on the entire cluster of modules.

Only as the orbit of the YZ-class surveillance platform whipped the satellite across the coast of Nova Scotia, did the ground control computers flash the GRU signals intelligence technician monitoring the satellite the alarming news that Pichuga's critical onboard systems were failing.

The technician was not alarmed at first. Redundancy, after all, was a key element built into all space-based systems. Every piece of equipment onboard the satellite, from the smallest integrated circuit chips to the most complex mechanical components, was backed up by a fallback system in case of damage or breakdown.

In the unlikely event that all systems failed, the satellite could be neutralized by remote control.

Because he had clearance to make low-priority operational decisions, the GRU signals intelligence technician keyed in the code sequence that would switch to backup systems designed to duplicate the functions of the failing modules and return *Pichuga* to full operational capability.

Confident that the problem had been corrected, and already choosing the language in which he would couch the actions he had taken and the reasons for taking them in the report he would file with his superiors, the technician waited a beat while the computer system's internal diagnostics checked telemetry from the spy satellite.

But the computer continued checking long after the few seconds the technician had anticipated. The seconds ticked on into minutes, and then....

The screen in front of him flashed the words:

FALLBACK SYSTEMS
FAILURE

The technician swore, now realizing that the problem that confronted him was far more serious than he had at first believed. It was not a minor malfunction as he had originally surmised. What was happening in space was nothing short of a full-blown systems shutdown.

Checking the satellite's position, the SIGINT technician noted that it had already passed the US-Canadian border and that its flight path had become a southward vector that was swinging the bird across the eastern seaboard of the United States from which, on a clear night, it would be visible as a faint dot at an approximate seventy-five degree azimuth to the horizon.

The corners of the technician's mouth turned downward as more whispered oaths escaped his lips in the darkened operations center. He did not like to be confronted with the prospect of owning the fingers that keyed in the mission abort command that would cause the four hundred million-dollar satellite to autodestruct.

Although taking such a drastic measure required the highest of all security clearances, and thus permission from his superiors, the arcane logic by which the Russian military chain of command distinguished innocence from culpability would nevertheless dictate that inordinate blame be placed on himself as well those in higher places.

However that might be, the SIGINT technician knew that he had little choice in the matter. He faced a problem of serious magnitude. He could no longer act autonomously.

Using the gooseneck microphone at the ground control telemetry console, the technician called in his chief systems engineer, briefly explaining the problem as the flashing Cyrillic characters on the console screen before him flung waves of multicolored light across the panels of his face.

In a few minutes, the chief engineer was beside him. Both men attempted to place other backup systems within the satellite on-line. Both failed to do so.

Noting that the satellite's orbital trajectory was now sweeping it over New York State and past Toronto, Ontario, the Chief Engineer had no recourse but to telephone his superiors for permission to abort the satellite's mission.

"General," he said, as soon as he was patched through to his GRU commander's direct line, "we have a problem. The *YZ* platform is behaving erratically. Backup systems have failed to respond to all commands. Permission to destroy the satellite is requested at this time."

Unlike the SIGINT technicians, the general was well aware of the covert nuclear device onboard *Pichuga.* A sudden spurt of adrenaline made him sit bolt upright at his desk. Sweat beaded his beetling forehead and his jaws worked for a few seconds without any words being formed.

"Give me its position!" he finally shouted into the handset. "Quickly!"

"Thirty degrees, north latitude," the chief engineer began, reeling off the readout figures appearing at the upper left of the view screen, "Fifty-degrees, south longitude, azimuth -- "

"-- Damn you!" the military intelligence officer, who had no technical background, cut in, "in plain language, *where is it!*"

"The northern border of New York State, general," the chief engineer replied with a fearful tremor in his voice, sensing from his superior's inexplicable panic that there was more going on than a systems failure, albeit onboard a new and costly orbital spy platform.

"Destroy it!" barked the general after barely a moment's pause. "Destroy it *immediately*."

"At once, general. I will initiate -- "

The satellite chose that instant to explode.

The blast registered as a flashing green cluster of words in the Cyrillic alphabet at the center of the view screen. The words, appearing and disappearing once each second, said:

CONTACT WITH SATELLITE LOST

"General," the Chief Engineer shouted into the handset, all control now gone from his voice, "the craft, it ... has just exploded."

"What do you mean?" asked the general, hearing the sudden terror in the engineer's voice. "Did you execute my order?"

"No, sir," stammered the SIGINT officer, "it -- it blew itself up."

There was silence on the other end of the line.

"General ..." the chief systems engineer shouted into the microphone, hearing nothing but silence from the speaker, "general, are you there? What is happening, general?"

When the chief systems engineer received no response, he broke the connection and alerted the Russian space agency, Roskosmos, at its central Moscow headquarters Moscow that something dreadful had happened at the general's office.

There had been, he said, what sounded like a single pistol shot before the line had suddenly gone dead.

Upon in turn being informed of events by Roskosmos, and reaching the general's office, the building's security detail found him slumped over his desk.

Blood spurted slowly from the hole in his skull and a Graz-Burya 9-millimeter automatic pistol lay to one side on the leather-topped desk.

The handset lay turned upside down, a few inches from its cradle.

Exactly where the general had dropped it when he had taken the Graz-Burya from the top drawer of his desk, placed it against his right temple and blown most of his brains out through the other side of his skull.

THIRTY-ONE

Metro New York. Although the explosion of the sixty-kiloton nuclear warhead in space was both invisible and inaudible to ground-based observers, its effects were immediate and catastrophic.

At the New York Stock Exchange, the banks of screens that flashed the minute-by-minute upticks and downticks in the daily trading volume suddenly exploded like bombs as a surge of power raced along cables linking them and their network hubs with the exchange's mainframe server cluster.

Thousands of splinters from glass fragments sprayed the packed trading floor with the velocity and wounding power of shrapnel blasted from artillery shell casings, severely injuring those trapped inside the perimeter of the killing ground that the exchange's Pit had become.

As hundreds of telephone handsets were picked up by commodities brokers positioned around the financial center's big room, they were amazed to discover that the lines were completely dead.

At the corner of Forty-second Street and Avenue of the Americas, the billboard that flashed the national debt stopped short at just over 2.7 trillion dollars, a solution to the federal deficit that neither Congress nor the House had ever anticipated.

Downtown, at Madison Square Garden, an audience that had been watching the concluding scenes of the *Walking with Dinosaurs* exposition, during which the house lights dim as the asteroid that doomed the giant sauropods strikes the earth, found themselves plunged into pitch darkness as the lights went off and stayed off.

Not even the emergency exit lights were functioning.

A traffic helicopter operated by WNYC FM had been hovering above the East River Drive -- on which a multiple pileup had started when a yellow taxicab collided with a tractor trailer, backing up traffic all the way to South Ferry -- when its radio went dead and its main a tail rotors suddenly stopped turning. Its electrical systems burnt out, the helicopter plunged into the East River, shattering on impact into hundreds of pieces amid a resultant fuel explosion and churning orange-black fireball.

On the highway below the falling chopper, as on every street and thoroughfare within the area effected by the exoatmospheric nuclear EMP blast, cars, trucks, buses and all other vehicles with electronic ignitions systems immediately stopped working.

The scream of tires was heard everywhere, as automobile crashes occurred across the five boros of the City of New York.

THE BLACKOUT HEIST

The explosions caused by thousands of exploding gas tanks made the damage and loss of life increase dramatically in the first few minutes of the catastrophe.

Customers at automated teller machines throughout the city were frustrated to find that the computer screens that described their transactions had suddenly ceased to function.

Several of these customers were also killed immediately as traffic on the streets and avenues outside the banks went out of control and crashed through plate glass windows, crushing their bodies to pulp against ATM walls.

Television and most radio transmissions ceased completely. Burnout was total. Shutdown was complete. The only sounds heard above the screams of the cataclysm's many victims were the sounds of utter chaos.

***

The tremendous destructive power of electromagnetic pulse (EMP) was a phenomenon first discovered after the detonation of the atomic bomb in 1947.

It was quickly incorporated into the then fledgling strategy of nuclear warfighting by both superpowers.

The EMP principle is as simple as it is destructive. A nuclear blast creates two primary effects: blast wave and radiation. It is from the latter that EMP is produced.

When a nuke explodes, clouds of gamma rays are generated in the first few nanoseconds of the burst. Gamma rays stream from the burst zone in all directions. If the nuke burst occurs in space, some of these bump into electrons in the air molecules of the upper atmosphere.

This creates a "Compton Effect," named for the discoverer of the EMP phenomenon. The gamma-charged electrons -- Compton electrons -- emanate from the collision sites at incredible speeds. When they encounter the earth's magnetic field, the electrons are deflected, producing a transverse electric current.

This transverse current, in turn, generates EMPs, which radiate downward toward the surface of the earth.

Even though only about one-millionth of the energy of a nuke burst is emitted as EMP, the net result is the near-instantaneous burnout of all electrical and electronic systems in the effected area.

Once exposed to EMP, these systems are permanently knocked out. They cannot be repaired. They will not recover on their own. They are ruined forever, fit only be junked and completely replaced.

The military importance of EMP is therefore enormous, especially when the principle of nuclear warfighting called "decapitation" is taken into consideration.

In military terminology, decapitation means destroying command, control, communications and computing (C4I) systems in the first phases of a thermonuclear exchange. Nuclear warplanners liken this scenario to cutting off the head of a scorpion.

THE BLACKOUT HEIST

Without the brain to guide it to a target, the scorpion's sting is useless. In some cases it might even be turned back on itself.

Minus the electronic network that links the sophisticated computer systems of a superpower's nuclear arsenal, its capacity to counterlaunch against a devastating first strike is greatly diminished. Even if only minutes are lost, the first combatant to attack could conceivably win the exchange.

While both the United States and the Russian republics have made plans to harden their existing C4I networks against EMP by using shielding and massive circuit breakers, few of these changes have been implemented by the US

This has not been the case with the Russians, however, and with the People's Republic of China. Captured, bartered or bought electronic components from both countries had long shown an almost universal adoption of tubes and electromechanical parts, all highly resistant to EMP.

Whether or not this was due to a superior policy of development and implementation, or to the technological inferiority of backward nations, had never been determined, and, in the aftermath of what the recovering US media later dubbed a "death pulse," probably never would.

THIRTY-TWO

Kesselman, underneath Manhattan.

Three things happened. All at once.

The eight-car IRT subway train screamed like a soul in torment as its electrically powered brakes locked up, catapulting its passengers forward, then savagely flinging them in the opposite direction as though they were rag dolls with the tremendous backlash of a sudden stop from high speed.

The lights throughout the train blinked off, instantly plunging all eight cars of the Pelham Bay local into total darkness as it lurched to a complete stop in the tunnel midway between two stations.

Shouts of terrified passengers echoed up and down the now totally immobilized row of cars.

For Bernard Kesselman, it suddenly felt as though someone had rammed a white-hot iron lance through his chest. Kesselman screamed in agony, making the last sounds that would ever take shape in his throat.

"Get the fuck off me, old man!" the dreadlocked Rastafarian sitting near Kesselman's wildly gesticulating body shouted in panic as the black shape beside him suddenly flopped across his lap, limbs thrashing insanely.

237

THE BLACKOUT HEIST

Kesselman's EMP-overloaded pacemaker had delivered one fierce jolt of electric current to his heart that threw it into a final frenzy before it stopped beating forever.

Nerve endings fired crazily as Kesselman's neurological, arterial and organ systems went haywire and his entire body was gripped by convulsive spasms. Within minutes, the thrashing man was a still, dark lump, barely visible as he lay stretched out on the filthy center aisle of the immobilized car.

More shouts echoed through the pitch blackness of the unlit tunnel. Some passengers were angry, not yet grasping -- or not yet prepared to confront -- the seriousness of their plight, while others became immediately terrified out of their wits.

What was most frightening of all was the fact that none of the passengers had any idea of what was happening to them.

Although most had experienced every type of emergency from track fires to marauding wolf packs of juvenile muggers in years of riding New York's slow, unpredictable and dangerous subway system -- and a few had even been marooned underground on 911 -- they had never encountered anything resembling this present situation before.

For one thing, whenever a train's lights had gone out in the past, emergency lighting from auxiliary power sources had always kicked right in. For another, there had always been the sensation of the train vibrating, of the conductor's announcements, of the tunnel lights twinkling and arc lamps of maintenance crews brightly flashing just beyond the flyspecked windows of the car.

Not this time, though. The tunnel lights had disappeared.

Utter darkness now engulfed the stationary IRT train like a burial shroud. The silent motors were as motionless and as utterly devoid of any sign of life as the still heart of a corpse.

***

In the cab of the crippled IRT local, motorman Willie Inskeep saw the indication meter on the console in front of him flicker off a moment before the interior lights in all eight cars winked into oblivion.

He had tried to restart the motor, but nothing he could think of doing had any effect on the immobile train. Believing himself to be caught in some kind of local power failure, Inskeep turned the goose-necked intercom mike toward him and depressed the talk button in an attempt to hail La Dollicia Shavers, the IRT local's conductor.

The intercom was silent.

Cursing, Inskeep picked up the handset of his portable communications radio. The radio had its own power source and should therefore not be affected by any power outage. He depressed the mike's talk button but heard only static.

At first he thought the machine might be inadvertently switched off, but playing around with the on-off switch did nothing and the battery indicator stayed a steady, glowing red.

It was at that point that Inskeep started hitting the panic button. Images of other tunnels, stifling dark, many meters beneath the stifling jungles of Sumatra and Borneo, began to flicker to life in his brain. Sudden beads of cold, young sweat stood thickly on Inskeep's brow.

The darkened motorman's cab was suddenly gone. He began to float in space and time as his shattered mind began to flash back to a jungle hell.

Oh sweet Jesus, he whispered, unable to suppress a shudder as he fought for control. *Don't let this happen, don't let this happen to me again....*

***

At the same time Inskeep was trying to contact his conductor, rookie conductor La Dollicia Shavers was attempting without success to raise the motorman on her own intercom.

A cold sweat broke out on La Dollicia's face as it had on Inskeep's. Only her third week on the job *and this shit had to happen.* When you thought about it, it was almost comical.

Here she was on a train without lights or power stuck in a dark tunnel with hundreds of half-crazed straphangers on the verge of going totally bananas on her. They sure didn't cover this one in the manual.

She had a vague impression that something terrible had happened above ground, something that was bigger than the power outage she, like the train's passengers, at first suspected was the cause of the sudden darkness, but she kept that thought at bay.

Suddenly there was no time left to think.

People were hammering their fists on the steel-paneled door of the conductor's cab. La Dollicia snapped the latch and swung the door open.

By now the passengers' eyesight had adjusted to the meager quantum of light that exists even in pitch darkness so that at close distances the outline of figures was vaguely discernible.

La Dollicia heard the shouts of people arguing, of fights breaking out up and down the central aisle of the stationary IRT local.

"What's going on?" someone asked her, the passenger's tone demanding that La Dollicia knew the answer, as though being an MTA employee would in and of itself place the knowledge in the cells of her brain.

"I don't know what's happening," she returned, sounding much calmer to herself than she felt. "Everybody just chill yourselves out, okay? The power'll come back on any minute now. Just relax."

"Bitch-ass ho', this ain't no fuckin' power failure," a gruff male voice off to one side bellowed. "I know power failure, and this ain't one. I been through the one in oh-six and the one in fourteen," continued the voice. "Know what I think? I think them muh-fuckin' Arab muh-fuckas bombed our asses. I think this is the start of World War fuckin' Three. I think we all as good as dead."

There were more shouts at this, some agreeing with the speaker, others calling him a liar and a fool, still others mocking, challenging, daring the speaker to fight. La Dollicia could sense that the anger of the crowd was now at the boiling point, smell the fear and animal tension and crazed rage rising from scores of bodies and minds.

This crowd's right on the edge, La Dollicia thought. *All it'll take is one wrong word, one wrong move....*

A sudden claustrophobic dread took hold of her. She remembered the feeling of being trapped from long ago. Still a child, she had cowered in a corner while her gangbanger father in the projects of Brownsville, Brooklyn, had beaten up on her mother, unable to do anything but close her mind to the inconceivable ugliness of what was taking place around her.

That was the same fear as now. The fear that comes of being trapped; trapped with nowhere to take refuge but inside your own head.

"There's a dead body in one of the cars!" another voice, a woman's, shouted, "some guy just started flopping around and then he just up and died."

"Maybe it's poison gas!" someone else shouted. "I heard on *Eyewitness News* they been experimenting with ways to kill us all down here like a bunch of fucking rats."

"Yeah, I seen that, *I seen that!*" someone else shouted, the shout being picked up and repeated by others in the stifling darkness in a domino effect. The fear deepened for La Dollicia. The fear that crippled, numbed....

"Chill out, people! Please!" La Dollicia shouted, desperately attempting both to control her own mounting sense of panic in addition to the crowd's.

"Nothing's wrong! Just stay calm and it'll be all right."

She decided to go get Inskeep. "I'm going to get the motorman," she told the passengers around her. "Let me through."

She couldn't get through, though. The bodies were far too densely packed in the aisle of the train car. La Dollicia decided she'd be better off exiting the car and walking along the stygian track bed to the motorman's cab at the front of the Broadway local. She felt better the moment she was free of the middle car's stifling interior.

***

While some passengers had returned to their seats and waited as instructed, many others were not content to heed the conductor's instructions for caution and calm.

In a blind panic, scores of passengers stampeded from the stalled train and began to stumble along the track bed in the all-enfolding darkness.

Unable to see what was directly in front of them, they groped their way along the sides of the tunnel like blind mice, hoping to find a lighted exit way giving access to street level.

None existed, though. And while they were only a few hundred feet from the nearest exit, not a single passenger suspected that they would not survive long enough to stand a chance of ever reaching it at all.

THE BLACKOUT HEIST

Book Two:
Darkness Visible

No light, but rather darkness visible.
-- John Milton; *Paradise Lost*

THIRTY-THREE

Perkins, Queens Airspace. On the last leg of a ten hour flight, the Air Europe charter flight from London's Heathrow Airport to JFK International in New York was cruising over lower Manhattan at an altitude of ten thousand feet when those passengers looking out the windows noticed the lights of the city vanish.

Their panic was matched in the cockpit as LED indicators suddenly went blank and dials in gauges nosed into the red as the EMP death pulse blew out the 747 jumbo jet's electrical systems.

The aircraft was lurched by a sudden severe bump that threw passengers not strapped into their seats into the aisles as both pairs of engines simultaneously flamed-out, trailing streamers of churning gray smoke from beneath each wing.

Captain Randy Perkins attempted to radio a desperate Mayday, however his VHF commo unit was as dead as the inertial navigation equipment and the four enormous Pratt-Whitney turbofans that had kept the plane airborne across three thousand miles of open ocean.

The giant aircraft began to quickly lose altitude as its propulsion system flamed out over Manhattan.

THE BLACKOUT HEIST

As Perkins toggled switches which clicked dumbly in the silence of the cabin without having any effect, and pulled throttles which refused to respond, he could hear the shouts and screams of the doomed passengers in the cabin beyond the locked cockpit door.

With the plane continuing to lose more altitude with each passing second, the cockpit echoed with the chaotic hammering of fists that furiously pounded on its door, desperate voices shouting questions at the crew which they could not answer, pleas for help to which they could not respond.

Perkins ignored the sounds of chaos from behind him, struggled to force them from his mind, focusing instead on grasping whatever slender thread might exist to save the lives of the crew and passengers of the crippled aircraft.

As the plane began to nose downward steeply, those who looked out through the portholes could see other aircraft drop like stones from the airspace above Manhattan and crash to earth with the sound of deafening explosions.

Already there were enormous fires burning below at the crash sites of downed aircraft sending plumes of black smoke churning high into the unforgiving grayness of the twilight winter sky.

They realized that what they were witnessing was a prelude to their own fates. Then, only a few hundred feet above the rooftops of the city below, the jumbo jet began to barrel-roll and the world turned upside down before final impact silenced the screams of those who knew they were about to die.

***

DAVID ALEXANDER

The cake for Mary's party had been brought in from the bakery on Worth Street a little after three P.M. She had not even had to try to act surprised.

Her coworkers' timing had been perfect. She had been asked to take the office postage meter to be filled at the postal station across the street by Mr. Flowers, her boss. Flowers had explained that the meter had gone dry just before a big mailing and that nobody else could be spared at the moment.

When she returned, twenty minutes later, the plate glass doors of the office had been draped with red, gold and silver tinsel and crepe paper bunting had been hung from the fluorescent lighting fixtures. Aluminized helium balloons declaring Happy Retirement! floated near the ceiling and hand-lettered signs wishing her a bon voyage had been taped to the frames of the office doors while hip-hop blared from somebody's portable boom box atop one of the desks.

Mary was shocked. Although she had been expecting her going-away party for weeks, the reality of it happening *now* was overwhelming. Her reaction was as real as if she had never suspected a thing. Tears of genuine surprise and happiness welled in her eyes as her coworkers ushered her into the office.

"Bon voyage, Mary!" shouted someone from among the group of applauding well-wishers that crowded the aisles between the office's desks and work cubicles, "here's to the beginning of the rest of your life!"

***

THE BLACKOUT HEIST

The Battery Park Commercial Center's West Tower lay directly in the path of the 747 that Perkins was furiously trying to land despite the failure of all onboard navigational and flight control functions and the imminence of a crash.

In a matter of seconds after its engines and its electromechanical and digital systems were neutralized by electromagnetic pulse, the jumbo jet began to plunge into the topmost stories of the West Tower, impacting with the deafening sounds of shattering glass and rupturing metal.

Inside the cockpit, the flight crew, consisting of Perkins, his copilot and another pilot "deadheading" a free ride to New York, was the first to die as their bodies were horribly mangled, then crushed to jelly-like pulp beneath tons of disintegrating metal wreckage. Their deaths occurred so rapidly that they did not even have time enough to scream in terror.

In the passenger bay behind the imploding cockpit, the tremendous pressures of the collision that collapsed the nose section of the plane, very much like an empty milk carton can be flattened beneath the sole of a foot stamped rapidly down on it, mangled and crushed the one hundred-ninety-seven passengers onboard to bloody biological wreckage in a split-second.

The highly combustible aviation fuel stored in bladders within the aircraft's thirty-foot wings caught a spark from the crunching fuselage of the jet and exploded microseconds later. Tremendously hot, the fireball of incandescent gasses immediately incinerated the wreckage of the aircraft.

DAVID ALEXANDER

Most of the three uppermost floors of the West Tower was blown out by the blast. Thousands of tons of glass, concrete and structural steel showered the streets below for a distance of a quarter mile in every direction.

The storm of wreckage killed pedestrians stumbling through the suddenly darkened thoroughfares of the Wall Street financial district. Razor-edged shards of glass and pieces of metal debris as sharp as reapers' scythes sheared away heads and limbs of hundreds in the initial seconds of the crash.

Those employees on the upper stories of the West Tower were killed instantly, their bodies incinerated by the searing heat of the fireball. They could not know it (nor would it have given them solace if they had), but they were the fortunate ones.

***

The lights had gone out moments before. Then the computer terminals all simultaneously crashed. The rap song from the boom box suddenly slurred to incomprehensible jibberish as the compact disk ceased turning on its spindle and the light of the laser scanning it died, providing satanic background music to a world turned topsy-turvy and gone up in a rush of hellfire.

Amoroso heard the confused cries of his fellow workers as he rose to his feet.

Suddenly everything appeared pitch black, and Amoroso's first impression was the chilling fear that he had somehow inexplicably lost the sight from his eyes.

THE BLACKOUT HEIST

But then he turned toward the windows and saw shadowy human figures scurrying against the lighter background of the indigo-tinged twilight sky, and the unfocused fear in his mind was suddenly given a sharp clarity that turned it into full-blown panic.

The thought registered in the back of his mind that there were no lights on in any of the buildings visible on the Manhattan skyline from the window of his office.

Before Amoroso could do anything else, somebody shouted to look toward the window.

What Amoroso saw filled him with a mute, primal terror that made his skin lose its warmth and his knees begin to buckle and the hair on his neck seem to stand on end.

Suddenly visible beneath the edge of the window, he watched the 747's nose dip groundward as the fuselage sharply canted diagonally. What next took place almost seemed to happen in slow motion.

The nose of the plane grew larger and larger. There was no sound at all, save for the eerie soughing of the wind. As the incoming jumbo jet's nose assembly continued to expand to almost fill the entire view from the window, the plane approached to only a few hundred yards from the taller East Tower in which Amoroso worked.

In the final seconds before impact, Amoroso thought he could see figures moving in the cockpit of the doomed jetliner that was backlit by the final rays of the setting late winter sun. Then there was an agonizing moment as the nose of the plane collided with the side of the glass-walled skyscraper.

A terrific explosion followed immediately, almost simultaneous with a fireball that blinded him and everyone in the office as the entire top section of the West Tower exploded outward in every conceivable direction.

Pieces of wreckage intermingled with the licking tongues of flame as the fireball lit up the sudden night and left in its wake a one hundred ten story candle that burned brightly amid the smoking depths of the artificial eclipse.

The sudden, blinding light shot fiery lancets of pain through Amoroso's eyes and he raised his hand in a futile attempt to shade them.

A heartbeat later, the floor beneath his feet shook with tremors as though an earthquake had just struck. The effect was produced, not by an earthquake, but by exploding gas mains that had caught fire from sparking power conduits overloaded by high-voltage transients generated by the EMP attack.

Amoroso fell to his feet, striking his head against a sharp corner of his metal desk as the rest of the people in the office fell into a blind panic to escape the madness that had suddenly, and without warning, closed in around them like the jaws of a shark.

THE BLACKOUT HEIST

THIRTY-FOUR

The Bronx. They noticed the streetlights blink out first.

All over the South Bronx.

Just like they were doing everywhere else.

***

In Mott Haven, a new terror held sway on the streets.

As soon as the streetlights went out, the cars began careening out of control.

The street people saw it happen, and although they did not articulate the thought, they understood. Their time had come. How and why was not important. All that mattered was that the world beyond the streets had, in a brief spasm of sudden flameout, relinquished all control. And now control was in their hands.

A wordless communication immediately took place, much like the kind that transforms solitary grasshoppers into swarms of ravenous locusts.

On the Grand Concourse, the wide avenue that cuts across the South Bronx, the passengers of stalled cars were pulled from their vehicles and beaten and robbed of any valuables they had on their persons. Shopkeepers nearby saw gangs of

252

young urban punks join together into an impromptu army of looters, killers, crazies, rapists and worse.

Angel Saldivar grabbed for his .357 magnum pistol as he saw a crowd of young kids, carrying baseball bats, knives and other dangerous implements, hurl a garbage can through the plate glass window of the small furniture store he had run for the last five years. He shot two of them through the chest before the rest ran into the store in a human wave attack that knocked him down beneath its inexorable onslaught.

The last sight Saldivar saw on this earth was one of the punks pick up a jagged splinter of plate glass and ram it through his throat, laughing maniacally as the blood gushed from the severed carotid artery. He did not see them pour the contents of a bottle of whiskey over his bloody corpse, light it up, and cremate him where he lay.

The police were just as powerless as the civilians. Without benefit of numerical superiority, and faced with the spontaneous violence that was breaking out all over, they were beaten by mobs of crazies and killed with their own side arms.

The rioting mobs ran wild all across the Bronx. Through the shattered windows of stores they looted furniture, groceries -- anything they could get their hands on. Through the twilit streets, the savage locust swarm of looters could be seen carrying their booty like a column of soldier ants sweeping everything in their path before them.

Others began committing random acts of arson, using any implements at hand. Looted booze was poured down their throats and over piles of looted goods to be burned for no better reasons than the urge to watch the flames lick skyward.

Then again, the spontaneous fever to burn might have been kindled by a spark that set off a long-suppressed human impulse that dated back to the caves. Or, then again, it might have started as nothing more complicated than an attempt to supply light by which to see by the oldest and most primitive method known.

Whatever the reason that underlay the setting of fires in neighborhood after neighborhood, the crackling of flames soon spread throughout the city streets. Within hours, fires were burning everywhere in the South Bronx.

***

Applebaum heard the explosions.

He ducked over to the window.

The things he saw were unbelievable. Although the lights of Manhattan across the river had been suddenly extinguished, a flickering glow, like the kind produced by major fires, hellishly lit up the horizon for miles around.

You could see the vague outline of the Manhattan skyline against that infernal flicker, as well as drifting clouds of smoke that rose up, and up, into the chill night sky.

The air too was filled with the noxious odor of choking, acrid smoke, that smelled like wind-blown combustion byproducts from the colossal smoke plume from the burning World Trade Center on September 11th, 2001. But tonight there were no police, emergency or fire company sirens wailing in the background. Vehicles stood immobilized everywhere in the streets below, littering the city's thoroughfares like the carcasses of prehistoric beasts killed, then preserved, by a sudden great freeze.

Applebaum could hear shrieks and cries coming from everywhere at once. Cries rang out from the corridor beyond his apartment walls. Someone pounded on his door. Then the pounding ceased, a man shouted, other doors slammed up and down the narrow corridor outside to the accompaniment of running feet.

Then there was the sound of someone else shouting for help, the sounds of more doors opening and closing in the corridor, the multiplying sounds of footfalls as people ran aimlessly about, congregating in their helplessness and fear and inability to comprehend the nature of what was happening all around them.

Applebaum ignored the pounding on his door and the shouts from the hallways. He sprinted instead toward the bookcase and pulled open the door to his hidden weapons room.

The light switch didn't work. Applebaum felt around in the darkness until his hands closed around his rechargeable combat flashlight. He flicked the switch located on its side.

The beam of light flashed upward, its shaft forming a circle on the ceiling, illuminating the darkened room. Applebaum propped the flashlight against some shelves, hearing glass shatter and somebody else pound on his door while he grabbed together his weapons from the Iron Maiden.

THE BLACKOUT HEIST

Although Applebaum was reasonably certain that the lead shielding he had lined his weapons room with had saved his flash from being neutralized by whatever it was that had knocked out electricity everywhere else, he didn't suspect that he was among the few who possessed a flashlight, or any other source of illumination, anywhere in the entire City of New York.

DAVID ALEXANDER

THIRTY-FIVE

Skerrit, Midtown Manhattan. None of the elevators worked. The fire stairways were the only means of escape. But the building was thirty stories tall. The narrow passageway was choked with jostling, panicking bodies, each trying to gain the street level a moment sooner than the others.

Caught in the savage press of the crowd after the lights had gone out in the restaurant in which they'd been having dinner, Rick Skerrit and Shyanne Robbins found themselves caught in the dark, congested stairwell.

Nothing moved now. The flow of people down the stairs had ground to an almost complete halt as more and more people from each floor of the blacked-out building saw the fire stairs as their only way out.

"Oh my God," Shyanne told Skerrit, holding him close against her. "I don't know whether to scream or piss my pants."

"You're not alone," replied Skerrit, who was pressed against the wall of the stairwell. The atmosphere was already beginning to grow hot as the air was fouled by carbon dioxide from hundreds of exhaling lungs. In the close-packed darkness, the odor of fear was as palpable a presence as the sound of panicked voices.

Skerrit thought for a moment. Apart from those posed by packing too many people into too confining a space, the situation did not present immediately life-threatening hazards.

"Stay close," he said, noticing that they were only a few feet from the exit door of the floor above.

Pushing through the crowd with Shyanne holding onto his arm, Skerrit and she made their way onto the floor. The crowd had already thinned out up there.

"Where are we going?" she asked. "Shouldn't we be on our way down instead of up?"

"Not necessarily," answered Skerrit. "We're in bigger trouble if we stick with the crowd. It's full of mean, scared people, and sooner or later somebody's liable to start throwing punches. When that happens, the rest of them will start going nuts. Let's see if there's another exit that's not being used," Skerrit went on, "if not, I think we should stay here until the crowd thins out."

Using his cigarette lighter to provide illumination in the darkness of the corridor, Skerrit and Shyanne found another exit sign. This particular exit was empty.

"See what I mean?" he said. "It's just a matter of person-see, person-do. The lemming mentality at work. They all followed each other without thinking."

Shyanne rubbed up against Skerrit. Suddenly he felt her hand on his crotch.

"Rick," she said, her voice taking on a breathily seductive tone, "I'm wet."

"You're ... what?" Skerrit asked incredulously.

"My pussy's sopping wet," she returned, tugging on his zipper again, her fingers clawing at the elastic waistband of his shorts, fishing for his cock. "You have no idea how this excitement is turning me on," she continued. "I need to get fucked right now, right here."

"Look baby," Skerrit told her, "this isn't the time or place. Anything could happen. We'll do it later, okay? For now, let's -- "

" -- No, Rick," she cut in. "I'm really fucking horny. My pussy's dripping down into my stockings. Fuck me. Here. *Now!*"

Skerrit was being turned off in a big way by Shyanne's misplaced hedonistic ravings. The world was going straight to hell and this woman wanted a poke in the bush. Suddenly he was sick and tired of Shyanne's sexual needs, of her insatiable hunger, of her insane caprices. Maybe it was his own fault or maybe it wasn't, but he'd had enough of her demands on his body.

"Let's go, baby," he said to her, his voice registering finality.

"Damn you, you bastard," she retorted sharply. "I want some fucking now. You do me or I'll get somebody else."

"Fine," he said calmly, "but I'm getting out of here." With that, Skerrit turned toward the exit door. "You can come or stay."

"Damn you, bastard," she spat, running after him. "I won't forget this. I won't forget this ever."

"Neither will I," Skerrit told her, hearing the fire exit door slam behind them. He meant it. If he got out of this alive, Skerrit resolved to hand Shyanne her walking papers.

**

The familiar scene on Fifth Avenue had been replaced by hellish visions straight out of one of the panels of a Hieronymus Bosch painting Skerrit had once seen in Spain's Prado Museum.

A crosstown bus lay half in, half out of the picture window of Bali of Switzerland. When it crashed it had burst into flames. The exterior of the bus was still sputtering as its diesel engine burned.

Those passengers who had been fortunate enough to get out staggered from the crash site with blood streaming down their faces and staining their clothes.

They were the lucky ones. The unlucky survivors were the ones who had been riding at the back of the bus at the moment when its fuel lines had caught fire.

They lay moaning on the sidewalk, their clothes singed and melted into their char-broiled flesh, their bodies hideously burnt.

Passenger cars too were piled up everywhere across the broad avenue. Some had crashed headlong into fire hydrants which gushed water into the air in fountaining, thirty-foot streams. Others had barrel-rolled and skidded on their hoods, so that they stopped with their tires spinning in the air, making them resemble giant upended beetles, helplessly thrashing to right themselves.

Both Bonwit Teller and Cashmere-Cashmere were the scenes of brazen looting by both gangs of street people who had been warming themselves above a steam grating near St. Thomas Church, and now emerged wearing furs and jewels over their rags and cramming their mouths full of purloined goodies from Godiva Chocolatier.

"Christ, what happened?" Shyanne asked Skerrit, a little calmer now but still inwardly fuming.

Across the street and a little farther down the block, a crowd of well-dressed pedestrians was swarming in through the shattered show-window of Cartier, oblivious to the threats of a lone policeman who raised his gun impotently, not knowing whether to shoot or to run, as looters hurried past him with their glittering and expensive prizes dangling from their hands.

"Exactly what I warned the bastards against," Skerrit distractedly returned Shyanne's question, a faraway look in his eyes.

***

At Fifty-sixth Street and Broadway, Skerrit left Shyanne at the CableMedia Building. Her television station already had a small crew standing by in the early hours of the catastrophe. Although the station was unable to do anything to report the news, its personnel waited in the wings as the events unfolded.

She'd be safe there, Skerrit knew, and he'd be rid of her. As he walked back into the street, Skerrit realized that Shyanne and he were finally finished. That was just as well. Skerrit had finally become aware that she and he were on two different wavelengths.

Skerrit began walking. He knew that he had to reach a police or fire station. Mobs were everywhere, mean, ugly, drunk on looted whiskey, high on openly dealt street drugs.

All around him, the city trembled on the verge of meltdown, teetered on the razor edge of panic. Not a soul knew what was happening. Those who did not participate in the spontaneous orgy of spasmodic looting and murder were scared, angry and hostile as only New Yorkers can be in an emergency.

If a nuclear attack of some kind had in fact been launched, where was the mushroom farm? So far no nukes had fallen in New York City or its vicinity, nor had there been any outward indication that hostilities had been declared.

On every block, Skerrit passed pedestrians looking up at the sky, their eyes wonderingly scanning the dark, smoke-shrouded heavens for signs of a detonating nuclear warhead, looks of horror twisting their faces into profane masks of agony and terror.

Skerrit passed a group of people clustered around a black kid with a suitcase-sized boom box. The kid had switched from disk to radio. An announcer's voice was coming over the air, but although the volume was cranked to the maximum, static and the thickness of the crowd made it hard to make out anything but snatches.

"Outbreak of terrorist attack ...." he heard the newscaster say, *"unconfirmed reports that ... Pentagon spokesmen advise alert ... President will address the nation... more as events unfold...."*

Some pedestrians were screaming at the sky, waiting for the weapons of mass destruction exploding overhead. Skerrit passed a man who shouted, "Get it over with! Kill us! *Kill us all!"* as he threw off his conservative business clothes and ran naked through the streets, only to be set upon by a group of homeless men and quickly lost in the center of a throng of savagely flailing bodies.

But Skerrit had a gut instinct about what had actually happened. His suspicion was that it was an accident -- not a nuke, be it a rogue missile, terrorist WMD attack, or otherwise -- although the precise nature of that accident was unknown to him at the moment.

With an average time of twenty minutes for an ICBM to cross between East and West, it meant that if a nuclear strike launched by North Korea or Iran, or even the neo-Soviet Union, had indeed occurred, the first airbursts should have already exploded.

Since they hadn't already, a half hour following the blackout, Skerrit reasoned that a nuclear strike could be ruled out. At the same time, this was surely no ordinary blackout.

Its totality immediately told Skerrit that something greater than a failure of the local or regional power grid was taking place.

Skerrit suspected EMP.

But therein lay the paradox. The generation of an electromagnetic pulse by exploding a nuclear warhead in space only made sense if it were being performed as a prelude to nuclear attack, and if nothing else, current world events made this possibility highly unlikely.

THE BLACKOUT HEIST

But if no nuclear exchange was taking place, where was the motivation for releasing a death pulse of EMP? Though Skerrit couldn't guess the answer, he could envision numerous enough explanations.

Covert weapons systems had been payloaded into orbit for decades by the US and the Russians both, and after that by North Korea and Iran. Skerrit had a strong hunch that one of those weapons systems had just behaved in a manner which those who had built it and put it in place had not been prepared for.

In Washington, Moscow, Pyongyang or Tehran, and in those and other global capitals, all hell was probably breaking loose.

***

Skerrit knew that there was a police precinct located near Rockefeller Center. On his way there he was forced to fight off gangs of punks and street people who eyed the vulnerable pedestrians who had poured from the office structures on the Avenue of the Americas like sharks watching schools of helpless fish.

Everywhere, the business class was being attacked by homicidal mobs of torch-bearing street people and organized gangbanger wolf packs. Skerrit watched these marauders beat and rob their bleeding victims, few of whom were able to put up much of a fight. They were dazed, helpless, perfect targets for the packs of pillaging savages who attacked them like hunters slaughtering seal pups in Newfoundland.

Skerrit couldn't do anything to help them. He had trouble enough protecting himself as he ran the gauntlet of looting, robbing street crazies.

Finally he found the police station.

A cordon of cops were holding back a human wave of bleeding victims. Many of them belonged to the business class that had worked in the skyscrapers above the streets.

Now they were in the streets.

In the dark streets.

Prey to the beasts of the night.

Transformed into beasts themselves.

THE BLACKOUT HEIST

Chapter Four
Call in the Americans

DAVID ALEXANDER

THIRTY-SIX

Richie's Crew, Lower Manhattan. At two minutes to zero-hour, Ace was grimacing as he forced the heavy duty cable cutters around the thick insulation of the underground high tension cable while Kingsley stood lookout.

Cutting the power main it had been more difficult than he had anticipated. The rubber bushing was inches thick, almost like cutting through steel rather than plastic. But he could tell that his efforts were paying off. He had sliced through most of it and only a little more work would enable him to cut entirely through the cable on schedule.

"Hey, what's going on down there?"

Startled, Kingsley looked up. An inverted face blocked out the murky Manhattan sky, framed in the circular opening to the manhole twenty feet above his head. Kingsley's heart thumped in his chest. It was a Metropolitan Consolidated Energy worker wondering about his presence down in the hole.

"Got some problems with the main," Kingsley shouted back. "Could be worse, though."

"Where's Fotopoulos?" the MetroCon man questioned, skepticism evident in his voice and his screwed up features. Kingsley thought above the silenced .38 caliber revolver riding the shoulder holster beneath the stolen MetroCon work overalls he wore. "I never seen you before."

Kingsley quickly considered his options. His back was to the questioner and a dead body could be hidden for awhile underground. If he could get him to come down, then he could shoot him and still take care of his end of the operation according to schedule.

"I'm usually over at Clinton," Kingsley shouted back. "It was an emergency and me and my partner took the call. Guess, the regular guy wasn't available."

Kingsley fought the instinct to reach for the silenced handgun and remain calm, though he felt the worst case scenario was a foregone conclusion.

"Yeah, okay," the MetroCon man up top called down. "Just wondering what was going down. You guys take care."

"You too," Kingsley said, barely able to control his relief as the MetroCon man's face disappeared letting the fading daylight drain back in. Seconds later he heard the sound of a vehicle door slamming and an engine turn over. After the MetroCon truck had left the scene, Kingsley checked his watch. Only thirty seconds remained to zero-hour.

He cursed as he strained every muscle to help Ace push the jaws of the cable cutter tighter around the recalcitrant cable that refused to be severed, as though it had a will of its own and would not concede defeat. He realized that only seconds remained until the timed charges they had placed in and around the Federal Reserve Bank of New York building across the street from the manhole would detonate.

Then, with a sudden loud snap, the tempered steel jaws of the cable cutter bit completely through the high tension wire. Sparks leaped as the current was abruptly cut off. Kingsley and Ace wasted no time in hauling ass up the side ladder and leaving the manhole cover where it lay. As they emerged from the hole in the street, they spotted a cop rounding the corner and coming their way at curbside.

The effects of the sudden power outage that slicing the mains cable had caused were already becoming evident. Lights in windows, neon signs, street lights and traffic signals all began to die. The policeman's neck craned from buildings to lamp posts, then back to the two electrical workers. Kingsley and Ace walked as calmly as possible toward the stolen MetroCon field truck as the cop picked up his pace. They gained the cab and got in, while Ace, behind the wheel, started the engine.

Then the charges place around the building full of gold blew with a very loud bang.

The cop was now looking in the direction of the Federal Reserve Bank office building. Dense clouds of noxious black smoke mingled with yellow flames that licked skyward were billowing from its upper stories. The two other bombs that had been placed in garbage cans and beneath parked cars outside the building had also detonated right on schedule and these added their blast, flame and thick black smoke to the conflagration that rose forty stories into the air.

269

THE BLACKOUT HEIST

Black smoke clouds were already drifting across the street as Ace pulled into gear and drove away from the cop who had now turned his attention back to the MetroCon truck. That was a bad break.

Officer Pete Wilson caught the license number of the vehicle. He quickly scribbled it down on his notepad and made a mental note of the face of the man climbing out of the manhole only an instant before the charges detonated. He would remember that face.

As Ace was careening the MetroCon truck through the narrow streets of the Wall Street area, Richie and Sister John heard the faint echo of the rumble caused by the explosion of the charges.

"What was *that,* Howard?" asked a matronly midwesterner directly behind them as the line of sightseers took the Federal Reserve Bank's Gold Tour.

"I don't know, Jan," her husband replied, "sounds like a bomb to me. Just our luck to be in the middle of another terror attack."

The group began babbling about terrorists but Richie was still wondering why the Fed's lights were still on. If Ace and Kingsley had screwed up, then they were all in deep shit. For the heist to go down right, Richie's crew needed to be in sole control of the building's electrical power for the next twenty minutes. If not, it was game over, with no escape routes available. In that case, odds were that everyone in the vicinity would be questioned by the cops, and Richie remembered what he thought had been the extra attention that the guards had subjected him to as he had crossed the lobby.

Then, all of a sudden, the house lights flickered and died. The delay had been due to an electrical ripple effect as backup systems failed. Ace and Kingsley had done their part! Or so Richie thought, not yet realizing the true extent of the power failure, and what had actually caused it.

THE BLACKOUT HEIST

THIRTY-SEVEN

Parrish, Staten Island. The Mall was getting cold as the sun began to set. About half of those who had been inside it when the lights had suddenly gone out had by now left to make their way home.

The remainder stayed inside, afraid to go out into the road. They had the safety of numbers inside the Mall, they reasoned. And there was food.

Others had quickly decided to keep as much of the scarce resources in the Mall for themselves.

Shoppers stormed the Spread 'N Buns Shoppe and grabbed as many edible items as they could lay hands on.

A big stainless steel coffee urn was overturned, scalding those close beside it. There were fights over the jelly donuts, knishes, quiches and frankfurters that the looters found inside.

Others headed for the high-tech shops on the Mall's duplex levels and began an orgy of looting. Within minutes after the blackout, the Mall had been transformed from a shopping center into a suburb of Gehenna.

***

"Hey, I don't want any part of this action," one Mall security guard said to another. The rest seconded this motion. Moments later, the rent-a-cops began leaving the premises in droves.

"No, wait," Parrish told them. "We have to at least help the shoppers leave. This is an emergency. We're paid to protect them."

"Not me, Parrish," said Joe Slattery, his second in command, as he threw on his coat. "My responsibility is to my family. I'm getting home anyway I can. See you around, pal."

Before Parrish could say another word, Slattery, Hauser, Gupta and the others had joined the crowd of shoppers scurrying away from the Mall in every direction over the highway that was choked with dead cars and disoriented motorists.

Parrish shrugged. *Go. Who needs you.*

Maybe it was because he didn't have any family. Or maybe it was due to some deep-seated sense of duty. Whatever the reason, Parrish turned around and walked back into the darkening Mall.

***

The door of the deserted guard station wasn't even padlocked. The guards had left in too much of a hurry to worry about closing it up properly. When the Aryan Death Squad arrived back in the Mall from the parking garage, in which they'd been hanging out, they noticed the guard office just as they entered.

Forcing the door was easy. Goodies awaited them within. They hadn't expected to find the room in back contained a gun locker. Or that the gun locker contained several Ithaca pump-action riot shotguns, plus boxes containing hundreds of rounds of ammunition. Or, finally, that the gun locker was also unlocked.

"We're in business," Suckdog yowled with glee as he cranked a shell into the chamber of his gun. His two-year hitch in the Army would finally do him some good after all. "We're really going to have a party."

The skins ran out of the guard office. There were still enough people left in the Mall to make their time worthwhile.

***

The sound of shattering plate glass echoed off the glazed brick walls of the Mall's corridors.

It was Kristallnacht all over again, the night of shattering glass when the Nazis had run wild in Berlin, Vienna and other cities throughout the Reich.

Suckdog's Aryan Death Squad had total control of the Mall. They were its masters. And, as befit a master race, they had their slaves too.

Pretty soon, the doors giving access to the Mall were closed. The skins had found lengths of heavy motorcycle chain and padlocks in a utility room near the abandoned security post they'd looted. The keys to the locks hung from hooks on the wall. Each was numbered for easy identification.

After they had chained the access doors to the Mall so that they could only be opened by the skins, the Nazi crew combed both levels of the Mall, rounding up whoever was left inside it.

In the end they had about a hundred people. All to themselves. Quickly, they set about robbing their captives at gunpoint, doing what came naturally.

While Suckdog quoted from Mein Kampf, they removed the valuables carried by their captives. Then they locked the captives in a room and began to loot the abandoned shops on the deserted walkways, listening to the wonderful cacophony of shattering glass as they hurried about their business of grabbing up booty.

***

Courtney Lassiter was scared. She was having a flashback. As she heard screaming coming from everywhere around her, she went back in time. To the night she lost her eyesight and her husband of only three months to a sadistic pack of creeps. Glen and she had been out for a ride on Glen's motorcycle.

Then there had been the blowout on the road that made Glen lose control of the bike. Dazed and bleeding, she'd stumbled toward the gas station down the road for help. Instead of aid and comfort, she'd found only terror.

In the dark of the garage, she had called out for assistance. Soon she'd heard footsteps behind her, and suddenly she had felt somebody grip her from behind.

Then she felt another pair of hands grab her breasts and heard the obscene laughter as the ghouls began to claw at her tight woolen sweater.

Courtney began screaming, but nobody heard her, or nobody cared. Courtney's unseen assailants dragged her by her hair and legs for a short distance. She heard a door slam and something make a rasping sound in the darkness.

A match flared and she caught a pink blur that might have been a row of faces hidden behind nylon stocking masks. Then there was a larger fire. She saw one of the goons holding a makeshift torch and smelled the odor of burning lighter fluid.

She thought there were cement walls beyond her now. She was in some sort of storage area. She could smell the odor of mechanic's grease and automotive oil, so thick that it made her gag.

She began to scream. Scream at the top of her lungs. Scream hysterically, beyond panic, beyond madness, becoming the scream that poured from her throat like water over a damn.

One of the goons kicked her in the jaw.

"Scream all you want, *biutch*," he told her. "Nobody cares."

While one of them held Courtney down, the one in front of her pulled down his jeans. His hardness was erect. He stepped close. Courtney felt his hand on the back of her head. Suddenly her mouth was crammed full of the organ.

"Suck my cock, you fucking cunt!" the ghoul screamed. Frightened and half conscious, Courtney did as she was ordered. She felt another one from behind maneuver her onto her knees. Her buttocks were roughly spread and the one behind her tried to force his organ into her vagina.

It was dry, however, and impenetrable, and he began to masturbate himself as he cursed until Courtney felt something hot and wet strike her naked buttocks.

Then the obscene ghoul in front of her exploded in her face. She cried out as the hot acid liquid stung her unseeing eyes.

But the ghouls just laughed. They continued their obscene violations for hours. And now, a lifetime later it seemed, but still bearing the scars of that terrible incident, she was blind and alone in the Mall, and every bit as trapped as on that hellish night, two years before, when Glen's bike had overturned on that dark stretch of road.

***

Parrish had been hiding out in the Mall. Because he knew about places that nobody but a Mall employee whose business was security would knew about, Parrish knew he could remain in hiding indefinitely. He had seen the gang of Nazi punks that he'd ejected earlier that day take over, but he had been too late to do anything about it.

By the time Parrish had spotted them, they had already armed themselves with the automatic weapons and shotguns stolen from the security room. Parrish cursed his fellow Mall security guards.

They were all criminally negligent in his eyes, and, he hoped, would be in the eyes of a court of law once this nightmare was over.

Anger burned hotly and fiercely in Parrish's mind. He hated the kind of scum that had gotten in here. They had come into this pure, clean place and infested it with their rank corruption. They had soiled this place. Made it foul. Stained it with their malign presence.

THE BLACKOUT HEIST

Parrish ached to wash away all signs of their presence from the clean, airy spaces of the Mall. But he was impotent to do anything now. For the present, all he could do was watch and wait. He realized the limitations of a single man against an armed band of violent crazies.

Whatever happened, it would not last indefinitely, he surmised, though. These drugged-out punks weren't rational. And therein lay their weakness.

When the adrenaline wore off, they would realize the one thing that Parrish had realized right away, but that had not yet occurred to the invading skinhead punks -- that they were now every bit as trapped in the Mall as the prisoners they held captive.

THIRTY-EIGHT

Richie, Lower Manhattan. Reacting just as they had drilled themselves to do, Mike and Vinh screamed a van to the entrance of the federal building. Wearing head-mounted night vision displays, they pitched flash-bang grenades in through the federal building's street-side doors and rushed the guards who manned the security checkpoint. The guards went down like the Dixie cups that the Department of Homeland Security's uniformed federal cops generally were as Mike and Vinh gun-whipped some and cowed the others into submission with their hands against the wall, whereupon their hands were quickly cable-tied behind their backs.

Reaching Richie and Sister John at the building's mezzanine level just behind, Mike and Vinh tossed them the extra H&K subguns they'd carried in slung across their chests on bandoliers while Quincy rolled and carried in the additional gear from the van they'd need. Most of this gear was portable Sun Guns to compensate for the absence of emergency lighting.

Mike fired off a burst to keep the captives in the Fed's lobby, now made up of tourists and potbellied or undersized federal cops working for DHS and herded them into the corner, the red beam of the laser emitter atop all the receivers of the subguns the crew carried adding to the effect of domination over the captives.

"Get out of the booth now," Richie ordered the guard manning the last checkpoint separating the team from the gold storage vault, "or I'll start piling up bodies."

The guard unlatched the door. Richie disarmed him and shoved him back into the booth, his hands cable-tied. Vinh handed him the keys to the area he had taken from the tour guide. Richie locked the guard in with the tour group as he and Sister John hustled down the corridor.

Under normal circumstances, the computer-controlled security system would have by now done three things. First, it would have sent two-inch thick steel bulkheads sliding down at choke points throughout the building. Second, alarms would have begun to sound, with direct links to the New York City police. Third, the Federal Reserve Bank's own security contingent of SWAT personnel would have been galvanized into action, making for the site of trouble pinpointed on a computer screen in their central control room.

But none of these things had happened yet, because of the loss of electrical power from the main that Ace and Kingsley had cut, followed instants later by the citywide power failure and blackout, whose first manifestations rippled in a domino-effect across the five boros. Richie had planned for a delay of several minutes before the building's own emergency power and computer backup systems kicked in. In those minutes, Mike and Vinh would have to empty the number three counting room of its stock of cash and make for the emergency stairwell while Quincy watched their backs would be waiting to carry the burden to the roof.

At the same time, Richie and Sister John were to use bolt cutters to open the steel wire mesh cage in front of the paletted gold, whose ingots of bullion bore the Nazi swastika and rampant eagle of the Third Reich, and wheel the pallet to the nearby freight elevator. Once there Richie would use his walkie-talkie to signal Harry Krishna in the Aircrane to winch the entire car up through the shaft with themselves and the gold inside it.

Knowing that every second was critical, Richie forced his way into the counting room with Mike and Vinh close behind. The trays of hundred dollar bills were stacked on the counting tables, with loose cash dropped nearby where the three counters had left them as the heist commenced.

"Just stay cool," Richie said as he herded two stunned federal guards into a corner, then turned the operation over to Mike and Vinh, who dumped tray after tray of currency into the burlap bags that had been compressed beneath their coats.

"Hurry it up," Richie told them, feeling every time-tick bringing them closer to blowing the entire operation as he turned to follow Sister John into the gold vault. "And don't lose anything."

"I'm hustling, boss," Vinh said. Richie could see that he had already filled most of the second bag.

THE BLACKOUT HEIST

That meant that two million dollars in unmarked currency were already stashed away in there.

Just then, the emergency lights in the corridor began to glow as shielded backup generators came online. Richie realized that their time had just run out.

"Let's go, we're through here," he shouted to Sister John as they bulled past the deserted guard booth into the gold vault as emergency alarms began to sound. Inside, Richie tucked his small automatic weapon inside the pocket of his coat and unshipped a pair of heavy-duty bolt cutters while Sister John did the same. In minutes they'd popped the locking mechanism and threw the mesh doors wide open.

"Look at all that shit," said Sister John. "Fucking Nazi shit."

"Talk later. Let's hustle," Richie said, and both of them strained to pull the bullion-heaped skid from its place in the vault by the steel handles at either side of the heavy-wheeled pallet.

It moved more easily than they had anticipated and they were a full minute ahead of schedule by the time they reached the freight elevator. Richie and Sister John began to manhandle the six-ton gold pallet into the elevator car.

Just then he heard the telltale sounds of boots clunking against the edges of the metal stairs. It told Richie only one thing: armed security guards were hustling up to the counting room area and would soon be near the elevator.

The logic was simple. Security systems were back up and reports must have already come in from the international gold repository in the subbasement that nothing was wrong down there. The counting room floor was the only other area likely to have been hit. The gold vault was considered impregnable. Still, events had overtaken them for the second time in a row. Richie hadn't counted on reinforcements arriving this quickly.

He unshipped the H&K subgun and by habit checked to see that the safety was off and the fire select button on full automatic. Waiting until the sounds of the SWAT team's progress up the stairs grew so loud that they had to be only a flight or two below, Richie cut loose with a burst of fire, angling it against the walls.

Shouts came from below as the team tucked down their heads. Richie pulled the flash-bang grenade from his pocket and pulled the pin. The black cylinder bounced its way down the stairs as its fuse ticked off the three second delay before it would detonate.

Richie and Sister John pushed the gold skid all the way into the car as the flash-bang went off, giving off strobing flashes of intense white light and a series of earsplitting reports. Sister John strained to force the two steel doors to move together on their tracks, and bullets spanged against the armored steel, pocking the doors as the SWAT team raked the elevator with automatic fire. Richie had bought them a few precious seconds, but that would be all they had.

On a flight path paralleling lower Broadway, Harry Krishnah heard Richie's voice in his headset and gunned the Aircrane toward the Federal Reserve

THE BLACKOUT HEIST

Bank of New York's rooftop. The chopper reached its objective in a few seconds of flight time. Krishnah pulled the pins on a cluster of three standard NATO fragmentation grenades and dropped them from the cockpit's side door. Counting to three, Harry heard them detonate on the final count.

"Fuckin perfect," he said to himself as he saw the glass cupola above the freight elevator shaft disintegrate in a spray of particles. Harry then released the automatic winch from the roof of the Aircrane's unique cargo bay behind the cockpit and sank it down the shaft until the digital readout on the dash indicated that it had latched onto the freight elevator's roof.

"You two fuckers hold on tight now," Krishnah advised Richie and Sister John with a laugh, getting into it now as he felt the lurch of contact and the Aircrane dip as the steel cables tautened against the incredibly heavy six-ton load that was nearly half the chopper's carrying capacity of eighteen metric tons. Pushing and pulling hard on the Aircrane's hand and foot controls, Krishnah felt the load begin to move up with the straining helicraft.

Suddenly, though, the chopper was slammed by an invisible giant's hand. *Downburst*, he thought, as below, inside the elevator, Richie and Sister John were slammed against the walls of the steel cube like roaches in tea tin. The Aircrane yawed heavily, and for a moment or two Krishnah's mind flashed on the chopper pitching into a critical azimuth where its seven-bladed main rotor no longer supplied vertical lift, and crashing in flames against unforgiving steel and brick. But then he felt the powerful rotors bite the air again, as the Aircrane righted itself, and with its turbofan jet engines to port and starboard screaming in defiance, rose straight up with the Fed's freight elevator hanging from its belly by a three-inch thick rope of steel fiber, and the pilot knew that he had won.

As the chopper continued to rise vertically to its translation altitude to horizontal flight, Krishnha already felt the Aircrane stabilize as the winch brought the payload up into the cube-shaped aperture of the cargo bay behind the cockpit. As soon as the whining of the ultra-heavy duty winch was replaced by the final thunk as the elevator car locked automatically in place behind the Aircrane's cockpit Krishnah worked the stick and throttle hard. The main rotor blades' pitch angled steeply forward and the chopper swung at its maximum fully loaded speed of better than one hundred miles per hour toward the Hudson.

"Get out of that elevator, you fuckers," Krishnah said into his walkie talkie. "We're airborne."

Richie and Sister John emerged from their steel crypt as Harry swung the chopper hard to starboard, heading over toward the Hudson river where the hide site they had prepared in New Jersey was situated, and Richie felt a wild surge of elation light up every nerve ending in his body. They had done it! They had pulled it off!

Now that the chopper cleared Lower Manhattan, he could look down through breaks in the rising smoke and see the activity below.

THE BLACKOUT HEIST

Emergency vehicles of every description, from fire trucks to police emergency bomb squad vehicles formed a swarm around the Fed, while other police vehicles had already sealed off the small streets feeding on the area and some of the larger arterial thoroughfares beyond.

From lower Broadway down to the South Street Seaport area, the section of Manhattan was sealed off. But this wasn't the case in the air. Here, it was a jumble of aircraft of all kinds, from newsmedia helicraft to police choppers. For a moment, Richie knew fear as he saw a chopper with blue and white markings with the word POLICE on its flanks hover close, but apparently the SAR paint job that Krishnah had given the Aircrane to disguise it had worked. The airborne cops flew right by them, rotors roaring, heading in the direction from which the Aircrane had come.

Richie turned to Sister John who was staring at him with a blank look on his big moon face.

"Shit," was all he managed to say.

"We did it, you ugly sonofabitch!" Richie shouted, and punched him hard, high on the right side of his chest. Sister John didn't even flinch.

"Shit," he said again.

Richie turned back toward inspecting the cityscape below the Aircrane. He had to keep his senses alert. This was a long way from Malaysia, but it was still a live fire zone.

If he didn't watch it, they could still wind up in some deep shit. Most of all, Richie thought about the two ground teams. Had Ace and Kingsley ditched the truck yet? Were Vinh, Mike and Quincy across the Holland Tunnel and into Jersey with the money bags as planned? Richie didn't know and for some reason communications were out.

He knew they shouldn't have been, but they were, and as the Aircrane completed the Hudson river crossing into Jersey and banked toward the hide site, Richie's gut told him something had gone wrong. And then, glancing out the starboard window, Richie saw the lights of Manhattan begin to disappear, winking out in a ragged line from Battery Park to its extreme northern limit of Harlem's Marble Hill. Richie knew in that instant that something else had happened, a citywide blackout that had occurred almost simultaneously with the heist.

THIRTY-NINE

Richie's Crew, Lower Manhattan. Ace drove the truck through the streets. His CB radio, tuned to federal emergency frequencies, brought him the news that the authorities believed that a terrorist attack on the city was currently in progress. Which didn't quite add up, considering the nature of the blackout. Also, he didn't realize that he had been made by the beat cop who had gotten his plate number.

Suddenly, Ace heard a description of his truck. Its license tag numbers were also being broadcast on police emergency frequencies. Ace thought about what to do as beads of sweat stood out on his face and brow. Should he run, or what?

He and Kingsley decided not to. The truck was speeding down Maiden Lane, not far from the Manhattan Bridge. If Ace got onto it they could across and into Brooklyn. There would be plenty of places to ditch the van in the warren of narrow, twisting streets that ran there. Ace hit the gas and swung around a corner, crashing a light.

It was a mistake. A police cruiser was waiting just around the corner. As they ID'd the MetroCon truck, they radioed for other police units to converge on the area. The dashboard tactical computer quickly displayed a route map of the area before its screen suddenly flickered and went dark.

Ace crashed the truck through the plate glass window of an audio equipment store on Maiden Lane. Shoppers fought to leave the store and ran in every direction through the streets outside. Ace and Kingsley were both armed, but neither had seriously thought they'd wind up using their weapons.

Ace snapped off some shots, but they were mostly for show and ineffective. A return volley of gunfire from the cops wounded him in the leg and stitched Kingsley across the chest, opening up a line of red-spurting pockmarks along the top of his MetroCon overalls as Kingsley spun like a rag doll and collapsed with a crash over a display table for the latest mobile phones.

Ace tried to make it out of the store, but a ricochet caught him in the side and he collapsed onto the concrete pavement. His head hit the sidewalk hard, and Ace lost consciousness as his skull cracked like an egg.

The last ambulance out of blacked-out Manhattan brought Ace across the Hudson, where the feds were waiting at a command post in Jersey City.

***

The feds turned Ace over to the CIA who shared the cross-Hudson facility, which had been set up as a clandestine detainee center, a black site to hold and interrogate terrorist suspects before covertly transporting them to secret CIA prisons overseas.

"We need to know about your accomplices," they said to him. "We'll grant you immunity from prosecution. Just answer our questions."

"Go fuck yourselves."

"Look, we can do it the easy way but we're prepared to go the hard way too, guy. It's your choice."

"I ain't got nothin' to say."

The spooks realized that they wouldn't get the information from Ace. But time was a critical commodity. They got rid of the feds and the New York cops. One of their doctors was an expert in administering truth serum. He'd had plenty of practice at the black site over the years.

"Hey, what's going on?" asked Ace as they strapped him down to the rolling hospital gurney bed.

"Just giving you a little therapy, that's all," said the doctor as he hooked the IV tube of the sodium pentathol-amobarbital mixture up on the moveable stainless steel stand. He swabbed Ace's arm and plunged in the needle.

"What are they doing?" Ace had noticed the rest of the Company men setting up the recording gear for the session.

"Don't worry about it," the doctor said. He opened the petcock and the pentathol-amobarbital flowed into Ace's veins.

"Who mastermind this."

Ace clamped his mind shut. He didn't want to say "Richie."

"Richie," he heard himself shout, "Richie Block."

He knew that if he thought about the words in response to the questioner's questions than he would speak it. He struggled to get free but the Velcro clamps held his arms and legs tightly.

"Calm yourself now," said the doctor. "Trying to fight it will only make it worse for you. Relax and it will go easy."

The doctor increased the flow of solution into Ace's artery. The subject of chemical interrogation thrashed around, but then subsided into a state of deep relaxation.

After all the questions had been put to the subject, the Company doctor looked at the spooks. One of them went over to transcription computer and closed the lid on the laptop, waiting until the flickering blue disk drive light finally winked off.

"What shall I do now?" the doctor asked the spook.

"Terminate him. He's a goner anyway."

The doctor nodded and increased the flow from the IV bottle to Ace's arm.

THE BLACKOUT HEIST

FORTY

Petrov, Moscow, CIS. The present Russian winter was the harshest since the time of Stalin. Snow had fallen as far south as the coast of Sebastopol on the Black Sea.

Even the residents of Moscow who were used to severe winter storms had had their hands full digging out from under three successive blizzards in a single month.

Despite the extreme weather conditions, an air conditioner hummed in the window of the conference room of KGB operational headquarters at the Lubyanka building in central Moscow, a location still retained by top Russian intelligence echelons despite new facilities located a short drive away.

Owing chiefly to the vagaries of the Lubyanka's central heating system, which had been installed just prior to the first World War, and had never been adequately modernized, some parts of the sprawling building received so much steam heat that it was necessary to compensate for the excess by air conditioning, even in winter.

DAVID ALEXANDER

And even with the benefit of the cooling apparatus that hummed in the window near his seat, Vassily Petrov was gripped by a stifling sense of slow asphyxiation.

Loosening his tie had not helped, and he was forced to mop his brow every few minutes to keep the sweat from dripping into his eyes.

Perhaps it was the fact that the meeting chamber was filled with the President's chief advisers that contributed to the stifling heat by which the Baikonur Cosmodrome's director felt so oppressed.

Assembled around the long table measuring at least twenty feet from end to end -- a table that dated back to the time of Czar Nicholas I -- were representatives of every policy-making body in the government's civilian and military branches.

Here, men who had been engaging in fierce internecine warfare for decades in the endless jockeying for position that once had characterized Soviet internal politics, and which persisted in somewhat more civilized form in later eras, now sat side-by-side, united by a common need to band together against an unprecedented crisis.

The crisis that had brought them to this room was one whose magnitude transcended all individual rivalries, all personal plans and professional loyalties. It might potentially, all of them realized, spell the end of every one of their careers, if not their very lives.

The unexpected detonation of the nuclear warhead hidden onboard the YZ-class surveillance satellite had sent a spasm of fear throughout the Russian federal hierarchy.

Throughout every directorate, department and office, the terror had swept like wildfire. It was obvious to anyone with a brain to think with that what they now faced could well be a prelude to nuclear holocaust.

Petrov, like a handful of others, had been aware for years that the former Soviets had been launching space vehicles equipped with nukes into orbit since practically the earliest days of their space program.

It had been a story told in whispers, but in a society where whispers still sometimes served as the most reliable newsmedia available, they were enough to convince Petrov that the story was the truth.

In the beginning, both the Americans and the Soviets had looked seriously at using small, lightweight nuclear power plants to generate electricity for the satellites they sent into orbit around the earth.

The Americans had soon decided, however, that nuclear power technology was still far too crude and inefficient to be worth consideration and bypassed it in favor of using solar energy instead.

To the less technologically sophisticated Soviets, it had made little difference by what method they powered their orbiting spacecraft. They had the added incentive of having a wealth of data on nuclear power recently stolen from the Americans and almost nothing available, and of practical merit, on solar energy. Nuclear power packs had been launched into orbit ever since.

From its infancy, that nuclear battery technology had evolved to the point where the Soviets had developed the capability of building compact, yet ever more powerful, orbital nukes with every space shot they carried out.

It had been a small step to equip *Pichuga* and each of its two sister satellites with a nuclear bomb that was both compact and reliable, as a viable clandestine countermeasure to the PATRIOT Shield initiative that the Americans were so stubbornly determined to deploy, despite protests not only from Russia but from their closest strategic partners in the EU.

At any rate, the Kremlin had believed the covert nuclear countermeasure to have been viable -- until one of the nukes had exploded in space subjecting New York City to an EMP-generated power failure and total blackout.

The speaker now called for questions, jarring Petrov from his sullen musings back to the business at hand.

"Sir," asked Petrov as a question suddenly formed in his mind, "why not order the destruction of the two surviving *Pichuga* reconnaissance satellites immediately?"

The speaker shook his head as many murmured agreement with Petrov's insightful remark.

"That is quite impossible," he told Petrov, immediately silencing the murmurs that had spread around the table.

THE BLACKOUT HEIST

"You mean to say that there is no autodestruct mechanism onboard the satellite?" asked another member of the assemblage, a high-ranking army officer with a line of medals and patches pinned to his tunic at chest level.

"No," the speaker returned. "There *is*. We can blow the circuits of the surviving orbital platforms to deprive the Americans of the technology aboard the satellites."

Pausing, the speaker swept his gaze from side to side to take in all the men seated at the table before continuing.

"*But* the nuclear device itself -- that will not be effected by this in any way."

"Why not?" Petrov asked the speaker.

"For two reasons," the speaker replied. "First, because the bomb's purpose itself is, after all, to explode, and that will probably happen in case of any attempt at tampering whatsoever. Secondly, because nothing short of blowing up the nuclear bomb contained inside the satellite would conceal the secret of the satellite's payload from the Americans."

"And the third reason?" asked the President himself who had been strangely silent throughout the unprecedented briefing session from his place at the long table opposite the speaker. "What is it, general?"

"The third reason, Mr. President," the speaker responded, returning the form of courteous address characteristically used by the Russian leader, "and perhaps the most important one of all, is because exploding the remaining exoatmospheric bombs, even without generating devastating electromagnetic pulses, would nonetheless create a high risk of sending enriched plutonium raining down on the American heartland. I need not draw the conclusions of such a disaster for you."

The Russian president paused for a moment as he reflected on what the speaker had just said, steepling his hands beneath his chin.

"Yes, general," he replied. "I quite see the problem. What then is to be done?"

The speaker's face grew somber, his eyes bored into those belonging to each of the men who sat watching him in the hushed conference chamber.

"There is only one choice," he finally said, "launch a Buran shuttle mission. Dismantle the remaining bombs before they explode."

"And," the President added pointedly, "before the Americans become aware of their existence."

***

It had taken another two days to prepare the CIS space shuttle for liftoff and to train and brief its three-man crew.

Now, the giant Energia launch craft, a larger and more powerful version of the Proton-K that had lofted the YZ-class satellites into orbit, sat steaming on the pad at the Baikonur Cosmodrome with the Buran -- *Blizzard* -- shuttle, christened Tchaikovsky, secured piggyback-fashion to its upper stage like a sucker fish attacked to the belly of a passing shark.

Vassily Petrov again oversaw the launch as the countdown neared the final seconds before liftoff.

THE BLACKOUT HEIST

In a rare display of cooperation with the Federal Space Agency, the Azerbaijani weather had produced a limited window of calm. No storm activity was anywhere in sight, nor was any inclement weather predicted for at least another forty-eight hours.

Visibility, atmospheric turbulence, prevailing winds and other launch conditions all appeared optimal. The countdown prior to launch had proceeded smoothly throughout, with no sign of trouble from any onboard or ground system. Even biomedical readings of the crew of cosmonauts onboard the shuttle were all excellent.

After the countdown had ended and the ignition of the Energia's powerful booster engines had filled the launch facility with clouds of smoke, Petrov watched as the shuttle slowly lifted off the pad. A cheer went up in the launch control center as the colossal launch vehicle soared skyward on a pedestal of flame and a geyser of smoke.

Suddenly the cheers turned to cries of dismay. To Petrov's horror, the control room's giant view screens showed that the rocket was beginning to veer wildly off course. Its angle of climb quickly became unstable, its vapor trail a crazily twisted streak in the azure blue sky.

The command center's loudspeakers transmitted the terrified sounds of the cosmonauts inside Buran struggling in vain to stabilize the rocket's path as the Energia workhorse nosed steeply downward, on a collision course with the steppes of Tayuratam below.

Suddenly a blinding fireball lit up the clear morning sky. And then there was nothing left of the shuttle or the Energia launch vehicle except a cascade of spinning fragments hurtling groundward, and plumes of white smoke that marked their earthward progress.

The shuttle's crew, realized Petrov, must surely be gone -- all of them dead. But unlike the deaths of the American shuttle astronauts, there would be little said to the press about the tragedy.

Only that a routine launch had resulted in the destruction of an unnamed spacecraft at an unspecified time.

Only more whispers in more dark corners, in a society where whispers still passed for truth.

But Petrov was also aware that there was far more to the significance of what had just taken place.

There would be no way to mount another shuttle mission in time to ward off disaster. Therefore, what had just transpired would call for unprecedented measures being taken by the Commonwealth's policymakers.

Petrov knew that the new coalition now had only a single choice left short of allowing the satellites to explode.

Call in the Americans.

THE BLACKOUT HEIST

MetroCon facility, Manhattan. On a steel-plate catwalk encircling a rectangular concrete maintenance bay extending thirty feet below the streets and sidewalks of lower Manhattan and filled with the bulking cylinders of giant electrical transformers, a MetroCon workman noticed the banks of overhead lights erratically blinking on and off.

Looking down into the huge transformer bay below him, the workman heard the steady, rhythmic thrumming of the machinery below him suddenly speed up in cadence and become a shrill, ugly hypersonic wail. Moments later, tongues of flame and gouts of acrid, brownish gray smoke belched from the overloaded power transformer banks.

The workman did not live long enough to determine what caused the problem, however.

In moments, one of the transformer banks exploded as millions of volts racing along the city's power mains overloaded the transformers too quickly for MetroCon's automatic circuit breakers to trip and isolate the machinery from the citywide power grid.

DAVID ALEXANDER

The tremendous surge of the killer electromagnetic pulse shorted the internal circuits of the transformers.

Hot blue-white sparks ignited the flammable PCBs that were used to cool the monster-sized units.

The PCBs spontaneously combusted, creating a massive fireball that ripped through the underground maintenance bay with devastating force, hurling a section of Wall Street into the air and slaughtering hundreds of pedestrians on the crowded streets directly overhead.

Although the immediate result of the explosion was in itself catastrophic, its ultimate effects were far more devastating.

The maintenance bay supplied power to the banks of giant pumps used by the Metropolitan Transit Authority to keep the waters of the East River from flooding the subway tubes that ran beneath the river, tubes connecting lower Manhattan with Brooklyn.

The pumps were augmented by a network of mechanical locks that prevented the river water from seeping into the tunnels where it could produce shorts in the electrified railway that could severely disrupt or entirely halt subway service.

The moment that the pump system failed, millions of cubic tons of river water were held back by nothing more than a few feet of aging concrete and brick.

The tunnels had been constructed at the turn of the century. They were among the oldest and the narrowest in the New York City subway system, as well as the most decrepit.

The tunnel system was like an old man suddenly finding a heavy burden placed on his frail shoulders.

At first, the walls of the tunnel held the river back, but it was only a matter of time before they would cave in beneath the immense weight bearing down on them. When that happened, the tunnels would flood.

***

In the blacked-out IRT subway tunnel beneath lower Broadway in the Wall Street area, the passengers of the immobilized Pelham Bay local train that Willie Inskeep had been driving were completely lost.

Inskeep couldn't understand why his flashlight wouldn't operate, nor why his radio had gone dead on him, despite the fact that its power indicator light continued to glow steady red.

Nothing made any sense. Like the rest of the passengers, Inskeep was filled with a cold, numbing sense of foreboding.

What in the name of hell was happening here? A small voice in the back of his mind warned him that something terrible had taken place, something unprecedented and catastrophic.

Inskeep thought suddenly of his family in Jamaica, Queens. Terrible images flashed through his mind like fragments of a nightmare recalled on awakening. His wife Claudette and their daughter Zeena all alone, crying out in the darkness, facing hordes of crack dealers who....

No. Inskeep fought to drive the gibbering voices of fear and the strobing images of terror from his fevered mind.

Nothing out of the ordinary was happening, at least for New York, he told himself. This was just some kind of power outage, no different from the blackouts Inskeep and millions of other city dwellers had experienced over the past twenty years. *Don't panic, stay cool, it'll all shake out before too long*, Inskeep told himself.

The first thing Inskeep knew he had to do was to reach street level. Get out of the tunnel. Out of the dark. Get back up topside where there were TVs and radios and newspapers and computers connected to the internet and other people and familiar landmarks. Back to the world, like they used to say in the jungles of Malaysia.

Ordinarily, there would be well-lighted emergency exits positioned at three hundred yard intervals along the walls of the subway tunnels. Inskeep knew, however, that such would not be the case in the present position of his train.

Stopped dead where it was, midway between Manhattan and Brooklyn beneath the East River, there would be no emergency exits located anywhere in the immediate vicinity.

There would be doors located nearby, sure. But these doors led nowhere except to service bays, generator alcoves and storage rooms.

What's more, they would almost certainly and without exception be locked for security purposes. In order to reach the safety of the city streets scores of feet above them, Inskeep and his passengers would have to trek the better than three miles of track in either direction.

Just then La Dollicia Shavers, the conductor on the IRT run, reached Inskeep. He could identify her easily by the outline of her conductor's uniform ball cap in the dimness of the blacked-out tunnel.

Other shadows which moved against the deeper shadows of the darkened subway tube, belonging to the other passengers, clustered around her.

The passengers were calling out questions, each shouting to be heard above the noise of hundreds of competing voices.

From somewhere in the murk around him, Inskeep heard a baby crying, its mother trying desperately to silence the bawling infant in a rapidly spoken foreign language that the motorman could not identify.

Inskeep had the uncomfortable feeling that the train's passengers were holding him responsible for what had happened, looking for a scapegoat on whom to take out their fear, anger and hopeless desperation. The fleeting image of a lynch mob stringing him up from the tunnel roof almost made him laugh despite the desperateness of the situation.

"Don't worry," La Dollicia shouted above the cacophony of voices in the stygian darkness of the tunnel. "There's nothing to be concerned with. There's been a problem with the power supply to the track mains. There's no fire here or smoke danger, so its okay. All we have to do is walk to safety."

"Bullshit!" a man's voice cried out from somewhere in the crowd. "This has nothing to do with a power outage. This is something really serious."

"Can't you radio for help or something?" a young woman's voice came from the center of the mass, her voice raising in a Valley Girl's interrogative on the final word.

"Yeah, call up the Transit Police for crissakes!" a gruff male voice seconded. "Have them send somebody to get us out of here."

"For *this* they keep raising the fares?" somebody else with a different foreign accent than the one Inskeep had heard before shouted, "for *this* lousy, stinking service?"

Despite the bleak situation, this remark was answered by a wave of laughter from several positions in the dark.

"I can't call. My radio's out," Inskeep told the crowd, addressing the dark, wraithlike forms around him in as calm a voice as he could muster. "It stopped dead the same time as the train did."

A murmur of fear now raced through the crowd trapped in the tunnel's blackness.

"We're all going to die!" a woman's voice hollered shrilly. "Oh, sweet Jesus, we're going to die here in the dark like a bunch of fuckin' rats."

"Nobody's going to die!" La Dollicia Jackson cried out to the woman. "Chill out, people. It's all right. All we got to do is walk to the nearest emergency exit."

"What exit? I don't see no fuckin' exit nowhere!" the gruff male voice that had spoken up before asked. "How far we gotta walk?"

"Well," Inskeep began, dreading the response he knew would come but knowing he had to say what had to be said, "we have two choices here. We're about halfway between Brooklyn and Manhattan. Nothing but river water overhead. It's about a mile-and-a-half in either direction."

"Please mister, I have a bad heart," an old man's voice cried out. "I don't think I can walk that far."

"That's okay, pops," a Spanish-accented voice from one of the shadows near the man who had spoken said, "I give you a hand, okay?"

"But where?" asked another voice, one Inskeep had not heard before. "Which way do we go?"

"Any direction's about as good as another," Inskeep replied. "My vote's for going back the way we came, though. But that's just personal. It's closer to where my family's at."

Again Inskeep struggled to keep the nameless dread from congealing into an image that frightened him even worse than he now felt.

"No way," a man's voice cried out. "I live in Brooklyn. Ain't no reason for me to go back to no fuckin' Manhattan. Fuck that shit."

Other voices seconded the man who had just spoken. It was finally decided to split up into two groups.

One group, headed by Inskeep, would go back toward the Manhattan side.

The other group, with conductor La Dollicia in the lead, would head toward the Brooklyn end of the tunnel.

The two groups began walking in opposite directions, neither of them aware that they were treading on a tightrope stretched over nothing, and on fire at both ends.

FORTY-TWO

Amoroso, Wall Street District. The earsplitting boom of the JFK-bound 747 exploding into a geyser of flame and knife-edged spinning fragments, as it crashed into the West Tower of the Battery Park Commerce Towers complex, brought Ellis Amoroso back to his senses.

As he struggled to get his feet under him, Amoroso could feel the one hundred ten story skyscraper shudder violently around him as though it were a sheaf of thin straws shaken in the fist of an angry titan.

Screams of horror rang out from every direction as the hell-flames lit up the night with strobing orange-white flickers that sputtered across the walls in grotesque patterns.

WHOOOOOOOOMMMMMMMMMM!

This time the enormous tower shook with enough force to send Amoroso crashing back to the carpeted office floor.

Terrified, he saw enormous fissures spread through the groaning walls in the light cast by the fires outside as torsion wrenched them savagely, followed by the tormented scream of rending, shattering metal as the support beams of the skyscraper tore apart like brittle plastic packaging under a blade.

With a sickening crash, part of the building wall gave way and began a seventy-six story plunge to the street, disintegrating in midair into a deadly shower of spinning, tumbling fragments, each weighing many tons and, each as jagged as fractured glacial ice.

All of this happened with such astonishing suddenness that the senses could not fully absorb the progression of events, the mind could not assemble it all into a coherent, understandable whole. The net result was that the senses reeled.

At first there was enclosure, then it vanished completely from sight, leaving behind only the hellishly fire-lit darkness of the wind-torn winter sky. Familiar points of reference were swept away in the terrible maelstrom so quickly that the survivors cowering in the darkness of the office were struck dumb, frozen where they stood, sat or lay.

A gust of intense wind that wafted burning embers into the shattered office interior washed over Amoroso as the side of the building completely gave way.

The wind's ferocity sucked human bodies toward the edge of the precipice, carrying its helpless victims over the side and into space like dry leaves blown about by the gusts of a sudden storm. The glowing embers blowing in from the burning East Tower set clothes and furnishings on fire, burning flesh and singing hair.

Those swept to the edge of the shattered floor space tried to hold onto anything to prevent themselves from being dragged by the overpowering suction over the edge of space into the gaping maw of death that awaited them beyond the brink, but the ferocious tug of the wind at that altitude was beyond their power to resist. Howling like some ravenous beast, it pulled them toward the shark jaws of doom.

Amoroso saw the bodies of his coworkers being dragged over the edge, swept out into the night, whirled like bits of torn newspaper into an empty void before disappearing with bloodcurdling screams into the flame-lit darkness of the savagely howling night.

Amoroso was fortunate to be positioned near the intact wall of the skyscraper.

Crawling on all fours, he struggled to fight the pull of the agonizingly powerful wind suction that was like the invisible hand of a giant demon desperate to pull him toward its famishing mouth.

Others around him were doing the same thing, grasping onto anything that could anchor them against the wind's savage pull.

After long, agonized minutes that seemed like eternities, Amoroso finally was able to crawl out of the office suite and into the corridor that bisected the floor.

Other employees, both of his company and from other concerns located on his or adjacent floors of the building, had managed to save themselves by crawling as he had.

They lay along the corridor's carpeted length, gasping for breath, too numb with horror to believe what had happened to them was reality, instead of nightmare.

***

Darkness blanketed the corridor. The odor of air that was contaminated by smoke permeated it thoroughly.

Although there nothing was on fire, the stench of burning flesh, wood and metal in the streets below was powerful enough to reach up into the upper stories of the East Tower of the commerce complex like a hand from the grave.

By the flickering light of the flames that illuminated the night with a ghastly red-orange glow, Amoroso and the survivors on his floor regarded one another.

Without speaking, they each gravitated together, their minds reeling from the sudden horror they had just experienced, struggling to understand what had taken place.

"Is it an earthquake?" someone finally cried out. "What in the name of heaven is going on?"

"All the power," another spoke, "it all suddenly just ... went out. Then the plane crash. I don't understand."

"What's the connection?" another cried out.

"It was the plane crash," someone else ventured, "the crash is what knocked out the power."

"No," another shouted out to contest this claim, "my computer display froze and went blank just before the plane hit the West Tower."

"That's right," somebody else seconded.

A group of men had risen to their feet and were frantically trying the elevator button.

Long after they realized that the elevator car would not respond to their efforts, they continued punching the buttons purely as a reflex, not willing to believe that they were trapped hundreds of stories above the street. Not even hearing the screams for help that rose from the elevator car trapped in the shaft a few floors below.

"What do we do?" a woman cried out.

"Wait for help to arrive," a man counseled. "They'll be sending over paramedics."

"You're out of your mind, buddy," another man shouted angrily. "The whole damned city's blacked out. We could be stuck here for days. Believe me, I know. I was stuck in an elevator for thirty hours in that last big blackout. I had to see a shrink for the next two years. It was worse than 911."

***

Along with the other survivors on his floor, Amoroso went down the emergency stairwell. The stairwell was clogged with masses of building personnel desperate to exit the West Tower. At first the crowd flowed sluggishly down the stairs. Then all movement stopped.

"There's something wrong," someone cried out as reports were carried back up the line from those at the front of the stream of people. "Down there, it's all blocked off."

Panic now spread like wildfire through the trapped crowd.

Suddenly, there was another explosion. The entire immense structure was rocked violently as the shock waves coursed through the skyscraper.

"There's been another plane crash!" somebody hollered. "Oh, Jesus, not again. Please not again."

"No! *A bomb!*" another shouted. "I swear it was a bomb!"

Immediately, Amoroso could smell the acrid, smoky odor of things catching fire that had never been intended to burn. That 911 smell that was a hideous mixture of flesh and steel and wiring and who-knew-what.

The air quickly became thick and heavy with the nauseating stench of burning office furniture, walls and carpeting.

Amoroso fought to keep from being stampeded to death as the crowd surged in mindless panic back up the stairwell to the corridor from which they'd originally descended.

THE BLACKOUT HEIST

FORTY-THREE

Applebaum, The South Bronx. For Mad Marty Applebaum, it was time to rock and roll.

His girlfriend Yolanda safely stashed in his apartment with instructions to keep the door locked, Applebaum wouldn't have to worry about her safety -- too much, anyway. Personal distractions cramped a merc's style, and for the action that lay ahead for Applebaum, he'd need all the powers of concentration that he could muster up.

Perched on his vantage point on the parapet of the rooftop of the Zoo's Building Five, Applebaum looked down through night-seeing binoculars that gave him a clear field of view in the already wine-colored twilight.

Through a glass darkly, Mad Marty witnessed nothing short of the incredible. Every light in every building and on every lamp post on every street corner, had been blacked out.

Not only across the entire boro of the Bronx had this happened, but -- a swing of the binoculars to the southwest told him -- across the big sewers they called rivers here, in Manhattan as well.

Here and there, Applebaum could see enormous plumes of bright yellow flame whooshing up against a backdrop of swiftly gathering darkness, illuminating the pillars of billowing black smoke that spread across the bloated underbelly of the brooding winter sky.

Something about the dark panorama below him reminded Applebaum of a passage he'd once read in the Book of Revelations that told of Apocalypse.

All well and good. Except that nothing Applebaum now saw jibed with the list of potential reasons for Apocalypse he ticked off in his mind. Although the situation certainly bore all the telltale signs of the first phases of a nuclear attack, other indications conflicted with such a scenario.

If the Iranians -- the likeliest suspects since they'd been bragging of their plans for just such an attack for some time -- had exploded a nuke in a suborbital airburst to blanket part of the US with EMPs to knock out command, control and communications, prior to a surprise nuclear hit using their long-range King Darius II missiles -- then by now Applebaum would have expected to have already been nuked to radioactive atoms.

The better part of an hour had passed, however, without any follow-up on the "blinding" phase of nuclear confrontation. No way, Applebaum guessed, that any rogue state, be it Iran or North Korea, would give our forces enough time to retaliate after pulling a stunt like that. The same went for the neo-Soviets, a far more likely source of a nuclear strike on the US eastern seaboard.

It made sense that if they'd gone to all the trouble of launching a surprise attack, they would have had to have already delivered the coup de grace. Why sacrifice the edge when you can shut the other guy out?

Since the sky mushrooms had not fallen, Applebaum had to assume that what was going down was some kind of nuclear accident. Catastrophic, maybe. Terminal, nah.

If disaster could strike at Chernobyl and Three Mile Island, and then at the nuclear facility at Peshawar, India, in 2015, why couldn't some other kind of royal-assed fuck-up go down? After all, both sides had all kinds of nuclear shit orbiting around up there in outer space. Along comes a meteor and -- blam! -- you got yourself a couple of megatons of nuke airburst there, partner.

This particular scenario made sense to Applebaum. Somehow, he reasoned, either the morons in the former neo-Soviet military or the morons on our side had blown a nuke warhead. He doubted that the morons in shit holes like Iran and North Korea had anything more concrete than bluster and threat.

Yes, that sounded about right. In fact, the more he thought about it, the more Applebaum was convinced that he was right on the money.

Hell, he thought, when you get right down to it, it was really only a matter of time before the inevitable happened. With the US fucking around with PATRIOT Shield technology in space and the Russians -- or God knew who else -- doing the same, except claiming they're not, an orbiting Chernobyl scenario wasn't that farfetched at all.

Applebaum smiled broadly as he checked the luminous dial of his Tag-Heuer analog wrist chronometer, noting that another ten minutes had elapsed without anything further happening.

If this is just an accident, he said to himself, *then what you'll have is total chaos for awhile. Then it'll be back to normal -- lawsuits, flag-waving, whopping compensation checks for fat-slob widows of slain cops, firefighters, sanitation men and subway maintenance workers, sweetheart bailout deals for giant corporations headquartered in the city, and above all, enormous graft from City Hall to real estate developers already slobbering over the money to be made remaking the five boros into a playground for rich lawyers and corporate fart-suckers like they'd done to Manhattan after 911 -- and life, for Marty Applebaum, would get boring again.*

In the meantime, you my man, Marty's dialog with himself continued, *can get yourself some target practice.*

Replacing his night-seeing binoculars in the web pouch at his belt, Applebaum applied camo paint to his face and cranked a live round into his shooter.

His Colt Commando Special Forces assault weapon in hand, he hightailed it through the rooftop entrance of the building's fire stairs.

***

Chooch and Majik Tajik were doing what came naturally. Cueball-headed and standing a little over six feet tall, Chooch was freshly returned from a stretch in the Ray Brook federal penitentiary upstate at North Elba, for the rape-murder of a seventy-year-old Manhattan schoolteacher. Having copped

317

a plea, he'd done ten years out of thirty and gotten his sentence commuted for snitching on a fellow inmate.

Majik Tajik was a little wiry dude, sporting a Detroit haircut that left his kinky hair thick on top and closely shaven on the flanks of his face. He had gangbanger tats all over his body and prominent track marks on both his sinewy arms, showing that even junkies can profit from fresh air and exercise.

Both were members in *baaad* standing of the Yanomamos, an Afro-Hispanic biker gang that ruled the mean streets of Mott Haven. Run by a Latino G called Cinco Muertes -- "Five Deaths" -- it was a law unto itself in the inner city combat zone that the Yanomamos called home.

"*Chingao!* Check this motherfucker out!" Chooch hollered elatedly as he heaved a corrugated steel garbage can through the plate glass window of the tiny refreshment kiosk tucked away in the lobby of the Zoo's Building Four. "We fuckin' struck gold here, my dog!"

"Yo, shit!" replied Majik Tajik, drawing close to examine the prize that fortune had cast their way. "You think they some bread in this box?"

"Only one way to find out, my homie."

Majik Tajik produced a crowbar and began prying open the door of a soda machine that stood against the kiosk's wall. It sprang open with a loud grating sound.

The coin box was next to go down. Both Yanomamos were gratified to discover that it contained several hundred dollars in receipts. To celebrate their good fortune, Majik Tajik and

Chooch began opening cans of warm soda and spurting the suds all over the kiosk and themselves.

Suddenly they heard the sound of a loud metallic click behind them. Turning their heads simultaneously, Chooch and Majik Tajik saw a guy in military camouflage fatigues who was pointing a mean looking weapon at their guts.

The momentary look of shock was replaced by broad smiles.

"That thing made outa plastic, candyass?" he asked the guy with the gun.

Applebaum smiled back. "You don't want to find out, piss eyes," he returned. "Now let's see you little faggots both try to give that floor a blowjob."

A look calculated to strike terror into the human soul spread across Chooch's mask-like, triangular face.

"Fuck you! Nobody talk to me like dat," he returned in a low growl. "I gon' kill you, muthafucka."

A nine-inch combat knife glittered dully in Chooch's fist, catching the last few rays of twilight. "Yeah, mothafucka," he said, "I'm gonna check your box."

Before the Yanomamos could lunge however, Applebaum squeezed the Commando's trigger and fired a burst pointblank into the onrushing Chooch's belly. Pieces of the gangbanger's intestines splattered the walls with a series of rapid, sloppy impact sounds.

Regardless of the fact that he was now minus most of his intestines, Chooch still kept coming and Applebaum emptied the clip of 5.56s into his head, watching it disappear in a crimson spray of pulverized bone organ tissue, leaving behind a ragged, bloody stump that sent red jets spurting up where Chooch's head had once sat.

Applebaum looked around, shining the flashlight here and there.

The little guy with Chooch had taken a powder. But Applebaum hadn't heard the patter of sneaker soles against concrete. A constricting sense of panic gripped Applebaum.

The little fucker was somewhere nearby, watching and waiting. Applebaum could feel cold mercury mice waltzing up and down his spinal cord as he ejected the spent clip and quickly reloaded. The gun in his hands suddenly felt like a huge magnet for trouble, a lightning rod for death. He experienced the maddening urge to hurl it to the floor and run away.

Suddenly Mad Marty saw something gleam on the periphery of the cone of his flashlight beam. An object flew at him and struck a glancing blow on his head.

A sharp, searing pain blossomed in his left shoulder like a poison flower. As a grunt of pain escaped his lips, Applebaum whirled and saw the little Yanomamo rear back his arm to stick the switchblade into him again. He reacted instantly, swinging the butt-end of the steel Commando's steel folding stock against one close-shaved temple of Majik Tajik's ugly, turnip-like head.

Blood instantly began spurting from the long, ragged gash on the side of the bantam dude's skull.

He gave out a bloodcurdling yell of pain and anger, but didn't fall and didn't run.

Instead, he tried to stab Applebaum again with the shiv. His lunge for Mad Marty's throat was wild and sloppy, though, and it wasn't too hard to block the clumsy and wide swing with the Commando's case-hardened steel frame.

But the sudden move threw Applebaum off balance. Both men fell to the hard, cold floor, grappling and grunting in the darkness as the flashlight rolled away.

Now Applebaum was in a fight for his life. The little fucker was incredibly strong. Though wounded, a psychotic fire burned in his black pushbutton eyes. Majik Tajik skinned back his lips and bared his teeth, growling from deep in his throat like a rabid dog.

Applebaum couldn't believe how strong the little dude's fingers were as the grabbed for Marty's assault rifle.

With his free hand, Applebaum managed to unship the Beretta 9-millimeter semiautomatic pistol from the holster on his hip and jam the muzzle smack dab against Majik Tajik's face, right between his beady black eyes.

High on his own adrenaline, Marty jerked the trigger over and over again, continuing to fire long after the head had completely disintegrated into an aerosol spray of pulped brain matter and pulverized bone and the ten-round clip of nines had run dry.

Now spattered with the gangbanger's blood, Applebaum pushed the headless, twitching corpse off him and crawled to retrieve the fallen flashlight.

THE BLACKOUT HEIST

He sat against a wall for a long moment, breathing hard, fighting back the waves of nausea that crashed inside him like waves on a storm-tossed beach.

It shouldn't be like this! he told himself, the thought running through his mind in a loop of madness. *This wasn't how I expected it to feel.*

But it *was*, nonetheless, and when he felt his strength return, Applebaum rose shakily to his feet and couldn't hold back the heaves a moment longer, vomiting all over the corpses lying at his feet.

Retrieving his flashlight and weapons he staggered into the darkened corridors of the Zoo.

He was beginning to feel much better now.

You ain't cherry no more, brother, Marty told himself. *Now you a fuckin' ho!*

DAVID ALEXANDER

Book Three:
Daylight

And the light shineth in the darkness;
And the darkness comprehended it not.
-- *New Testament*, John, 1:5

FORTY-FOUR

Richie, North Jersey. Harry Krishnah set the chopper down in the hidden compound. Mike, Vinh and Quincy pulled in as Richie, Sister John and Harry were struggling to unload the bars of Third Reich gold into the back of a waiting refrigerator truck using a hydraulic lift.

With a little grunt work from all six hands, the straining lift mechanism heaved the six-ton pallet into the trucks' cargo bay where Richie and his crew maneuvered it further inside, lashed it down, and covered it with vinyl tarp.

Richie then paid each member ten thousand dollars in cash out of his own pocket as an advance against the proceeds stolen. The stolen currency was hot and would be handled in a separate fencing operation.

Most of the hot money would be converted into diamonds to be smuggled into Liechtenstein and turned back into cash, in the form of euros deposited in numbered accounts in all five names. Though small enough to represent a whistle-stop through Switzerland, which surrounds and envelopes it, and which Americans passing through it generally believe it's a part of, Liechtenstein is a nation apart, whose banking secrecy laws remain unaffected by dictates from Washington. The euro accounts were to remain untouched for two years, but they would be safe from tampering or garnishment by Interpol or European cops.

A portion of the hot cash, however, would find its way into safe deposit boxes at some of Manhattan's most prestigious banks -- boxes rented under Norman Judson's name, and also containing documents easily interpreted as detailing the plans of the Fed heist. An anonymous tip would also lead cops to the hide site after Richie and his accomplices were long gone, where law enforcement personnel would find a drugged, but otherwise unfettered Judson. The idea was to give them a convenient Saddam in a convenient hidey-hole so they could conveniently hang him.

The only sour note so far was that there was no sign of Kingsley and Ace and neither Richie nor anyone else at the hide side could raise them via portable radio communications or cell phones. Richie concluded that the worst had happened to them. But there was nothing anybody could do. They'd all known the risks and had accepted those risks from the beginning.

"Now get going," Richie told Sister John and the others.

"You won't try to rip us off, will you Richie?" asked Mike.

"What to you think?" he answered.

"Sorry, it's just that's it's a lot of money there, partner."

Sister John put a hand on Richie's shoulder.

"I'd stake my life on my dog here," he told Mike and the others. "I staked it in Afghanistan and Malaysia and Richie saved my ass more than once.

If you can trust any human being in this bullshit world, it's my dog. Word up."

***

The two getaway cars left with Sister John and Harry Krishnah in one vehicle and Mike, Vinh and Quincy in the other. Both cars -- Black Lexus SUVs with all their paperwork in good order -- broke away from the hide site to roll west through Pennsylvania by different routes. Two more hide sites were waiting in Indiana and Ohio with changes of cars, forged ID and the services of expert cosmetic surgeons who would be paid in cash. After a brief stay at the second hide sites, the two getaway teams would cross over to lay low in the comfort of Europe's most scenic cities.

Richie and Maddie were left alone with the drugged Judson after the two vehicles had departed the safe house. The end of the game was near.

Richie quickly slotted the barn where the helicopter was housed with plastic explosive demolition charges. The plan was for when the cops arrived Judson to be semiconscious in the house. Motion sensors would trigger the charges as the law arrived to blow the chopper and any evidence, including fingerprints and DNA, that the Aircrane might contain.

Before his and Maddie's departure, Richie went back into the house to check on Judson.

"Put up your hands."

Judson was pointing a gun at Maddie whom he held in an arm lock. Richie froze.

"I'm sorry Richie, he was too quick," she said.

"It's all right," said Richie, putting up his hands Judson demanded.

"You thought you were going to make me the fall guy, huh?" A maniac's laugh exited Judson's mouth. "You know what? I'm going to make you both the fall guys."

"The cops are closing in, Judson," said Richie. We're all going to take the fall."

"You think I give a damn?" Judson returned. "When they come you're going to be dead. Because by then I'm going to have shot you both in self-defense. You kidnapped and drugged me, you see."

"We've got enough on you to send you to prison for a long time, Judson," Richie said. "Let's cut a deal."

"Who cares?" Judson said. "I give the authorities you two and information on the others. They'll close the case and not bother with me. No deal. Outside."

Judson gestured with the gun. Richie walked outside into the compound. Judson was pointing them at the barn. As Richie walked he saw one of the motion sensors in the grass. As Richie passed it, the initiator charge went off and triggered the rest of the demolition charges slotted across in the barn around the Aircrane.

The big bang of the explosion startled Judson. Richie was prepared. He reached down, unholstered the backup .38 on his ankle and shot Judson in the face. He pulled the trigger again and again. Judson went down and dropped his gun.

THE BLACKOUT HEIST

Richie thought quickly. He took out his wallet and photo ID cards including his drivers license. He put those in the dead man's pockets.

"Get the car started," he told Maddie as he dragged Judson's body toward the flames that were now beginning to crackle from the barn as the chopper's fuel tank ignited and exploded in a balloon of flame and smoke.

In a matter of minutes everything inside the barn would have become an inferno. Richie dragged Judson's body inside the barn and ran to the truck. Climbing behind the wheel, he got in beside Maddie and rolled the vehicle down the road.

They passed the police heading toward the site of the safe house. The cops didn't notice them since they were disguised and driving a clean vehicle and not doing anything to attract attention. Richie continued driving until they reached a Hilton directly across the river from blacked-out Manhattan. Richie had booked a suite as a precaution, and was now glad he'd done so.

"You stay here until whatever happened to the city is fixed, and we'll meet up later as planned," he told her.

"I want to come with you," she challenged.

"No way, kid. It's too dangerous. You just stay put. You're clean. I'll let you know where I am in a few weeks after I've fenced the gold."

She went upstairs. When she turned to look back at Richie, the truck was already gone.

DAVID ALEXANDER

FORTY-FIVE

The White House, Washington, DC. The phone on the antique Resolute desk in the Oval Office buzzed.

"The President is on the line, sir," the President's secretary announced.

Thanking her, President Johnson Ubutu Ubuto Ebong picked up the handset and put the call on speakerphone. In front of him, positioned on the two comfortable sofas beyond the Great Seal on the office rug, and seated in chairs flanking the fireplace at the opposite wall, members of his cabinet and the National Security Council listened in. The voice over IP phone system included a mobile teleconferencing screen that had been wheeled in by aides and positioned in front of the sunny French windows on the east wall of the oval room. The large screen showed real-time imagery of the two heads of state, captured by small webcams on their respective desks.

"My apologies, Johnson," Russian President Grigory Leshenko said to the US President, using the familiarity developed at Leshenko's recent visit to Helsinki to represent the CIS in the 2019 G-25 economic summit.

"We are dealing most severely with the individuals responsible for this disastrous piece of adventurism. I promise you that there will be a full report available to your military and scientific people as soon as it is ready."

"Damn it, Grigory," the president responded with genuine anger. "How the hell could your military let this kind of a thing happen? What about those treaties we signed against nuclear weapons in space? This is a direct violation of our bilateral agreements. How am I going to explain that to my countrymen?"

"The blame will be placed squarely on the shoulders of those responsible," replied the president, "this I can completely assure you."

The President was silent as he weighed the possibilities, inclining his head as one of his aides whispered a comment into his ear.

Blaming the Russians was one thing, but there was another important aspect to be considered. Ebong had been the prime mover behind the East-West nonproliferation treaty, ramming it home despite heavy opposition in the Senate and the House well before any unilateral moves by the United States to sharply cut its own WMD arsenal in the wake of the Russian Federation's reunification of territories lost in the USSR's breakup decades before.

This accident -- if it was indeed that -- would make him look like an idiot. He would never stand a chance of reelection come next November.

"Fine Grigory," said the US president, resigned to the fact that there was nothing he could do. "Keep me posted. I want to know what your people find out as soon as possible."

The CIS president smiled to himself in his office at the vast Kremlin complex, watching an echelon of red-breasted Siberian geese fly past the window that overlooked Red Square, and remarking to himself that the first thaws of spring were only a short time away. He had read his opposite number correctly. Like himself, the president was a political animal.

Whatever fundamental differences lay between the two men, the ideologies they represented or the forms of government which defined the two countries, they had one very important thing in common; the need to cover their asses.

"I am glad we understand each other, Mr. President," the Russian President said. "*Bud'te zdorovy.*"

"Take care, Grigory. My regards to your wife."

The President replaced the handset on its cradle. He leaned back on his chair and steepled his fingers beneath his chin.

The first thing that had to be done, he reasoned, was damage assessment and control. He leaned forward and punched his intercom. He wanted to see a damage-control team assembled on the double. The only fly in the ointment was that the American president had chosen to mention his wife. The Russian president would now have to take an antacid tablet.

***

THE BLACKOUT HEIST

Like Marty Applebaum in the Bronx, Rick Skerrit too had surmised that what afflicted the City of New York was some form of unprecedented nuclear accident rather than a loose-nuke strike or a prelude to full-fledged nuclear attack on a larger scale.

From the outset, however, it had been apparent that there was no ordinary power blackout in effect. Instead, something of far greater magnitude was certainly taking place.

Not only had electrical power lines been knocked out of commission, but self-contained pieces of equipment that ranged from heavy-duty electromechanical systems like automotive vehicles and industrial appliances, to laptops and mobile info-appliances like cell phones, were also rendered inoperable.

Vehicles of all types were stalled by the thousands on streets and highways and computers from the micros in people's homes to the mainframes the banks used for their automated teller networks were reduced to useless pieces of junk.

There was only a single phenomenon that Skerrit knew of that was capable of producing such widespread damage to electrical and electronic systems, and that was electromagnetic pulse.

Yet the only force capable of generating EMP in large enough quantities to cause such widespread damage was a nuclear warhead detonated in low earth orbit. If that happened, Skerrit knew, the damage would spread outward from the epicenter of the nuclear burst in a radius whose area was determined by the force and magnitude of the explosion.

Although the only conceivable motivation behind triggering such a detonation would be a prelude to armed attack or some other form of highly disruptive action, such as cyberwar, Skerrit had ruled out these possibilities for practically the same reasons as Applebaum, in the South Bronx.

A full-fledged attack had not swiftly followed the severe power outages that had blanketed the city and outlying regions. New York City was still intact, albeit without electric power, transportation or communications.

An accident. That was the most likely explanation for what had happened. And it would be an accident that was surely the result of negligence by one of the handful of world powers, large and small, known to toy with exoatmospheric military systems.

***

The scene at the Emergency Command Center (ECC) that had been set up at City Hall was grim. Skerrit had been brought there from the police precinct he'd reached in the aftermath of the mega-blackout.

An armored NYPD personnel carrier, guarded by a detail of cops armed with riot shotguns -- a vehicle normally used only for SWAT action -- had shuttled him to the building.

The truck was one of the few vehicles with electromechanical ignition systems in service in the city, and as such had remained unaffected by the killer EMP burst.

THE BLACKOUT HEIST

The interior of the spacious circular room was illuminated by emergency power from the basement of the facility. The building was guarded by a cordon of police armed with riot control equipment and M16 assault rifles.

Barricaded from the streets of lower Manhattan surrounding the mayor's offices and the seat of city government, City Hall had been turned into an impregnable fortress.

Inside City Hall, the mayor and Police Commissioner Farooq Ibrahim had been assembled, along with a corps of advisors.

Skerrit had been appointed to head the Emergency Command Center by the mayor who had asked for the expert on EMP to be found and brought to him right away.

When he'd been informed that the country's foremost authority on the phenomenon had been fired just that morning, the mayor had exploded into one of his famous tantrums.

"Find me that guy," the Kaiser had shouted, "or so help me, heads will roll!" And find Skerrit they had.

Because limited radio communications existed, the ECC was in contact with the Department of Energy's Emergency Electric Power Administration (EEPA), mandated to manage electric power allocation and restoration during times of national energy emergencies under its Department of Homeland Security charter.

EEPA had informed Skerrit that they were working on the problem but that Washington had been hard hit too. It would be at least another forty-eight hours before New York City could expect large-scale federal aid.

"You heard it," Mayor DeKeyser had said, "we're on our fucking own."

Skerrit spread one of the crisis center's maps of the five boros in front of him on one of the several trestle tables that had been set up as makeshift desks. On the map were marked the sites of the power transformer stations throughout the city. In each of the five boros, the transformer stations were indicated by red circles and matching numerical geolocation coordinates.

On those sites that updated news reports indicated had been destroyed by explosions or by fire, Skerrit had placed round yellow garage-sale stick-on dots. He used red stickers to mark those facilities that were still functional or otherwise intact.

Roughly half of the stickers on the map were red, while the other half were yellow.

The first order of business, Skerrit knew, would be to salvage those sections of the power grid that were still intact. Although the EMP death pulse had happened too quickly for most to survive, some sections had been shunted off-line in time to preserve their critical infrastructure by quick-thinking personnel.

The digitally enabled systems that controlled the grid were now completely knocked out, but some of the older electromechanical systems were still in place at several locations throughout the five boros, primarily as emergency backups.

These older, backup systems might allow teams to reactivate part of the citywide energy grid, but there would be considerable grunt work involved in manually re-routing cables and operating complicated switching systems that had been out of use for well over a decade. It could be accomplished, though, Skerrit reasoned.

From here on in, the NYPD would have their work cut out for them as well. So would the National Guard and other rescue units as the few operational vehicles and salvageable emergency equipment was gathered together and deployed out on the streets of the city. As many units located in metro New York as possible would need to be mobilized, because hard-hit emergency services from surrounding exurbs had found themselves with their hands full maintaining order and were unavailable at present. The city was on its own, and the next few hours would be critical.

Whatever ultimately happened, Skerrit knew that if they were able to restore even some of the power to the sprawling city by next morning, they could forestall a major catastrophe. If they were unable to, however, then it was a sure bet that New York, isolated by a deadly surge of ionized electrons the way New Orleans had been by a tidal wave years before, its streets already an urban battleground, would soon become the earthly capital of hell.

DAVID ALEXANDER

FORTY-SIX

Suckdog, Staten Island. While his Aryan Death Squad kept their riot guns trained on the cowering crowd, Suckdog went down the line of shoppers, his boot soles cracking like pistol shots on the Mall's tiled floor.

Behind him walked his skinhead lieutenant, named Thrasher, holding a big plastic garbage can that had been taken from the hardware department of the Mall's Alexander's outlet.

The Mall was now Suckdog's concentration camp, a little Auschwitz to call his own.

"*Achtung!*" Suckdog shouted, his voice echoing off the tomblike walls of the shopping center. "As of now you are all prisoners of the Aryan Youth Resistance Movement. You will obey the orders we give you. The penalty for disobedience is death.

"Throw all your valuables into the can. I mean everything. Watches, jewelry, wallets, everything you've got on you." Suckdog added, "anybody who doesn't turn everything over gets a bullet in the head. Like this -- "

Turning swiftly, Suckdog put the muzzle of the shotgun he carried against the head of the first of a line of a dozen mannequins that stormtrooper Pooch and some other skins had brought from a store display window.

337

THE BLACKOUT HEIST

As the first head was blown to smithereens, Suckdog went down the line until the gun ran dry and the dummies lay on the cold floor, minus their plaster noggins.

Some shoppers screamed, while many others fainted.

"In case any of you have trouble getting the message," Suckdog barked at the crowd of prisoners, "the next demonstration will be on live targets."

One woman had trouble handing over her jewelry. "Yo, Suckdog," one of the skins called. "Check this out." He held up the golden chain he'd ripped from the woman's neck. "A yid," he said, showing gaps in his teeth, "a fuckin' yid."

Suckdog noticed that the woman's eyes were unfocused. "She can't see," he said. "You blind, is that it?" he asked.

Courtney Lassiter didn't want to whimper in front of the scumbags. She said nothing. Suckdog told one of his Nazi skins to drag her into a back room somewhere and rape her.

Courtney shouted for help as she was dragged off by three burly stormtrooper skins, begging and pleading every inch of the way. None of the hostage shoppers moved from their line, though. Suckdog smiled as he nodded.

"That's good," he said to the group of cowering captives, "that's very, very good. That's they way they did it back in the good old days of Hitler. We are the strong. You are the weak. That is the eternal order of the world."

DAVID ALEXANDER

Suckdog looked around him, disgusted and elated at the same time. The maggots were showing him what he longed to see for so very, very long. They were showing him fear, raw, naked fear. It was in their eyes, in the way they stood, in their whining and begging to be let go. It rose from them all like a smell that hung heavy in the air.

A sweet smell.

Suckdog realized that for the first time in memory he was in complete control.

All his life, he had been under somebody else's thumb. First his fucking Polack old man who beat him and his mother. Then the reform school. After that, a succession of employers at shit jobs who pushed him around and ran his ass ragged. Other people controlled what he said, thought, ate and even dreamed. Sick and tired of not having any shred of control over his life, he had joined the Nazi party to get even.

Now, Suckdog knew he had been right all along. This is what he had been born for. To give the orders and let others jump to them or suffer the consequences.

The emotions that now whirled like amphetamine dervishes through his brain were exactly the feelings he had known all along he would experience when the time came. This experience was worth whatever might happen to him hereafter. Even death. To be in total control, even for a day, even for an hour, was worth any price.

THE BLACKOUT HEIST

"Listen up," he told the cowering crowd of Mall hostages. "Now I want you to take off all your clothes."

At gunpoint, the members of the crowd began to strip. Suckdog watched with unconcealed glee.

He had the women separate from the men and stand where his Nazi skins could inspect them. Most of them were dogs, but two of the teenyboppers looked pretty fuckable.

Suckdog would have his fun with them later. Man, this shit turned out to be so fucking easy. For now, he had more important matters to attend to, though. Fun would have to wait till later.

***

The Mall's shops yielded a bountiful harvest to Suckdog and his crew. A harvest of pain. Through the smashed-in windows of the stores that lined the shopping center's walkway levels they came out carrying artifacts of every description.

The corridors of the Mall echoed with rap music from ipod players and boom boxes confiscated from a Sonic City Record and Tape Metropolis, many of which still functioned due to the quirk of EMP which left some electronics unaffected while others were rendered completely useless.

There was plenty of food from Los Alamos, the Mall's Mexican restaurant, too. Suckdog's skins pigged out on enchiladas, tortillas and tacos, and washed it all down with five different blends of cappuccino and latte from the Mall's Starbucks and Cosi.

DAVID ALEXANDER

Motorcycle chains and padlocks taken from the hardware department of Alexander's provided the skins with the makings of great entertainment.

It wasn't hard to pick out the kikes in the group of captives from the names on driver's licenses and from the ostentatious *Jew*-elry they wore on their necks. The niggers and the spicks were even easier to spot, of course.

The two kikes and one nigger they had hung from the balcony of the Mall's upper level by a couple of lengths of motorcycle chain tried to hang tough at first. One of the kikes was a big guy who managed to haul off at one of the skins, breaking his nose.

The kike had paid for that outrage, just like all of the little weaklings that Suckdog held hostage at the Mall would eventually pay. While three skins had pinned his arms and legs, their wounded Aryan brother had worked the kike over with the stock of his Ithaca riot gun until his face was a bleeding red mess.

Now the kikes and the nigger were dangling upside-down by their ankles. It was easy to take pot shots at them. The rifles were easy to fire. The noise of shooting went well with the incessant thudding of the boom boxes blasting the place out with the white noise of urban hip-hop.

***

Parrish hunkered in the darkness of a section of aluminum ventilation ducting directly behind a square wire-grid register panel set in a wall. He was sickened by what he saw as he looked around him.

THE BLACKOUT HEIST

How would he escape? What would he find? None of the radios from the Radio Wave franchise outlet he had broken into, even emergency band units he'd found, were functional. And forget the phones from the Horizen phone store he'd also tried. They were all totally trashed.

Fortunately, he was able to find the old vacuum tube model radio set gathering dust in a back room of the store. It was either a novelty item or a piece for somebody's trophy case, but who cared. The set worked perfectly with the addition of a couple of batteries.

And from its speaker grille had come the truth about what had happened. Coming through the ether faintly, the news report had originated from a station in Vancouver, Canada. The federal authorities weren't sure yet, Parrish heard, but they thought that it was some kind of Russian nuke that had exploded in space. Apparently, only part of the Eastern seaboard had been effected.

Parrish heaved a sigh of relief. At least it wasn't all-out nuclear terrorism. It was some kind of freak accident instead. But even so, Parrish knew he might not survive until things got back to normal.

He knew that he was trapped in the darkened Mall without easy access to food, and with no electricity or transportation available. Furthermore, the Mall was in the hands of the gang of skinhead crazies which had already beaten up on several shoppers and would eventually start killing innocent people sooner or later.

Parrish decided to lay low until he could see which way the wind blew. If there was a chance to escape, he'd take it.

Odds were that the National Guard or other EMS units would be called in soon.

That was maybe a good twelve hours away, though, according to what he was able to estimate from the news reports he'd heard. And, the way things were going, John Henry Parrish figured that twelve hours might well wind up being the rest of his life.

THE BLACKOUT HEIST

Chapter Five
Sublevels

FORTY-SEVEN

Museum Row, The West Side. Bucky Genesis was finally a man with a satisfied mind. All alone in the Guggenheim Museum, two aerosol cans of Red Devil spray paint in each deep pocket of his tattered overcoat. Who could ask for anything more?

Everywhere, the works of the so-called masters hung on the walls, mocking him as they had every time that Bucky had gone to the museum and beheld them on its walls.

Picasso, Klee, Dali, Kandinsky, Van Gogh, and the rest of the modern masters. And the old masters too, represented by the museum's collection of Rembrandts, Vermeers and Goyas.

What right did they have to the fame their work enjoyed, those fucking, shitty frauds who had managed to masquerade as great creative geniuses?

The giant graffiti throw-ups that Bucky had painted on the walls of buildings and the sides of subway cars from the Bronx to Staten Island were works of true genius, not the degenerate garbage that these self-adulating phonies had churned out as thralls to crass commercialism.

THE BLACKOUT HEIST

Yet while their bogus artistic creations received the accolades, Bucky's were reviled as urban eyesores.

Because the art world had turned its back on him, Bucky had been forced to make his living as a "can man," scavenging for thrown-away bottles in public trash receptacles. But now, Bucky would finally have his revenge.

And revenge would be sweet. He had brought enough spray paint with him to create the ultimate graffiti art masterpiece, a mural to rival anything on the Sistine Chapel ceiling. The so-called "art" of the famous phonies that surrounded him would make the perfect canvas for Bucky's truly masterful creations.

Fate had delivered his enemies into Bucky's hands, and now they would pay the ultimate price. He was a Luddite in the midst of the debris of the postindustrial revolution, a latter-day Iconoclast, eager to smash the hated graven images in the heathen temple of corporate piffle and crass commercial kitsch.

Taking the first aerosol can of red spray paint from his pocket and shaking it almost reverently, Bucky went to work. Hours later, the long, curving wall of the Guggenheim's second floor gallery was covered with immense whorls and cresting swirls of dripping primary colors, while empty spray cans littered the floor at Bucky's sneakered feet.

Exhausted at last from his Herculean artistic labors, Bucky flung his final empty aerosol can to the museum's floor. He had emptied himself as completely as the spray cans that now rolled and clinked around him, poured out his creative fire in a burst of magnificent splendor. The graffiti art that he had created today would remain as an eternal monument to Bucky's unyielding genius and adamantine will.

In a transport of ecstasy, Bucky stepped back to admire his work. Unfortunately, he did not see the empty aerosol can directly behind him.

As he stepped on it, the can rolled backwards, catapulting Bucky over the guard rail of the Guggenheim's second floor gallery and sending him hurtling to his death on the main floor below where, as fate would have it, Bucky's corpse was impaled on a sharp protruding corner of a freeform stainless steel sculpture.

The name of the sculpture happened to be "Genesis."

***

St. Patrick's Cathedral was aglow with the brilliance of many candles. By the hundreds, they gave off enough light to illuminate the many who had gathered inside the church, taking refuge from the chaos surging all around them.

The sound of prayers echoed off the walls as a late mass was being conducted. Outside the cathedral's doors, hundreds more frightened people lined Fifth Avenue for many blocks in either direction.

On Lexington Avenue a few blocks uptown at Temple Emmanuel, a similar scene was being played out. Candles glowed. The sound of prayers ascended to the heavens.

THE BLACKOUT HEIST

Those few police patrolmen and national guard units that could be spared formed a cordon around these houses of worship, as they did around City Hall and One Police Plaza.

Despite the absence of functional radios and transportation, the message had spread by word of mouth: there was safety at those places. Assemble there. Wait out the night.

And scores of thousands of New Yorkers had heeded the call. Some had come together spontaneously, as the crowd that had gathered at Times Square.

While human wolf packs and armed gangs scavenged the crowd's periphery, the numbers of those gathered there gave each solitary individual in the immense assemblage a communal sense of security and hope.

There was no LED-diode ball descending luminously as on New Year's Eve, but thousands of candles and cigarette lighters were held aloft against the encircling darkness.

For many New Yorkers, it was the first time in recent memory that they could be near one another and draw comfort, instead of hostility, from one anothers' presence.

***

Lindsay Weems pushed her husband Morton over the balcony of their thirty-sixth story duplex apartment in Battery Park City. Betty had been planning to poison her husband when the lights had suddenly gone out and changed everything.

She'd decided to turn the situation to her advantage when Morton had gone out onto the balcony to study the situation from their vantage point high above the darkened metropolis.

It was easy to get him to stand against the luxury condo's balcony where he could easily be sent tumbling downward to his death.

Lindsay had suggested a blowjob. On her knees, she sucked Morton's dick until he was about to erupt a sticky load into her mouth. When she felt him beginning to ejaculate, Lindsay gave Morton a quick, hard shove that sent him doing and end-over-end onto the pavement below.

With any luck she could convince the authorities that he had fallen in the dark and killed himself. Lindsay had no doubts that she'd be able to pull it off. She knew she was a very persuasive liar when she needed to be. That and her skills at sucking cock gave her all the confidence in the world.

***

The Divine Assembly Building was aglow. Around its perimeter, the dark streets were deserted. Most of the residents of the gentrified neighborhood were cowering behind locked doors.

"I say unto you my children," proclaimed Reverend Nehemiah Lux to his flock, "that the Lord has declared this to be the hour of reckoning. Go ye forth, do battle in his holy name!"

"Amen, amen!" came the resounding assent from the Reverend's assembled minions. "Amen unto the Lord!"

"Go my children. The Lord awaits you."

And Reverend's spiritual children went forth into the darkness. They would do good work in the streets. The first group of the Reverend's followers was armed with sophisticated weaponry. They offered food and clothing. But there was a price.

In return for the food and the clothing and the shelter which the Divine Assembly offered the residents of the neighborhood surrounding the cult's headquarters, the residents would be required to sign release forms.

The releases deeded their homes and worldly possessions to the reverend and his Divine Assembly. It allowed the holy man and his flock to expand outward into the neighborhoods with impunity.

The Reverend Nehemiah laughed out loud. The Lord had indeed smiled on the faithful this day. But then again, the reverend had never doubted in his heavenly master's plans.

The Lord had come to him in a dream and, along with a revelational prediction of the Endtimes, had given him the knowledge of what mission he was to fulfill when Judgment Day arrived. Now that it had come -- amen, for he was ready.

The Divine Assembly's shaven-headed acolytes went through the streets, pounding drums and chanting the holy songs that their holy shepherd, the reverend, had taught them. They carried food with them and water. They gave out the food and the water to all souls they passed in the blacked out streets. The food and water were laced with powerful hallucinogens.

The residents of the Queens neighborhood went crazy as they lapsed into convulsions, falling to the concrete pavements, cracking skulls and breaking bones. The shaven headed acolytes moved on, singing and chanting as they smiled beatific smiles into the shining face of the moon and the twinkling lights of the stars.

In the basement of the Divine Assembly Building, the reverend had constructed a gas chamber apparatus. The gas chamber used automobile exhaust funneled from the building's underground garage to pump carbon monoxide into airtight chambers.

The exhaust was generated by a large truck with a dirty carburetor. Now the first of those to be gassed were placed in the chamber. The Reverend's followers told them that they would be given lodging momentarily. Then the doors were shut. Tightly.

Once the vehicle engines were turned on, those condemned to die in the gas chambers began to fight ferociously for life. But it was all to no avail. They would expire in only a few minutes. After that, the Divine Assembly's faithful would cart away the bodies which would be burned in large crematorium ovens. Thus the property rights that they had sought to deny the Reverend Nehemiah's flock would be granted him by the one who watches from on high.

From dusk until dawn, the chimney of the Divine Assembly Building produced a great deal of fire and smoke beneath the leaden-hued firmaments that had rained down a death pulse to punish the wicked. Or so the reverend told his flock.

***

A great swarm of homeless persons had developed from an aimless march of the destitute that had spread outward from the Upper East Side drop-in center.

The swarm was many hundreds strong. It was big and it was mean. Like locusts, the identities of solitary individuals changed when thronging together. Years of pent-up anger at the haves of the world was now given free reign with nothing to stop it from assuming any form it wished.

Real estate developer Roland Stone had decided to sit tight in his palatial office on the penthouse level of Stone Mountain, the enormous plate glass skyscraper that overlooked Manhattan's First Avenue. Stone had everything that he needed to wait out the catastrophe.

The building was equipped with gasoline-powered generators for the production of emergency electricity. Stone's security force was tantamount to a small, well-trained army, the Praetorian Guard of a latter-day Caesar.

There was plenty of food available, and in enough quantity to last a full week at the least. Stone felt more secure in his well-defended tower bastion than anywhere else on earth. Stone knew that no harm would come to him within the mighty ramparts of his private castle.

The swarm of the homeless had other ideas, however. They overwhelmed Stone's Praetorian Guard stationed in the lobby of Stone Mountain and climbed the stairs to Stone's inner sanctum on the penthouse level of the sky-challenging glass tower.

There they found Roland Stone standing atop his desk, arms outstretched in a Tae Kwon Do karate stance, daring the mob to take him on with a snarl on his perpetually snarling lips.

Not all the king's horses or all the king's men or even the power of Tae Kwon Do, however, could keep Stone from being pitched out his office window to begin a seventy-story plunge to eternity. And after that great fall, nobody would ever put Roland Stone back together again.

THE BLACKOUT HEIST

FORTY-EIGHT

Inskeep, underneath Manhattan. Inskeep had set them collecting.

The track bed of the subway tunnel had yielded up dowel-shaped lengths of scrap lumber, snippets of newsprint, oil-stained rags, discarded candy wrappers and other oddments of debris.

The passengers had supplied strips of fabric torn from their clothing and bits of thread, string and elastic material. Strips of cloth and paper had been wrapped, layer upon layer, on the ends of the wooden dowels, until it formed large knots.

String-like materials had been used to securely bind the fabric wrappings onto the sticks mummy-fashion. Fluid from cigarette lighters, whiskey from pocket flasks -- anything capable of being poured, and flammable enough to burn when lit, next soaked the bulbous ends of the sticks.

Matches had ignited the makeshift torches, and by their wan, flickering and malodorous light, Willie Inskeep and his group of passengers began making their way along the tunnel floor towards the Manhattan end of the long subway tunnel.

La Dollicia Shavers, the IRT local's conductor, and her group of subway riders were already out of earshot as they made their way in the opposite direction, toward the tunnel's Brooklyn side.

Before setting out, Inskeep had taken a fast head count. His group numbered thirty-six people in all.

There were five torch bearers in the group, not including himself, and the torches gave out enough illumination for them to be able to see approximately six yards in either direction.

Inskeep had also assigned Korean passenger, Jing Duk Soo, to watch the passengers' rear. Although Inskeep didn't think there would be any danger of attack presenting itself, it paid not to take unnecessary chances.

A lot of homeless people used the subway tunnels as places to squat, after all.

There were hundreds of thousands of them all over the city and most of them -- despite the media's protestations to the contrary -- were mental cases. Often dangerous ones.

Inskeep heard the rapid cadence of footsteps crunching on the track bed beside him.

"Smoke, my man?" The construction worker shook his half-empty pack of Luckies so a few were exposed above the torn-off top of the pack.

Inskeep took one of the cigarettes and placed it between his lips, accepting a light from the passenger. By doing so, he was breaking a vow made to his wife two years before that he would quit smoking for good.

But Inskeep's nerves were unraveling, coming apart strand by strand like fur in a cat's claws. He needed the nicotine. She would forgive him for weakening now, Inskeep knew, even if he could not forgive himself.

"My name's Buddy Coyne," said the man with the pack of Luckies. "What do you think's been going down here?"

Inskeep shrugged as he dragged tentatively on the cigarette, tasting the forgotten though familiar bite of the burning tobacco against the walls of his lungs. "Damned if I know," he returned. "Some kind of almighty fuck-up, that's for sure."

"Don't think its World War Three or nothing like that?" he asked with a self-conscious laugh that sounded forced. "I mean you got to admit this is some weird shit that is happening here."

"Not war, man," Inskeep returned, shaking his head as he took a drag of the first cigarette he'd smoked in two years. "We would have heard the blasts by now. I worked the Kumpulan Mujahideen tunnels in Surinam. They burrowed thirty, forty, sometimes sixty feet down and when the artillery started shelling, you could feel the whole jungle shake around you."

Inskeep drew on the cigarette again, "No," he concluded, "there ain't no war going down. Not yet, anyway. They nuke the Apple, we'd have known it by now, believe me."

A woman near the end of the line called out suddenly. "Excuse me," she asked, "but don't you hear anything funny? I mean like a rumbling noise?"

Suddenly the group stopped. Inskeep listened in the silence that was broken only by the popping and crackling of the makeshift torches.

Faintly, as if he were listening to the sound of a waterfall in the distance, Inskeep thought he *did* hear something.

It was indeed a rumbling sound. Moments went by and the rumbling seemed to grow louder.

Inskeep was perplexed. Then suddenly he had a chilling thought. *The river. It was above them!* The rumbling sound might be the sound of running water.

"What could it be?" asked someone else.

Inskeep was suddenly afraid. His thoughts flashed to the giant pumps that the Metropolitan Transit Authority used to prevent the East River from entering the hundred-plus year-old tunnel system that ran beneath it from East to West.

The thought had not occurred to him before, but now he realized that if all the power had been shut off, then the pumps and the giant blower system that ventilated the tubes would also be knocked out.

The roaring sound from above them had grown louder in the few minutes since they'd stopped to listen. Suddenly one of the torches hissed angrily as its flame sputtered.

"I felt water fall on me!" someone cried out in panic. "Oh God -- *there's water dripping from the ceiling!*"

Others echoed this cry. Inskeep could feel the water dripping down on his head. He looked up and could see the cracks in the flat concrete roof of the tunnel by the guttering light of the torch he carried in his hand.

THE BLACKOUT HEIST

"What's happening?" passengers cried out in panic. "Why is there water dripping on us?"

Inskeep looked around him. Up the line a little, there was a metal door set into the brick wall.

He had noticed the dull gleam of metal a few minutes before, figuring it for a door, but knowing that a door didn't necessarily mean an exit. Inskeep sensed that the door most likely led to a storage room rather than or a way out of the tunnel.

"Let's go," he said, knowing there was no choice now, "just up ahead." The passengers began to run helter-skelter toward the door.

Reaching the door, Inskeep used his MTA motorman's utility key in his belt to unlock it.

Then -- *E X P L O S I O N !*

Tons of concrete flew from the tunnel wall as the wall finally gave under thousands of cubic tons of water pressure from above.

Foaming, bubbling, howling like a rampaging beast, the river above poured through the rapidly widening breach like an invading army bent on slaughtering every living thing in its path.

By the light of the torches they carried, Inskeep and the passengers could see a torrent of river water spewing through an enormous rupture in the tunnel wall that had just gaped open under the tremendous pressure of the river above them.

The water spilled and splashed along the track bed. Scant moments later it had already risen to ankle-height.

"Quick!" shouted Inskeep as he hustled the last of the passengers into the storage room and shut the door behind him. Outside he could hear the

terrible rushing noise as the tunnel became submerged.

Then there was something else.

Pounding.

From the other side of the door.

"Mommy!" a child's voice shrieked to Inskeep's side. *"Where's my mommy?"*

***

Someone in La Dollicia Shavers' group cried out. Turning, the twenty passengers in her group saw the wall of water screaming toward them in the darkness of the tunnel.

Before they could react, before their stunned brains could even form coherent thoughts, their shrieks of horror were cut short as the tunnel roof collapsed and the tunnel was almost instantly submerged.

La Dollicia held her breath as long as she could, her horror-widened eyes watching the human bodies hurled with pulverizing force against the walls of the tunnel, shattering bones and tearing flesh.

Limbs thrashed in a mad frenzy before going limp and still in death, yet no sound was made. Only the rushing of the cataract from hell that claimed their lives.

And then her aching lungs could no longer hold out against the overwhelming urge to draw breath.

Letting finally go, La Dollicia allowed the East River to enter her mouth and her lungs like the swollen organ of a cold, mad lover bent on penetration.

THE BLACKOUT HEIST

Again she drew in the icy stream of liquid and the world began to fade to darkness.

La Dollicia joined the rest of the corpses that floated like alien underwater plants in the now completely flooded IRT tunnel.

DAVID ALEXANDER

<u>FORTY-NINE</u>

Skerrit, Uptown Manhattan. The ancient doors creaked open. A musty smell of decaying masonry filled the dank air. Waste water puddled the concrete deck and peeling plaster walls.

Rick Skerrit's flashlight glanced jerkily across the cobweb covered banks of electromechanical switching machinery, momentarily pinning a large brown rat in its beam before it scurried into a hole, squealing as it ran.

The Ninety-fifth Street transformer station had not been entered for almost twenty years. It smelled, felt and looked it.

Now the "outmoded" equipment would enable the power utility to get back online.

Not even Skerrit had realized the extent to which the city relied on its electrical power and communications. He had not dreamed of the savagery waiting to be unleashed the moment that the light of civilization was extinguished.

But this is precisely what had happened. "Mere anarchy," as Yeats had put it long before, had been "loosed upon the world."

All across the City of New York, gangs of street people had erupted into spontaneous orgies of violence, looting and arson. On reflection, that might

361

have been expected. New York was a pressure cooker even on good days. Increase the pressure, even by a little, and you inevitably produce an explosion.

What had not been as predictable, perhaps, had been the chaos that prevailed as ordinary citizens of the city found themselves suddenly confronted by the unthinkable. Without warning, the checks and balances of society that had underpinned their lives had fallen by the wayside. The result was madness.

In bedroom communities across the city, supermarkets, corner groceries, dollar stores and candy stores had been the scenes of savage food riots. Men and women who only hours before would never have considered criminal actions were now fighting like junkyard dogs over canned soups and dried noodles.

Reestablishing even a small part of the power network was vital, Skerrit knew. But how would he be able to do so in time for it to even matter?

Inspecting the equipment that had lain rusting with neglect and disuse for over two decades, Skerrit realized that it would take a miracle for it to be made operational again, let alone within the next twenty-four hours.

Yet a miracle was precisely what was necessary now. Nothing less would suffice. Skerrit knew he had to make this miracle happen.

They had thrown him out for daring to sound the clarion of warning, for having the integrity to speak the truth that they had not wanted to confront, despite the danger it posed to his own career.

Secure in their personal fiefdoms, neither the MetroCon energy utility's chief executive officers nor the movers and shakers in city government had wanted to hear that the black wolf of power failure was scratching at the door.

They had installed their multi-billion dollar digital switching system and that high-tech network had failed, precisely as his study had predicted. Now it was Skerrit's turn. He would get the power grid back online, one way or another. And then they would all pay for their overarching arrogance.

"Rig me up a temporary splice on section oh-seven-hundred," Skerrit told his crew chief, Billy Chu. Chu studied the schematic of the transformer station spread out atop a packing crate in the beam of his flash and frowned, shaking his head.

"That stretch of cable runs right under Broadway," Chu told Skerrit. "That's no man's land out there. People are getting shot and stabbed in those streets."

"That's what the cops and the National Guard are for, Bill," Skerrit told the crew boss, an edge of anger in his voice. "Get it in gear, no fuck-ups, no excuses. Do it!"

The crew boss shrugged and walked out.

Skerrit remained alone in the darkened room, for the first time in a long time feeling like he mattered.

***

A gang of squatters confronted the detachment of troops. The National Guard sergeant ordered them to disperse immediately. When they failed to obey, he had his men fire a warning salvo over their heads.

The troops and the cops were met with a fusillade of stones, bottles and other garbage hurled at them by the street people as they advanced on the armed emergency personnel.

Their next action was to fire into the crowd. Some of the squatters fell immediately. The rest broke ranks and fled, hunkering on the sidelines in the darkness like whipped dogs.

"Okay," said Billy Chu after the street people had dispersed, "set up the kliegs."

The truck-mounted mobile gasoline generators were set up and banks of powerful klieg lights were placed in position.

In moments, the gas-operated generators chugged to life and the powerful halogen-arc beams described a circle of blinding illumination across the operations site.

Spreading the schematic of the power grid out on the hood of one of the generator trucks, the crew boss indicated to the members of the emergency power restoration team the precise coordinates of their repair zones.

They scattered to the sites and began to work. Chu lit up a cigarette and watched the meat wagon collect the bodies.

***

The mayor felt like a general commanding troops on the battlefield as he sat in one of the armored personnel carrier that the NYPD used for special tactical operations.

The military armored Apache APC had been purchased from the same company that manufactured tanks for the US Army. Guarded by a contingent of rifle-toting cops, the mayor used a field telephone system in the mobile command center to keep abreast of breaking events as they unfolded.

"Call's coming in now, Chuck," the mayor's aide said to him. When the mayor picked up the handset, he was on the phone to the governor.

Governor Renso Franco told him that the National Guard detachments that were expected from Bridgeport, Connecticut, would be on their way soon, but couldn't get there for another couple of hours.

"There's pure chaos here," the mayor told the governor. "We don't have enough manpower even during normal conditions for God's sake," he went on. "I don't even know if we have minutes, let alone hours."

"I know Chuckie," replied the governor, "but we have our hands full up here too. Hell, the entire country's been hit by this. Do you have any idea of how this stuff has screwed up the computer networks the banks use? And the military, they're even more fucked up. They tell me it could be years before it's all straightened out again, if ever."

"I don't give a flying fuck about the banks and even less about the military," the mayor responded, feeling his pulse rise and making a mental note to do the calming breathing exercises his doctor recommended he perform when he was under stress.

THE BLACKOUT HEIST

He held out his hand in a "V" for Valium which his aide immediately brought him. He didn't want to give himself another stroke. Especially not now and definitely not here.

"You gotta get me those God damn troops, Renso," the mayor said, "as soon as you damn well can or there won't be anything left of this city come tomorrow afternoon but a pile of smoking garbage."

"Got another call coming in, Chuckie," the Governor said, "it's the White House. Talk to you as soon as I know more."

The mayor heard the click in the earpiece as the connection was severed.

"Fuck you too, Renso," he said under his breath as he racked the receiver.

The five milligram Valium had a bitter taste on his tongue as it slid down his throat and he stared gloomily out the small window of the armored personnel carrier at the MetroCon maintenance crew working in the circle of intense light.

Right now the mayor wished he hadn't wanted that fourth term so damned badly.

FIFTY

Applebaum, The South Bronx. Marty Applebaum pulled two Stingball stun grenades from the military webbing that crisscrossed his camos and prepared to hurl the flash-bang grenades at a group of looters who were running wild in Building One of the Bronx Zoo.

He hunkered on the fire escape watching them go through an elderly couple's apartment, carrying out the TV, stereo and whatever cash and jewelry they could grab.

The flash-bangs went off with a series of loud concussions and strobing flashes that temporarily, yet completely, disoriented the looters and froze them right in their tracks.

Applebaum was not about to make the same mistake he'd made at the kiosk in Building Six. This time it was take no prisoners. Show no mercy.

Holding the Heckler Koch MP5 submachinegun at his hip, Applebaum sprayed the interior of the apartment with automatic fire. As the zigzag of bullets hit their marks, the looters did crazy puppet-like dances as the walls were splattered with their blood. Mad Marty turned and ran down the fire escape, slinging the H&K across his back by its carrying strap.

***

Reloads, he needed reloads.

THE BLACKOUT HEIST

Applebaum had reached his twentieth-floor apartment in Building Six via the fire escape that ran outside it. Squatting on the steel fire escape platform, he tapped on the window, expecting Yolanda to let him in.

Through his night-vision goggles, Crazy Marty saw that the interior of his apartment was a total fucking mess. Applebaum smashed the window and swung in, weapon at the ready, seeking target acquisition.

"Yolanda?" he called out, but there was no answer.

Okay, room by room. The H&K's buttstock was cradled in the crook of Marty's arm as he leaned against the side of the door leading to the kitchenette and bedroom beyond the central living room area.

Taking a deep breath, Applebaum launched himself from hiding, tucking to the right as he moved into the small foyer linking the apartment's three rooms on a half crouch. *Where are you, mothers?*

The barrel of the MP5 subgun swept back and forth, three short arcs to take in each corner of the kitchenette.

Clean. The room was clean. *Go to the next room, the bedroom.* Applebaum felt the sweat drip down into his face.

He ignored the sting of the salt water and focused his attention toward the shadows of the bedroom. Again, he repeated the procedure he'd conducted in going from the living room into the foyer.

The bedroom was also clean. The apartment was empty. Applebaum slung the H&K from his shoulder and sat on the bed.

He could feel the organs pumping madly inside him beneath the tautly stretched envelope of his flesh. Heart, lungs, even brain overstimulated by adrenaline, by fear, and yes, also by raw-edged excitement.

They had not found Marty's crisis room. The bookcase was intact. Behind it, the concealed, padlocked door to his Iron Maiden was intact.

By the light of his flash, Applebaum replaced empty ammo magazines, replenished stocks of grenades, armed himself with the firepower his imagination and instincts told him he would now require.

Applebaum thought of it as his Big Boy, his pride and joy. The M60E4 Squad Auto Weapon was the centerpiece of his gun collection. It had cost him thousands, but at the moment he considered the money more than well spent.

Applebaum slung ammunition belts containing 7.62-millimeter NATO-caliber rounds across his chest and snapped a box magazine containing one hundred rounds onto the underbelly of his Big Boy, threading the belt into the SAW's receiver.

Now he was ready. *Show the fuckers, show them they can't mess with you and live.* Ready to go where he had been wanting to go for a long time now. *Lock and load, take no prisoners. Waste all the fuckers.*

THE BLACKOUT HEIST

They had sent him a message. The street scum had sent him a message. *Come and get it,* said the message, *come and get it if you dare....*

The message, Marty knew, had been sent by Cinco Muertes. The gangbanger was undoubtedly holding Yolanda prisoner. And there was also no doubt as to where he was keeping her captive.

The crack house on One Hundred Thirty-second Street, the fortress manned by a small army of hard case ghetto warriors.

The place the neighborhood referred to with completely warranted fear as "The Mosque."

FIFTY-ONE

Battery Towers, Wall Street District. Flames engulfed the West Tower of the Battery Park Commerce Towers. The West Tower had a ragged gash substituted for the place where most of its top floor section had once been.

Many of the survivors of Ellis Amoroso's office story were trapped inside the elevator that was stalled in a shaftway three floors below.

The cable from which it was suspended creaked as the strands of tautly stretched filament steel snapped strand by strand, unraveling moment by moment. Amoroso and the rest of those on the floor with him could hear the screams for help from the trapped passengers.

In a very short space of time, the car would plunge more than sixty stories straight down to kill them all at the end of the drop.

Ordinarily, circuit breakers would have ejected steel prongs to break the elevator's fall, but the EMP death pulse had neutralized the elevator safety mechanisms. The elevator now hung by a slender thread, and it was a long way down.

THE BLACKOUT HEIST

Amoroso had succeeded in climbing down the shaftway and entering through the emergency trap door on the top of the immobilized elevator car.

Once the passengers had been hauled to safety by means of a fire hose tossed down from the floor above where several men from Amoroso's office were waiting pull it up, Amoroso readied himself to grab the end of the hose.

It was at that moment that the last strand of the cable chose to snap. The elevator car beneath Amoroso fell immediately away from him, crashing, moments later, many stories below with a thunderous report. The fire hose was jerked from the hands of those who held it, vanishing down the windy shaftway.

Amoroso fell several stories before he even had a chance to scream. He groped blindly as he tumbled to his death at the concrete bottom of the shaft.

By some miracle, Amoroso managed to grasp hold of a severed power cable that dangled uselessly from the side of the wall. It broke his fall and saved his life.

However, Amoroso's skull struck the concrete, opening a huge gash along one side and knocking him unconscious. Bleeding, he lay for long minutes before finally regaining his wits.

***

"What will we do?" cried Mary Koslowski. She and the rest of the survivors of Amoroso's office floor huddled like trapped rats a few stories above the shaft.

"He's gone. I heard him scream as he fell," someone answered her.

"We have no choice," put in Daniel Furness, who was the assistant office manager. "I vote we try to make it out of here without Amoroso."

"No, he's alive I tell you," Mary shouted, "I know it."

In the end, a small group of twelve persons waited for Amoroso's return. The remainder of the group went their own separate way.

The group of twelve who stayed were the only ones who survived. Those who left were destroyed in a sudden flash fire caused by an exploding propane tank in a cafeteria kitchen a few stories below. Their bodies, now aflame, were catapulted through the plate glass windows of the tower like living bonfires.

Those still inside the building thrashed around before death claimed them, human torches with their centers burning black, wreathed by crackling tongues of fire.

**

Flames licked the walls of the elevator shaft when Amoroso regained consciousness. Noxious black smoke poured from the burning floors below, almost choking him.

Unknown to Amoroso, a fire started by the tremendous power surge had detonated a cache of highly combustible propane tanks stored in a cafeteria a few floors down.

This explosion rocked the building's upper stories as he climbed upward through the steel framework of the elevator shaft, finally reaching a narrow ledge.

Amoroso staggered to his feet and started to pry open the elevator doors in front of him. The doors remained stubbornly closed, though, blocked by something in the corridor beyond.

He had no choice but to climb to the next floor up, although the smoke was so thick that he couldn't even see in the zero visibility and made it hard to breathe.

Climbing up the elevator shaftway by finding handholds in its steel superstructure, Amoroso barely managed to gain the floor above him. This time the elevator doors opened easily. He crawled on hands and knees into the corridor beyond. Calling out, he discovered that the hall was deserted.

Amoroso knew that the fire would reach his level in minutes. He had to find a way to get the people trapped ten floors above him out of harm's way. He looked around him.

The first office yielded nothing, so Amoroso ran back into the corridor. Holding his shirt in front of his mouth against the choking smoke that was already billowing from the ventilation ducts, Amoroso managed to locate another office.

Inside this office, Amoroso discovered materials that he believed might provide him with a means of escape from the burning skyscraper.

It was a long shot at best, but there was no other way out that he could see. Amoroso gathered up the materials and returned to the elevator shaft, prepared to begin the long, hard climb up to the floors above him.

Reaching his destination on the floor he had originally come from, Amoroso outlined his plan to those few of his coworkers who had remained behind. It involved flinging a rope across to the West Tower. They would attempt to shimmy down the rope, reach the other tower and from there rig up an improvised breaches buoy.

The survivors discussed the rescue plan and decided they had just run fresh out of options. Help would take hours to arrive, if it ever arrived at all, and they realized that they didn't even have minutes left to wait.

THE BLACKOUT HEIST

Low earth orbit. Its tiled hull glittering in the light of the sun, the US space shuttle Pioneer cruised soundlessly one hundred fifty miles above the surface of planet earth that hung in the inky black sky like a shining sphere of polished blue crystal.

At the controls of the American shuttlecraft, Air Force Major Jim Magnus saw the radar blip that indicated the proximity of the first of the remaining two *Pichuga* reconnaissance satellites.

Magnus was a veteran of four shuttle flights and a NASA veteran, having been trained as an alternate for the first manned Mars mission planned for the next decade.

The rest of the five-man crew that had been hastily assembled in the aftermath of the explosion that had destroyed the Buran shuttle Tchaikovsky on the launch pad at Baikonur was made up entirely of civilian personnel.

Two of those personnel were Russian and two were American. Magnus was the only veteran astronaut onboard, and the only crew member capable of piloting the space shuttle.

Because of the overriding consideration that both American and Commonwealth members of the emergency team have flown a mission together before, there was room enough onboard for only one career shuttle jockey.

In fact, only four candidates for the crew existed: four men and women who had served on a joint US-Soviet shuttle mission the previous year.

Although the Russians had claimed full responsibility for the chain of events so far, they had nevertheless insisted that it would be a bilateral team that would dismantle the two remaining *Pichuga* satellites.

The Americans had been forced to accede to the Russians' demand. Despite the imminent danger to the entire world that was posed by the hidden bombs onboard the YZ-class satellites, a unilateral act by the US would certainly be interpreted as an act of overt hostility by their nervous colleagues.

The Russian president had made his country's position clear in a second, follow-up direct hotline call to President Johnson Ubutu Ubuto Ebong via the Rapid Initial Communications Kit desk phone system that gave the system the code-name Hammer Rick. The US president had had no other choice than to give the mission his full approval, which meant that a presidential finding stating the particulars of the mission was already In preparation for the chief executive's signature to make it official.

The Pioneer shuttle would fly with Commonwealth and US personnel onboard, and God help them all.

The bird had sat on the launch pad astride its Ares launch vehicle, with its hastily briefed crew, within thirty-six hours of the two leaders' conversation.

Protocol for the mission had determined that it was to be the Russians who dismantled the satellites.

The Americans were to fly the shuttle and provide logistical and technical support. Canaveral and Baikonur would be linked by telecommunications satellites to create a joint US - Commonwealth ground crew.

"Okay, people," said Magnus, his voice picked up by the headsets worn by the rest of the crew, "Radar shows target number one dead ahead. We'll have visual contact in thirty seconds."

"Roger that," came the reply from Canaveral, which had picked up the commo. "Proceed on your present course heading. Good luck."

"Thanks," Magnus said back, "we'll sure need all we can get."

***

The curved doors of the shuttle's cargo bay opened slowly on pneumatic arms. When they were fully deployed, cosmonaut Rasputin Tokmakoff perched on the lip of the Pioneer's gaping equipment bay. He gripped the hand control of the Manned Maneuvering Unit (MMU) strapped to his back. The MMU would enable him to maneuver in space without a guy line to the shuttle by means of micro-burns from small rocket nozzles on the backpack which, in effect, was a miniature rocket engine.

A moment later, the invisible blast of gases hurled him through space toward the gleaming cone-shaped satellite that was his destination.

As Tokmakoff was launched, the space shuttle Pioneer cruised toward the radar-designated position of the second of the two Bright Star satellites, leaving Tokmakoff to handle the dismantling of the nuclear device by himself. The marginal time frame in which the shuttle crew was forced to work necessitated this hasty departure.

Working single-handedly would pose few problems, however. Tokmakoff had the required expertise and the satellite could be maneuvered in orbit by a single astronaut if necessary.

In any event, Tokmakoff was in constant touch with both the shuttle and the joint US-Commonwealth ground crew. The Pioneer would be near enough to be reached in minutes if an emergency arose.

"I am approaching the satellite now," Tokmakoff spoke into his portable in-helmet commo mike.

"Very good," the voice of Vassily Petrov, on the ground at Baikonur, returned via the lightweight headset he wore. "We are tracking you on radar. You must lose some weight, Tokmakoff," Petrov added, "it is difficult distinguishing your blip from the satellite."

"My wife's cooking," Tokmakoff returned, as he executed a small yaw to prevent overshooting the satellite. "Ah, here we are. I have almost reached it."

THE BLACKOUT HEIST

Tokmakoff's gloved hands grabbed a rung built into the satellite's hull for use by cosmonauts who serviced it while in orbit. The maintenance hatch he was looking for was located on the opposite side, however.

Moving slowly because even the slightest movement produced enough inertial force to send him spinning out into space, Tokmakoff found the hatch and maneuvered himself into position to remove it.

"Move quickly," he heard Petrov's voice speak in his ear. "Computer predictions show the second device will fail in less than twenty minutes."

But by then Tokmakoff was already pulling the malfunctioning component card from the interstices of the satellite and placing it in the Velcro pouch at his waist.

"I have beaten both you and the satellite to the punch, my friend," Tokmakoff said into his commo mike. "Out here, even a fat man moves quickly."

DAVID ALEXANDER

FIFTY-THREE

Inskeep, beneath Manhattan. The improvised torches of the trapped passengers from Inskeep's IRT train illuminated a cavernous underground vault.

By the flickering light of their makeshift firebrands, they could see a ceiling that rose dozens of feet overhead, as high as a cathedral's. Waste water, black and streaked with an oily surface scum, trickled over the bare concrete deck and dripped from many cracks in the decaying walls.

One of the passengers had not made it through the door. The frantic pounding had stopped suddenly as the current had swept the nameless woman away down the length of the tunnel to her certain death in a nameless concrete grave. The sound of her orphaned child's crying filled the flooding utility chamber like a death knell.

Cold turbid water was now pouring in through the edges of the door that had been designed to keep smoke out from track fires, and not water flooding in from the river above. Inskeep didn't know how much longer it would continue to hold against the onrushing flow of current in the flooded tunnel beyond.

For that matter, Inskeep had no idea how much longer the storage room itself in which they had taken refuge would hold up against the crushing pressures of the river above.

Holding his torch high and throwing back his head, Inskeep strained to see if there were any cracks in the ceiling, but the flickering light wasn't able to penetrate the deep shadows.

"We'll all be killed here!" a woman screamed, her face contorted with a fear so intense that it gnawed at the edges of her sanity, her hands going up to the sides of her head.

Other passengers tried to calm the hysterical woman who would not stop screaming. Finally someone slapped her. This only made the woman more hysterical and led to a fight that Buddy Coyne had to break up.

"We need to find another exit," Inskeep said, "or we'll all be drowned. Every second you spend pissing and moaning is a second gone forever. Now get your asses in gear, all of you. You want to live so bad? Then look around you. Find that way out!"

Silent now, the passengers in the group began looking around them. Inskeep searched along with the rest of the survivors, straining his eyes to make out details in the storage area by the inadequate light of the guttering torch.

The walls didn't seem to have any doorways in them, though. Nor could Inskeep detect any outlines that might have marked the places where doors had once existed before being bricked over.

These, he knew, could be potential passageways into another section of tunnel, a way out of the nightmare that was closing in on them all.

Already the water level had risen to ankle-height. A few minutes more and --

"Look! This way!" an old man's shout rang out from a corner of the supply room, "I feel some wind coming from back here."

Inskeep quickly crossed to the old man. There, behind a stack of haphazardly piled crates, there was a small vertical gap in a bricked-over section of wall.

Inspecting the narrow fissure, Inskeep could see that the brickwork had not been recent. It had been done years, perhaps decades, before.

Hope flickered dimly in Inskeep's mind. Beneath the streets of New York, he knew, ran an invisible subterranean network of corridors and catacombs.

These were the result of public works projects performed over the course of the city's almost three hundred year history that had left a labyrinth of burrowings beneath the asphalt and concrete.

Sewer lines, conduits for electrical cable, abandoned subway stations, and even other passenger rail tubes were all intertwined beneath the city's streets.

Many of these had been long-ago abandoned and long-since forgotten, recorded only on musty plans filed away in city archives.

Due to the very abundance of tunnels and their proximity to one another, most of the tunnels in the New York subway system were interconnected in some way to this labyrinthine network.

THE BLACKOUT HEIST

Sometimes the connections were the result of unplanned tapping into other nearby tunnels. Usually these breaches were hastily covered up.

"Help me move these crates away," Inskeep called out, trying not to think about the water level that was already lapping at their knees. Coyne and one of the other passengers waded over and together the three men managed to heave the heavy crates away from the side of the wall.

Playing the light of his torch across the section of wall they had just uncovered, Inskeep placed his face close to the brickwork and felt a rush of musty air on his cheek.

Suddenly there was a rhythmic thumping sound coming from the door to the storage room.

"What's that?" someone cried out, their voice shrill with panic.

"The tunnel outside's flooded," Inskeep yelled back. "Something outside's bumping against it as it's washed past in the current."

"Oh my God!" yelled Patty Scarfone, a legal secretary. "Look! *Look at the door!*"

The gaps in the door's edges had widened, puckered like a sheet of waterlogged cardboard. The river was now pouring into the room, its roar the sound of an angry predator thirsty for blood.

The floor was steadily filling up with cold, murky water. Each passing moment brought the level dangerously higher.

Clearly, they had to do something very quickly or they would end their lives in this lonely warren of tunnels beneath the bed of the river.

Casting about him, Inskeep found a piece of scrap iron left over from maintenance work long ago. He went to work on the bricks, his muscles driven by the galvanizing dread of a death that was both near and horrible to contemplate.

The welling water, now at navel height, helped to dissolve the ancient cement that had already turned to sand between the points.

The bricks gave way quickly as old, rotting cement crumbled and fell away in chunks, disappeared into the swirling black eddies.

Together with other passengers, Inskeep pulled away the bricks, until his fingers bled from the effort, revealing a hole in the wall roughly five feet in diameter.

Inserting his head and shoulders, Inskeep waved the torch back and forth.

Ahead of him he saw a circular tunnel. The tunnel smelled foul with dry rot. But there was no sign of flooding, except for the water pouring into it from the vaulted room. The sides, roof and floor of the tunnel were otherwise mercifully dry.

Inskeep guessed that it was some kind of old sewer main, long since disused by the city.

"Okay," he said. "Everybody inside that hole on the double."

"But where does it lead?" asked one of the passengers.

"Even if it leads straight to hell," another passenger answered, "we don't have much choice."

He was right. The water level had risen to chest height. Another few minutes and the room would be completely submerged.

THE BLACKOUT HEIST

Suddenly, the door buckled, then burst with a thunderous sound. Water spilled into the room. The killer had entered.

Casting desperately about him for something with which to plug the hole, Inskeep found an old nail barrel. Backing up into the hole, Inskeep pulled the barrel in after him, succeeding in wedging it into the edges of the aperture to form a temporary seal.

So far it would keep out the river. But for how long?

***

At first they were forced to crawl through the narrow tunnel on hands and knees. Then the tunnel widened so that they could walk normally.

"Where are we?" somebody asked Inskeep.

"I think I know," a middle-aged man in a Mackinaw jacket replied. "We're in the old sewer lines under Wall Street. I hear there are crocodiles down here."

"Alligators," someone answered, correcting him.

"Bullshit, there's nothing down here," a third put in. "Just roaches and water rats."

"Button your lips," Inskeep called out. "Keep your eyes open for a hatch or a door or a hole in the concrete. The idea is to get out of this place and reach the street."

Inskeep knew that these tunnels stretched on for miles, twisting and turning in every direction.

Somewhere, though, there had to be a place where they connected with either the basement of a building, another tunnel system or the city streets above.

DAVID ALEXANDER

Almost an hour later, Inskeep called out for the passengers to stop. Without saying anything, Inskeep held his now faintly sputtering torch aloft, studying the ceiling of the tunnel and its walls for several long moments.

Nodding to himself silently, Inskeep confirmed what he had been growing to suspect.

The had been going around in circles.

The tunnel they had taken refuge in had taken them around in an endless loop. It was a labyrinth that curved back in on itself.

A sickening fear that had been coiled inside Inskeep's guts suddenly released itself, shooting shock waves along his nervous system. For a moment Inskeep felt a withering claustrophobia that made him want to scream out loud.

Fighting to get himself back under control, Inskeep turned and faced the other passengers who were looking at him with questioning glances.

"We're lost," somebody stated before he could utter a word. "Damn, I knew it," he continued when Inskeep nodded. "I knew this place was starting to look familiar."

"Don't panic," Inskeep told them all. "There's a way out of here, I know it." He didn't sound convincing, though, not even to himself.

"Why are the torches getting so faint?" a woman with a Brooklyn accent asked.

"Oh, Lord Almighty," the man in the Mackinaw jacket bellowed. "*That's because we're running out of air!*"

Mackinaw was right. They were running out of air. Fast. Already Inskeep could feel his heart thunder in his chest and his lungs strain from lack of oxygen.

This time the fear was too great to resist. He cut loose with a bestial scream that reverberated across the sewer main's walls.

FIFTY-FOUR

Amoroso, Battery Towers. "Here we go," Amoroso said as he held up the contraption he had managed to assemble from scrap materials scavenged from various items of equipment and furniture found in the office.

The device was constructed from the guts of a Xerox copier, the metal frame of a desk drawer, wires from a lighting fixture, and other miscellaneous items hastily dog-robbed from broken-into storerooms.

The makeshift grappling hook might hold fast. Then again, it might not.

Fortunately the rope he'd woven from spliced lengths of electrical cord looked strong enough to serve the purpose Amoroso intended it for.

Amoroso, an amateur rock climber, had spent his weekends scaling the cliff faces Pywiack Dome in Yosemite Park and the North Face of Canada's Mount Waddington.

Nodding at one of the group near him, Amoroso heaved back and tossed the grappling hook across the several score yards that separated the East Tower that he was in from the West Tower, aiming for the fire-lit interstices of a deserted office.

The throw would have been impossible if not for the fact that Amoroso was aiming at floors of the East Tower on a lower level than the one he was located on.

Nevertheless, the first several tosses proved unsuccessful. The grapnel failed to find purchase on anything solid enough to hold it anchored securely.

On many tries it seemed to hold at first, but then a solid tug always dislodged it, and Amoroso was forced to reel the grapnel back in and try again, arms aching, eyes hot and stinging from windblown particles of ash from the fires below.

Casting the hook was a lot like a game that Amoroso had played as a child when his family had vacationed in the Poconos. There, a gum machine had required the manipulation of a metal claw in order to snare a prize from a heap of baubles nestled within a glass dome.

In a flash, Amoroso's memory swept him back across the years, replaying the frustration he'd felt as a child as he groped for the glittering toy he had set his heart on, felt it fall from his claw, tried again --

-- and the sudden elation as he gaffed the prize.

On Amoroso's fifth attempt, the grapnel finally found purchase on something solid within the flame-illuminated office in the West Tower. The crowd cheered and he was slapped on the back.

DAVID ALEXANDER

Understandable reactions, but premature, Amoroso knew. There was a great deal more to be done before anybody could begin a round of congratulations in earnest.

Tying the line fast around the leg of a heavy steel desk, Amoroso stood perched on the windowsill and pulled on a pair of work gloves he had found in a janitor's storeroom.

He would need the gloves to provide him with a firm grip on the rope as he shimmied down it to the opposite tower, hanging in space above a seventy-odd story drop to the street below.

"Please don't fall," Mary Koslowski called out as Amoroso began his rope climb. Amoroso thought to himself that this was the understatement of the decade.

***

The wind was fierce, slashing at him with talons at once insubstantial and punishingly strong, fed by the inferno from the burning stories below, and funneled upward by the concrete canyons of the Wall Street district into a rapidly spinning vortex.

Here the winds gusted at hundreds of miles per hour around Amoroso as he began his diagonal descent, causing his body to sway precariously on the rope as he moved cautiously down its tautly stretched length.

Amoroso had known about the winds beforehand and had factored them into his preparations for the rope-climb.

Several people had tried to scale the Battery Towers in the two decades since they'd gone up to replace the World Trade Center.

391

THE BLACKOUT HEIST

There had been three parachuting attempts and two human fly attempts. Each media-hungry daredevil who had made an assault on the complex's twin towers had reported encountering violent winds.

Looking down below him, Amoroso saw the flames of burning stories in both towers leap toward him like cat's claws reaching for a bird that was just out of their reach, eager to pull him toward death's hungry jaws.

Choking black smoke stung his eyes and made breathing difficult. The night air was numbingly cold as it sluiced past him, making him shiver despite the flames crackling below and the precautions he had taken to wrap his body in many layers of clothing scavenged from a variety of empty offices.

Amoroso averted his eyes as he shimmied only a few feet. Staring ahead of him, he could see where the grapnel had found purchase on the West Tower.

From his present vantage point, he had a workable, although extremely limited, line of sight through the shattered windowpane into the office beyond and below him.

The office's dark interior showed no evidence of a human presence. Its furnishings were strewn about everywhere, papers covered overturned chairs and desks, the drawers of filing cabinets hung open and fractured sections of drywall and drop ceiling littered the room.

Amoroso stopped as a sudden gust of wind more fierce than the others made him wobble precariously on the guy rope. There was a moment of panic as he felt the rope suddenly slacken as the grapnel shifted position.

It was tempting to just go with the force of gravity and attempt to slide down the rope, but Amoroso's climbing experience had taught him that surrendering to this urge could prove a deadly error.

Moving too fast was an invitation to disaster for several reasons. If he moved too suddenly he would sway from his center of gravity, becoming vulnerable to a gust of wind that might catch him, and if severe enough, blow him off his precarious perch to his death in the inferno many stories below.

Amoroso began to cautiously move again, inching forward like a caterpillar on a dry twig, using his muscular arms to haul himself forward and his knees to brace his body against the edges of the guy rope.

A treacherous gust of wind suddenly caught him on his side and turned him on the axis of the rope like the blade of a propeller. Amoroso's panic-jolted heart hammered in his ears as he hung from the rope, suddenly upside down, dangling precipitously over the distant streets far below.

Above the maddening roar of the flames he heard the faint sound of his group of survivors calling out to him from their vantage point somewhere above him.

Although he could not make out what they were saying above the din of the inferno, it made no difference. At this point, nothing they could say or do could help him.

THE BLACKOUT HEIST

With his last remaining shreds of strength, Amoroso hauled himself up and looped his legs around the rope once again until he was in a stable position above it.

He remained like that on the swaying rope, resting and willing his pulse rate to slow, not daring to wipe at the sweat that ran down his scalp into his eyes, stinging them with their salt, blinding him.

Swallowing hard, he fought back the numbing panic that held him frozen in place.

Just a little bit more, he told himself. *Then you're inside, out of the wind, with a floor under you again.*

Gritting his teeth, Amoroso summoned up his courage and began to shimmy the rest of the way toward the shattered, flame-lambent window.

Long minutes that seemed like eternities later, Amoroso had reached the broken window's edge. Maneuvering himself to a sitting position on it, he swung his legs around and hopped down into the room, laughing out loud as he felt his knees wobble beneath him.

Now standing at the window, Amoroso waved to the group he had left behind in the East Tower, giving them the signal that he had made the crossing safely and to stand by for the last part of the rescue operation.

Then Amoroso collapsed against the wall nearest him. The tremendous stress of his dangerous high-wire act had not manifested itself before, but as the adrenaline that had been coursing through his system began to ebb from his veins, the shock suddenly hit him with the crushing force of a sledgehammer blow.

Amoroso pulled the flask out of his pocket and took a long drink to steady his nerves, grateful that he had found it at the bottom of an otherwise empty desk drawer. Then he wiped the sweat off his brow with the back of his hand and looked out the window.

The first of the group was in position. As agreed, it was Dalwit Darwish, a former boy prostitute from New Delhi who had emigrated to New York and now worked as a part-time file clerk to help pay for a sex-change operation while attending law classes at nearby Pace University.

The breeches buoy they had rigged up under Amoroso's guidance was a masterpiece of improvisation. Normally, a life preserver suspended from a rope and propelled on pulleys would function as a device to evacuate victims of emergencies across empty space.

Those riding the buoy to safety were supported by the life preserver's rim beneath their armpits, while their legs dangled below.

But Manhattan skyscrapers were not equipped with life preservers, and instead, Amoroso was forced to make do with the next best thing; a toilet seat.

If undignified, it was also an effective substitute. Finally, it was their only chance at survival.

Amoroso watched Dalwit wave to him, signaling his readiness to begin the descent. He caught the control rope that had been tossed down to him by his boss Murray Jackman, and held it in his gloved hands to steady it. Then he waved back, signaling that he too was ready.

Moments later, seventy-plus stories above the shattered street and over twenty stories above the tips of the fiery tongues that licked satanically into the savage night, the makeshift breeches buoy began its long, agonizingly slow descent above the crackling flames directly below it.

FIFTY-FIVE

Rockaway, Queens. Under the boardwalk. They weren't falling in love. They were roasting a nineteen-year-old girl they had found wandering aimlessly through the streets.

They had stuffed large steel drums with garbage and pieces of planking ripped from the boardwalk to make pitch pots.

They had soaked rags in gasoline which they had siphoned from the gas tanks of disabled vehicles and they had set fire to the heaped trash inside the drums.

The burning pitch pots were arrayed in a long line along the windswept Atlantic beach.

The homeless had been in Rockaway for as long, it seemed, as the Atlantic ocean had lapped at its sand beaches. They were there even before they had become a common sight elsewhere on the streets of the city's many neighborhoods.

Rockaway Beach had become their Mecca when urban renewal had lain waste to endless stretches of neighborhoods that had once been the fashionable seaside resorts of another era.

In time, the area had become a wasteland of moldering structures, fit only for those without any place else to live. They were soon overtaken by platoons of derelict squatters.

THE BLACKOUT HEIST

Now, with police presence absent, the street denizens of the former seaside resort had found easy victims in the drivers and passengers of stalled vehicles, and, with the force of numbers on their side, had dragged them out into the gutters. Some they had robbed, some they had raped, and some they had killed on the spot.

This particular group had surrendered to a latent streak of cannibalism, though. A latent streak that had now risen to the surface.

Killing her parents, they had dragged the freckle-faced girl from the new Lexus SUV, spitted her like a pig on a long, sharp, wooden stake cut from a telephone pole, and roasted her over the pitch pots they'd set up on the beach.

The roasted girl-flesh tasted sweet, although at first it stank in their nostrils and made many of them vomit onto the sand.

Now they each took turns feasting on the succulent flesh of the young high school student they had captured and devoured with relish.

Under the boardwalk, boardwalk....

***

Cruising at forty thousand feet, the specially modified Boeing 707, redesignated the E-6 by the Pentagon and code-named Looking Glass, carried the president and his chief advisors across the post-death pulse landscape of the northeastern United States.

Since the beginnings of the Cold War, it had been standard procedure for the chief executive to be flown above the continental US from where he

398

could issue directives in the event of nuclear war or catastrophic national emergency.

Although the member nations of the Commonwealth of Independent States had disavowed any sinister purpose behind the explosion of their *Pichuga* YZ-class satellite, the Strategic Air Command headquarters had revised the Defense Readiness Condition, or Defcon, level, to Defcon Three, the second lowest state of nuclear preparedness.

It paid not to take chances, especially where (so many veteran commanders still believed) duplicitous Ivan was concerned.

Even if the Russians were sincere in their insistence that what had occurred was a freak nuclear accident and not a prelude to a surprise military attack, President Johnson Ubutu Ubuto Ebong felt it prudent to let the Russians know that the United States was not taking the situation lightly.

When the Chernobyl reactor facility had blown up in a radioactive death cloud and nuclear fallout had rained down across Eastern Europe and as far west as the English countryside, the Defcon status had been similarly reassessed for the duration of the blackout disaster crisis.

It was a good idea to send the Russians the message that the United States regarded even their fuck-ups as a provocation of sorts. It would help to keep them honest.

Furthermore, the Looking Glass aircraft was one of the few in the US fleet that had been hardened against EMP damage. Ground-to-air communications could be carried on despite any attempt by the Russians to interfere with, spoof or scramble them.

The president relaxed with a glass of Perrier in the cushions of his couch in the situations room that formed the rear of the aircraft's fuselage. Around him were clustered his advisers.

Direct telemetry connected him by phone to both SAC headquarters and NORAD in Cheyenne Mountain, Colorado.

"So you're telling me there's no indication yet of anything serious, Mike?" the president said into the mouthpiece with his trademarked bluntness.

A microprocessor onboard scrambled his transmission which was transmitted from the forty-foot-long antenna that trailed behind the aircraft by ultra long radio waves that were highly resistant to EMP interference.

"That's right, sir," the SAC commander returned. "Satellite reconnaissance shows no evidence of Russian launch vehicles anywhere. Looks like what we've got here is another Chernobyl instead of the overture to Armageddon."

"Okay, Mike," the president returned after several moments' thought. "Downgrade Defcon status to four. And Mike, I want regular situation reports as soon as new data becomes available."

"Roger that, sir," the general answered and the connection was severed.

The pilot's voice came over the intercom after a few minutes more informing those in the conference chambers that the Looking Glass aircraft was approaching the perimeter of the zone effected by the EMP burst.

As the President looked out the window of the plane, along with the others onboard the aircraft, they saw a sight of overwhelming horror.

The lights were out in New York City. The metropolis that had nightly cast a glow of such magnitude that the lights of Broadway had become a readily identifiable landmark visible to astronauts in space, seemed to have vanished off the face of the earth.

In place of the lights, there was darkness. And, as the darkness began to give way to the murky gray twilight of dawn, those onboard the aircraft could see the pall of smoke rising from the stricken area below.

"What a mess," the president said to those around him. "What a God-awful mess. What's the condition of the White House now?" he asked his aide a moment later, "or do we still have one left?"

Washington, DC had been partially blacked out too, partly as a result of the overload to the national power grid caused by the devastation in the epicenter of the strike zone, partly because the effects of the Russian YZ-class satellite's explosion in orbit had reached as far as the nation's capital.

After checking, his aide reported that the White house was now back on line.

President Ebong picked up the phone and punched the button connecting him to the cockpit.

"Turn this bird around and get me back to Washington," he ordered.

THE BLACKOUT HEIST

Then he reached for the over-the-counter calcium based stomach buffer in his pocket. This one was giving him a massive case of heartburn. Besides, these tasted just like candy.

***

Half naked, Mindy Wagner had found herself rubbing up against the guy in the center of Times Square. It was incredible, but she felt herself responding sexually.

Under ordinary circumstances, Mindy would have had nothing to do with it. She would have screamed for the cops. But a man she had met had turned her onto Ecstasy. She had heard a lot about the drug; how it made you feel loving and warm and at peace with the world.

"Word up, bitch," he'd said, urging her to swallow the capsule filled with white powder. "Look around you, everybody here's doing E."

A glance told Mindy that he was right. People all around her were indeed popping Ecstasy capsules into their mouths. And she could understand why.

Wasn't she eager to turn the terrible fear she felt into happiness? Didn't she want to replace the entrails-gnawing emptiness in her guts with a feeling of warmth and belonging?

Mindy had swallowed the capsule that her newfound friend had given her.

"Aren't you taking any?" she'd asked when it had gone down.

"I already took mine," the guy told her with a smile.

It was not long before the first mellow rush of Ecstasy hit her. Mindy felt it warm her entire consciousness and penetrate deeper, into the inmost reaches of her heart and soul.

When anonymous hands pushed up her skirt and groped for her buttocks, she smiled and giggled a little.

"Yeah, bee-yutch," a voice behind her rasped. "You so wet. Open for me, ho."

Mindy allowed the rigid penis to be inserted into her from behind. Nestled among the thousands of bodies that formed a communal group against the cold and the darkness, Mindy felt totally at peace as the organ inside her ejaculated.

"Mmmm .... yeah, ho," she heard the voice rasp in her ear. "Give it up, bee-yutch."

When another was inserted into her vagina from behind, Mindy accepted the phallus into the semen-slick genitalia.

She eagerly crouched down on all fours and took another organ into her mouth. Beginning to suck, she felt the head of the penis come a rush of semen down her throat.

On Ecstasy, Mindy's only thought was to submerge herself in the crowd like a fish in the ocean.

It was amazing how many others in Times Square were copulating spontaneously, just like herself. She somehow knew that when the crisis was over, she would convince herself that this had never happened.

For the moment, however, all Mindy wanted to do was lose herself in the oceanic delight of being an anonymous receptacle for discharging penises, drench herself in wave after delicious wave of orgasm, surrender herself to Ecstasy.

And then suddenly, she realized something very different was beginning to happen to her. Pleasure had unexpectedly been replaced with pain. The mouth between her legs that had been making her feel so good had now switched from licking to biting.

Mindy screamed as part of her vagina was torn away in a bloody flaying of throbbing, bleeding flesh. Her agonized screams intensified as more hungry teeth ripped into her abdomen, her arms and her thighs.

They were silenced forever, as an uprooted parking meter crushed her skull and a woman with mad eyes and an ear-to-ear grin, dipped her tongue in Mindy's bloody brains.

A woman, like Mindy, caught in the throes of Ecstasy.

FIFTY-SIX

Skerrit, West Side. From his vantage point inside the armored command center, Rick Skerrit watched the emergency repair crew on the banks of monitor displays.

Tracked by special low-light surveillance cameras mounted on masts atop the van, the repair crew negotiated the wreckage-strewn streets of the Hell's Kitchen neighborhood as though they were the first wave of an army of invasion.

In a way that's exactly what they were. The tenderloin area on Manhattan's Upper West Side, despite being repackaged by developers as "Clinton" or "Midtown West" for rich yuppies, had always been a forgotten section of the city in which empty warehouses brooded over fenced-off lots and the derelict remains of the old West Side Highway. Its waterfront strip still had its share of them.

When MetroCon had selected which transformer stations were to be phased out completely and which were to be retrofitted with new computer switching machinery, a factor in their arriving at the decision had been the location of individual sites.

Those like the dockside Westhaven facility, already located in a pocket of growing urban decay, were doomed to be sliced from the power grid like cancer cells from a healthy body because they stood in neighborhoods that were already dying.

Because the new computerized systems were faster, fewer individual switching stations were needed. An individual transformer station would now be able to service an area five times as great as had been possible in the past.

At the same time, as families and businesses relocated from the older neighborhoods to sections of the city under development, there was less of a need for the switching stations they had depended on before.

And so Westhaven, like scores of other electrical switching stations throughout metro New York, had been forgotten. Until now. Now, with the destruction of their successors, the old stations were the only hope Skerrit saw to lessen the blow that had eclipsed the city under a plague of deadly darkness.

Yet not every station would be capable of being put back on line, at least not quickly enough. When the switching stations had been removed from the power grid, there had been a wide disparity in the way they had been treated.

Some had been dismantled entirely and were now little more than rotting concrete shells. Others had been cannibalized for parts on an ad-hoc basis, while at still other stations the switching machinery had been sold by MetroCon to other municipalities at bargain basement prices.

Few records had been kept, and so Skerrit had no way of knowing which stations were still serviceable except by direct inspection.

This process alone used up valuable time during the emergency where every moment was critical, and the necessity for on-site inspection put his work crews at risk. Before the EMP burst had hurled the city back to the stone age, these forgotten neighborhoods were urban combat zones.

Skerrit and his men had no choice. In addition to escorts of cops armed with automatic rifles and riot gear, his people carried shotguns.

As matters presently stood, Skerrit had a dozen electrical repair crews fanning out across the stricken boros of Manhattan, Brooklyn, the Bronx, Queens and Staten Island, each attempting to reactivate the corroded switching junctions that had been taken out of active service and forgotten almost a quarter century before.

His walkie-talkie suddenly chirped.

"Rick, this is Billy Chu." Skerrit rogered Chu's transmission. "We're inside the transformer facility now," he went on. "So far looks good."

Chu shone his flashlight on coils of cables. Covered with inches of dust, they were nevertheless attached to the banks of step-down transformers that were required for the transmission of AC power.

"How's the main transformer assembly look to you?" Skerrit asked Chu.

"Good," Chu returned. "I think Westhaven's a winner. Out."

407

THE BLACKOUT HEIST

Skerrit told the engineer to keep him posted and crossed his fingers. They had put a dozen sites through a fine-meshed screen and had come up with a short list of precious few that were in good enough condition to be utilized again.

Only three of them so far were near a state of readiness to be put on line. Skerrit wanted to wait for as many as possible to be ready before he would recommend the switch being thrown.

EEPA had allocated ten million kilowatts of emergency power pooled from generating stations in the Midwest. These would be enough to supply power to sections of Manhattan and the Bronx only.

It would do little more than scratch the surface of the problem, but it would have to do for a start.

Skerrit's strategy was to attempt to at least bring some power back to the city on a neighborhood-by-neighborhood basis.

Even if a few neighborhoods could be returned to something resembling a normal power-availability status, the crisis would simmer down a little.

For openers, Skerrit wanted to light up Midtown. The Empire State Building would be a beacon seen for miles in every direction. Mobile trucks carrying searchlights were in position too.

While no one could do anything to bring back television reception because the electronic components in almost every set in town had been shorted out beyond repair by the electromagnetic pulse, at least some basic utilities could be restored.

Right now, even that looked pretty good to Rick Skerrit.

DAVID ALEXANDER

***

As the third emergency repair team worked at the 95th Street site, the street people watched them from the shadows beyond the maintenance perimeter.

They had come from the shantytown near the FDR Drive. They figured that the men working had money on them.

Creeping up silently, they overpowered the cops that were guarding the trenches in the street where workmen were inspecting underground power cables.

The scream of the utility man whose throat had been cut from ear to ear by a wickedly honed straight-razor alerted the rest of the guardians of the repair crew.

They began firing into the street people, killing some and driving away the rest. But others who had weapons attacked the cops and sent them running for cover themselves.

Suddenly, a Molotov cocktail appeared in the hand of a man with long, greasy dreadlocks and wild black eyes.

He flung it with a shout at one of the NYPD's mobile troop carriers in and behind which cops were taking cover, sending it up in a fireball of destruction that was heard halfway across the clty.

***

The mayor had a fit when he heard what had happened to the repair crew that had been blasted by the street people.

He shook his fists and hollered for police commissioner Farooq Ibrahim who promised to get

409

some more men down to the scene of the violent confrontation as soon as possible.

Staring gloomily out at the klieg-lit expanse around his Mobile Command Center, the mayor made another "V" for Valium and hollered for his aide.

***

The first generator was finally on-line. The power transmission cables were intact, since no physical damage had been done to them by the EMP burst.

This had been determined by taking readings of the lines prior to sending out the crews.

Skerrit had only chosen those sections of the electrical power grid that were still reasonably intact.

His criterion had been that the sections he would try to salvage would have to encompass at least twenty blocks of city neighborhood, have at least one transformer station capable of being salvaged, and have street lighting that had not been completely blown out by the blast.

Fortunately, Skerrit had found that a remarkable number of areas had survived intact.

It was amazing considering the scope and intensity of the nuclear EMP burst that had caused the damage.

While most of the municipal power grid had been immediately incapacitated, there were entire sections where rudimentary salvage was a definite possibility.

This was due to two factors. The first was that some of the wiring and transformer stations were

410

old, and therefore more resistant to electromagnetic pulse damage.

The second was that these older sections were equipped with more reliable circuit breakers.

The net result was that there were at least ten areas throughout the city that could be salvaged. Some of these were located in all five boros.

Nevertheless, the strategic location of Skerrit's repair crews ruled out all but Manhattan as the site of the first attempts to get the MetroCon system back on-line.

The nature of the problem facing Skerrit was not so much that no power was available. On the contrary, there were millions of kilowatts ready for generation to New York City from outlying areas unaffected by the blast.

The problem lay in the inability of the energy to reach its destination along the existing network designed to transport it.

This was because electric power did not flow directly, like water through a pipe, but instead was transmitted through a series of discrete steps along the route it traveled.

The key to this process were banks of transformers, which turned the high-voltage DC power into the more controllable AC power that came out of electrical outlets.

Not only had the EMP attack physically burned out many power cables beneath the streets of the city, but it had also destroyed several of the transforming stations through which the current needed to flow.

411

THE BLACKOUT HEIST

Many of those that had not been destroyed shut down automatically, however.

With the wiring intact, all that was necessary was to reactivate the operational transformer stations that had been shut down and plug them all into the grid.

A few decades ago, this would have been relatively simple. But the digital packet switching system that had rendered the power grid so vulnerable complicated this process.

Right now, Skerrit's men were working to disengage the power grid from its computerized controls; to put the human operator back into the loop.

Once that had been accomplished, they would have to reactivate the manual switching apparatus. The entire process was complicated. And risky.

But there was no time left for sophisticated checks. An additional problem existed: burnout.

If power surged back on too strongly for the grid to handle, it would create a new overload condition and do even greater damage than the original burnout. For this reason Skerrit decided to play it safe. He had designated only two city neighborhoods to receive the first jolt of newly switched-on power.

"Activate stations one and two," Skerrit spoke into the commo link with Chu's team. "Put the system on-line. Light the fucker up!"

"Roger," came back Chu's reply. "Am instructing my men to do so right away."

In moments Skerrit heard the explosion caused by the transformer facility at which Chu was stationed blowing up.

"Damn!" Chu's voice came stridently over the communications link speaker a moment later. "She blew to smithereens! Everything's on fire."

"Any of your people hurt?" asked Skerrit.

"Don't know for sure yet," Chu said back, "but I'd be surprised if we didn't have -- hold it -- yeah, we got two guys with serious burns."

"What about the second station?"

"She's holding, Rick," Chu returned. "But -- *shit, there she goes!"* Skerrit clearly heard the explosion of the second overloaded transformer facility blowing up and saw its flash briefly light up the sky.

"Nice try," Chu said finally, "but I'm afraid we don't win the kewpie doll this time. Out."

For a few brief moments, those in the area serviced by the second transformer station had seen streetlights flicker to life, only to be plunged again into the primeval darkness of night a heartbeat later.

Skerrit racked the communicator's mike and pounded the wall of the Mobile Command Unit, angry and disappointed.

"Light up, damn you!" he cursed under his breath, addressing the city that taunted him with its stubborn refusal to respond, a physician anguished by his medicine's inability to save a dying patient. *"Damn you, light up!...."*

THE BLACKOUT HEIST

Chapter Six
The Sound of Prayers

DAVID ALEXANDER

FIFTY-SEVEN

Central Park, Manhattan. It was almost like Woodstock. Somehow, almost as if by telepathy, the huge crowd had begun to come together at Central Park's fifteen-acre Strawberry Fields. The former Sheep's Meadow had been named after the Beatles tune following the death of John Lennon by a deranged fan's bullet that had cut him down as he was entering his multi-million dollar condominium apartment at the Dakota.

Spencer Garfield had been one of the many who had found themselves coming out of the primeval darkness that had descended on New York City to find comfort in Strawberry Fields, as the slain rocker's fans had done long ago in sympathy for the ex-Beatle.

He had first seen the many candles, like a sea of glowing lava, illuminate the park from his prewar apartment on Central Park West.

Garfield had at first decided to stay put behind the locked doors of his apartment.

He was one of the few New Yorkers allowed to own a gun. Garfield's wealth had secured the much coveted full-carry pistol permit. His family connections in City Hall had helped too.

But some inexplicable something had made Garfield want to come down from the security of his darkened apartment and join those congregating in the park below him.

There he had found many like himself, people who had been similarly attracted to Strawberry Field by a magnetism they could not understand or explain.

Young and old alike, rich and poor, native New Yorkers and those recently transplanted from other places, had come together in Strawberry Field to wait out the savage night and take solace against the plague of darkness that had overcome them like some ancient judgment out of the Bible's pages.

Many had brought guitars and other musical instruments, and groups of people singing the old folk songs that had given them courage in the sixties were everywhere on the grass.

Except for the fact that the singers and listeners were older and had shorter hair, it could have been a replay of a be-in out of the Summer of Love.

Yet the energy transmitted by the crowd was exactly the same as in that bygone era.

There was a communal warmth present here. Garfield could feel it flow through him. Despite the cold and the darkness, there were smiles on people's faces. They had found something that many had long forgotten existed.

Garfield had found himself "adopted" by a group of total strangers. Generally hostile, New Yorkers were letting their guards down, forging contacts they would never have dreamt of making before. One of his group had produced some marijuana and soon all were high on a cloud of pot.

DAVID ALEXANDER

As the night wore on, the minstrels in the park began to fall silent. People left Strawberry Field or drifted off to sleep. Garfield had been one of those latter.

Now, as dawn approached, Garfield got up to answer nature's call. Gingerly, he stepped over slumbering bodies, to make his way into the bushes to urinate. As he was finishing up, he did not hear the sound of footsteps behind him.

His throat was slashed and the blood was pouring out of it before he even realized it and many hands felt through his clothes for his wallet and beneath the cuffs of his sleeves for his Rolex only moments after the corpse hit the ground.

***

The Mall's ventilation system was cramped, a network of crawl spaces barely wide enough for a full-grown man to move through on hands and knees. It had not been designed as passageway for anything but air.

Yet to security guard John Henry Parrish, the dark, claustrophobic shafts were a safe port in a turbulent storm. The ventilation system ran everywhere throughout the Mall. It could take him anywhere, even out of the Mall entirely, if he wished it, he knew.

Parrish, however, had no intention of leaving the Mall. Not yet, anyway. Apart from the fact that there was no place else to go, he still had a score to settle with the human garbage bags who had turned the Mall -- *his* Mall -- into their own personal concentration camp.

THE BLACKOUT HEIST

Parrish would revenge himself upon them. The Mall was more of a home to him than his apartment, the shoppers the only family Parrish had.

The gang of young neo-Nazi punks had brought a sickening madness into his place of sanity, befouled the wholesome corridors that Parrish loved, uprooted him from the single place in the entire world that he felt he belonged to and which belonged to him in return.

Yes, the fuckers would pay. Oh God yes the fuckers would pay, would pay....

Suddenly Parrish heard the clamor of voices from somewhere nearby. Several men's voices, laughing, taunting. And a woman's higher voice. The woman screaming, pleading. The men responding with laughter, shouts, threats, slaps. Parrish's blood ran hot in his veins.

Yes, the fuckers would pay, would pay. Oh how the fuckers would pay pay pay.

He followed the sound as it echoed through the aluminum walls of the narrow crawl space, growing louder with each foot he moved.

Finally he was almost upon the source of the sounds. It was coming from a room used for the storage of maintenance equipment on the Mall's second level, the same level on which the skins were holding their prisoners hostage.

Frozen in place, Parrish listened. The woman was pleading. She was telling them to stop, not to hurt her.

Parrish had heard enough. He couldn't move on them from where he was, he knew. He'd have to find an air vent that led to another room.

DAVID ALEXANDER

Parrish crawled back up the ventway, finding a side branch of the crawl space network. Peering through the ventilation grating high on the concrete cinderblock wall, he saw that this next room was empty. Parrish pushed out the grating and jumped into the room.

Pay, pay, make make make the fuckers pay....

Creeping along the corridor, Parrish had his .38 caliber revolver out, the hammer cocked, a round in the chamber. But then he saw something else. It was a fire ax that hung from the wall on a bracket.

A broad grin lit up Parrish's face as he put the revolver back in its holster. Taking the fire ax down from its fasteners on the wall, he hefted it in his hands. Its weight felt reassuring, filling him with a sense of power.

Parrish was inside the door in seconds. By the macabre flicker of candles they had lit to provide them with light, he saw the naked woman, the two goons, the smiles on their faces suddenly turn down at the corners.

Lashing out with the fire ax in a short, horizontal arc, Parrish sent the head of one Nazi skin flying in a stream of blood as laughter suddenly forced its way from his lips.

Pay, pay, pay, make make pay....

As the second skinhead goon dived for the Ithaca riot gun that he'd stupidly left leaning in the crook where two corners of wall dovetailed, Parrish sank the blade of the ax into the goon's back so that the razor-sharp cutting edge emerged through his abdomen, its length coated with blood that gleamed

419

darkly in the light of the candles. Parrish pulled out the blade.

The punk skin was whimpering now, begging Parrish not to punch his time card. The laughter bubbling from his lips like uncorked champagne, Parrish pulled the ax high overhead, gripping it securely with both hands. Then he brought it down as hard as he could, cleanly chopping off one leg at the hip.

Pay, oh yes, oh yes, pay!

The punk vomited a bloody gruel. His lips moved, as though struggling in vain to form words, but only bubbles of dark blood popped as he sputtered meaningless sounds.

Parrish chopped the other leg off. The punk made gagging noises, choking on his own blood and his own vomit.

Then Parrish hefted the ax above his head again, until he could feel the weight of the ax-head pulling him backwards. With a mighty grunt of exertion, he now brought the blade down with all his might, cleaving the punk's face in half along its vertical axis. He had to admit that it felt pretty damn good.

But then inspiration struck Parrish.

A buzz saw.

A buzz saw might feel even better....

FIFTY-EIGHT

Applebaum, The South Bronx. Well protected behind a twenty-foot high perimeter fence of welded cast iron and manned by a crew of streetwise hoods armed with automatic weapons, the Mosque -- so called because it had been the burned-out shell of an actual mosque before the drug dealers took it over -- deserved its bad reputation as a crack gang's urban stronghold.

But Mad Marty Applebaum knew that no matter how well-fortified or protected, any target was breachable. This, as their instructor at merc school had told his class, was the principle behind special forces tactics and strategy the world over.

As often proved the case, a couple of well-trained, highly motivated Davids could overcome an army of Goliaths.

His face cammied up in non-reflective squiggles of olive-drab and black camouflage paint, Applebaum crouched behind the tiled parapet that ran around the rooftop of a building across the street and a few hundred yards to the south of the Mosque.

Raising his binoculars, he swept them across the operations zone looking for holes in the security perimeter that he could exploit.

THE BLACKOUT HEIST

They would be there, Applebaum was sure. There always were. No matter how secure, there was a way inside. Once he knew the weak points, he could then plan his strategy.

The thing you got going for you is that these guys are crude shits. Look at the way those two pissbags hanging out in front of the place are shucking and jiving. They think the Uzis they got under their coats make up for the hernias they got for brains.

How many would there be inside? No way to tell, Applebaum knew. But he guessed that an estimate of at least twenty punks, each armed with an automatic weapon, wouldn't be too far off the mark.

The building was four stories tall. A couple of the windows were boarded over, the rest didn't have shades covering them. Activity went on behind them, right out in the open, for all the world to see.

In one of the windows, Applebaum saw figures moving back and forth and caught a flash of a pair of large naked breasts. The figure framed in the window suddenly moved downward. Then came the jerky up-down movements of one shoulder before the figure passed completely from view.

Sweeping the binoculars from the Mosque to the street in front of it, Applebaum noted that stalled cars made a jumble where they had been abandoned by their drivers at the moment of EMP detonation.

Some of the cars had crashed into the lower floors of the apartment buildings across the street.

Applebaum made a mental note of the cars and their positions -- they could provide him with cover.

Applebaum checked his watch. It was already three A.M. In another couple of hours it would begin to get fully light again. Applebaum would wait only a little longer. He'd make his move soon, at the triple witching hour before dawn.

***

Cinco Muertes, the drug lord of Mott Haven Avenue, was talking to his troops in his war room on the second floor of the Mosque. The Shark was one mucho angry dude. He wanted something done now about those scumbags at the Bronx Zoo. As of now.

Didn't the streets of the neighborhood belong to Cinco Muertes? Weren't the cops paralyzed now? Didn't that mean that it was time to go into their homes, take their money, exact a heavy price for their years of persecution?

The drug lord's war chieftains were troubled. This was crazy shit the gangbanger was talking. The cops were still in charge. The cops would *always* be in charge.

Let's get real here, they thought. Cinco Muertes was a dude drunk with his own bullshit. A dude like that, he was plenty dangerous.

These last few days, the G had gone crazy. Now he goes and starts kidnapping the straights from the housing projects. What would happen next, they wondered? Maybe he'd declare the neighborhood a new banana republic?

Now Cinco Muertes wanted to see the new women he'd had brought into the Mosque. He

423

especially wanted to see that *puta* from the Bronx Zoo. This was the crazy one's woman. *El Mujer de El Loco.* He would see for himself what made this *puta* so fucking special. He would go at once to the cell in which the woman was being held.

Yolanda struggled to get free of the ropes that they'd tied her hands with. Suddenly she heard the sound of the door crack open. Cinco Muertes walked in, high on crack, shit-brown, bloodshot eyes lit with a psychotic fire.

"You see this, *puta*," said the gangbanger, taking his cock out of his pants. "I want you to watch what I do with it."

At a snap of Cinco Muertes' fingers, two of his Yanomamo warriors held Yolanda down while he came closer, pumping his organ in his fist. Between his lips was a crack reefer, its smoke sucked deep into the gang lord's lungs.

"Ahhhh," he cried out, masturbating all over Yolanda's breasts.

"That be just for openers," he said when he finished. At a snap of Cinco Muertes' fingers, the two goons flung Yolanda down on the bed and brought his Viagra.

***

Night time. It was the right time to kick somebody's ass. Applebaum had already tactically scoped out the area and figured out what his strategy would be. The ins and outs, the ups and downs. All of it was not programmed into the old noggin.

He'd snuck behind some of the derelict cars and planted timed charges of C-4 plastic explosive.

Not enough of the plastique to cause any major damage, but certainly enough to make a great deal of noise, smoke and flame.

When the Yanomamo mouth-breathers guarding the gates of the Mosque ran out to investigate, Applebaum would go in shooting from the hip. He knew he should be shitting his pants at the thought of walking into the lion's den, but he wasn't.

In fact, he was feeling good. The adrenaline was flowing through his veins. He was on what those in the merc business called a combat high.

Applebaum waited down the block counting down to the point of blast off. Twenty seconds, ten, five .... then the plastic detonated. The cars went up like the Fourth of July fireworks display at Coney Island.

Grated auto parts pinwheeled up into the air for thirty feet, then cascaded back to earth, spinning and burning, hitting the street with loud plopping noises. That was what those in the merc business called high-visibility damage.

The effect on the Mosque's protectors was just as Mad Marty had predicted. The Yanomamo guardsmen broke ranks, whipping iron from under their clothes and ran right into the street to see what was happening, in the process making perfect targets out of themselves.

Didn't even cross their minds that somebody might be out there gunning for them, he thought as he cut loose with a figure-eight burst of 7.62 NATO rounds from the chattering M60 Squad Auto in his fists.

THE BLACKOUT HEIST

Moving from cover, Applebaum sprinted across the street to the Mosque's sidewalk entrance. Darkness cloaked the building's lobby, but in the darkness, something moved.

Applebaum saw the eyes of the Yanomamo goon guy widen like dinner plates as he saw him coming. The gangbanger said something in Spanish and dipped under his ski jacket.

He was faster than Mad Marty thought he'd be. The inner-city triggerman almost managed to get what he was carrying out into the open where it might do Marty some damage.

As Applebaum saw the telltale shape of an Uzi Micro subgun, he triggered a burst of the M60 in his hands. Game time came for the Yanomamo seconds later. The heavy caliber NATO slugs ripped a zigzag of holes across the G's fatigue jacket.

Again, he hollered something in Spanish as the Uzi flew from his hands and he tumbled backwards, arms windmilling, legs doing a spastic soft-shoe number in reverse, taking four jerky steps before thudding into a wall, collapsing to a sitting position and finally sliding sideways to die with his butt against the wall and his cheek on the cracked tile lobby floor.

Mad Marty Applebaum pulled the specially smoked visors over his eyes and prepared to pitch a flash-bang grenade into the dark interior of the Mosque. Like he had promised his mother long ago, he never came to a party empty-handed.

FIFTY-NINE

Inskeep, Underneath Manhattan. There. Up ahead. Amazingly, it was there. Had not Inskeep and his ragtag assemblage of passengers stopped precisely where they had, they might not have noticed it.

That they had not sighted the half-hidden aperture in the torch lit caverns of the old city sewer main was understandable. It was no more than a small, shadow-shrouded notch, easily overlooked in the wan light cast by their torches.

Playing his sputtering torch over it, Inskeep could just make out a rusty access ladder threading down to a lower level below the floor of the passageway. Something glistened in the chamber far below them, throwing back the flicker of smoky torch light as a series of sparkling fragments of reflected brilliance.

"Try dropping something into the pit," someone suggested. There was plenty of debris lying scattered along the dry bottom of the sewer tunnel. Picking up a chunk of concrete the size of a large pebble, Inskeep let it drop down and heard the splash of water after an interval of no more than two seconds.

"No way of telling how deep," Inskeep said, trying not to let the disappointment in his voice show. "Could be just a couple of feet maybe."

"I volunteer to go down and take look," said the messenger. The short, wiry Korean was a likely choice to fit down the hole.

"Tunnels go underneath Korea," he explained, however. "Dug by communists in Pyongyang. When I with South Korean army, I in charge of filling tunnels up. Many times get flooded, either by rain or underground water. I know how to handle situation," he concluded.

While the others combined the light of their torches to give Jing additional light as he prepared to climb down the ladder, the messenger took a few tentative steps. Soon his head was below the surface of the hole.

"See anything yet?" Inskeep called down.

"No see yet," Kim's voice came back up, reverberating off the slimy brick walls. "Wait, I get back in minute." They heard him splashing around in brackish water many feet below them.

Down in the hole, Jing Duk Soo had to feel around in the cold brackish water that covered the floor almost to ankle height.

"Don't see anything here," he called up. "No door, nothing. But water is not very high."

Inskeep thought for a moment. There had to be some connection with another tunnel system. The ladder wouldn't have been positioned near another level so close to the surface without there being some purpose for its presence.

"Feel beneath you," Inskeep called down. "See if there's a plate or a manhole cover."

More splashing sounds came up through the dark hole as Jing Duk Soo squatted and probed the slime-encrusted floor of the bay. Suddenly his hands closed around something that felt like a handle.

"Yes," he called up. "I have got hold of something now. Yes, this definitely a handle."

"Can you pull it open?" Inskeep called down.

"I am trying," replied Jing. There were sounds of exertion as he strained to lift the door. "It no good," the Korean finally called up. "Cannot make door to budge."

Inskeep came down and together they managed to pull open the trap door with a groaning sound as more than a century of metal rusted to metal by layers of oxidation separated protestingly. At once, the brackish water rushed down the cavity that had opened and sluiced through into the sublevel below.

The sputtering torches came back to life as a gust of musty air rushed up from the level below.

"Let's go," Inskeep hollered as the group of passengers hustled down the ladder.

***

With the torches now freshly wrapped with rags scavenged from the tunnel and re-lit, the group made its way through the newly uncovered sublevel of the caverns.

429

THE BLACKOUT HEIST

Down here there was plenty of air. Inskeep was certain that this was a good indication of there being a connection with the surface somewhere close by.

There was no light shining through from casemented ventilation ducts above them, however.

Although Inskeep was certain that the group was no more than a few hundred yards from the streets of Manhattan above them, they might nevertheless spend many hours more down here before hitting on a way out.

Of course, if no way out presented itself, then they could very well die down here. The pangs of hunger had been gnawing at his innards for hours. The rest of the passengers were certainly hungry too.

How long could a person survive without food or water? A week, two weeks, a month? How long before the human body grew too weak to continue walking? Yes, Inskeep supposed that it was entirely possible to starve to death down here. Very possible indeed.

Nevertheless Inskeep didn't think that this would happen. There was a way to the surface, he knew it. In fact, as Inskeep saw it, the real problem was the situation to be faced when they finally reached the street.

Who knew what was happening up there? Anything was possible. Inskeep's mind flashed him scenarios from an invasion by men from Mars to the aftershock of a massive earthquake.

What if they'd exploded some kind of a dirty nuke up there? One of those babies could knock out electric power and kill millions of people without hardly making a sound. *There could be nothing but corpses left up there,* thought Inskeep. *And my family, my family too....*

"What the hell is this place?" someone asked, startling Inskeep from his reverie. "It's giving me the creeps."

"Some kind of drainage tunnel," Inskeep returned, the terrible images fading in his mind as he faced the immediate situation. "Yeah, that might be what it is," he added with a nod.

Huge concrete bulkheads filled with stagnant water jutted out along both sides of the long, rectangular passageway whose walls were made of poured concrete and whose terminus was lost somewhere far off in the shadowed distance.

Massive pipes snaked along the ceiling and up and down the side walls. Touching them, Inskeep felt no evidence of condensation. The pipes were dry and cold. Obviously no water had flowed through them for years.

The only evidence of activity was a sluggishly moving stream of brackish water that flowed sluggishly along a narrow trough running along the center of the passageway, about six inches in depth. Inskeep guessed that sewer lines still fed runoff after heavy rains into this system through water percolating through cracks in cement walls.

"Hey," someone called out. "There been people down here pretty recently. Check it out. There's some wino nests here!"

Scattered about the concrete deck, the flattened corrugated cardboard boxes that had contained refrigerators and washing machines, old rags and empty whisky bottles and soda cans were certainly strong evidence that the abandoned drainage tunnel had been inhabited in the recent past, or even that it was currently inhabited by persons as yet unknown.

There was nothing surprising about this. As their numbers expanded with each passing month, the scores of thousands of homeless in New York delved into every nook and cranny of the city for places to sleep.

The network of caverns snaking and twisting beneath the city's surface had long become as familiar to them as the streets above were to most New Yorkers.

The discovery of wino nests was encouraging. It meant that there was a way out of the tunnel close by, an exit used by the human moles who called this subterranean labyrinth their homes.

"Okay, don't worry," Inskeep said. "Keep together, it'll be all right."

The group of passengers moved cautiously along the dank floor, noticing the graffiti scrawled on the walls in the flickering light of the torches they lofted in their hands.

Something was wrong with the graffiti, though. Inskeep couldn't place the source of the anxiety he felt. Then, in a flash, it came to him. The graffiti was the same kind he'd seen on the news about groups of satanic ritualists.

As the group probed further into the drainage tunnel, they saw other disquieting signs left behind by the tunnel's inhabitants.

432

Dried bones and desiccated pieces of body parts belonging to chickens, cats, dogs and other small animals littered the concrete deck.

"No! No! *NOOOOOOOOOOOOOOOO!*"

Shocking them all into starting en masse, the woman's bloodcurdling scream reverberated off the dripping concrete tunnel walls. Pivoting toward the source of the scream, Inskeep was just in time to see the kicking legs thrashing as the body of the female victim was quickly dragged into deeper shadow.

At least three men, probably more, were now coming at Inskeep's group. Two had already grabbed Jing Duk Soo and were dragging the Korean messenger into a side corridor as the Korean's pathetic screams echoed off the concrete walls.

Screaming maniacally as he lunged at the legal secretary's breasts with some kind of long, sickle shaped hook that caught her in the throat, another homicidal mole man with long dreadlocks suddenly jumped down into a nearby pit, pulling the thrashing secretary in after him. There was the splash of water and the woman's screaming abruptly ceased.

Inskeep stuck his torch into the face of another mole man with no hair on his bald head and a bushy black beard who was coming after him screaming, laughing and swinging a meat cleaver.

The guy's beard instantly caught fire as the mole man brayed like a wounded mule and staggered backwards. Inskeep touched him again with his torch, setting the oily rags on his back on fire.

THE BLACKOUT HEIST

The mole man thrashed and rolled on the floor, desperate to quench the flames engulfing his body and managing to stumble to his feet, then run off, still smoldering.

Inskeep turned and waved his torch at another couple of mole men who were hunkering on the shadows, screaming and laughing as they brandished an assortment of knives and other makeshift cutting weapons.

"*Shag it! Go!*" he told the passengers while he and Buddy Coyne held them at bay with their torches, finally flinging his own torch into the mass of hunkering mole men when the last of the passengers in his group had passed him. Then he and Coyne booked like jack rabbits down the tunnel.

They had been running along the length of the corridor for many long minutes when Inskeep hollered for them to stop.

"Hold up," he yelled, out of breath.

They stopped running and listened. There were no sounds of pursuers.

"We must have lost them back there," he said.

"Where do we go now?" someone asked.

"There's only one way to go," Inskeep said, pointing to his left. Let's see where that side tunnel leads us."

Turning, the group went into the new tunnel. Although neither Inskeep nor the passengers he led were aware of it, they were at that moment directly beneath an opening that led directly to the subbasement of a department store on Cortland Street.

Had they taken that exit, they would have reached the surface of the street within minutes.

But they didn't take the exit.

Instead they continued to go deeper and deeper into the claustrophobic darkness of the twisting subterranean corridor.

SIXTY

Battery Towers, Lower Manhattan. Daniel Furness regretted his bravery the moment he was seated in the makeshift breeches buoy.

What in the name of hell was he doing hanging from this contraption hundreds of feet above the streets of downtown Manhattan?

It was too late to change his mind, however. Every second counted, Furness knew. If he stayed where he was, he would die anyway. In the short space of the past few minutes, the flames had already consumed another three building stories. It was either try his luck this way or die staying where he was.

Down the diagonal line of rope he could see Amoroso in the shattered window of the West Tower office that was to be his destination.

Amoroso held the guy rope taut in both hands and signaled up for the man behind Furness to secure the rope on his end.

Moments later, Furness was sliding down the length of rope, the makeshift breeches buoy swaying precariously in the flame-fed updrafts streaming up between the two towers.

Although neither Amoroso nor the other survivors could hear it above the roar of the flames, he was also screaming "Hail Mary full of grace," over and over again at the top of his lungs.

***

Within the space of twenty minutes, a little more than half of the occupants of the East Tower's office that Amoroso had originated from had been successfully evacuated to the West Tower.

There was no time to lose, however. The flames that were consuming the middle and lower floors of the skyscraper were inching their way up the tower at an ever-quickening pace.

Only minutes remained before the floor containing the survivors was consumed like the ones below it.

Another of Amoroso's coworkers took their place dangling from the breaches buoy as it came back to the window on its return to the East Tower.

Because they needed to hurry the procedure against the rising flames, and despite the danger it posed, it was decided to start running two at a time.

A fat woman who worked in bookkeeping now shared the breaches buoy with an accountant who hung onto the rim of the buoy. A tug on the rope was the signal to move.

The buoy swayed precariously in the fiercely gusting wind. Amoroso stopped pulling on the guy rope until the winds died down somewhat. He began pulling once again after daring to wait as long as he could.

Suddenly, without warning, a fierce updraft of hot wind from the explosion that came from one of the burning floors below rocked the breaches buoy, tipping it over.

437

THE BLACKOUT HEIST

With a horrible scream, the fat woman tumbled end-over-end from the buoy, lost almost immediately in the billowing black smoke choking the air below.

The man who had left the burning East Tower with her, struggled to hold onto the guy rope for all he was worth. He succeeded in raising his body somewhat and repositioning himself on the buoy, when suddenly a tongue of flame whooshed upwards, obscuring him from view for several seconds.

When the buoy again was visible, hanging from it was a smoking firebrand that was no longer human.

The accountant was now reacting in a blind panic beyond the powers of rationality to effect.

Flailing and thrashing his arms, the burning man tumbled out of the buoy and was quickly lost in the rising pall of choking black smoke from the fires below.

Those trapped inside the East Tower tried to pull the chair toward back them.

It reached the window a half minute later, somewhat singed but still serviceable.

Inside the office, the six people remaining began fighting among themselves for a chance at saving their lives, realizing that only one of them stood even a prayer of making it.

One man larger and stronger than his coworkers managed to push the others aside and haul himself into the breaches buoy.

Almost as soon as he had ensconced himself within it, though, hands reached out and tore him out of the hard plastic ring. Moments later, he was roughly hauled back inside the derelict office.

Then the man reemerged and, bypassing the buoy altogether, attempted to scale the rope hand-over-hand.

He swayed precariously at first as his momentum combined with the fierce winds created severe torque, then stabilized himself.

He only managed to get a few feet down the rope, though, before a belch of incandescent gasses from the flaming stories beneath him caught him and burned him where he hung.

With a bloodcurdling scream, the man released his grasp and plummeted to his death.

Those in the window of the West Tower looked on in mute horror.

Another figure tumbled out, preferring to hurl himself to his doom rather than perish in the all-devouring flames.

Soon the rest of the faces were lost to view beneath the thickening smoke that obscured the East Tower.

***

Amoroso hustled the rest of the shocked survivors in the room with him out of the office in which they had taken refuge.

"There's nothing we can do for the others," he screamed above the crackling of the inferno. "We've got to try to save ourselves."

At first they moved with zombie-like slowness, but then survival instincts took over. In moments the rest of them were out in the corridor.

THE BLACKOUT HEIST

The elevator was dead, of course, as were the lights, although the glow of the burning tower next to them illuminated their path with an eerie flickering brightness.

Amoroso found the door leading to the fire stairs. The stairwell was littered with debris of every description although otherwise free of major obstructions.

The group raced down the stairs, taking level after floor level at a fast run. For the first time, they believed they would reach safety.

They did not know that the lobby was filled with a slowly spreading lake of gasoline, nor did they smell the fumes it was releasing....

SIXTY-ONE

Applebaum, The South Bronx. A jagged line of automatic fire ripped hunks out of the drywall to Applebaum's right as he sprinted up a flight of stairs to the third floor of the Mosque. Jagged fragments of wood and plaster flew past his ear, cutting his face badly enough to draw blood.

Dodging for cover around the line of fire of the stairwell above, Applebaum fired the M60 SAW, hearing grunts of pain from the next landing up.

The thud of falling bodies that followed a few seconds later was sweet music to his ears.

Another moment and two dead Yanomamos rolled down the stairs to land immobile at Applebaum's feet. Applebaum turned them over with the hot barrel of his smoking machinegun. They were dead as they came. And holler than Swiss cheese.

Upstairs, Applebaum heard Yolanda screaming for help. Flattening against a wall outside the door at the landing of the stairs, he took a couple of deep breaths, then dodged through the doorway on a half crouch, swinging the M60's barrel from side to side.

441

THE BLACKOUT HEIST

A gangbanger appeared suddenly from a doorway to his left, whipping an automatic pistol up to draw a bead on Mad Marty. The Squad Auto burped once long, once short, and a butterfly of steel-jacketed bullets sent the pistolero straight to rat heaven on angel's pinions of hellish flame.

The corridor now clear, Mad Marty sprinted toward the source of Yolanda's screams, the frame of a doorway that had once been the entrance to an apartment about eight feet down the tile-floored corridor to his right.

Yolanda screamed again as Marty reached the entrance, ducking in on a low crouch that he hoped would bring him under the line of fire of any Yanomamo torpedo who might be waiting with a drawn shooter.

Applebaum was glad that he did, as a gangbanger's bullet sang over the top of his head before auguring through the wall beside him.

In a split instant, Mad Marty took in the source of both the hot lead and the screams.

While one gangbanger held Yolanda down on a filthy mattress that served as a bed, another Yanomamo was leveling a wicked-looking Colt Python magnum at him. Applebaum could see the cylinder turn as the street punk squeezed the heater's trigger.

Ducking, Marty scored a tight, eight-round pattern on the shooter that took his head clean off at the neck, throwing the headless corpse back against the wall in a spray of blood and gore with its arms stretched out scarecrow-fashion at either side.

Yolanda screamed again, pulling her clothes up around her. At the same time Cinco Muertes pulled the second Yanomamo triggerman in front of him in a fast save.

Applebaum riddled the drug dealer's human shield with a short, lethal burst. The sacrificed gangbanger shrieked and writhed in agony, his arms and legs convulsing as spasms of terminal pain lit up his nervous system with the fires of retribution. Then the guy went limp.

Cinco Muertes pulled a silver Colt semiauto from under his coat and fired at Applebaum, forcing him to duck for cover. Moving fast, the gangsta sprinted from cover, throwing Yolanda aside as he took flight. Applebaum grabbed her up off the floor and raised her to her feet.

"Forget him," she screamed, "let's get out of this place."

Applebaum ran down the stairs, pushing his girlfriend in front of him. He and Yolanda narrowly avoided the angry hit squad of several more gangbangers that ran after them, guns drawn and curses on their lips. Applebaum, however, was saving his best shot for last.

He'd filled one of the stalled cars with a large brick of C-4, all that remained of his stockpile of the demo putty. As he ran, putting the wrecks between them and Cinco Muertes' crazily firing goon crew, Applebaum fired a long M60 burst of white tracers into the car.

The enormous explosion triggered by the incendiary-tipped bullets belched a stream of flame and debris sky-high. The gangbangers who were crouched here and there on the street and sidewalk dived for cover behind a wall of fire and smoke thrown up by the sudden pyrotechnic eruption.

Some who were too close to the blast-shattered vehicle died in the blaze, their bodies thrashing and flailing as the human torches ran around before dropping to the street and lying still as the flames consumed flesh, blood, organs and bone.

From the top floor window of the Mosque where he had taken refuge, Cinco Muertes was one pissed-off hombre. Nobody waltzed into his turf and did shit like that to him. Nobody. Especially that fucker from the Zoo. That crazy fucker who hadn't seen the last of Cinco Muertes, the king G of Mott Haven.

***

"We gonna get them motherfuckers," Cinco Muertes hollered at his gangsta troops. The Yanomamos, or what was left of them in the wake of Mad Marty's one-man death squad, were holed up in the wreckage of a burned-out department store on Pelham Bay Parkway. Torches illuminated the interior of the derelict home appliance store.

"What's the point of this?" one of his soldiers who went by the handle of Chunks, asked. "Who needs this cowboys and Indians shit? We gonna all be up on murder raps."

A murmur of assent rippled through the ranks of gang members wearing the Yanomamo's colors.

Heads nodded. Cinco Muertes' cold black pushbutton eyes slid over all the faces around him, calmly assessing the situation. He smiled at the end, smiled cruelly. Cinco Muertes was confident they would do what he told them to do. He was the top G and his homies would follow his orders.

"The point of this, Chunks, mah dog," he began, "is that we gots us something to prove. And that something is the fact that these streets belong to us G's. Not to the cops, not to *los blanquitos*, but to *us* G's and us G's alone. Got dat?"

Again, a murmur rippled through the crowd, but it was shorter and less loud this time.

"Now you pussies get your muh-fuckin' *culos* in gear and follow me," Cinco Muertes ordered.

And, as the gangsta honcho had never doubted, they all rose and followed him, chains swinging in their fists, bats propped over their shoulders, knives and guns at their hips and holstered beneath their arms, ready to do battle for absolutely nothing.

***

Mad Marty had a new perspective on life as he looked out over the city from his vantage point atop Building Three of the Bronx Zoo.

Now visible in the gloaming, smoke rose up from the city in dense, acrid palls for miles around.

In the immediate vicinity, the plaza on which stood the towers of the Zoo was littered with debris.

Outside the apartment complex, figures scurried through the streets of the barrio.

The night of terror was effectively over, for now, Marty realized. But if something were not done to restore power and services, the next night would surely be worse.

THE BLACKOUT HEIST

Mad Marty shook his head. What kind of government was this anyway?

They had let everything degenerate. The air, the water, the very freedom to live your life without fear of punishment or even death, often for a trifling infraction or circumstances totally beyond your control. Now disaster had struck, and nothing was being done.

Suddenly there was a sound behind him.

Turning, Marty saw the figure. It was one of his neighbors.

"My kid's been hurt," he cried to Marty.

Marty put down his weapon. He accompanied the man downstairs.

The child was injured. He was barely breathing. The gash in his abdomen was huge. It would turn gangrenous unless he was able to dress and bind up the severe stab wound.

Fortunately, Marty had his first aid kid handy in his pack. He boiled some water and attended to the child's injuries.

The father was one of those who had laughed at "Mad" Marty before.

He wasn't laughing now. He regarded Marty the way Marty had seen cocker spaniels regard their masters in the past, with a mixture of awe, love and fear.

"What we do now?" the father asked Marty.

"We prepare for the worst," Marty replied.

SIXTY-TWO

National Strategic Highway System. Following President Johnson Ubutu Ubuto Ebong's directive to revise the US strategic forces' defense readiness condition level back to Defcon Five after it had been determined conclusively that no attack was forthcoming, units of the National Guard were mobilized to relieve the stricken New York metropolitan area blacked out by the EMP death pulse.

Unfortunately, these units had their hands full merely in coping with the problems that arose in their own EMP-affected operational areas.

The highways and roads leading toward New York were hopelessly clogged with stalled vehicles of every make, model and description.

While some stranded motorists had found lodging in nearby homes, motels and rest stops, many more were still waiting by their immobile vchicles for Red Cross relief to arrive. With the roads impassible, only aircraft stood any chance of getting through to New York.

A transport plane was being loaded with medical supplies, food supplies and other items to treat the disaster victims at Offut Air Force base in Nebraska.

447

THE BLACKOUT HEIST

Unfortunately, the loading process was slow. Computers across the country, even in areas not directly effected by the nuclear EMP blast, were operating at no greater than twenty-five percent efficiency.

This was because most large computers were linked in a wide area network to share information, and many of these were located in the EMP disaster zone.

A fleet of Pave-Low helicopters, capable of making a long-range run into the afflicted area was standing by awaiting orders to take off.

It would be many hours yet, however, before relief in any significant form, could begin to trickle into the totally blacked out city of New York.

***

Revolving dome lights flashed red atop the lone ambulance that tended to the injured men who had been pulled from the burning wreckage of the Ninety-fifth Street transformer station.

The ambulance's doors were closed and the paramedics sped off toward Harlem Hospital, where a skeleton crew of doctors was on call.

Rick Skerrit sat in the police mobile command center and decided to give the order to hold off on reactivating the remaining transformer stations.

If another major overload and power outage took place, then the entire power grid serving New York might well collapse like a line of dominoes. In that case, there would not be a second chance to make repairs.

The city would be completely blacked out for several days, and it might be months before current was completely restored.

The extra time would allow final preparations to be made to shunt electricity from the pooled power reserves that EEPA had allocated the city through the still intact network of power cables and transformer banks that linked New York State to the rest of the country's Northeast corridor.

The cables and transformer stations situated along most of the power transmission network were still largely intact. But any number of things could go wrong -- and once the switch was thrown, putting New York back on the national grid -- there would be no turning back.

***

At the Seventy-fourth Street transformer facility, the MetroCon repair crew was faced with a dilemma.

The power transforming equipment was in a precarious state. It was holding steady at present, but it could destabilize at any moment.

The crew boss was faced with the potential of an accident occurring if he waited too long.

On the other hand, he had to hold back until the rest of the stations got on line before throwing the switch.

Suddenly, the station was surrounded by a crowd of street people. Some of them carried guns. The street people took all the money that the members of the repair crew carried.

A big guy, with Indian features and with a black du-rag tied close around his head, was their leader.

THE BLACKOUT HEIST

Without warning, he emptied a small, .22 caliber target pistol into one of the repairmen in the crew.

He told them that the same thing would happen to the rest of them if they didn't do exactly what he said.

"Why are you doing this?" asked the crew chief.

"To you this is hell," he was told. "To us, it's heaven. We like it the way it is now. Dark. The darkness is our gift, your curse. We want to keep it that way."

The street people poured gasoline all over the repair site and set it on fire.

As the repair crew's survivors fled, the transformer station blew sky-high, consumed in an incandescent fireball.

DAVID ALEXANDER

SIXTY-THREE

Low earth orbit. Cosmonaut Illyana Gretschkova angled herself toward the last YZ-class satellite still in orbit, *Pichuga*-3. The magnesium-monel alloy hull of the CIS military reconnaissance satellite reflected the light of the sun back at her in a blinding beam.

Despite the polarized filter of her helmet visor that screened out most of the solar radiation, the intense glare was so painful that it made her squint.

Behind her, the US Space Shuttle Pioneer hung against a black starscape, the doors of its open cargo bay resembling the wings of a gigantic seagull.

With the successful dismantling of the second *Pichuga*, all that would now be required would be to neutralize the nuke onboard this final satellite and the mission would be successfully completed.

Suddenly Gretschkova's helmet intercom crackled with static. One hundred fifty miles below her, and ten times that distance to the east at Baikonur Cosmodrome, Vassily Petrov's voice came through the lightweight headset as clearly as though he were standing right beside her.

"How far are you from the satellite?" Petrov asked Gretschkova. In front of him in the darkened

451

mission control room, he could see the computer's minute-by-minute progress report on the systems status of the final satellite.

The picture did not look good. The failure rate of the microprocessor chip onboard *Pichuga* was increasing with every passing minute.

It would have to be dismantled quickly.

"Are you within working distance of it?" Petrov said into the microphone at his lips. "Can you get to the plate of the maintenance cavity?"

"Yes," Gretschkova replied. "I have made contact now." Gretschkova had grasped a protruding handhold on the satellite's hull and was working her way around to the access bay to the component module that housed the warhead arming microprocessor. The eyephone over his left eye showed him a close-up schematic view. "It will be a few more minutes."

Petrov frowned. She might not have another few minutes. The computer display was indicating that the microchip was on the verge of imminent failure.

If the circuitry module containing the defective microchip was not removed very quickly, the resulting explosion would not only claim Gretschkova's life, but the lives of the remaining five astronauts and a very expensive American shuttle as well, to say nothing of plunging most of the American Middle West into the same state as its East Coast.

Ripping open the spun Kevlar lid of her tool pouch, Gretschkova pulled the ratchet wrench from the pouch and brought it to the first of the four hexagonal nuts that secured the access plate to the satellite's hull.

Even through her air-conditioned space suit that was constructed of highly reflective fabric to keep it cool, the cosmonaut could feel the intense heat of the sun that radiated back at her from the spacecraft's polished alloy skin.

Gretschkova attached the ratchet wrench to the first hex nut and began to turn it, but it would not budge. *The sun,* she thought, *the damned sun!* Because the plate was located on the side of the satellite in full sunlight now, the intense solar heat had made the bolts expand within their threaded sockets.

The computer began flashing a warning sign. Petrov turned to the technician seated at the screen.

"Not long," the technician told him in answer to his unspoken query, his voice grim. "Maybe seconds."

"How far along are you?" Petrov said into the transmitter mike with as much calm as he could muster. "Have you removed the plate yet?"

If she had, Petrov knew, then there might still be minutes required to disconnect it from the four small connector interfaces that secured it to the satellite's internal wiring.

"Negative," came Gretschkova's reply. "I have the first two bolts free." She could see the gleaming hex bolts sparkling like miniature stars as they floated off to one side.

She had used all her strength to loosen the swollen bolts from the satellite's hull and her hands ached from the effort. "Am beginning to loosen the remaining bolts now."

The computer flashed the word:

FAILURE

"The chip has failed," Petrov shouted into the microphone. "Repeat. *The chip has failed!* Explosion is imminent. Return to the shuttle immediately."

Gretschkova struggled with the final bolt securing the access plate to the satellite's hull. She had heard Petrov's shouted warning, but knew that if she could only remove the plate then all she would need to do would be to pull the circuit board from its bus.

To her chagrin, however, the final bolt was stuck tight. No matter how much force she applied to the ratchet wrench, the hex nut would not turn.

Panic now started to well up in Gretschkova's throat. She looked toward the American shuttlecraft. Though she knew that it floated no more than a few hundred meters from her present position, it seemed to be light years away.

"Return to the Shuttle," Petrov's voice again shouted in cosmonaut Gretschkova's ear. "Get away from there immediately!"

"Negative," Gretschkova said back into her helmet mike, her voice hard with resignation. "I will do what must be done."

She let go of the ratchet and grasped the handhold of *Pichuga*-3 firmly with both hands.

Then she activated the personal propulsion unit strapped to her back, opening it up full-throttle and angling the propulsion nacelles away from the

454

American spacecraft. In moments, she had propelled herself better than fifty meters into space.

The radar operator at Baikonur Cosmodrome noted the icon moving across the screen.

"What are you doing?" Petrov shouted into the mike. "What in the name of hell is happening?"

But then, the flight director realized what Gretschkova was doing and fell silent, turning to watch the icon that moved from the American shuttle at an ever-increasing rate.

Petrov was aware that Gretschkova had done the only thing possible under the circumstances. She had sacrificed her own life so that who knew how many others might not have to die.

Onboard the shuttle, commander Jim Magnus at the helm saw what Gretschkova was doing. "What the hell are we going to do?" asked copilot Larry O'Hare.

"If she can manage to give that thing enough of a shove," he returned, "maybe there's still a chance." Magnus pulled the gooseneck console mike to his mouth and punched the broadcast button. Both of the Russian crew members spoke almost perfect English so he knew that he'd be understood.

Speaking quickly, Magnus told Gretschkova to use her last reserves of fuel to propel herself away from the satellite at the last moment.

They would have to hope that *Pichuga*-3 gained enough momentum so that it would be far enough away from both the shuttle and the earth do be rendered harmless when the nuke onboard exploded.

THE BLACKOUT HEIST

"No," came Gretschkova's reply. "There is no hope. My great, great grandmother died at Stalingrad. She gave up her life for a reason. I do the same thing now."

"You're crazy," Magnus shouted into the console mike. "There's still a chance."

"There is none." Gretschkova turned her thrusters on full force. She was constantly gaining momentum. Already she had traveled the better part of two kilometers. *A little further,* she thought, *just a little further and it will all be all right.*

The American shuttlecraft had grown much smaller now. Gretschkova turned, mentally saying good-bye to the world she was leaving behind forever.

"*Do svidaniya,*" she said, before the rapidly expanding fireball incinerated her at its incandescent heart.

SIXTY-FOUR

Suckdog, Staten Island.

"Fill your hand!"

At the sound of the voice Suckdog spun on the heels of his military surplus Malaysian War jungle boots. He saw the guy with the buzz saw. The guy had a second buzz saw that he was kicking toward him.

Suddenly Suckdog realized that he was alone. There were none of his Aryan Death Squad pards around him to watch his back. As a spurt of adrenaline made his heart thunder in his chest, Suckdog realized that it was now one-on-one between himself and the guy with the buzz saw.

"The choice is yours, chickenshit. I shoot you dead or you fight it out."

Saying that, Parrish revved the buzz saw he held in his hand, making it growl angrily in the silence of the candle-lit Mall.

"You're crazy," Suckdog hollered. "Thrasher! Gorgo!" he shouted, confident that his skins would come despite what the crazy mo' fo' with the power saw had told him.

457

THE BLACKOUT HEIST

"Meathook! Pig Pink!" His shouts were met only with silence, though.

Parrish flung something at Suckdog. What he flung looked like a bunch of melons or coconuts tied together. They made a kind of sloppy-wet, hollow-inside sound as they thudded against the floor and rolled a little way before coming to rest at the tips of Suckdog's boots.

With a sudden sickening feeling in his gut, Suckdog saw that what the security guard had flung at him wasn't melons, coconuts or any other type of vegetable.

They were the severed heads of Meathook, Thrasher, Pig Pink and two other neo-Nazi skins, tied together with nylon fishing tackle from the Mall's Bait 'N Switch sport shop.

"No more fucking Indians left on the wall," the security guard said in a strange, nasal voice that was tinged with a demented laughter, pulling the chain on his buzz saw and filling the Mall's corridor with the sound of its revving motor.

"Just you and me, babycakes."

He patted the buzz saw.

"And my buzz saw here makes three."

As the guy with the buzz saw advanced menacingly on Suckdog, the Aryan Death Squad honcho realized that he was now in the presence of something he'd never before thought existed, and certainly had never seen anywhere else before.

He realized that this was a guy who was way fucking crazier than even he was.

***

DAVID ALEXANDER

Suckdog grabbed for the power saw that Parrish had kicked toward him. At first, as he fumbled with it, keeping one eye on the grinning guard, he thought it was coated with something slippery, some kind of oil he'd put on it to make it slide out of his hands.

Then he realized it was his own sweat that was making the buzz saw difficult to get a good, solid grip on.

Vroooom! Vrooommmmmmmmm!

The sound of Parrish revving his buzz saw echoed through the corridors of the Mall. Suckdog fumbled with the pull-chain, hearing the saw in his own hands suddenly awaken.

Now that he had it running, he was even more scared than he'd been before. Funny how that should be, but it was. This was because now Suckdog realized he'd have to fight the dude. A duel of buzz saws. Shit. This was too fuckin' *real.*

Suckdog moved forward, sweeping the buzz saw in a shallow arc ahead of him. As he did, he watched his opponent's eyes carefully. Watch the eyes, he knew, you could tell when the opponent was going to make his play. Suddenly Suckdog saw the guy's eyes dart to the left. He feinted left, then dove sharply right.

Vroooom! Vrooooooom!

Parrish had faked him out. At first Suckdog didn't feel anything. Then he saw the wetness on the floor at his feet, heard the sound of something spilling out, striking hardness of the surface.

459

Only then did he realize he'd been cut in the side. Oh God, this *was* real. Oh shit, this wasn't no *game* no more. Suckdog was frightened.

Bending suddenly, Suckdog swept the buzz saw in a surprise lunge at Parrish's feet, attempting to slice him off at the knees. But Parrish sidestepped the move easily. Then, on the follow-through, he brought his buzz saw blade up in a blur of light.

Vrooooooooommmmmm!

It was an angry, drawn-out sound now. The sound of some vicious prehistoric monster beast tasting prey-flesh. Suckdog felt a pitchfork of pain stab him hard in his left shoulder.

With sudden horror, he saw his left arm hanging against his body by a narrow strip of pulped flesh. Arterial blood squirted from the huge red gash torn in his army surplus camos. Suckdog screamed. The shriek was high and girlish. When it tapered to silence, Suckdog turned and vomited all over himself.

"No more," he begged, throwing down the buzz saw. "Please, I surrender, I fucking surrender!" He raised his vomit-stained, bloody arms in a gesture of utter defeat.

Vroooom! Vroooommmmmmmmmm!

Parrish pulled the chain on the buzz saw he wielded, revving the gasoline-powered engine. The flames of the many candles surrounding them, and garbage burning in smudge pots made from steel drums, illuminated his blood-smeared face.

The guy was really insane, Suckdog realized. The guy was crazy, totally, certifiably, crazy.

"*No way*," Parrish hollered, shaking his head. "No compromises. No surrender. *No prisoners*."

Then he brought the tip of the buzz saw down and held it close to Suckdog's face. The whizzing tip of rotoring steel teeth was so close that Suckdog could feel the wind that it made as the chain sent the hooked outer cutting edge spinning around at many hundreds of revolutions per second.

"*No*," Suckdog said in a voice made whisper-soft by fear, "Please. Don't ... k-kill me!"

Parrish laughed. "Crawl," he commanded him.

Using his good hand and his legs, Suckdog sucked floor and made crabbing backward movements across the deck of the Mall, leaving a slippery blood track behind him.

As he crawled like some crustacean picked apart by a hungry seagull on a beach, Parrish kept the tip of the buzz saw blade poised a fraction of an inch from his face. Finally Suckdog felt himself backed up against a wall. There was nowhere else left to crawl to.

Cornered, up against the wall, suckdog raised his head and looked up into Parrish's face. The security guard stood there, breathing heavily, not moving while the buzz saw blade was kept poised near the bridge of the Nazi skin's nose.

Then Parrish smiled. He saw what he had wanted to see. *Fear.* A lifetime worth, compressed into the space of mere, fleeting moments. Moving quickly, yet precisely, he touched the tip of the buzz saw blade to the tip of Suckdog's nostrils.

Blood spurted from the raggedly severed stump. Suckdog screamed. He screamed and screamed, gibbering like an ape, delirious from the pain. This was a nightmare. He would wake from this nightmare any second now.

This was a nightmare. This was a nightmare. Blood was dripping from the nose stump into his mouth, pouring down his throat because he was breathing too heavily to keep from swallowing it. This was a nightmare. He would wake up any minute. The pain was incredible. *Vrooooommmmmm.* The buzz saw purred. This was a nightmare.

"Please, oh God please...."

Parrish smiled as he waved the buzz saw above Suckdog's body like a revving, wailing, belching, magician's wand. Then he touched its tip to his groin.

Suckdog's penis and testicles dissolved in a sudsing red froth. A bloody cascade spouted up from between his legs. Parrish revved the buzz saw. This was a nightmare. He would wake up any minute. He would wake up any minute. This was a nightmare.

ThiswasanightmareThiswasanightmareThiswa saniiiiiii

Vroooommmmmm! Vroooooooom! VroooooooooommmmmMMMMMMM! ThiswasanightmareThiswasanightmareThiswasaniiii iiii. *VrooooooooommmmmMMMMMMM! VrooooooooommmmmMMMMMMM!*

ThiswasanightmareThiswasanightmareThiswasa niiiiiiii

Blood poured down Suckdog's throat in a frothing red torrent tasting of brimstone and bile and madness and piss. His eyes seemed to be swimming in blood. There was a red haze he was looking out through like windows on his soul.

Everything moved in slow motion now. The maniac with the buzz saw seemed to bend forward, almost lovingly, bringing the buzz saw down across his legs, passing it across his knees.

Time speeded up, a film jerked back into synch.

Vrooooom!

A grisly fountain of blood mixed with chunks of bone flew up from Suckdog's severed knees. Parrish laughed with delight, tasting the blood that splattered his face with his tongue, pushing harder on the buzz saw to cut and to chop.

Vrooom! Vrooom! Vrooom!

This was a nightmare. He would wake up any minute. This this this this this this this this this

Parrish suddenly stepped behind Suckdog. He bent forward a little, bringing the revving tip to Suckdog's ruined and demolished groin.

"When you see your boy Hitler, give the fucker my regards," Parrish sang, and sliced Suckdog down the middle into two neat, though extremely bloody, halves, like butchering the carcass of a cow into slabs of beef at the slaughterhouse," remember me to East Berlin."

This was a nightmare. This was a nightmare. This was a night --

VroooooooooommmmmmMMMMMMMM!

Suckdog didn't hear the sound of Parrish throwing the gore-spattered buzz saw over the

THE BLACKOUT HEIST

balcony of the Mall's second level. He was already
much too dead by then.

DAVID ALEXANDER

Inskeep, underneath Manhattan. Inskeep and his group of passengers had already been trudging through the abandoned sewer main network for several hours and had lost track of time. Now they found themselves in the dark side corridor which branched off from the storm drain tunnel they had fled from.

Although none of the mentally drained and physically fatigued wanderers realized it, they had long ago passed a point directly beneath an exit to street level and were now walking back toward the flooded section of subway tunnel they had left behind long ago.

They had one final escape option left to them.

It lay in an access door to an abandoned subway pumping station that led to a cross-tunnel. The cross-tunnel terminated in a subway station from which stairs led up to the street.

THE BLACKOUT HEIST

The opening was located approximately five hundred yards ahead of them. But it was hidden from view, and in the shadows could be easily overlooked.

For the moment Inskeep and his people were glad that they were out of danger and that the air was better here. Currents of wind wafting faintly from hidden cracks in the ceiling and walls made breathing easier and allowed their torches to burn more brightly than the fitful light they had cast deeper down in the tunnels.

The light of the torches illuminated the walls of the tunnel sufficiently for them to see that the walls here were free from graffiti, and the concrete floor was clear of any sign of human habitation.

"Let's take five," Inskeep suggested. The rest of the passengers were only too eager to second him.

Of the thirty-six passengers that had originally set out from the point in the tunnel where the IRT local had stalled, only a dozen had survived.

The passengers settled in along the dank tunnel walls. They stared ahead with the blank apathy of combat short-timers.

By the watches that still worked they could tell that the passage of time they had spent in the tunnels could be measured in hours. But the gut reality of their trek argued that it had actually been a matter of lifetimes.

Inskeep rubbed his hot, tired eyes. He was having trouble breathing.

Hellish memories of the jungle warfare that had claimed his soul, long bottled up in a dark, secret place inside him, now rose to the surface of his mind. The numbing, paralyzing, claustrophobia was returning. He had believed he'd left it behind, in the terrorists army's tunnels of Surinam.

But Inskeep had not left it behind, not completely anyway, he now realized. Checking his self-winding wrist watch, he decided to give the group a couple of minutes more to rest.

When that time limit had passed, Inskeep hauled himself erect and motioned for the others to get up too.

Groaning and protesting, the tired passengers rose to their feet and trekked through the dank, slime-encrusted tunnels while the light of their torches flickered across the crypt-like cement walls.

***

They continued walking, stopping every few feet to play the light of their torches across the slabs of concrete to either side in search of doorways or other openings that might lead them to the surface.

Mrs. Ida Schuhmacher, slumped on the shoulder of her nephew Royal, was becoming weaker every minute that passed.

She had almost passed out a couple of minutes before, and now she felt the telltale signs of another attack about to come on.

It was her "aura." A ringing in the ears accompanied by a severe headache and photoluminous flashes that she continued to see even if she closed her eyelids.

Mrs. Schuhmacher's aura was getting deeper. She tugged on her nephew's shirt sleeve.

"An attack," she whispered hoarsely, "*Oy gevalt! I'm going to have another attack!*"

As she slumped to the cold, hard concrete, Royal reached down and held her jaws open.

"Quick!" he screamed. "Give me a pencil, anything to put under her tongue."

"What's happening?" someone cried out as they clustered around the woman who was now writhing in agony on the floor, the flickers of their torches playing over her convulsing form.

"An epileptic seizure," Royal said.

Inskeep handed Royal a pen which he jammed under Mrs. Schuhmacher's tongue.

The instant that he released his grip on her jaws she champed down with manic strength on the pen and her thrashings became more frantic still.

"Somebody help me to hold her down," Royal called out.

Haj Yacoub, another passenger, grabbed one of Mrs. Schuhmacher's arms. Incredibly, her manic strength was enough to hurl the wiry ghetto youth several feet to one side.

"Shit," Haj exclaimed as he landed dazed against one of the walls. "Whassup wid' dat shit?"

One of the passengers, a fat woman in a down jacket, came over to help Haj up as Mrs. Schuhmacher began to recover from her fit.

"Hey, you guys, look over here!" she shouted.

Inskeep came over. He couldn't believe his eyes. It was an ancient doorway. Stooping, he could feel a current of cool, dank air coming from beneath it.

As his eyes adjusted, he could now discern faint motes of light from beyond the closed door.

"It could be a way out of here," Inskeep said. "Give me a hand."

Buddy Coyne the construction worker and Haj helped Inskeep pound down the door. It gave way with a crunching of wood. Inskeep and Haj went in to investigate.

They saw a flight of old cast iron stairs leading upward. There was light up there. Inskeep and the Rapper tentatively mounted the steps. The flight of stairs led to a darkened room.

"Looks like our bad luck's still holding," Coyne said.

Inskeep didn't answer. He wasn't so sure. He stepped up to one of the walls of the large store room and tapped on the shiny black surface.

"This is glass," he said, excitement in his voice. "Not cement, but glass!"

Coyne and the Rapper were beside Inskeep in a second flat. "Damn, it sure is!" one of them agreed. Without having to discuss the situation, the three of them grabbed up pieces of debris and hurled them through the plate glass.

As it the window shattered, Manhattan daylight spilled through. Although there wasn't much of it, it was bright enough to make them squint.

They looked out onto a subway station. Although the platform was empty, a flight of concrete stairs led to street level.

"Follow me," Inskeep hollered down the stairs to the rest of the passengers still below. One by

469

THE BLACKOUT HEIST

one, they filed up towards the pale shafts of gritty New York daylight.

DAVID ALEXANDER

SIXTY-SIX

Applebaum, The South Bronx. Most of the Zoo's tenants who had chosen or been forced to take shelter in the huge housing complex had holed up in the lobby of the main building.

Marty recognized many of his neighbors. Often he had been angered to the point of rage by their remarks about him, but now he felt the joy of triumph.

He was finally somebody in their eyes. His unique skills, his special know-how, finally counted for something.

No longer was he the village idiot. Now Mad Marty was the guy to whom they all turned to save their lives.

Marty decided he would help them save their lives. But it would cost them. What Marty did, he did for a fee.

"You want to live?" he asked. "Okay, I'll help you live, but it won't come free." Marty found a garbage can. "Turn over all your valuables. That's my price. I'll take whatever you have."

A murmur arose from the assemblage in front of him.

THE BLACKOUT HEIST

"Go ahead, talk it over," he said to them with a smile. "But do it fast. Pretty soon those geeks will be back. The longer you take to get ready, the less prepared to deal with them you'll be."

***

It didn't take very much discussion before Mad Marty's fellow tenants decided to cough up the payment for his services. Marty took the plastic garbage can around, collecting donations from each one of them.

At the end of the haul, Marty had collected a couple of thousand dollars in cash, jewelry and other negotiables.

It wasn't big money but it would do for a start. He had payments coming due on a lot of special tactical equipment he'd bought.

"All right people," Mad Marty announced after pocketing the cash. "You're all going to learn a little about what it takes to defend yourselves against the scumbags and fuckers out there."

Marty called for a show of hands of all of those who had gone through any kind of military training. Two kids raised their hands.

One of them looked too young and under questioning broke down and said he'd been lying.

The other kid had been through Army basic training and knew a little about combat techniques and weapons.

Next, Marty asked for any of those who had any firearms in their possession.

Again, he got two hands. One of them had a handgun, the other had a rifle. Both weapons were kept in their apartments.

Marty sent them off to get their weapons, escorted by the kid from basic training to whom he handed his M16A41 assault rifle.

"Now, ladies and gentlemen," Marty told his crowd, "here's where the soup starts sticking to the spoon."

***

Mad Marty Applebaum knew that the attack would soon materialize. In only a couple of hours it would be dark again.

Man's primeval bloodlust went back for millions of years.

The programming for violence was locked in the human genes.

Attacking at night was as instinctive as the urge for sex, food and sleep. Marty had no doubt that Cinco Muertes and his gang would come at them again, and hit as hard as they could.

The attack would be all the more savage because Cinco Muertes must know that it would be his posse's final chance to overrun the Zoo.

There had been no war. In the modern world the pace of events proceeded at a fixed rate.

Crises were measured in hours these days. Cinco Muertes had to have surmised that by tomorrow or the next day, at any rate very soon, the authorities would have regained some measure of control, perhaps enough to land his gangsta ass in jail.

Mad Marty and the kid who had army training helped prepare barricades out of stalled cars that they pushed around the lobby of the main building.

THE BLACKOUT HEIST

They siphoned gas from the tanks and filled empty bottles with the high octane fuel that some of the women and kids had scrounged up.

Others were put to work tearing strips of clothing to make fuses for the Molotov cocktails.

Some of the cocktails were filled with a mixture of gasoline and liquid detergent.

The detergent would give a stickiness to the burning fuel, making it stick to anything it touched. It was a kind of makeshift napalm. Not as effective as the real thing, but in a pinch better than nothing.

With the six additional rifles available to them, Applebaum positioned a crew of "sharpshooters" at various points at the perimeter of the makeshift barricade.

Applebaum had serious doubts that they would be able to hit the broad side of a barn, but at least they would go down throwing lead.

As for Applebaum, he prepared himself to wage a one-man guerilla war outside the periphery.

The Army kid asked to go along. Applebaum considered. Maybe he could use a hand after all. He gave the kid an extra BDU suit and both of them cammied up.

***

Cinco Muertes' goon battalion ringed the Zoo. The gangbangers from the Mosque prepared to attack. The winter sky had clouded over, blocking out what little sunlight there was to begin with. An early twilight would give them the advantage.

Cinco Muertes would personally reserve getting his hands on that gun-crazy motherfucker who had humiliated him in front of his Yanomamo warriors.

474

When he did, he would carve his initials on his chest with the blade of his Jamaican gravity blade. That was a promise. And the Five Deaths was a homie who always kept his promises.

THE BLACKOUT HEIST

SIXTY-SEVEN

Battery Towers, Wall Street District. The fierce explosion caught the six persons still alive in the skyscraper complex's East Tower completely by surprise.

As the highly combustible diesel fuel from the crashed tanker ignited, it sent a white-hot sunball of flame belching upward through the ceiling of the East Tower's main lobby.

The shock waves were enormous. They shook the entire one hundred and ten story structure like the hand of some invisible colossus.

Falling debris crushed Cappy Templeton, the operations manager. The middle-aged Templeton, known for his ribald office jokes, had survived every obstacle that had lain in the group's path so far. Templeton had appeared to lead a charmed life.

Now he died with sickening suddenness as a jagged edged shard of glass three feet long penetrated his stomach and exited through the small of his back.

Blood gushed in a bright red plume from Templeton's mouth. His eyes bugged and one popped from its socket to dangle on braided red nerve strands across his pinstriped shirt. His lips moved as though he had meant to say something, but the mouth, unplugged from the brain, couldn't manage to get out the fatally wounded man's final words.

Templeton staggered forward and collapsed in a crumpled heap.

Amoroso and Billy the Ear, the boss's hatchet man, realized instantly that there wasn't a damned thing they could do for Templeton.

On the contrary, the survivors were all resigned to the imminence of their own deaths.

They struggled to grab onto anything that would afford them handholds as the entire building trembled and swayed with a horrible sound of thunder, debris pelting them as the walls and ceilings began to disintegrate.

Suddenly, the floors beneath their feet sagged and then gave way completely as the structural steel and concrete crumbled into jagged confetti. For a moment, they hung in space. And then, as though gravity suddenly remembered them, they began to fall through a cloud of dust and debris with the sound of the collapsing floors above and below them in their ears.

"Drop down to the next level," Amoroso cried out, struggling to be heard above the terrible din. "It's our only shot."

They let go and felt themselves hurtle through dark, dusty space.

Amoroso hit with a savage lurch that made his head reel. He felt something sticky run down his face. At first he couldn't feel his arm and was afraid that it had been torn off.

Blindly, Amoroso groped around and crawled a few feet through the choking smoke and piles of debris.

"Billy? You there, Billy?" he cried out. "Frank? Nan? Anybody alive, shout out!"

"It's me, Nan Bruckner," a woman's voice said weakly. "I-I think my leg is broken."

Amoroso crawled over. The secretary was pinned beneath piles of smoldering wreckage.

Amoroso inspected Nan's leg. It was badly swollen at the ankle but it didn't otherwise appear broken. Amoroso strained to pull the wreckage off of her.

"Try to walk," he counseled, "hold onto this to prop you up," he handed her a piece of wreckage to use as a walking stick.

One by one, figures appeared from the debris or called out for help from beneath piles of rubble that had collapsed on them and pinned them dazedly beneath a mountain of rubble.

Billy the Ear didn't make it. The office spy had been crushed by a steel I-beam that had severed his head. The headless body was horribly mangled.

"What do we do with Billy?" Tony the messenger asked, "it's not right to just leave him there, even if he was a guy you loved to hate."

"You're right, it's not," Amoroso agreed.

Stooping, he picked up Billy's bloodstained body that felt feather-light and frail as that of a child's.

Suddenly, Amoroso noticed the odor. *Oh God, don't let it be. Not after all that. Not now.* Again, the smell. Unmistakable now.

Gasoline!

The air was filled with the powerful stench of gasoline fumes. It was choking, nauseating, sickening. Amoroso saw the source of the fumes in a moment.

The tanker truck.

The broken body of its driver lay sprawled half in and half out of the cab. A tremendous rupture in the side of the huge fuel storage tank atop the long low-loader trailer hitched to the diesel cab of the semi was still leaking a stream of the high octane mixture. The lobby floor of the West Tower was covered with a greasy and highly combustible fluid.

Only by some miracle had the fumes not yet ignited. But they were all living on borrowed time, Amoroso was all too well aware. All it would take would be a single spark to set off a massive explosion.

Amoroso looked around. And froze as a cold, numbing panic raced along every nerve ending in his bruised and battered body.

There. In the ceiling. Dangling from the ruptured concrete. *Gas mains.* Broken pipes hissing with gas.

Amoroso's mind fast-forwarded to a flashpoint minutes, maybe seconds ahead of them in time. *The ceiling would give way. Metal pipe grating against metal pipe. A spark ... only one single spark....*

And yet, they could make it. He knew it. Through the shattered plate glass that was all that remained of the lobby's windows, they could see the street outside.

All they had to do was to crawl down from the mezzanine level to the lobby. Negotiating the heaps of rubble would be treacherous. But it would take minutes. *Did they have minutes?*

Amoroso helped pull the survivors of the fall from the wreckage. Nan Bruckner, Tony the messenger and Murray Jackman, Amoroso's boss, were all okay. They helped get everybody else out. The survivors were at street level.

"Where's Mary?" someone asked.

Amoroso didn't see the old lady. He swore. He knew he had to go back inside and search for her. He told the other survivors to get away, that he'd go back in, telling Jackman to help them away from the danger zone.

He waited for a moment, watching the others head toward the safety of the Richard Cheney Memorial Plaza directly outside the complex's street-level mezzanine. There was a sudden longing in his heart to join them.

But then he thought of the old lady back inside the shattered lobby, maybe still alive, pinned helplessly beneath some wreckage she was too weak or too injured to move. Amoroso couldn't leave her. He had to go back inside.

The overpowering stench of the gas fumes seemed doubly choking as Amoroso stepped between the shattered panes of glass and stepped over piles of wreckage, his shoes splashing on the gasoline-saturated deck.

"Mary?" he called out. "Can you hear me?"

Suddenly there was an answer. Mary's voice called feebly from within the wreckage-strewn expanse.

Amoroso made his way toward the source of the tremulous voice. The old lady was pinned beneath a fragment of the huge Calder stabile that had formed the lobby's centerpiece. She had fallen on the outer edge of the rest of the group and hadn't been seen. Amoroso worked to free her. He held her frail body in his arms.

Oh no, please no!

Suddenly there was the sound of rumbling that Amoroso knew presaged another slide of many tons of debris from the ruined levels above him.

Frantically he clutched the woman to him and dragged her a few feet, but Amoroso knew that it would not do either of them any good. The next thing he knew, there was a crash as steel beams snapped like tinfoil. The resulting spark ignited the gasoline-saturated air.

The fireball almost instantly incinerated Amoroso and Mary together as it blew sections of the East Tower for many miles across the Wall Street area.

***

Wordlessly, too numbed to even think, the survivors staggered from the wreckage of the Battery Park Commerce Towers complex toward the level of the street.

THE BLACKOUT HEIST

Darkness was falling. The early twilight was deepening into the deep magenta of evening. The winter air was cold, yet despite the fact that none of them were wearing coats or sweaters, they felt nothing, neither pain nor pleasure, neither joy nor sorrow, nor even hope.

The survivors looked around them, dumbstruck, stunned and shocked to the cores of their beings at the devastation they had witnessed.

Their stunned amazement was heightened by the knowledge that only a day before, they had walked these streets as they had on countless other mornings and afternoons as part of what had been for many a familiar work routine.

With shocking suddenness, that familiar routine had been utterly shattered with a savagery and a finality that their minds refused to grasp or accept.

Cars were piled up amid the wreckage of countless shattered windowpanes. Fires had turned the trees in the nearby park to charred, blackened stumps.

"What happened?" asked Murray Jackman. "What in the name of God happened?"

Nan Bruckner, the closest person to him, didn't reply, nor did any of the other survivors.

Whether or not the question had been directed at them didn't matter.

All that did matter now was moving away from this terrible place as fast as they were able and not looking back. If they did, they were afraid they might lose their minds.

SIXTY-EIGHT

Skerrit, West Side. A Draconian choice now confronted Rick Skerrit. Whether to turn on the power or not to turn it on.

If he guessed wrong, then the multi-kilowatt surge of electricity could very well short out the remaining sections of the power network that were still left intact and in some semblance of working order.

It he waited too long, however, the city would undergo another night of terror. Even if power were partially restored, reasoned Skerrit, it could make a difference.

Just knowing that the worst of the crisis had passed, that the city was once again plugged back into the mainstream of contemporary civilization, might be enough to reduce the tidal wave of senseless, atavistic violence that had turned the streets of New York into a suburb of hell.

But Skerrit would not act on his own initiative. This had to be a direct order from the mayor. He would not accept the sole responsibility -- the burden had to be shared by everyone concerned, not just himself.

THE BLACKOUT HEIST

Skerrit was patched by radio link into the City Hall communications network. The mayor cursed and told him to do what he thought best, and to let him know when all the lights were back on.

"That's not good enough, sir," Skerrit told him. "It has to be your decision. I just run down the options. You act on them."

Skerrit was through taking all the risks and all the shit. This time it would be the movers and shakers who would go out on a limb and take any heat after it was over.

"Okay," replied the mayor after a long pause, in which Skerrit heard the sound of a palm clapped over the phone's mouthpiece for a long interval. "Do it, God damn it."

Then the line abruptly went dead as the mayor hung up. Skerrit allowed himself a laugh. The brass didn't like it when scapegoats were not available. Well, fuck 'em.

Skerrit turned to his crew boss, Billy Chu. "Think this'll work?" Chu asked.

"I don't know," Skerrit replied, "but there's really no other option at this point." He turned to the diazo schematic stretched out in front of him. "What sections of the grid would be energized?" he asked.

"Let's see," said Chu, bending over the schematic and putting on his reading glasses to see better, "Yorkville, the Upper East Side and Midtown."

"Would that include the Empire State Building?" asked Skerrit.

Chu nodded.

"Okay," he said after a moment's contemplation. "Here's how we play it. First we get the Midtown section online. If it works, some of those buildings will stand out like beacons."

"Surges will blow out a hell of a lot of equipment that hasn't been already damaged."

"Not our problem," Skerrit returned. "Ours is just to get the lights turned back on as fast as possible."

Skerrit picked up the field phone and signaled the work details to switch on the power for Midtown.

"We have contact," the voice came back over the line. Suddenly, Skerrit could hear cheering in the background.

He climbed up onto the roof of the van. The center of the city sputtered to life as thousands of windows flickered to brilliance in formerly darkened windows of high rise office buildings.

The city cops and the National Guard detail posted around the emergency van also sent up a wild cheer.

Skerrit climbed back inside the van.

"Put the rest of the grid on-line," he ordered Chu over the radio, confident that the worst of the crisis was finally over.

***

They heard the first explosion at the South Bronx's Zoo. The housing development's defenders immediately assumed that it was the sound of Molotov cocktails exploding. But then one of the lookouts that Mad Marty had posted on a third floor window ran down to tell the others what he had seen.

THE BLACKOUT HEIST

"It's over," he shouted, telling the others that he had seen the lights of the Empire State Building in the boro of Manhattan across the river suddenly come on.

"Look!" someone from the crowd shouted, pointing through the plate glass window of the Zoo's lobby. Outside, the streetlights were blowing and popping like water balloons.

As current again surged through the wiring, televisions, radios, VCRs, lighting fixtures, anything that ran on electric energy suddenly overloaded. The explosions continued, growing louder as individual explosive reports merged into several long, echoing booms that shook the night.

Cinco Muertes' goons stopped short of the Zoo's main building. They saw the searchlight beacons crisscrossing the sky overhead. They knew that they were not the lords and masters of Mott Haven's streets any longer. And so they quickly retreated back into the shadows of the busted neighborhood, scurrying into the holes like rats.

"Where you going?" bellowed Cinco Muertes as his gang deserted him. "Come back or you're all dead! *Todos muertos!* Do you hear me, *fucking hombres muertos!*"

But nobody paid attention to the Yanomamos' chieftain anymore. Cinco Muertes now stood alone, clenching his fists in the Zoo's main plaza. Then he heard somebody whistling. Cinco Muertes looked up to where the sound of the whistle had originated.

In a third floor window of the Zoo's main building, he saw something that made him simultaneously burn with hatred and recoil in mortal terror. The gangbanger honcho of Mott Haven saw Mad Marty standing tall, high above him, and flip him the bird.

A moment later, beneath a hail of NATO-caliber bullets from Mad Marty's machinegun, Cinco Muertes was turning tail and running from the Zoo as fast as his gangsta legs could carry him.

**

"Amazing sight, Chuck," the mayor's aide, Francisco Zapata said to him. Charles DeKeyser looked out across Broadway and saw the glow of the newly lighted Empire State Building's tower.

Zapata was right, the Kaiser acknowledged to himself. It certainly was an amazing sight. All the more amazing considering how many had taken it for granted for so long.

"The National Guard units from Bridgeport should be here pretty soon," Zapata added.

"Coordinate with the cops," the mayor told his aide. "Just remember that this is New York. I don't want the Big Apple turned into a police state, even for five minutes," he went on.

"Do what has to be done, but make sure we don't create worse problems administering the cure than fighting the cause. And turn over control to the cops the minute that you're able."

"Right," Zapata told the mayor, and left the command post.

The mayor turned to Commissioner Ibrahim who was seated nearby, adjusting his turban and preening his beard. "I'm getting too old for this," he complained.

THE BLACKOUT HEIST

"Why don't you quit, Chuckie?" asked Ibrahim with a smile on his bearded face, already knowing the mayor's response.

"If I did that," he answered, matching the commissioner's smile with one of his own, "how would the other twelve million victims in this town get along without me?"

A couple of minutes later, Zapata came back in to inform the mayor that he'd arranged everything as instructed. Suddenly, the mayor flashed Zapata a "V." Zapata turned automatically toward the desk where the mayor's medications were kept.

"What are you doing?" DeKeyser asked his aide.

"You just flashed me your sign for another Valium, didn't you?" Zapata returned perplexedly.

The mayor laughed and shook his head.

"No, Francisco," he told Zapata. "This time I actually meant *'victory.'*"

DAVID ALEXANDER

SIXTY-NINE

Metropolitan New York. By the time that the National Guard units that had been dispatched from Bridgeport, Connecticut arrived in the devastated city, it had been almost forty-eight hours since the *Pichuga* orbital recon satellite had exploded, saturating the city of New York with its EMP death pulse.

Units from elsewhere in the tri-state area augmented those of the Guard already posted in the metropolitan disaster zone were well-organized and were able to establish order quickly. A ten P.M. curfew was instituted and the streets of the five boros cleared.

Thousands of arrests were made in the space of a few hours. Because the local jails couldn't hold the thousands of offenders in police custody, former detention centers for suspected terrorists and federal prisons along the Brooklyn and Bronx waterfronts were pressed into service as makeshift holding facilities.

The citywide post-disaster cleanup effort might have been difficult, but it was smalltime compared to the job of countering the massive damage done to the vital digital information infrastructure on which the entire nation depended.

An untold number of computerized bank records was destroyed beyond all hope of salvage or recovery. Telephone communications were in a complete shambles and would take months, if not years, to be fully and reliably restored.

As extensive as the damage to material things was, the damage to human lives was beyond calculation.

The death toll numbered in the multiple thousands, an early count indicating a final body count at least twice as great as that of 911's aftermath. Also at an early stage, it was apparent that the elevated level of fatalities had been caused as much by human savagery as by the immediate aftereffects of the EMP disaster.

The enormous casualty figures were all the more incredible given the relatively brief duration of the disaster.

These figures would be studied by members of think tanks the world over for decades to come. They would have lasting impacts on federal policy, strategic military plans and international law, with the United Nations and the World Court in the Hague, Netherlands, acting in the name of the citizens of the world's nations in the aftermath of the disaster.

***

In the days after the restoration of electrical power to the City of New York, Washington, DC, and the many other municipalities large and small across the effected eastern seaboard of the United

States, Rick Skerrit was summoned before the MetroCon energy utility's corporate board of directors.

He was told that he could name his own price to take on the post of chief of MetroCon operations. The mayor himself had told the utility that he wanted Skerrit for the job. Skerrit told them he wasn't interested at any price. He was leaving the city, having decided that New York wasn't that important to him after all.

Maybe somewhere else people wouldn't kill each other like stone age savages the minute that the lights went out.

He didn't bet on finding such a place, he added, but he aimed at least to try his luck.

One thing -- New York was finished for him. He had seen beneath its glitzy veneer this time, and Skerrit knew he'd see the Apple forever differently than he had before death pulse struck the five boros.

For Skerrit the city would always be a place where the facade that its residents put on masked a malignant evil that always lurked just beneath it and would never go away.

The city would always be a place where most people lived lives so close to the brink of madness that they only needed the slightest push to shove them completely over the edge and into a lost world of anarchic violence.

The lights going out had put New York City over that fine line that divided sanity from madness, order from chaos.

THE BLACKOUT HEIST

Skerrit had seen what lay on the other side of that line.

He had hated what he had witnessed and was determined to wipe the image from his mind forever.

***

Christmas Island.

Skerrit had looked up the place on a whim. What he had read had interested him. An island smack dead in the middle of the Pacific Ocean, as far away from civilization as a man could get.

A school, a postal station, a general store and a hospital. A few Australian residents and local natives.

He had liquidated his cash holdings and booked tickets on a direct flight to Auckland, New Zealand. A charter flight had taken him the rest of the way.

Now, baggage in hand, he walked along the small airstrip away from the chartered twin-engine Cessna that had taken him on the last leg of his journey. Finally he would be away from the manipulators, the users, the mindfuckers. Maybe, just maybe, Rick Skerrit could now find peace, or at least some reasonable facsimile thereof.

***

Mad Marty Applebaum finally got the email he had been waiting for. The job called for a mercenary to snatch back the kidnapped daughter of a woman whose Egyptian husband had spirited the kid away to the Middle East.

Applebaum accepted the assignment. It had come along just in the nick of time. For the moment, he was a hero. But, then again, Arnie Maltz, the notorious "subway shooter," who had blasted away at a gang of punks on the A-train, had been dubbed a hero too, at least at the beginning.

A vacation was just what the doctor ordered. A long vacation. A long vacation somewhere far away. The Middle East fit the bill nicely. Marty had heard a lot about the dry heat. Now he'd have a chance to experience some of that dry heat up close and personal.

SEVENTY

The Pentagon, Arlington, Virginia. The magnitude of the EMP disaster as well as the lightning speed at which it had turned the world's largest city into a vast killing ground, had astonished the entire world.

Both the CIS and the United States had quickly signed sweeping and unprecedented bilateral agreements to not only tighten existing bans on space-based nuclear weapons, but to sharply curtail the military exploitation of exoatmospheric orbital space around the planet.

Both countries promptly forgot their treaties, however, and put more space-based defense research on their secret military agendas.

They each reasoned that if one country possessed such formidable weapons, then it had others as well that were every iota as lethal, and that military space capabilities that were known to the intelligence agencies of either power represented the tip of a much larger iceberg.

Besides, the problem with *Pichuga* had not been that it had not worked, but that it had not

494

worked well enough. If a relatively low-yield nuclear warhead exploding in orbit could wreak as much havoc over as wide an area as the one aboard *Pichuga* had done, then the potential for a space-based weapon that could deliver a truly devastating knockout punch -- purely in the interests of national defense, of course, and never, ever for offensive use -- was a capability worth a few covert research and development dollars -- or, for that matter, rubles.

Both sides believed in learning from their past mistakes. Such was the basis of all human progress, after all was said and done.

***

One hundred twenty miles above the surface of the earth, the Albatross-2 orbital surveillance platform passed over Moscow.

The American satellite was a new generation of spy platform, so powerful that, from its orbit in space, it was capable of reading the license plate on a car not merely parked on a city street, even through dense cloud cover, but -- using high-energy terahertz frequency radiation -- through the roof of a parking garage, a feat that had previously been beyond technical reach.

Unknown to everyone but a handful of CIA officials, the Albatross carried onboard a hidden nuclear warhead, intended to release a burst of EMP to cripple Russian communications in time of armed conflict -- conflict, which key analysts had, in a secret national intelligence estimate, deemed likelier now than it had been throughout the Cold War years, albeit for different reasons and toward

495

changed strategic goals. Continuing destabilization in the CIS might give rise to a Russian Napoleon yet, proposed the intelligence analysts, and proactive measures would need to be taken.

Albatross-2 had been secretly launched just prior to the launch of *Pichuga*, and plans existed for a future shuttle mission to dismantle the nuclear warhead onboard in order to comply with the terms of the newly signed bilateral US-CIS non-proliferation treaty.

American plans and international treaties, however, had no bearing on the flight trajectory of a chunk of primeval debris that had been formed during the solar system's birth pangs.

It had been orbiting within the broad band of space rubble that formed a belt of cosmic detritus between Mars and Saturn for untold millions of years, until a collision at around the time of the dinosaurs in the late Jurassic period had dislodged it from its orbit.

Twenty centuries later, the meteoroid's flight path had been deflected by the moon of the big blue planet that orbited three in from the sun. The blue planet's gravitational field had then taken over, drawing the tiny rock inexorably toward it at a speed of more than five hundred miles per hour.

Ordinarily, the pebble-sized meteoroid would have burned up in the earth's atmosphere, except that a metal object many times larger than it floated directly in the meteoroid's path.

At the speed it was traveling, the meteoroid struck the Albatross-2 surveillance satellite with enough inertial force to rip easily through its shielded magnesium-aluminum alloy hull.

Because it was night in Moscow, the explosion that instantly followed lit up the sky and was visible for many miles in every direction.

THE BLACKOUT HEIST

EPILOG

DAVID ALEXANDER

SEVENTY-ONE

Richie, Zurich, Switzerland.

Richie put down the morning edition of the *International Times*. The robbery of the Federal Reserve Bank of New York had faded from the news. The feds had drawn precisely the conclusions that Richie had intended them to draw.

Judson had been branded the mastermind of the biggest gold heist in history. Security cameras had been knocked out by the massive power outage, and likenesses of the disguised members of the team were available only through police sketches from the unreliable recollections of witnesses. There might be covert repercussions, but Richie's protection, in the form of the damaging evidence of the Nazi gold bars themselves, was insurance against that.

As for those ingots of bullion that had been forged in the demonic crucibles of the Third Reich's final throes, the gold had been sold to a fence in North Carolina at better than the going exchange rate on the international black market. Richie and

499

his crew were all extremely wealthy as a result of the transaction. And as far as Richie was concerned, the gold, most of which had come from the possessions and even the dental fillings of millions of the Nazis' victims, belonged to nobody in particular, and to anybody who had the balls and brains to snatch it.

Richie took the cell phone from the pocket of his suit jacket and dialed a long distance number. He reached Maddie's voice mail.

"It's me," he said. "I'll call back."

A moment or two later his cell phone jingled. It was Maddie, returning his call.

"It's time," Richie told her. "Pack your stuff, babe."